# THE JALOPY CHRONICLES

BOOK III

## A PARALLEL WORLD

## BY CAELI ENNIS

Illustrations by Elyzabeth McDonald,

Brigid McDonald, Martin Webber, and Caeli Ennis

**Canoe Tree
Press**

Canoe Tree Press is a division of DartFrog Books
301 S. McDowell St.
Suite 125-1625
Charlotte, NC 28204
www.DartFrogBooks.com

*For Eva O'Reilly, the brightest and warmest soul.*

*"May the road rise up to meet you.*
*May the wind be always at your back.*
*May the sun shine warm upon your face;*
*the rains fall soft upon your fields*
*and until we meet again,*
*may God hold you in the palm of His hand.*
*– Irish Blessing*

*"Broaden your minds, my dears, and allow your eyes to see past the mundane!"*
– *Professor Trelawney,* Harry Potter and the Prisoner of Azkaban, *by J.K. Rowling*

# The Jalopy Chronicles


Book 1: Across the Universe
Book 2: Lost in the Time Belt
Book 3: A Parallel World

# Contents


Author's Note ................................................................11
Chapter 1 - A Universal Request .............................13
Chapter 2 - The ERA's Newest Employees .............25
Chapter 3 - Case: Confidential ...............................39
Chapter 4 - Clorin Reborn ......................................51
Chapter 5 - Babies and Blueprints .........................63
Chapter 6 - A Noisy Surprise ..................................73
Chapter 7 - Mission Stardust ..................................87
Chapter 8 - The Dark Astromarket .........................99
Chapter 9 - Trouble at the Border .........................113
Chapter 10 - THESIS ............................................125
Chapter 11 - Project Bakerloo's Innovation ..........139
Chapter 12 - The Pilot Test ...................................149
Chapter 13 - Celebration of Life ...........................157
Chapter 14 - The Entrance to Reprisa ...................163
Chapter 15 - Thera ................................................177
Chapter 16 - Meet the Bunker ..............................189
Chapter 17 - The Cantileery Family ......................201
Chapter 18 - Fadre's Farmacy ...............................219
Chapter 19 - Gwympy's Predictions ......................233
Chapter 20 - Stenolly's Overture ...........................243
Chapter 21 - The Athenaeum .................................263
Chapter 22 - Fantasly's Lair ...................................281
Chapter 23 - Insomnyus Reunited .........................293
Chapter 24 - Battle in the Bunker .........................305
Chapter 25 - Elbina's Decision ..............................315
Chapter 26 - A Message from the Beyond ..............323
Acknowledgments ................................................339
About the Author .................................................341

# Author's Note

Hello, Reader! Thank you so much for being here. Before you start on this book, I wanted to put forth a couple notes to put your brain at ease.

First, there is a slightly puzzling time continuum aspect to this book that was introduced in book 1 of this series *(Across the Universe)*. You may remember that when our heroes, the McHubbards, returned to Earth from planet Harvinth, they went back in time by seven and a half years from the initial colonisation date on Harvinth. The colonisation date was July 2, 2220. Seven and a half years later from this date, the McHubbards returned to Earth. If we subtract seven and a half years from July 2220, we reach January 2213. This is the time period in which the story continues in the pages to follow.

Now that this information has been brought to light, I also want to say that our characters' ages are being treated as their biological age rather than their chronological age. Biological age is how old their body is. Chronological age is the time between their birth and the time that the book starts. Biologically, our characters on Earth are the age as if they are in the year 2228, but it is actually 2213.

You may be asking yourself, "Why did Caeli Ennis decide to incorporate such a difficult time concept into her book?" And I would answer with the following: "I ask myself this question every day." It was my first book that I ever wrote, so we're going to roll with it!

The second note I will point out has more brevity to it and is far less confusing than the first note. It is something that I would want to know as a reader, especially when there are animals involved: The dog survives.

Thank you again for allowing me to live out my dream as an author. Happy reading, and I hope you enjoy *A Parallel World*!

Always,

Caeli Ennis

# Chapter 1

## A Universal Request

Griffin McHubbard watched with bulging eyes as the grand room before him filled with the most peculiar creatures he'd ever seen. Some were in protective Perspex bubbles because they were too tiny to see, even under the strongest microscope, while others were the size of a lorry. Some had fangs that could slice through him with the gentlest touch, and others were merely small blobs without any defining features. The creatures were all colours of the rainbow, including some beyond the human visible spectrum, judging by the fact that some of the creatures appeared to be greeting thin air. Several creatures were made of steel, a few were made of fire, and others possibly some sort of gaseous element.

The creatures seated themselves around neatly prepped white tables in Danforth Commons in the White House in Washington, DC. The Earth Rehabilitation Association, or ERA, was headquartered in the White House. The ERA was Earth's last hope of survival; their predominant focus was ensuring that the planet's ecosystem didn't completely die off. Breathable gases constituted very little of Earth's atmosphere in the current year of 2213. The destruction of the atmosphere about two hundred years prior had forced all of Earth's surface water to boil and evaporate. All plant and animal life became extinct, and humans fled indoors, never to set foot or lay their eyes on the outside world again. No one in 2213 really knew firsthand what Earth's desolate surface looked like. All they knew was that if they were to somehow breach the barrier that protected them from the outside world, they'd meet instant death by vaporisation.

Griffin jumped as one particularly slimy creature suddenly appeared in his periphery, having emerged from a giant glass door. Danforth Commons had cylindrical glass tubes along one wall of the room where the creatures entered and exited as they travelled to and from their home planets. The late-arriving creatures scuttled, slithered, hopped, and flew to their seats around the tables, causing some of the chinaware to crash to the floor. The muffins and carefully crafted fruit ensembles were instantly devoured by the creatures, sending crumbs and splotches of fruit splattering across the room.

Griffin, best known as Riff to those close to him, pulled the lapels of his green ERA lab coat closed across his chest, in a sense hoping to conceal himself from the peculiar beasts. He slumped in his chair. Luckily, his table was filled with humans he wasn't scared of. Perhaps they would protect him from any harm.

Knitsy, Riff's grandmother, who was sitting to his left, punched him in his shoulder, quickly knocking him out of his trance.

"Griffin McHubbard," she spat, "you are twenty . . . something years old. Pluck some courage up like your sisters and be a man, for heaven's sake!"

Even though Riff was deaf, he could read his grandmother's lips and he could interpret her tone with no problem, since she was usually bothered about something. At such times, her mouth quivered in fury, and he noticed that some of her white hairs popped out from her usually perfect coif. Knitsy fell into a coughing fit after her rant to Riff, catching the attention of the creatures at a few neighbouring tables.

Riff shot a baffled look back at his grandmother. "Nan, chill out. You're mental," he mouthed back to her.

"Sit up straight!" she barked between coughs, rapping the back of his chair with her cane.

Riff sighed and pulled his chair in, sitting up straighter but still slightly hunched. He ran his fingers through his messy red hair, catching glimpses of the room through his fingers.

A sharp tap on his right shoulder startled him again. This time he met the gaze of his sister Ann Lou, just turned twenty, the youngest of the McHubbard siblings. She pulled her left arm, a metallic prosthetic, back to her side. Ann Lou had a sweet face and kind, bright blue eyes. Her long blonde hair hung in two braids across her shoulders. She smiled warmly at him and signed, "You okay?"

Riff relaxed slightly, unclenching his fingers from his face and taking a deep breath. He nodded and smiled at her.

"For someone who survived the Time Belt, I'm surprised you're such a scaredy-cat," signed his oldest sister, Luna, who sat just across from him.

Twenty-five-year-old Luna had dark reddish-brown hair and hazy, clouded corneas, reminding Riff of the visionless world in which she lived. He watched as her left hand traced through a Braille textbook. Remembering Luna's insult from a few moments earlier, Riff shuddered slightly at the thought of their recent escapades. Although he and Luna had been successful in destroying the Time Belt and saving all the innocent creatures trapped inside, allowing them to return to existence and their home planets, the horrors of the depths of the Time Belt still wounded him. He recalled seeing his mother tethered to a rope in Mortalok, trying to get past a vicious creature in one of the towers in Galalok, and watching Ernesteen Bowser III (known by many names, including Father Time; her nom de plume, E. Bowser III; and mastermind behind the Time Belt) sucking up creatures in her skeletal hands to make them eternally disappear from existence.

Ann Lou nudged Riff again, and he dropped his tormented gaze and instead adopted an annoyed one, now focused on Luna. He furrowed his brows at her and said, "Some of the creatures in Vivalok were cute. These blokes are . . . well, there's one over there who just ate his chair, so figure it out for yourself."

Ann Lou laughed as she watched the last leg of the chair disappear inside the creature's body. Riff then met the gaze of the boy seated between Ann Lou and Luna. He was anxiously adjusting his tie and rubbing his forehead, which was visibly leaking sweat.

"Try to relax, mate," Riff said in an anxious tone.

The boy looked at him squarely, his left eye twitching. "Oh yeah, because *you're* the one who needs to address them all. Thanks for the advice."

Hayden Murphy was the current acting US President and Earth's delegate to the Universal Union, a group consisting of thousands of representatives from across the universe who promoted peace and wellbeing in the universal community. The last few delegates were still entering the room (the ones who could fit, of course).

At nineteen, Hayden held more responsibility than most adults. The sheer power of his position overwhelmed him at times. The McHubbards were at this Universal Union meeting to back him up should he stutter or faint, both of which were likely considering his delicate constitution.

A giant, spherical, rock-type creature with one menacing eye and two protruding, muscly arms rolled to the front of the room and cleared its raspy throat. In an instant, the creatures in the room ceased their various grumblings, hissings, and flappings and focused their attention on the rock—a delegate from planet Rhothgo who served as the Universal Union's leader.

Riff tapped Ann Lou gently on her knee. "Can you translate for me?" he whispered.

She nodded and activated her microchip translation by tapping her left wrist three times. Knitsy, Luna, and Hayden did the same. Soon, the grumbles from the Rhothgan turned into an English translation for the humans. Ann Lou held up her hands to sign the meeting for Riff as she focused her attention on the speaker.

The Rhothgan's menacing eye poked around the room and even met Riff's for a split second, forcing him deeper into his seat, followed by another rap from Knitsy's cane to the back of his chair. Riff watched the mouth of the Rhothgan start to move while Ann Lou's hands translated.

"What's the first order of business for this meeting, Pomber delegate?"

A purple-skinned, squishy and skinny-bodied creature nervously stared at a handheld device that displayed the agenda and recorded the meeting minutes. The Pomberian shook as it replied, "R-rations f-for planet Tortoine, s-sir."

The Rhothgan's eye met a small, blue-green, turtle-like creature whose spiral shell wrapped around its midsection.

The Tortoine delegate spoke up with a weak and croaky voice. "Please, Universal Union. I beg of you. My community is suffering from a lack of dihydrogen oxide."

"So, water?" Luna said so quietly that only the human table could hear.

The Tortoinian continued. "Our nearest sun is becoming a supergiant and dried our lands. We need supplies quickly, or we will all perish."

The Rhothgan growled and swept the crowd before him with a ferocious glare. "Who can provide di . . . hy . . . oxi . . . argh!—the compound planet Tortoine needs?"

The Cipton delegate, a blob creature, bounced in its seat excitedly. "We have plenty of that compound in our polar ice caps! The community of Cipto would love to provide as much as we can!"

"Thank you so much, Cipto delegate. How ever will I be able to repay you?" The Tortoinian was nearly in tears and slowly reached out a leg in praise.

"Next order of business," the Rhothgan droned.

The Pomberian stood up with its three shaky limbs. "N-next is—"

"We have another problem here," the delegate from Casper interrupted.

Everyone's heads spun toward the Casperian. The delegate had a large watermelon-shaped head to hold its enormous brain, and long nasal appendages that were held up to hush the room.

"Tortoine's sun will drain Cipto's dihydrogen oxide once it's transported over. We need to solve that issue."

The Tortoinian lowered its head in defeat.

The Casperian spoke up again. "Say, Tortoine delegate, do you actually need your sun?"

The turtle slowly raised its head in confusion. "No. Our community thrives on dihydrogen oxide alone, no matter how hot or cold."

"Then let's blow it up," the Casperian said, whipping its nasal appendages out in all directions. The Tortoinian's microscopic eyes bulged out of their sockets.

"Your sun, I mean," the Casperian clarified.

The Tortoinian relaxed slightly.

The Casperian continued, "We have recently developed a new technology to blow up stars."

The Rhothgan's normally angry expression became one of confusion. "Won't that put the planet in danger?"

"It is possible," the Casperian explained. "The star will turn into either a black hole or a nebula. Let's hope it's a nebula."

The Tortoinian quivered within its shell and shot a terrified expression at the Rhothgan, who didn't seem to notice.

"All right," the Rhothgan said. "Seems like a better chance at survival than doing nothing at all. It's settled. Planet Casper, please blow up planet Tortoine's closest sun, and then, Planet Cipto, please provide as much of your di . . . hydoidian . . . oxidian as possible."

The Cipton bounced, the Casperian nodded, and the Tortoinian's jaw dropped in fear. Before it could continue to speak, the Rhothgan spoke up again.

"Pomber, on with the agenda!" he boomed, slamming his fist into the wooden podium and smashing it in two.

The Pomberian leapt out of its chair, fiddled for its device, and closely inspected the tiny screen. "A t-transport request f-from Earth, s-sir," it piped before quickly sitting back down in the chair.

The Rhothgan scrunched in his spot and locked his single, menacing eye onto the human table.

"Earthlings?" he grumbled. "Elaborate."

Hayden breathed out slowly, then gingerly stood up from his chair. He swayed slightly, his dark skin blanched a bit, and his green eyes started to drift upward. Ann Lou must have sensed his light-headedness and temporarily moved her hand to his side to steady him. Hayden blinked himself back to reality, cleared his throat, smiled brightly with his famously flashy smile, and addressed the crowd in his usual suave manner.

"Hello, everyone. Thank you for congregating on Earth today. I know it's very far for some of you. Well, all of you."

Hayden paused to allow the creatures to laugh or unclench their horribly large muscles to diffuse the tension in some way. But not a single creature flinched or broke the silence. All eyes or analogous body parts were glued to Hayden.

Hayden cleared his throat and continued, wiping a stray bead of sweat hurrying its way down his cheek. "We need a Jalopy. Specifically, one that—"

"I see several right over there," the Rhothgan huffed, pointing its fist toward the Jalopy Cabins across the room. "Plus the boat, among many others under our control."

"N-no, a different kind of Jalopy. Specifically, one that travels quite a long distance. One that can travel to . . . another universe."

Every creature in the crowd burst out in synchronous laughter. Even the Rhothgan chuckled for a moment, but then he quickly regained composure and smashed a fist onto the already split podium, which was now in quarters.

"We need order in here! Now!"

The crowd stopped laughing mid-chortle and returned their gazes to the Rhothgan. He angrily continued.

"Let's all remember that the Earthlings aren't the smartest of creatures."

"I second *that*," the Casperian snarled.

Riff watched as Luna pursed her lips and stuck her nose into the air. He knew how much she despised being categorised as intellectually inferior, and he almost let out a chuckle watching her reaction.

"Can someone fill us in on why we can't get another Jalopy?" Ann Lou asked bravely as Hayden's knees wobbled.

"Because there hasn't been enough research done," the Casperian whined. "To get to another universe, you need to travel through black holes. Black holes can be terribly dangerous if they are not properly ventured through in the correct way. It would take loads of verification and validation before we could even attempt passage through a real black hole, plus a hoard of resources that probably aren't readily available."

The Rhothgan ignored the Casperian. "Why do you need such a Jalopy?"

The McHubbards gulped simultaneously. The reason was heart-wrenching. It was difficult to even speak about. Riff wondered if they'd be shown any mercy since the issue was a personal one concerning their family.

"Elbina McHubbard," began Hayden, his voice cracking, "my darling . . . erm, I mean, a very influential scientist in the Earth Rehabilitation Association, has been abducted."

"And why should we care about one measly Earthling?" the Rhothgan growled.

"Because . . ." Hayden trailed off.

Riff knew what Hayden wanted to say. He wanted to beg and plead the Universal Union to bring the love of his life back to him. Even though Riff felt grossed out by the thought of his sisters ever falling in love and simultaneously utterly confused about people falling in love with them, a gut-wrenching feeling bubbled inside him. He feared he might never see his younger sister Elbina again. He wanted her back just as much, if not more, than Hayden did.

"'Because' is not a strong argument. If that's all, then the request is denied. Next on the agenda—"

"We destroyed the Time Belt," Luna said forcefully, standing up from her seat. The crowd stared at her in confusion.

"What do you mean, 'destroyed' it?" the Rhothgan asked mysteriously.

"We were all there," Luna said, gesturing to her table. "We saw the horrors within, who was controlling it, and what they did to innocent lives. We solved the mystery and shut it down. Now no one has to get stuck there ever again. Our universe, which is called Coloratura, and all the others, should be thanking us."

The Rhothgan scratched his rocky head and looked to the crowd for some assistance.

The Casperian stood again and gulped hard. "It pains me to say that I actually believe the Earthling is correct. We have been noticing a different time continuum on Harvinth and its neighbouring planets. It is no longer reversed."

"It was E. Bowser the Third. She was behind it. She used her grandmother Ernesteen Bowser Senior's time machine to build it, and she used other creatures' time to become immortal. She's the one who took our sister," said Luna.

"That poet from planet Thera? That's all the way in the Reprisa universe," said the Casperian delegate.

"Yes, exactly; that's her," Luna nodded. "And that's why we need to go to a different universe, specifically one that is parallel to ours. Our sister is stuck on Thera!"

The Rhothgan peered dubiously back at the McHubbards. "I'm still not convinced this is a good idea."

Hayden collapsed in his chair as Luna continued. "Think of it as a benefit for the whole universe. We'll have the capacity to research new lands, develop new technology, connect with other populations, and . . . bragging rights as the superior universe."

The Casperian's appendages lifted in support. The crowd whispered among themselves.

"I think it's a brilliant idea," the Sinx delegate squeaked as it wiggled into a sinusoidal shape.

"The most amazing idea of all time!" bounced the Cipton.

"I can't wait to tell everyone back home," flapped the Antympanican.

The murmurs in the crowd gradually crescendoed to a roar of support for Luna's proposition.

The Rhothgan slammed his fist for order. "All right, *all right*," he bumbled. "Who is going to take on this development of a multi-universal Jalopy?"

The Casperian flung its appendages into the air once more. "We on Casper are clearly the only ones capable of such research and development."

"And me," Luna said sternly. "You'll need me."

Riff's face purpled from holding in his laughter. Luna was intellectually superior to any human he'd ever met. Although he knew she most likely was nowhere near as intelligent as the average Casperian in terms of brain capacity, it was still hilarious to watch her try to show them up.

"Absolutely not," started the Casperian. "Your brain is much too small—"

"It's settled. The lanky Earthling will be of assistance." The Rhothgan could sense the Casperian's annoyance. "If she truly did destroy the Time Belt, she has worlds of knowledge beyond yours."

The Casperian's nasal appendages reddened and curled into a fist. "I—how dare you insult—the absolute nerve of you!" the Casperian sputtered, trying its best to formulate words to maintain its superiority. Riff watched a smile broaden on Luna's face as she sat down. He even saw Knitsy clap a few times.

"I've had enough of this today," groaned the Rhothgan. "The next meeting will be held on Vignet, for those who are anatomically able to go. Bring sun protection. I recommend at least an SPF 25,000. Meeting adjourned." The Rhothgan's fist smashed what was left of the podium, leaving a pile of wood chips.

The creatures scuttled out of their chairs and hurried in a disorderly fashion toward the Jalopy Cabins. Before leaving, the hungry and hairy Kilo-209 delegate sauntered around to each table and finished off the rest of the food as well as one of the tables. It belched out a table leg onto the floor just before the Jalopy Cabin door closed.

Riff watched as Ann Lou helped Hayden regulate his breathing and Luna continued reading her book. He tapped the table, and Luna looked up toward him.

"So you're off to planet Casper, then? Too good for Earth?" he smirked.

"Trust me, if I could hide out on a different planet for the rest of my life reading and writing stories, I would. But I need Elbina. We all do. I don't feel whole without her."

Riff's heart sank upon the mention of Elbina's name. "Do you think she's okay? Alive, even?" His voice trailed off.

"Don't you dare think like that, Griffin." Luna swallowed hard.

Riff leaned back to allow some space between them. He knew Luna felt particularly sensitive about the subject of Elbina's disappearance. The two of them were best friends; inseparable, even. He thought better of continuing the conversation and allowed her to read in silence.

Riff's thoughts strayed to what Elbina might be doing at that moment in a far-off foreign land. She had to be scared, wondering where her family was, maybe even trying to escape. But now, with the support of the Universal Union, there was a glimmer of hope of finding her.

# CHAPTER 2

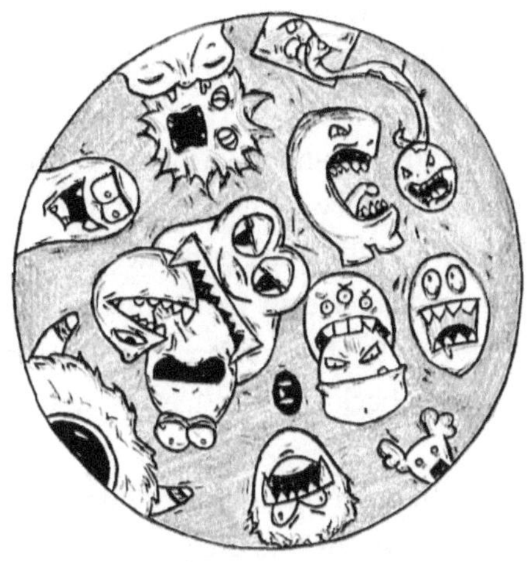

## THE ERA'S NEWEST EMPLOYEES

Later that day, in the depths of the White House in one of the ERA laboratories, an array of dim light bulbs hung above where Riff sat. Stools lined long rows of tables covered entirely in soil. This artificial soil was nearly identical in appearance to soil back in Earth's more atmospherically affluent days; however, one might receive the occasional electric shock while handling this soil because of its chemical instability. Dr. Jung-hoon Kang—a materials scientist at the ERA, as well as Riff's new boss—handed Riff a pair of safety goggles and some thick rubber gloves and gestured that Riff should put them on.

Riff obliged with a sigh, not excited at all to be replacing Elbina at her job while she was missing somewhere in an alternate universe. He snapped the goggles to his eyes and floppily fit the gloves onto his large, freckled hands. He caught Knitsy in his periphery dancing around the room with her cane and a watering can. He laughed to himself. Even though the misery of losing his sister loomed over him, at least he had Knitsy to make him feel better.

Peering back toward Jung-hoon, he noticed the scientist eyeing Knitsy with a particularly nervous expression. Riff patted Jung-hoon's arm and said, "Don't worry, I'll make sure she gets to work."

Riff swivelled around gracelessly on his stool, nearly knocking both himself and Jung-hoon to the floor. "Nan," Riff announced once he and Jung-hoon were sturdily back on their feet. He waved his arms to get her attention.

Knitsy stopped mid-boogie and glared at him. "What?"

"You're getting water everywhere except where it needs to be going," he said. "Try boogieing closer to the tabletops."

Knitsy stuck out her tongue at him but obeyed as she angled the spout of the watering can over the soil that was covering the tables. She slowly wobbled her way along the row of soil, spraying water unevenly. As Knitsy watered the last patch of soil of the row, she received a rather unpleasant electrical shock, causing her hair to point in all directions. Rather than looking sorry for herself, Knitsy swore profusely at the flowery watering can and threw it at the wall in a surprising moment of strength.

Riff met Jung-hoon's eyes with a nervous smile. Jung-hoon rubbed his temples slowly and fluttered his eyes, then focused his attention on Riff's task. "What I want you to do is continue inspecting the shoots that are growing from the soil. Do you remember what to look for in the microscope?" He pointed to a dingy-looking contraption on the other side of the room.

Riff shrugged. "Kind of. Remind me again why I'm doing this?"

Jung-hoon furrowed his brow over his usually kind almond eyes, then closed his eyes for a few seconds and sighed deeply. "Our team is verifying whether we can artificially grow viable plant life with our recently developed artificial soil. When you look at the cells under the microscope, they'll either be similar to this . . ." He tapped his left wrist five times, and a cartoonish holographic diagram of a plant cell displayed just above his wrist. It was a green blob with a colourful array of organelles, a nucleus, and membrane layers. ". . . Or they will look nothing like this. Keep a record of which ones are viable and which ones aren't. Understood?"

Riff felt his mind drifting to some lyrics by The Death Brigade. His head started to nod to the music. Luckily, Jung-hoon took that as confirmation of Riff's understanding.

"I'll be upstairs if you need me. Knitsy, please wear your rubber gloves. Dr. Loria has run out of the shock ointment, so we can't have any more injuries until she gets more." With a swish of his green lab coat, Jung-hoon turned abruptly and marched up the stairs. Knitsy grumbled something rather distasteful under her breath.

Riff sighed when Jung-hoon was out of sight, then clumsily stood up from the stool. He leaned down to eye level with the table and crept slowly down the row, looking for small shoots of plant life. He found none immediately. He thought it was strange how difficult it was to re-engineer plant life. Other than the forests on Antympanica, Riff wasn't even sure what a plant looked like beyond the renditions in history books. He wondered how different the plant life on Earth was from that of Antympanica, his last home, where he had spent nearly eight years.

He waddled along the rows of tables thinking about Antympanica and the fun he'd had there. He remembered the foul smells of the local pub that he frequented, the Cabbaged Egg Inn and Bar. To get there, one had to drive a small boat on a glittery purple lake. He recalled conversations with his old Antympanican friend, Tony, who knew the gossip of everyone within a thousand-mile radius. Best of all, his two closest friends from growing up, Matt and Joe, had lived there with him as well. He smiled as he thought of his bandmates. They, too, were recruited to the ERA to work on various rehabilitation efforts for the Earth. The hole in Riff's heart from the loss of Elbina was filled slightly by his friends' presence. They even had a band called the GeoLads, and there was a practice planned for after work today.

A tiny sliver of orange popped into Riff's visual field, snapping him out of his trance. The neon-orange shoot stood out in stark contrast against the gross brown synthetic soil. Riff stood up straight, stretched his back, and pulled out a pocket knife from his trouser pocket. He cut a small sample off the shoot and brought it over to the microscope.

Riff sat down, placed the sample on a clear slide, and positioned it gingerly underneath the lens. He hunched his back over the small instrument and pressed his eyes against the eyepiece.

A thwack to his shoulder caused him to fall directly off the stool. Riff stared up at a disappointed Knitsy.

"Nan, why can't you *gently* get my attention?" Riff barked at her, stumbling to his feet.

"Can we switch?" she whined, holding up the watering can. "It's *sooo* heavy . . ."

Riff snatched the watering can from her and bobbed it up and down. "Nan, it's empty."

"Well, I'm bored! I'd rather listen to Luna read one of her books to me again." Knitsy rolled her eyes and hung her head.

"Did you water all the rows of tables?" Riff asked suspiciously.

"Yes," Knitsy replied, curtly. Her eyes darted away.

Riff sighed at her blatant lie but knew she was better off doing something else. "Fine. Tell me what you see when you look through here." Riff pointed to the eyepiece on the microscope.

Knitsy excitedly hopped onto the stool, tossed her cane to the floor, and shakily put her eyes to the eyepiece and started moving her mouth.

"Make sure you look at me when you're speaking, Nan. I need to read your lips," he reminded her with a hint of annoyance.

Knitsy met his eyes. "Check this out!" she said giddily. "They're attacking each other!"

Riff raised an eyebrow and peered through the eyepiece. Sure enough, hundreds of cells in shades of red, orange, and yellow were racing around trying to engulf each other as quickly as possible. One cell, a red one, was noticeably larger and faster than the rest. Riff pulled away from the binoculars to look directly at the sample. It had turned from bright orange to bright red.

"Well, sample number six-two-three is not viable. Just like the rest of them," Riff said through gritted teeth, recording the finding in a memo stored within the microchip in his left wrist.

Riff and Knitsy spent the rest of the afternoon searching for shoots. They found a total of eight in the room, each with a different mutation and none of them viable. After inspecting the last of the samples, Knitsy kicked the watering can and left the room in a huff. Riff recorded the last failure in his memo and followed Knitsy up the stairs to another laboratory. This one was filled with high-tech computers with dozens of ERA ferociously typing on keyboards. Riff spotted Jung-hoon, whose face lit up with a mixture of anticipation and exhaustion.

"Anything?" Jung-hoon asked, ceasing typing his rather boring report on the concentration of fertiliser on planet Coniston.

Riff shook his head. "Same as every other day. I just sent the memo through to you."

Jung-hoon slumped into his chair in defeat. "I should've figured that was the case by the way Knitsy stormed past me. I thought we were getting close. We've been working so hard!" He slammed his fists on the desk, causing some labmates around him to stop typing and stare for a few seconds before returning to their respective reports.

"Don't give up, Jung-hoon," Riff said. "Think of my mum. She didn't stop until the very end." Riff felt a lump in his throat and swallowed hard. His mother had been the acting director of the ERA until her untimely passing. When all the other humans had been relocated to other planets, she had stayed behind and orchestrated a successful, gargantuan effort to take down the GeoLapse, a terrorist group that, until recently, had threatened the human population. Riff had learned recently that his mother and Jung-hoon dated for nearly ten years. He felt a connection to Jung-hoon, possibly in place of his absent father, who, he had also learned recently, was a member of the GeoLapse.

Jung-hoon matched Riff's solemn expression and nodded. "You're right. You're absolutely right. We have to keep going. For Henrietta." Jung-hoon strained to smile.

Riff nodded and turned on his heels swiftly, glad that Jung-hoon didn't want to discuss the subject of his mother any further. He strode out of the room and hung up his green lab coat messily on the rack next to the exit.

He sped into the lounge, where Knitsy lay open-mouthed and asleep in one of the chairs. Riff snorted at the scene and continued down the long, marble corridor to a dusty, unused room on the left. There, Matt and Joe were gently tuning their makeshift guitars. Matt's was made of wood he had carved from a bed frame, and Joe's was some malleable metal he'd nicked from one of the ERA laboratories. Their strings were some taut twine and shoelaces. Riff smiled.

"Riff, my boy! The highlight of the GeoLads is here!" sang Matt, tossing his fists into the air.

Joe nodded in Riff's direction.

"How did my little bro do today?" Matt asked regarding his younger brother, Hayden. "Did he get through that meeting alive?"

"Barely," said Riff. "But I guess I wasn't far behind him."

"Those creatures freak me out," Matt shuddered. "I'm glad I'm the musician and he's the politician. He deals with the trouble, and I dish out the treble." He continued plucking at his guitar strings.

"Lads, this is lame," said Joe, his floppy brown hair covering his eyes.

"Why do we even bother practising if we don't have real instruments?" He kicked his guitar-ish thing to the ground and huffed to himself.

Matt, on the other hand, smiled as he tightened one of the shoelaces.

"I dunno, mate, but I'm digging this light, bassy sound. Who cares how soft it is?" He started bobbing his head, his puffy dark afro nodding along on a slight delay.

"C'mon, Riff, I know you can feel this beat!" Matt beamed at him, still strumming and tapping his toe.

Riff swaggered over to his makeshift drum set in perfect rhythm with Matt's taps. Joe rolled his eyes and slumped to pick up his instrument.

Riff sat down in front of the pots and pans he had swiped from various racks and hangers in the White House kitchens. He picked up a pair of chopsticks and started tapping on his drums to Matt's beat.

"Yes, Riff! I'm diggin' it! Keep it up!" Matt enthused, dancing around as he played. Joe even started nodding his head slightly along to the tune.

This was the usual interaction between the boys. Joe would whine, Matt would cheer everyone up, and Riff would be lost in his own musical world. Whether it was drumsticks or chopsticks, they felt like additional appendages on Riff's hands. He couldn't hear the beats, but he could feel them as vibrations. The sounds he imagined emanating from his drum set were way better than the actual clashes and pangs Matt and Joe heard, but they still played along with him.

Riff hit his "cymbals"—little tea plates, already cracked, which broke upon being struck with the chopsticks, though Riff didn't notice with his eyes closed and his moppy red hair flying about. It wasn't until Joe stomped on the ground in front of Riff that he stopped and noticed his entire drum set had completely fallen apart.

"That's the third set this week, Riff," Joe scolded him. "Junghoon's never gonna let us practise again if you keep smashing all the kitchenware!"

Riff's face reddened, and he dropped the chopsticks to his sides while Joe stormed out of the room.

Matt approached Riff. "Don't worry, mate, he's been in a sour mood lately. He just hates working here, that's all." Matt placed a reassuring hand on Riff's shoulder.

Riff saw Knitsy hobble in with her cane twirling above her head as she jigged around the room.

"I liked that song. Especially the part where the shards of plate nearly took the sassy one's eye out!" Knitsy heaved with laughter, which then led to a series of coughs.

Riff jumped up and ran to Knitsy's side, clapping her back to help her cough up the fluid in her lungs.

"Nan," barked Riff, "if you don't wear your patch, I'm ironing it onto you! Where is it?"

Knitsy grumbled and looked away from him.

"*Nan,*" Riff said sternly.

From her skirt pocket, Knitsy begrudgingly pulled out a plastic tube that connected a small, square patch with a face mask.

"Why did you take off your mask?" Riff asked, maintaining his strict tone.

Knitsy suffered from breathing problems and had frequent bouts of coughing. The face mask provided a regular flow of oxygen, and the patch helped her body utilise the oxygen, although she never liked wearing them.

Knitsy let Riff affix the patch to her upper arm, but she baulked at the mask. "I don't want"—she coughed—"to wear that"—cough—"wretched thing! It makes me feel"—cough—"OLD!"

Riff snapped, "I hate to break it to you, Nan, but you *are* old!"

Knitsy scoffed and continued resisting Riff's attempts to place the mask securely over her nose and mouth. Luckily for Riff, he was used to her distaste toward the mask and learned how to counterattack her resistance.

Once the breathing apparatus was successfully wrangled onto Knitsy, she, Riff, and Matt left for Danforth Commons to grab some dinner. The gigantic, elegantly appointed room where myriad creatures had assembled that morning was now bustling with hungry humans. ERA members in green lab coats were lined up around the periphery of the room, heaving heaps of mush onto their plates from the buffet.

Riff spotted Ann Lou and her husband, Apollo, in deep conversation at one of the tables. Apollo hailed from planet Epiton, which was where Ann Lou met him while she lived there. Luna and Joe sat alone at the next table, Joe sulking into his mush, and Luna reading a book in Braille.

Riff led Knitsy and Matt to Ann Lou and Apollo's table, and Ann Lou glanced nervously at them as they sat down. Riff had been able to lip-read only the tail end of her last sentence: ". . . so we need to act fast."

"Sorry to interrupt," Matt said. "But, Annie Lou, do you know where I could find El Presidente?"

"He's up in his dorm," Ann Lou replied.

"He could probably use some big brotherly love after that meeting earlier. I'll catch you all later." Matt smiled, waved, and walked away, bobbing his head as he wandered out the door.

"Did we actually interrupt something important?" Riff asked.

Apollo huffed and curled one of his two giant claws into a tighter curl.

Ann Lou placed a gentle hand on his arm. "It's fine, Apollo. Remember, they already know."

Riff said, "That's a pretty bold statement. I rarely know anything that's going on."

Ann Lou pulled her hand back and placed it on her stomach, which showed a slight bump.

"Clorin!" Riff exclaimed. Clorin was Ann Lou and Apollo's son, not yet born. The McHubbards had met him in the Time Belt by happenstance.

Luna and Joe poked their heads up from the other table.

"Shhh!" hushed Ann Lou. "Let's not announce it to the entire ERA!"

"Sorry," Riff said sheepishly.

Apollo grumbled.

Ann Lou rolled her eyes. "We're naming him Clorin. I know Sulien was your great-great-great-grandfather's name, but Clorin is the name he chose in the Time Belt. He has much better memories with that name than he does with Sulien."

Apollo huffed.

"Hmph." Knitsy stuck her nose into the air.

"Nan, what's the matter?" Ann Lou asked, doing her best to hold back an annoyed tone.

Riff didn't quite catch Knitsy's response because she was looking away from him and Ann Lou, but based on Ann Lou's response, he knew more or less what she had said.

"I understand that you're upset, Nan. But this baby is coming whether you like it or not."

Riff tapped Knitsy's shoulder. "Nan, you've met Clorin! Have you already forgotten? We've only been back for . . . erm, how long have we been back from the Time Belt?"

"About two months," Ann Lou said.

"Two months already? Feels like ages, even though technically no time passed while we were stuck there. That place really messed up my sense of reality," Riff said.

"And how long ago was it that you and Apollo got married on Harvinth?" Knitsy said with one eyebrow raised.

Ann Lou gulped. "About . . . two months."

"Hmph." Knitsy stood and hobbled her way over to the dinner queue.

Apollo's mouth moved as he hissed and huffed in conversation with Ann Lou. Riff couldn't understand Apollo's Epitonian language, and microchip translation didn't work for him because of his hearing loss, so all Riff could decipher were hisses and growls from his lips.

"No, Riff has every right to be a part of this conversation," snapped Ann Lou.

Ann Lou leaned close to Riff. "Remember when Luna told you about that memory that she and Clorin saw when we were back in the Time Belt?"

Riff nodded. "I can't remember the exact details, though."

Ann Lou fidgeted with her hands and glanced at Apollo. He huffed, rose sharply from his chair, and stormed off.

"Okay, I'll make it brief," Ann Lou sighed. "Luna and Clorin visited one of Clorin's memories from the future. We were on Epiton, and the bottom half of my body was completely wasted away. The flesh, the muscles"—Ann Lou slammed her eyes shut—"they were shrivelled and dead. And it was all because of my pregnancy with Clorin. And then, well, some bad things happened between me and Apollo, but that's not important. What I've been discussing with Apollo is that we should focus on rehabilitation, mental health checkups, and eating a stricter diet so that I don't get sick and go all mad. So they don't . . . lose me." Ann Lou's voice cracked and her chin wobbled.

"And he's not in favour of that?" asked Riff.

"He is, but it means that we need to cut back on sweets, and I can't overexert myself with Pyroll," Ann Lou explained.

"What on Epiton will the man have left?" said Riff sarcastically.

"I know," said Ann Lou. "The bloke needs his Fava cakes."

Riff continued: "So, when is Clorin . . . due? Seven months–ish?"

Ann Lou shook her head. "The gestation period for Epitonians is significantly shorter than that of humans. But a Human–Epitonian mix . . . I'm not sure. Jung-hoon put me in contact with an OBGYN from the ERA's health sector. Supposedly they have a procedure in mind. But it might be tricky. I'm scared, Riff."

Riff held Ann Lou at arm's length and stared at her in awe. "Ann Lou, the Pyroll Champion of the Coloratura universe *and* Luge Crash champion of the Time Belt, is scared of having a *baby*?" Riff donned a dramatic expression, causing Ann Lou to laugh. "Your family has your back. Okay?"

Ann Lou smiled, and then something on the other side of the room caught her attention. "Look, Jung-hoon's coming over here. He looks serious."

The two siblings watched as Jung-hoon walked in their direction and stopped at the table next to them to engage in a brief discussion with Luna. He held a stack of papers and passed each one to Luna to read. She quietly traced her finger across each page, nodded when she was ready for the next page, and asked Jung-hoon a question or two once she was finished. He scanned her left wrist with a small pocket scanner and then left Luna to her book. Joe didn't seem to care about their interaction as he continued depressingly shoving mush into his mouth.

"What was that about?" Ann Lou whispered to Riff.

"Dunno."

They slid their chairs over to Luna's table. Joe scowled, annoyed at the invasion of his privacy, so he took his plate and marched to another table on the opposite side of the room.

"Ahem," said Ann Lou.

Luna continued reading.

"What did Jung-hoon want?"

Luna's finger continued tracing as she spoke. "It was the paperwork for my visa to planet Casper. I'm leaving tomorrow."

Riff's jaw dropped.

"Oh, geez! Thanks for the heads up!" snapped Ann Lou.

"Well, it's not like I've had time to process it yet!" Luna barked back.

"Why didn't we need visas to go to Epiton, Antympanica, Cipto, and Harvinth back in the day?" Riff asked.

"Because that was a state of emergency," Luna replied. "And Casper doesn't let just anyone visit. You have to have supplemental documentation of a major planetary or universal accomplishment."

"What was yours?" asked Riff.

"Um, only destroying the Time Belt," answered Luna.

"Oh, right. Well, is it safe to go there alone? Can your trip wait a little longer?" asked Riff.

Luna slammed her book closed. "There is no time to waste! Our sister is gone! Alone on some strange planet that we don't have access to. Stop being such a scaredy-cat and start thinking of others first!"

Luna slid her chair away from the table and stormed off toward the exit of Danforth Commons. A sea of eyes followed her as she left.

"Don't take it personally," said Ann Lou, warmly. "She's been a bit on edge. I don't blame her. She's lost her best friend. Although, it feels like we all have."

Riff sighed. "Speaking of unusual behaviours, what do you think is up with Nan?"

The siblings watched as Knitsy started a fight with one of the more senior ERA over the last steak in the buffet. She pulled one side of the steak with all her might, eventually ripping it from his hands.

"And Bob's your uncle!" she yelled, teasingly waving the steak above her head.

As soon as Knitsy's back was turned from the buffet, the kitchen replenished the vat of steaks.

"She's certainly been acting a bit differently since returning from the Time Belt," said Ann Lou. "Although maybe I'm just imagining things. She's always been a bit off."

"I've heard her muttering about Grandad Mack during some of her naps," Riff confessed. "It seems like her mission on Focalok, when she saw him again, really affected her."

Knitsy rejoined them at the table and hacked away at her steak, eating it at a surprisingly speedy pace.

"At least she still has her appetite," Ann Lou chortled.

# CHAPTER 3

## CASE: CONFIDENTIAL

The McHubbards, Apollo, the Murphy brothers, and Jung-hoon held a cramped going-away party for Luna that evening in one of the small ERA laboratories. The endeavour was fairly last-minute, and it showed: the refreshments were the leftovers from dinner, the decorations were used banners and streamers from an ERA member's retirement party (Riff had crossed out the *Retirement* in 'Happy Retirement!' and replaced it with *Travels to the Melon-Headed Planet*), and the music that blared from the loudspeakers was none other than The Death Brigade, Riff's favourite band, who played the heaviest of heavy metal.

Luna stayed for only about twenty minutes. She had never been big on social interaction, but she despised The Death Brigade's musical catalogue even more. She shook Knitsy—who had somehow managed to fall asleep in a chair despite the head-banging music—then helped her to her feet and guided her out of the lab, slipping away before anyone could say goodbye to them.

"I'm beat," Ann Lou said a few minutes later. Her eyes were bloodshot. "I'm at the point in this pregnancy where I could just collapse at any moment from the fatigue."

She bid goodnight to Riff, and she and Apollo retired to their dormitory upstairs, hand in claw.

"I need to be up early for a conference with the UN. I'll catch you all later," Hayden said, flashing his shiny teeth and striding out of the laboratory.

"Well, if the honouree isn't going to stay, then I might as well get back to work," Jung-hoon said, gulping the last of his coffee. "I'll just get some more of this first." His hands trembled as he reached toward the coffee machine.

"Dr. Kang, let me handle things in the lab tonight. You've been working nonstop the past few weeks," said Matt in a sweet tone.

"I'm so close to a breakthrough, though," Jung-hoon said, clenching his hands into fists. "I just need to keep running a few more trials, and—"

"Running trials while you're physically drained isn't the best strategy. Besides, Joe is on his shift now. He'll only drain you more," Matt said with a chuckle.

Jung-hoon closed his eyes in defeat. "You're right. A good night's sleep would be best." Then he perked up. "But I'll be back to the lab at oh four hundred hours. The chrysanthemum will have started to bloom, and I need to be there to—"

"Again, I've got it covered," Matt smiled.

Jung-hoon sighed. "Okay, I'll see you at breakfast."

"That's the spirit!" said Matt. "What the heck—have a lie-in and push it to lunch!"

"Oh, I could never," Jung-hoon said dreamily as Riff dragged him by the elbow toward the door.

Riff waved goodbye to Jung-hoon before returning to Matt. It was only the two of them left at the party.

"Some party, eh? If this whole science thing doesn't work out, we might be able to go into the event-planning business," said Matt with a laugh.

Riff shuffled his feet.

"You off to bed too, mate?"

"I feel a bit anxious about Luna leaving tomorrow. I just don't like it when we all get separated. Luna and I didn't exactly have the nicest interaction earlier today, either. There's no guarantee that we'll . . . see each other again. Like Elbina."

Matt placed a gentle hand on Riff's shoulder. "Luna is going to be fine. She bloody destroyed the Time Belt! And she loves you; don't forget that. As for Elbina, I know she's out there. You'll see her again. I promise."

"You're surprisingly comforting," said Riff warmly.

"I have this same conversation with Hayden every night," said Matt with a twinkle in his eye.

Riff nodded glumly.

"Come hang out with Joe and me on our shift tonight. It'll be fun. It'll take your mind off things," said Matt.

"Okay, that sounds good."

The friends walked out of the room and down the hallway to a slightly larger laboratory than the one they were just in. It was a dimly lit room with monitors of all sizes spread across all four walls, strange-looking plants in incubators, test tubes and flasks strewn about, giant bottles of various chemicals, and Joe. He was slumped in front of a computer typing very slowly. His head was bobbing every few seconds in and out of a doze.

"Good evening, Joseph," said Matt.

Joe jumped out of his slumber and spun his chair around, wearing a frightened expression that quickly turned into pure frustration once he saw his friends. "Nearly gave me a heart attack," he spat.

"How's the study coming along? Is the chrysanthemum doing anything interesting?" Matt asked.

The boys redirected their attention to a sorry-looking plant in a small but thick-walled glass incubator on Joe's desk. It had one drooping, sickly yellow stem with two and a half leaves (half of the third leaf cracked off before their eyes) and a single black bud the size of a pea. Riff quickly concluded that this plant had no chance of survival. No wonder Jung-hoon was so burnt out.

Joe sighed. "No, of course not. It's like watching paint dry."

Joe ran trials on various plants that Jung-hoon and his sector of the ERA were developing. If they could be made viable, there would be hope of reintroducing plant life on Earth. Joe's reports were given to Jung-hoon's team to develop more ideas for trials.

"Want to hear what I've written so far?" Joe asked. He cleared his throat. "'Chrysanthemum variant number twenty-six was tested with Solifican 8-B soil replacement {see Appendix A for full compositional details}. The plant was treated with UV rays for thirteen minutes, a water massage for twelve seconds, and verbal encouragements for five minutes. The results have shown that this plant is a useless piece of sh—"

"You might want to leave that bit out when you give it to Jung-hoon," said Matt.

"Lads, this job is doing my head in. I can't take it anymore. It's taking away from my musical creativity. I—I need to get out of here." Joe leapt up from his chair and sped toward the door, his hands clenching fistfuls of his hair.

Riff blocked him and encouraged him back to his seat.

"Riff, mate," said Matt, "he does this at least three times per shift. I usually just let him go. He always comes back for snacks."

Joe slumped in his chair and slammed his fist on the keyboard, adding a growing row of fs to his abstract.

"Come sit by my desk. My work is only slightly more interesting." Matt patted a chair between his and Joe's desks.

Matt worked in document control for the ERA. His role was reviewing all sorts of reports and procedures and approving them for widespread distribution on the ERA's internal quality management system. He had access to everything the ERA had access to—and more.

"I just have some reports to approve for Dr. Kang. Hey, it looks like this one was the study from earlier that you and Knitsy worked on!"

"Nothing interesting in there, I'm afraid, mate," said Riff.

Riff slumped in his chair as Matt read through the memo, correcting spelling errors and deleting a few curse words that Knitsy had added for fun. Riff was about to doze off when an email notification popped up on Matt's screen. Matt switched over from the document to his email. Riff read over Matt's shoulder as Matt inspected the new message:

*Matthew,*

*This is an urgent request. Drop all current priorities and attend to this immediately. Overtime work is expected. I just received some additional information on Project Piccadilly. Read through and add the information to the vault. Alert Dr. Kang when the information is stored so he can handle the matters accordingly. And please, no wandering eyes.*

*Regards,*

*Dr. D. Delevio, PhD*

*Director of Earth Rehabilitation Association (ERA)*

"Well, he seems lovely," said Riff.

"He's awful," said Matt. "I'd rather listen to a lullaby from nails on a chalkboard than this bloke any day. And he's the one in charge of all of us."

Riff's throat tightened. This Delevio guy must have taken his mother's position after she died.

"Project Piccadilly? What's that?" asked Riff.

"There's names for each project within the ERA. Just random words they assign to organise things. Like the viable plant project is Project District. Apparently, all the project names are from the old underground transport routes in London. Though I can't remember what Piccadilly is. I don't hear much about that one."

Matt looked in Joe's direction, his eyes bulging.

Riff quickly turned to face Joe. "What did you say?"

"It's the GeoLapse," said Joe.

Matt's face drained of colour. "D-don't say that name, Joe. We agreed—"

"Relax, it's okay," said Riff. "I need my two best friends to be able to speak freely around me. Besides, I can't change my past."

"I'll just do this later. It can wait," said Matt.

"Seems like Delevio doesn't think so. Besides, he's a nasty bloke. He'll rip you to shreds if you don't follow orders. Just do it now. I don't care," said Riff.

"But I have to do it in secret. 'No wandering eyes,'" said Matt in a hush.

"Bollocks," snapped Riff. "Who am I going to tell? My nan?"

Matt sighed. "Fine. Don't tell anyone you were here."

Joe rolled his chair closer to Matt and Riff.

Matt clicked the attachment that Delevio had emailed over. A dialog box displayed, and Matt quickly typed something. The document that came up had the word CONFIDENTIAL in bold red letters at the top. It read:

*The ERA European Surveillance sector reported today, 31 March 2213, that members of the GeoLapse terrorist group have been spotted in central London, United Kingdom. Many of the sightings have involved GeoLapse emerging from and disappearing into*

*unidentified tunnels. We do not have a count of GeoLapse existing within these tunnels, but they are thought to be numerous enough to have thwarted a counterterrorism operation two months ago, part of the regional effort in the Universal War. There is no current awareness of other GeoLapse tunnels on Earth, but if there is one in London, there are likely many more elsewhere.*
*Please find below the list of GeoLapse members we have been able to identify in this outbreak. Their profiles should be updated in the GeoLapse Vault for traceability.*

Riff expected to see five, maybe ten names maximum, but as Matt scrolled down the document, the names spanned many pages—fifty-five, to be exact. Fifty-five pages of GeoLapse hiding out in London. And that wasn't necessarily all of them.

"How did they all survive?" asked Riff. A knot formed in his stomach.

Matt and Joe stared slack-jawed at the list.

"It's going to take me all night . . . all *week* to get this stored in the vault," said Matt breathlessly.

"Do you think the ERA missed some locations?" asked Joe.

"Must have. I had a strange suspicion that four regional GeoLapse headquarters for the entire world was too few. Think of the sheer number of the GeoLapse," said Matt, scratching his chin.

"How many are there? Or were there?" asked Riff.

"There were millions," said Matt. "They had a bit of a slow start back in the sixties. But their growth shot up exponentially after that."

"Why would anyone want to join the GeoLapse?" asked Joe with a raised eyebrow.

Riff gulped. He had seen the formation of the GeoLapse when Knitsy completed her mission in the Time Belt. He had seen her memories of how his Grandad Mack was killed by his own brother, Burl Gorgan, another member of the GeoLapse.

"The promise of prosperity, money, food, the ability to go anywhere outside in special suits, free rein of the universe, just to name a few," said Riff gravely.

"I'd better get going on this list," said Matt.

The first name on the list read "Abecker, Alvin." Matt clicked a lock icon on his desktop. Again he was prompted to enter a lengthy password. A scanner at the top of Matt's monitor beeped, then analysed his eyes.

"What's this?" asked Riff.

"The GeoLapse vault. A profile of every member who ever existed. Or at least who the ERA could get a record on. Most of the GeoLapse don't have microchips, so they've been hard to detect. We rely on the surveillance team to spy on them and gather their information."

Matt typed 'Abecker' into the search bar, and a pixelated image of Alvin popped up. He wore a black suit that covered him from head to toe, and he held a lit torch. Glints of golden light reflected off the letters *GL* on his badge.

Below his picture, there were a few bits of information.

| | |
|---|---|
| *Status:* | *Dead* |
| *Last seen in:* | *Cardiff, Wales, UK* |
| *Rank:* | *Sergeant* |
| *Year joined:* | *2210* |
| *Height:* | *5' 11"* |
| *Weight:* | *218 lbs.* |
| *Notes:* | *Prone to using fire as a weapon.* |

Matt updated Alvin's status to 'Alive' and his location to 'London, UK.' He was just about to search for 'Addel, Kurt' when Riff said, "Let me take over."

Matt and Joe simultaneously said, "What?"

"Just swap seats with me," Riff said hotly.

Matt obliged and offered him his chair.

Riff typed 'Gorgan' into the search bar. Two results appeared: Burl and Willie.

Willie Gorgan's information read:

| | |
|---|---|
| *Status:* | *Dead* |
| *Last seen in:* | *Glasgow, Scotland, UK* |
| *Rank:* | *Private* |
| *Year joined:* | *2165* |
| *Height:* | *6' 2"* |
| *Weight:* | *278 lbs.* |
| *Notes:* | *One of the founding executives. Died in Battle of Watertown.* |

Willie looked important in his picture. He wore a tuxedo and sat in an elegantly upholstered chair. Smoke puffed from his nose. He was balding and had a round stomach. It seemed the GeoLapse's founding fathers were treated well. But what astounded Riff most of all was that this man, this evil man, was his great-grandfather. Not only did Riff have GeoLapse blood running through his veins, it was a founding member's blood. The thought made him sick to his stomach.

Next, he pulled up Burl's profile. It read:

| | |
|---|---|
| *Status:* | *Dead* |
| *Last seen in:* | *Portsmouth, England, UK* |
| *Rank:* | *Private* |
| *Year joined:* | *2169* |
| *Height:* | *6' 1"* |
| *Weight:* | *243 lbs.* |
| *Notes:* | *Strong influencer. Recruited a large percentage of UK membership. Died of natural causes in 2205, according to medical records obtained.* |

"Who's that?" asked Matt.

"My grandad's brother. He tried to recruit my grandad, but he refused. Burl killed him." The memory caused Riff's voice to croak.

Matt patted him on the arm.

Riff continued searching, this time typing 'Icketts.' Just the sight of the name sickened Riff even more.

"That's my dad's real last name—and mine, technically," said Riff aloud before the other two could ask.

There was only one result: Valents Icketts. Riff's heart dropped. The picture was of an evil-looking man smiling broadly. One of his front teeth was missing, and the rest were crooked. He had a circle tattooed around his right eye and a scar along his left cheek. His hair was completely white, although Riff was told his hair used to be red, like Riff's. The man looked like he'd kill anyone that stepped within five metres of his space. His profile read:

| | |
|---|---|
| *Status:* | *Unknown* |
| *Last seen in:* | *Washington, DC, USA* |
| *Rank:* | *Sergeant Major* |
| *Year joined:* | *2207* |
| *Height:* | *6' 4"* |
| *Weight:* | *195 lbs.* |
| *Notes:* | *Extremely dangerous!* |

Sweat dripped from Riff's forehead. "Where's that list of the GeoLapse you had earlier?" he said in a low voice.

Matt took the mouse and opened up the document that Delevio had sent. Riff scrolled through the pages looking for familiar names. Luckily there were no Gorgans—they were surely dead. His heart was pounding now. He passed the remainder of the surnames beginning with G, scrolled through H, and finally reached I.

*Please no,* he thought to himself. *Please be dead.* His eyes scanned the names.

*Ibman, Alley*
*Ibmuth, Ramsey*
*Ichfarm, Randall*
*Icketts, Valents*

"No!" Riff yelled, standing up from his chair. "No, no, no, this can't be happening!"

He began to pace around the room. He felt light-headed and nauseous. How could he be related to this monster? Three monsters, to be exact. And who knew how many other members of his family were linked to the GeoLapse. He felt a burning hatred toward his father— how could he have betrayed his four children and their sweet mother like this? How could the GeoLapse have caused so much devastation and homicide, including the incident in which Ann Lou lost her left arm as a young child? Riff wanted to rip his heart out and end it all. He didn't want to share DNA with Valents Icketts.

Riff hyperventilated and collapsed on the floor. Matt and Joe rushed to him and propped him up to a sitting position.

"Look at me!" Matt said, patting Riff's face. "You are not him and he is not you, okay? You are Griffin McHubbard, drummer extraordinaire, best friend, brother, and peaceful citizen of Earth and the wider universe. Do not even entertain the idea that there could be any similarities between you and that murderer."

Joe nodded in agreement with Matt. He even placed a steady hand on Riff's back. Riff glanced back and forth at his friends and wept. He held them tightly, wanting to keep close to him the people who made him feel happy, free, and fun-loving. He didn't need a father to do that for him—he had his best friends and bandmates, his sisters, and his grandmother to keep him authentically Riff.

Riff felt Matt and Joe release their grip on him. He wiped a tear on his sleeve, then looked up and saw that they were back at Joe's desk. Before he could question them, he could already deduce where their focus was fixated. The chrysanthemum was vibrating and glowing with neon-yellow light.

# CHAPTER 4

## CLORIN REBORN

Riff followed his friends to the blooming flower—if "blooming" is the right word to describe a violently vibrating plant that had shaken off the last of its leaves.

Riff felt footsteps in the room. He turned to see Jung-hoon running toward them while clutching his chest.

"Over . . . slept. Did I . . . miss anything? Has it . . . bloomed?" he said, completely out of breath. His eyes bulged at the sight of the chrysanthemum. He pressed his hands and nose to the incubator in fascination.

"Erm . . . I think I need to update my abstract," Joe said, sliding into his chair.

"Marvellous, absolutely marvellous!" Jung-hoon squealed, bouncing giddily in front of Matt and Riff. "It's blooming!"

"'Vibrating like mad,'" Joe said as he typed.

The black bud had turned red-hot, and the stem was glowing yellow.

"Blooming? It looks more like it's about to explode," said Riff.

Without hesitation, the plant did just that. It burst and splattered all over the inside of the incubator. Solifican and artificial plant goo dripped down the walls of the now plantless enclosure.

"'And exploded,'" Joe concluded.

Even with the unfortunate occurrence, the smile couldn't be wiped off Jung-hoon's face.

"Now this . . . is science," he beamed.

"I don't mean to burst your bubble, Dr. Kang, but I have an urgent matter to discuss with you regarding one of the projects," said Matt, biting his bottom lip.

"Which one?"

"Erm . . . Project Piccadilly."

Jung-hoon's face twisted in confusion. "That can't be right. Project Piccadilly was completed months ago."

Matt opened his mouth to speak, but no words came out.

"Very well," said Jung-hoon. "Let's find a place to speak privately. Riff, your sister is leaving for planet Casper in a few hours. I suggest you get some sleep so you can say a proper goodbye."

"Yeah, right. I'll head up to my dorm now," replied Riff.

"Oh, and Joseph," said Jung-hoon, "I want a full study on that chrysanthemum on my desk at oh six hundred hours."

Jung-hoon and Matt quickly left the room to discuss the urgent matter. Joe just banged his head on his keyboard, adding several lines of zs to the study.

* * *

"Argh!"

Riff was awakened several hours later by a sharp rap to the shoulder from Knitsy's cane.

"Wake up, lazy bones! For heaven's sake, we're going to be late to see your sister off!"

Knitsy started into a fit of coughs, all while still waving her cane at Riff.

"Nan, get your breathing patch," said Riff sternly.

"No!" wheezed Knitsy.

"Then no breakfast," said Riff, shrugging his shoulders.

Knitsy's lips twisted. "Fine," she said. She reached into her bra, where she occasionally stored her breathing apparatus, then slapped the patch onto her arm and snapped the mask contraption around her face.

Riff and Knitsy shared a dormitory within the White House. Knitsy had the entire king bed to herself and Riff was stuck on the trundle. Someone had to keep Knitsy under control, and Riff was the only one of the McHubbard grandchildren who could do just that. Riff was also secretly Knitsy's favourite grandchild. The two of them bickered constantly, but Knitsy also laughed far more with Riff than she did with the rest of the grandchildren.

Riff helped Knitsy get dressed in her usual long skirt and turtleneck. He ordered her to brush her teeth, threatening no desserts if she didn't. About ten minutes later, both he and Knitsy were ready. They made their way to Danforth Commons, which was empty except for a neat array of round tables and armchairs. The tables were perfectly set up for a formal event, with crystal goblets, flowery ceramic dishes and tea cups, golden cutlery, and serviettes folded into the shape of swans, which apparently were some sort of creature that had gone extinct a couple hundred years before.

The only other people in the room were Luna, Jung-hoon, Ann Lou, and Apollo, all standing in front of one of the Jalopy Cabins, the glass walls of which were frosted instead of clear like usual. Luna carried a small rucksack over her shoulder and was reading a book feverishly with her finger. She was expressionless, almost as if this journey wasn't troubling her at all—as if it were just a part of her day-to-day activities.

Ann Lou eyed Riff in an uncomfortable fashion. She held her stomach with her prosthetic hand. Riff noticed her trembling slightly. He opened his mouth to ask if she was feeling all right, but she shook her head to stop him.

No one spoke a word until Jung-hoon broke the silence. "Got all the paperwork, Luna? You certainly want to make sure you're prepared for Casper. They're not the most welcoming community when it comes to little inconveniences that might waste time."

"I've got it all sorted," Luna replied, continuing to read.

Silence again. After a few moments, Knitsy coughed, possibly purposefully to break the tension.

"What exactly are we waiting for?" Ann Lou asked.

"A Casperian is arriving to escort Luna on her journey," said Jung-hoon.

"But isn't that the whole point of a Jalopy . . . to escort yourself wherever you need to go?" asked Riff, scratching his forehead.

Jung-hoon nodded and sighed. "Yes. The Casperians are still feeling a bit wounded after that last Universal Union meeting where the leader told everyone that Luna was cleverer than the lot of them. So, they're being a bit stubborn and chauffeuring her in case she 'confuses the Jalopy.'" He chuckled to himself for half a second. "For peacekeeping reasons, let's do as they wish."

A slight rumble alarmed the group, and the frosted glass suddenly appeared clear again. Just behind the glass was an eerily familiar figure.

The large-headed Casperian stepped out of the Jalopy Cabin and smacked his appendages to his head. "Not again!" he cried.

"Tycho?" Luna gasped.

It was indeed Tycho. Back in the Time Belt, the McHubbards had frequented the book shop where Tycho worked. He had often scowled at their existence and belittled their brain capacity. Nonetheless, he'd been helpful in providing Luna with the information necessary to destroy the Time Belt.

"Why is it that you continuously find ways to pinpoint me in this vast, seemingly unending universal structure?" said Tycho hotly, balling up his nasal appendages into a fist. Like all Casperians, Tycho had been required to learn most of the universe's languages in the Casperian equivalent of preschool, so his English was excellent. Human and Casperian anatomy were similar enough that Riff had no trouble reading Tycho's lips.

"Technically, you found *us* this time," said Riff.

Knitsy snorted next to him.

Turning to Luna, Tycho growled, "I request that you be silent during our three-and-a-half-Earth-hour journey to Schingmaning, the capital city of Casper. Now, give me your visa to inspect. Considering your species' microscopic brains, I'm sure it is riddled with errors."

Tycho yanked the paperwork from Luna's hand with his appendages, turned on his heels, and marched straight back into the Jalopy Cabin to carefully inspect the paperwork.

"Well, this is goodbye for now," Jung-hoon said, reaching out for a hug from Luna, who patted him awkwardly on the back. "One more thing," he said, reaching into his pocket. "The ERA has finally been able to focus on other projects that were put on hold due to the GeoLapse. Our medical engineering team recently designed this device."

He handed Luna something that resembled a surgical headlamp.

"It has a sensor that grabs a picture of your surroundings. The picture is then sent via electrical impulses to your occipital lobe, which allows you to 'see' a set of images. It's not perfect yet, but—"

"No, thanks," said Luna, holding up her hand. "I don't feel like being a guinea pig for a device that may not work. I can cope with my other senses. I am quite comfortable as I am."

"I know you are, but we want you to have all the tools you might need—"

"My most powerful tool is here," said Luna, pointing to her brain. "That's all I need to help find Elbina."

"Very well," said Jung-hoon. His head drooped.

"Well, I'll see you lot later," Luna said.

Riff tensed up. "That's all you can say to us?" He so desperately wanted to tell Luna about what he had found out in the lab overnight, but now wasn't the right time, especially with Jung-hoon in the room. He wasn't sure if there ever would be a right time to tell her.

"What do you want me to say?" Luna spat back.

"Just—just that you'll miss us or something. I guess."

Luna scowled. "When have I ever said that?"

"I dunno. It's just that you've been so on edge lately, and I don't want you leaving like this. We're a team," Riff said.

Luna huffed. "Our team isn't complete right now."

Tycho cursed something in Casperian, then stuck his head back out from the Jalopy Cabin and rolled his tennis-ball-sized eyes. "Miraculously, your papers are acceptable," he said. "You must have procured some external Casperian assistance on this."

Luna turned her back on her family and strode inside the Jalopy Cabin. The window turned opaque, the cabin made a small rumble, and when the glass turned clear again, Luna and Tycho were gone.

"I'm going to head back to work," said Jung-hoon. "Lots to do. I'll see you two on your shift later," he added, pointing to Riff and Knitsy. Then he exited Danforth Commons.

Riff caught a glance from Knitsy, who looked visibly upset. "Nan, what's wrong?"

Knitsy wiped away a tear. "I don't like you kids fighting is all. That's my job to rile you up. It's hard saying goodbye."

"She'll be fine," Ann Lou said in a strained voice. She was still holding her stomach. "Nan, have you eaten yet? There's a pudding buffet in the canteen downstairs."

Knitsy perked up.

"Apollo, why don't you take her down? Riff and I will meet you in a few minutes," she added, wincing slightly.

Neither Knitsy nor Apollo looked thrilled at this request. Apollo hissed something at Ann Lou, to which she replied, "I'll be fine. It's not until later this week."

Apollo begrudgingly walked over to Knitsy and held out a large claw for her to take, but she swatted at him and led the way out the door. Apollo glared back at Ann Lou, his eyes red-hot.

Ann Lou just shrugged. "Follow her. Make sure she doesn't end up in the walk-in freezer again."

Once the Epitonian and the elderly Earthling had vanished out of the door, Ann Lou gripped Riff's arm.

"What's wrong?"

"I'm . . . in so much . . . pain."

Riff gasped. "We need to get you to the medical team, now! Why didn't you say something earlier?"

Ann Lou shook her head. "I didn't want Luna to worry. And Apollo, he's been so helpful with making sure I'm comfortable. I can't keep bothering him. *Ouch*!" She gripped her side.

"Ann Lou, Apollo loves you! He wants to know how you're feeling at all times," said Riff.

"Argh!" Ann Lou cried. She collapsed onto the floor in the foetal position.

Riff knelt down beside her and held his hand to her forehead. "Bloody hell, Ann Lou! You're scorching!" Sweat started pouring from her forehead, and her cheeks reddened. The rest of her body began to sweat profusely.

"Hold on!" Riff tapped his left wrist to activate a voice message, then picked up his youngest sister and cradled her in his arms. As he ran out the door of Danforth Commons and headed downstairs to Jung-hoon's laboratory, he verbalised a message to send to Jung-hoon.

> Riff McHubbard: *Jung-hoon! Get Ann Lou a doctor now! I think she's in labour!*

Jung-hoon replied within seconds. His reply popped up as captions in holographic form above his left wrist.

> Jung-hoon Kang: *Already? She's not due for another few days. The caesarean section isn't until later this week.*

> Riff McHubbard: *I don't care whether she's due or not. She's burning my arms!*

> Jung-hoon Kang: *Okay. We'll make space for her.*

Riff barrelled into the laboratory, his chest heaving as he took gulps of air. Ann Lou was breathing almost as hard. Jung-hoon raced over to them, knocking over a canister of Solifican, and led them to a space in the middle of the room where he had pushed aside some of the tables and chairs.

"Is there a doctor who knows what to do for her situation?" Riff asked nervously.

Jung-hoon nodded, helping Riff lower Ann Lou to the ground. "I've just alerted Dr. Gressfeld. She is aware of the procedure for Ann Lou and Clorin." They propped Ann Lou's head up with a pile of lab coats.

Within ninety seconds, the laboratory door burst open and Dr. Gressfeld charged in. She was a sturdily built woman with a tight grey bun, a unibrow, and a crazed look in her bloodshot eyes, and she was holding a pair of obstetrical forceps above her head. A team of three resident doctors followed, pushing an equipment cart. Riff thought some of the equipment looked strange for a pregnancy, particularly the giant pot, the oven mitts, and the flaming torch.

"Put her on ze sheet!" ordered Dr. Gressfeld.

The residents unrolled a sheet of metal and placed it on the floor beside Ann Lou. They then lifted Ann Lou on top of it; a button push somewhere on the equipment cart activated the metal sheet, and Ann Lou levitated on her back to everyone's chest level.

"Prepare ze surgical field!" snapped Dr. Gressfeld.

In a well-choreographed flurry that took about twenty seconds, the residents spun Ann Lou in midair, undressed her, covered her legs and torso with cloth drapes, and disinfected her abdomen with something so odorously strong that Riff worried that he'd never smell anything good ever again. He might as well ask Dr. Gressfeld to chop off his nose after she was done with Ann Lou's procedure.

Ann Lou's eyes bulged as she spotted the torch. Riff, also panicking, said in as calm a voice as he could, "A torch is nothing compared to the extreme heat of Epiton." He spread a fake smile across his face and held Ann Lou's hand.

"Anaesthetise ze girl!" Dr. Gressfeld continued shouting, jabbing her forceps at the residents to encourage speed.

One mousy-looking resident held up a giant syringe, then injected something into Ann Lou's neck. Ann Lou flinched, then instantly relaxed, her eyes fluttering half closed. Riff nearly fainted.

"Scalpel!" Gressfeld shouted.

A second shaky resident squeaked as he passed the sharp instrument to his attending.

"Prepare ze pot!" Gressfeld continued.

The third resident, who was the tallest of the three but no less timid than the others, dumped water into the pot, followed by a handful of a white powder. The water instantly began to boil.

"If you no like blood, you leave!" Gressfeld said to the room, but her eyes were focused on Riff.

Riff stared in horror as Gressfeld dragged the scalpel across Ann Lou's abdomen. Blood poured out, but Ann Lou seemed unaware that anything was happening. Riff tightened his grip on her hand and said, "Keep going,

Ann Lou! You're doing great," even though his voice was filled with terror.

Gressfeld reached her hands within Ann Lou's abdomen and started to tug on something.

"Yarrr!" she bellowed. "Ze egg has grown since ze last ultrasound! It will not fit!"

"What do we do?" Jung-hoon shrieked. "This was the plan you said would work!"

Gressfeld furrowed her brow at Jung-hoon. "Out you go!"

"B-but this is my lab," squawked Jung-hoon.

"OUT!"

Jung-hoon fled the room. Riff so badly wanted to follow him but couldn't leave Ann Lou behind.

"Now I crack ze egg," Gressfeld said in a tone of finality. She selected a small, sharp rock from the cart and raised it above her head. All three residents covered their eyes. Riff slammed his eyes shut until he heard a crack and felt something sharp and goopy hit his face. He opened his eyes and wiped his cheek. A piece of eggshell. He peered at Gressfeld. Her face and hair were covered in goop and eggshell, but she still wore a victorious grin.

"Get ze shell out of ze girl when I pull out baby!" she barked.

Gressfeld put on the oven mitts, then tenderly reached into the incision in Ann Lou's abdomen and pulled out what looked like a flaming ball of goo.

Riff couldn't see any defining features in the ball, but his heart nearly leapt out of his chest with relief. "Clorin," he breathed with a smile.

Gressfeld gently put the flaming ball of Clorin into the pot of boiling water. "Get baby to NICU," she ordered. "Keep him in pot and torch on bottom of pot."

One of the residents held the pot while another held the lit torch beneath it, and they swiftly exited the room.

"Help me get girl to ICU," Gressfeld ordered the last remaining resident.

They each gripped one side of the metal sheet on the ground, lifted it, and guided it toward the exit. Ann Lou was still completely out of it, and her floating body swiftly exited with the pair of doctors.

Riff followed them. "Is Clorin—the baby all right? And Ann Lou? Will she be okay?"

Gressfeld bumped Riff's shoulder, and he nearly bounced off the wall. "Both not in good shape. I surprised they both not dead yet!"

Gressfeld and the resident disappeared around a corner with Ann Lou. Riff fell to his knees. He couldn't lose another sister. He felt so alone. First Elbina was kidnapped, then Luna went to a strange planet, and now Ann Lou was on her deathbed . . . and on top of all that, he had the blood of the GeoLapse.

Riff dug his fingers into his hair. In his mind, he spoke to his sister and nephew. *Ann Lou . . . Clorin . . . if you can hear me, please pull through. For Elbina. For Mum. For me.*

# CHAPTER 5

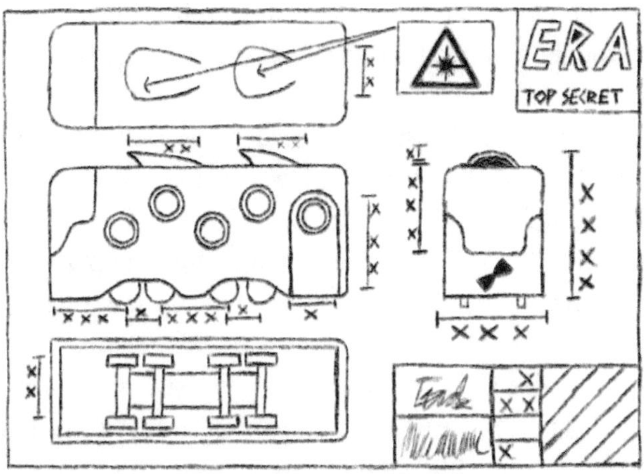



## BABIES AND BLUEPRINTS

Ann Lou and Clorin spent the next few weeks in the hospital, which was just a small section of the sixth and topmost floor of the White House. There wasn't much need for a hospital since the only people who lived at the White House were the ERA members and President Murphy. Aside from Clorin, there was only one other infant in the NICU: a human baby named Alphabeta Zeep, who was the new daughter of two ERA employees. Riff hadn't been able to visit Ann Lou and Clorin until Gressfeld gave the okay, and today was finally that day.

Riff visited Clorin first. This consisted of peeking through a window into the nursery. He pressed his face against the glass to see how the babies were doing. Alphabeta squirmed in her bassinet. She was a very cute baby with a tuft of black hair and squishy cheeks. Just to her left, in a very different type of bed, was Clorin. He had unfolded somewhat from the ball formation he was born in, and he was now in a much bigger pot of boiling water. He was still aflame. Riff could see a tiny claw poking through the fire, almost as if he were waving to his uncle. Riff smiled and waved back.

Riff felt something brush his shoulder. He looked to his left and saw two ERA employees, a man and a woman, whom he recognised, although he didn't know their names. Both were tall and had creamy brown skin and black, ultra-curly hair, although the man had a large bald spot in the middle of his head. They wore big, bulky glasses, which made them look nerdy.

"First-time parent?" the woman said with a sigh and a smile.

"Oh, no," said Riff. He pointed to the pot. "That's my nephew."

The man said something, but he turned away from Riff's face midway through.

"Sorry?" said Riff, pointing to his ear.

The man spoke again, but Riff still couldn't quite read his lips.

"Erm, could I possibly ask your accent?" said Riff, embarrassed.

"Spanish. Apologies," the man said.

"Ah, gotcha. Thanks, mate. Sometimes that really helps me with lip reading."

"How intriguing!" the woman said. "That's our daughter, Alphabeta. She was born on the same day as your nephew."

"Oh, you're the Zeep family. Nice to meet you. I'm Riff," he said, holding out his hand to shake.

"Nice to meet you as well. I'm Flora, and this is my husband, Garold," said the woman.

"Pleasure to meet you, Riff," said Garold, shaking his hand. "Which department do you work in?"

"I work in Jung-hoon Kang's plant lab as an environmental scientist."

Garold nodded. "Oh, Dr. Kang is the best employer to work for in the entire ERA."

"And he's so hardworking," added Flora. "Even after all he's been through, having lost his partner all those years ago, he still generates a tremendous amount of research."

Riff gulped. They were talking about his mother. He desperately wanted to change the subject. "Which department do you work in?"

"I'm on the medical engineering team," replied Garold. "And Flora works on the universal communications team. This is the hardest worker in the ERA, closely followed by Dr. Kang," said Garold, proudly putting his arm around a blushing Flora.

Riff, Flora, and Garold watched as Dr. Gressfeld adjusted some of Alphabeta's tubes. Alphabeta wailed and kicked her legs every which way. Flora let out a meek, "Oh, dear." Gressfeld then lit a torch and made her way over to Clorin. She waved the torch gently over Clorin's pot to keep him aflame.

When Gressfeld caught sight of the three onlookers behind the window, she started thrashing her arms, including the torch still in hand, in their direction.

"Go now! You disturb ze peace! Out of my NICU!"

The three of them backed away, then strode swiftly down the hall to the waiting room.

"That woman scares me," said Flora, once the three were sitting comfortably in chairs. "But she's supposedly the best in the business, so I have to trust her."

"She certainly runs a tight ship," said Riff.

"Oh goodness, yes! She kicked poor Garold out of the operating room because he was 'smiling too loudly,'" Flora said with a small chuckle.

"What can I say? Birth is the most breathtaking miracle in the world," Garold beamed.

Riff smiled at the Zeeps. He felt a warm comfort around them—the feeling he used to get at home in England, back when all of his family was still together. "Well," he said, "it's been really nice chatting to you both. I have to go check on my sister."

"And you, Riff. Come visit our labs anytime. You know where to find—"

"ZEEP!" yelled a man's voice.

Flora and Garold suddenly looked afraid. Riff saw a young man with a chiselled body and an overabundance of mousse in his slicked back hair angrily storming up the hallway. Flora quickly stood up from her seat.

"Dr. Delevio. Is everything okay?"

"Do I look like everything's okay?" Delevio spat, crossing his arms and tapping his foot. "You've been away from your desk for sixteen minutes. Are you not aware of the current situation with Project Piccadilly? We need all hands on deck for all hours. No excuses!"

"I—I was just taking my lunch break. We're visiting our daughter. She needs her mother to check in on her. I just needed to see her," Flora said, her lip trembling.

"Your child does not concern me. You are to report back to your desk with me immediately."

Delevio grabbed Flora's arm firmly. Garold stepped in.

"Dr. Delevio, please let go of my wife. It's my fault she's away from her desk. Do not blame her!" pleaded Garold.

Delevio yanked Flora's arm. Incensed, Garold grabbed his hand and tried to break the grip on his wife's arm, but he couldn't. With his other hand, Delevio shoved Garold to the floor.

"Stay out of my way, Zeep." Delevio angrily pointed a finger toward Garold. "You're interfering with important matters. I'll have you sacked from the medical branch before you even get a chance to hold your daughter." Then he dragged Flora down the hall and out of sight.

Riff helped Garold to his feet.

Garold dusted off his trousers. "What a horrible man. I hate that we all work for that monster."

"Is there anywhere else you and your wife could work around the area?" asked Riff.

"Flora is on a contract with the ERA to finish the projects she's working on. Like Project Piccadilly. She's been on that one for years—ever since she started here. And now it's just popped up again, so she has no choice but to stay on. Otherwise, they'll pull our home, our savings, basically our whole lives. We'd have nothing without the ERA's help."

"What has Flora told you about Piccadilly?" asked Riff.

Garold shrugged. "Dunno. She's not allowed to tell me. I can't imagine it's a fun project if it's making Delevio act like that."

"I'm sorry about your situation," said Riff.

"I'm grateful, kiddo. I've got my wife and daughter. That's all I need to be happy. Anyways, speaking of family, you'd better tend to your sister. I'll bet she needs you by her side. See you later." Garold waved and walked away, limping slightly.

Riff couldn't help but feel bad for the Zeeps. They were such a nice family, and they were being treated so poorly.

Riff made his way to the ICU, which was just a short walk down the hall from the NICU and on the opposite side. He walked in to find only one occupant in the unit: Ann Lou.

She was peacefully asleep in her bed. Her wild blonde hair was beautifully surrounding her head like a halo on the pillow. Riff tiptoed up to her, nervous to see how she was doing. She was covered in a blanket from the neck down. He wondered if her legs would be saved, or if she would end up the way she looked in Clorin's memory back when they were stuck in the Time Belt.

Riff gently shook her arm. "Ann Lou?"

Her eyes fluttered open, and she blinked a few times, contemplating the scene around her. "Riff? Where is Clorin? Where am I?" She scrunched the blanket in her fists and started panning the room.

"Relax, Ann Lou. You're in the hospital still. Clorin is doing just fine."

Ann Lou clutched her chest and lay back down. "Thank goodness."

"How are you feeling?" asked Riff.

Ann Lou closed her eyes. "Everything hurts." Within seconds, she had the same thought as Riff and peeked under the blanket that covered the lower half of her body. Her sigh of relief gave Riff all the confirmation he needed.

"I'm okay," she said with a tear in her eye. Her chin wobbled.

"Well," said Riff heartily, "that's bad news for the rest of the universe. Looks like you'll keep beating everyone to a pulp in the Pyroll arena!"

Ann Lou smiled, tears now spilling down her cheeks. "I was so worried that I wouldn't be able to play anymore. That—that I'd lose Apollo. And . . . my baby."

Riff hugged Ann Lou tightly. The two exchanged a few more tidbits about Clorin's upcoming feeding schedule (three hot stones per hour for the next two weeks, then graduating to eight burning logs per day for six months), Riff's recent encounter with Delevio and the Zeeps, and the gross hospital food that was brought in by a nurse (some mush that looked like haggis but tasted like the cabbaged eggs from planet Antympanica). Their visit was rudely cut short by Dr. Gressfeld, who swatted Riff out of the room with her surgical mask in hand.

After Riff passed the NICU and fit in a secretive peek at Clorin, holographic letters popped up just above his left wrist.

Jung-hoon Kang: *Riff, report to my laboratory now.*

Riff tore off in the direction of Jung-hoon's lab, speeding down the hallways and taking stairs several at a time. When he arrived at the lab door, Knitsy was already asleep in a chair next to Jung-hoon, who was feverishly typing an email.

"You all right?" Riff gasped for air. "Did I not need to run?"

Jung-hoon spun in his chair to face Riff. "I'm glad you arrived punctually. An emergency top-secret meeting has just started. Only the leads of each department will be there. But I want the two of you there as well."

"What's wrong?" Riff asked as Jung-hoon tapped Knitsy to wake her up. She stirred unhappily, groaning about evil hats that had infiltrated her dreams.

"You'll soon find out. Don't ask any questions. Just follow me and keep quiet."

Riff took Knitsy's arm, and the pair followed Jung-hoon around the maze of the White House until they reached the great doors of Danforth Commons. Jung-hoon pulled the D-shaped brass handles, and the doors opened on a meeting in progress. A panel of five people sat on one side of a long oval table, addressing about fifteen others who were seated across from them. Riff recognised Flora Zeep among the fifteen, and a couple of other familiar faces. One of the panellists was speaking. Riff immediately recognised one of the neighbouring panellists as Luna.

His heart started to race. Why was she back already? Was she hurt? Unlikely, he quickly decided, judging from the look on her face. It was her usual expression—the one that said, "I'm much too important to be here." She looked perfectly healthy.

"Ah, Jung-hoon," snarled Delevio, "it's so kind of you to actually join us." Delevio was seated next to Luna. The rest of the attendees robotically turned their heads in the direction of Jung-hoon, Knitsy, and Riff.

From behind, Riff couldn't tell what Jung-hoon had said in reply, but he hoped it was something along the lines of, "What's that supposed to mean, you arsehole?" Riff had been spending way too much time with Knitsy.

The three found seats on the side of the table opposite the panellists. Riff helped Knitsy sit down, and he made sure her breathing patch was secured—the last thing this crew needed was a top-secret meeting being interrupted by Knitsy's hacking coughs.

"What have we missed?" Jung-hoon asked the panel. "Oh, and by the way, Luna, it's Jung-hoon, your brother Riff, and your grandmother Knitsy who have just entered the room."

Luna gasped and perked up in her chair. She smiled slightly, then regained her composure. "Thank you for joining us," she said quietly.

Delevio snapped, "Jung-hoon, if you'd like to ensure no one's time is being wasted, we'd appreciate it if you would demonstrate your concern for the critical work being done at the ERA by showing up to meetings on time."

Riff was disappointed to hear Jung-hoon's response, a meek "Sorry."

"Anyways," continued Delevio, "this meeting is in relation to the recently added Project Bakerloo, which is to build a Jalopy that has the capacity to travel between universes. The creature will provide an update."

Tycho, the Casperian, who sat on the other side of Luna, stood and formed his nasal appendages into what seemed like a rather obscene gesture toward Delevio. "We have come to request additional materials. The current design is still preliminary, but we have deduced that there needs to be an energy source to keep the Jalopy and its inhabitants safe as they travel through black holes to other universes. This is the most important piece of the project—"

"This is where your team comes in, Jung-hoon," interrupted Delevio. "We need you to retrieve the materials."

Jung-hoon's face froze.

Flora piped up. "Mr. Tycho, would you be able to tell us what kind of materials you are looking for?"

"Certainly," Tycho replied, waving his appendages giddily. "We are looking for pure stardust, one of the most difficult compounds to come by."

"But we have plenty of stardust in the lab," said Jung-hoon. "There is a whole vault of it. We find it in meteorites. You can have as much as you want."

"Sadly, that's not *pure* stardust," said Tycho. "The purest form of it can be found as soon as it's formed."

"But that's . . . oh," said Jung-hoon.

The attendees started scratching their heads in unison and murmuring to one another.

"What?" Riff said aloud. "What's the problem? Luna, tell me what's going on."

Delevio slammed a fist on the table. "Jung-hoon, my underling scientists would *never* speak up unless spoken to! Get your employee in line!"

"No, he has a right to know," said Jung-hoon. "Riff, pure stardust forms during a supernova."

Riff's face scrunched as he thought back to his last science class in secondary school. "The thing that happens when stars die?"

"Yes," said Jung-hoon. "The star explodes, and the particles from the explosion come together and help birth new stars."

"So . . . how are we supposed to get pure stardust?" asked Riff.

"I think I have the same question for the panel," said Jung-hoon. "Why my team? We don't have any pure stardust."

"Your team is the most knowledgeable about materials," said Delevio. "And the most disposable."

"What?" gasped Jung-hoon.

"Your team has been volunteered to make the journey," said Delevio.

"By whom?" said Jung-hoon, his whole body shaking with fury.

"Me," said Delevio, with an evil grin. "Only three can go, though. Two from your team and one from the universal communications team. The Jalopy we have for the journey is available in the storeroom, but it needs a few repairs first. Creature, the blueprints." Delevio snapped his fingers.

Tycho pushed a button on the table in front of him, and blueprints of the Jalopy formed as a hologram in the centre of the table.

"Ricardo," said Delevio, "as head of the space transportation team, you need to review these drawings to repair the Jalopy. When can your team have it repaired?"

Ricardo, a balding, scrawny man who sat two seats down from Riff, began nervously darting his eyes across the complicated technical drawing. There were at least a hundred different dimensions, notes, and complex symbols that Riff had never seen.

"Well, Ricardo?" growled Delevio.

"Erm, well, I'd need a good look at these with my team to really provide a proper—"

"Give me a timeline now."

"Six weeks," said Ricardo, starting to sweat.

"Make it next Friday."

"Erm, that's not possible, I'm afraid," squawked Ricardo. "We could get it down to four weeks, minimum, if the team works weekends, but only a week is nearly impossible—"

"Next Friday it is," repeated Delevio.

"Excuse me," piped Flora. "Ricardo said it's not feasible. Shouldn't we take the subject matter expert's say on this?"

"Zeep, you're just like that insufferable husband of yours. Bold, arrogant, speaking out of turn. Who is the head of this work site? I am. Not any of you uneducated fools," said Delevio, his face purpling.

No one in the room spoke. All eyes were on Delevio.

"That's what I thought," Delevio snarled.

Tycho waved to get the room's attention. "We must be off now to continue our research. We look forward to receiving the pure stardust." His appendages roped around Luna's arms, and he started leading her to the Jalopy Cabins on the other side of the room.

"Wait!" shouted Riff. "I need to talk to my sister!"

But Tycho continued forward, gripping Luna tighter. Luna looked back in Riff's direction and mouthed, "Sorry."

Within seconds of stepping into the Jalopy Cabins, the two were gone, somewhere in the vast depths of space.

Delevio cleared his throat. "Now, Jung-hoon, I suppose these two employees whom you brought with you today are your volunteers to get the stardust?" said Delevio, staring menacingly at Riff and Knitsy. "Welcome to Project Bakerloo."

# Chapter 6

## A Noisy Surprise

Over the next week, Riff's work in the plant lab was severely uneventful. Knitsy neglected her watering-can duties, but Riff didn't have the energy to scold her. He was nervous about the journey that awaited them. Delevio was expecting them to jump into a rickety, hastily repaired Jalopy and travel to the depths of a supernova, just to collect some dust for a different Jalopy that might or might not be able to survive a voyage through a black hole. Riff was starting to think that there was more chance of his father giving up his lifestyle as the GeoLapse leader and becoming a monk than of him surviving this assignment.

Riff, Matt, and Joe held a few more jam sessions that week, and Ann Lou and Clorin were finally discharged from the hospital. Riff was pleased to see Ann Lou, Clorin, and Apollo sitting together at breakfast one morning in Danforth Commons. Riff beamed as he saw baby Clorin, who was just as cute as his slightly older self whom Riff had met in the Time Belt—even with the claws, the red eyes, and the horns atop his head. Aside from those Epitonian features, Clorin resembled his McHubbard kin, with his sandy hair and his pale skin.

Riff and Clorin locked eyes from across the room, and Clorin immediately flailed his limbs about and squeaked, "Wiff!" Clorin remembered him, even though he was still a baby! Riff rushed to their table and scooped up his nephew, kissing his hair and the horns atop his small head.

Apollo hissed something at Riff and slammed a clawed fist on the table.

Riff shuddered and practically dropped Clorin back into his mother's arms. Apollo placed a hot stone into his son's mouth. Clorin spat it across the room, narrowly missing the head of an ERA member who was naively strolling to get breakfast.

"Come on, honey. Eat the rock. It's yummy! Mmm," said Ann Lou with an exaggerated expression of delight on her face while placing another steaming rock in front of Clorin's face.

"No!" chirped Clorin.

Apollo hissed at Clorin.

Clorin gulped, took the hot stone in his claws, and started suckling it.

"Aww, he loves his daddy," cooed Ann Lou.

Apollo hissed something lovingly at Ann Lou, then got up from the table.

"Bye, love," said Ann Lou, kissing Apollo's forehead as he bent down to their son. "Apollo's got Pyroll practice," she said as an aside to Riff. "Will Aithne be at practice today?" Aithne was Apollo's mother and a Pyroll teammate of theirs.

Apollo grumbled in reply.

"Honey, I don't care if your mother desperately wants to see him. Clorin is much too young to bring to Epiton. Dr. Gressfeld said he needs to become acclimated to napping in the fireplace first before we even think of taking him on trips," said Ann Lou.

"Grrr," growled Apollo.

"Don't you growl at me!" said Ann Lou, pointing a finger at her husband. Clorin went to bite her outstretched finger.

Apollo groaned in surrender.

"Next time," she smiled.

Apollo huffed, patted both Clorin and Ann Lou on the head with a heavy claw, and darted out of the room at his rapid Epitonian speed.

"I can't wait until I can play Pyroll again," Ann Lou said to Riff while slipping another hot stone into Clorin's throat. "I'm so jealous he gets to go every day."

"It should be soon, right? Has Gressfeld given you the go-ahead yet?" asked Riff. He was sipping a giant mug of tea.

"No, she doesn't think Jalopy travel will be good for my healing. Shouldn't be too much longer, though."

Clorin regurgitated the stone, and Ann Lou's quick reflexes caught it in her prosthetic hand and sent it right back into his throat. He cooed happily.

"I don't think travelling in a Jalopy is going to be so great for me, either," said Riff, alluding to his upcoming journey.

"Don't be so dramatic. You'll be fine," said Ann Lou.

Riff snorted. "You have too much confidence in me. As soon as I reach that supernova, the Jalopy will implode and you'll never even know. Maybe it won't even make it out of the White House. Oh, by the way, if you do miraculously hear that I was blown into smithereens, my drum set can go to Clorin."

Ann Lou rolled her eyes. "I'm sure Clorin will *love* the shattered cups and plates that you plan to pass on to him. Listen, just keep Nan safe. We can't lose her again." Her expression grew glum.

Riff gulped. She was referring to losing Knitsy in the Time Belt on their first journey through to Harvinth. They watched her get sucked into a vortex, and they were all convinced that she had died. "I'll keep my eyes on her."

Ann Lou put a gentle hand on Riff's. Clorin followed suit and placed a tiny claw on top of her hand.

"Erm, Riff, there's some people walking toward us." Ann Lou's eyes flicked somewhere behind him.

Riff turned around and saw the happy faces of Garold and Flora Zeep. Their daughter, Alphabeta, was in Flora's arms. Alphabeta squealed with joy upon seeing her fellow NICU buddy, Clorin. Flora sat down next to Ann Lou, and the two babies started to swat at one another playfully.

Garold took a seat next to Riff. "Riff, great to see you again." He shook Riff's hand gently. "This must be your sister! Pleasure to meet you. I'm Garold, this is my wife, Flora, and this is our daughter, Alphabeta."

Ann Lou awkwardly shook Garold's hand with her prosthetic. "Nice to meet you. I see Clorin has a new friend." Clorin had already tangled one of his claws in Alphabeta's dark, curly hair. The two continued to squeal and laugh.

"We are so thankful Clorin and Alphabeta were in the NICU at the same time. We think he's the reason she pulled through," Flora smiled.

"Riff, I was wondering if you wouldn't mind stopping by my office a little later today. I have something for you," said Garold.

"For me? What is it?" asked Riff.

"I can't spoil the surprise!" said Garold giddily. "Find me in the prototyping lab. It's just past the vending machines, a few hallways from Dr. Kang's plant lab."

Riff knew exactly where the vending machines were. He ate from them at least four times per day.

"Anyways, we'd better get back to work, or else Delevio will have our heads," Garold said, drawing a finger across his throat. "I'll see you later.

And Ann Lou, it was a pleasure."

"Bye," said Riff and Ann Lou in unison. Clorin and Alphabeta waved to one another, their eyes teary.

Clorin decided that this was an opportune time to throw up on Ann Lou's shoulder. Riff burst into laughter, prompting Clorin to do the same.

* * *

Later that day, after lunch, Riff walked out of the plant lab and started for the prototyping lab. He walked past the vending machines, took a few steps back, pressed the pattern of buttons for a Nectarine Nutty, and then continued his stroll. He arrived at a clear glass door, where he could see a lot of commotion on the other side. At least a dozen engineers filled the lab, some wearing large protective goggles while welding, others hammering wooden frames together, and one fever-ishly coding on a computer.

Riff didn't know whether to knock or just walk in, but one of the goggled welding engineers waved to him and removed his goggles. It was Garold. He met Riff at the door, opened it, and shook his hand.

"Thanks for coming by! There's lots of excitement going on here. Let me take you to the back lab where there are fewer distractions." Garold guided Riff through the chaotic lab. "This is Riff, everyone. He works on Dr. Kang's team," said Garold aloud to the room as they walked.

Riff received several welcoming nods, waves, and a "Hello, World!" greeting from the programmer. The programmer snorted and Riff laughed awkwardly. He never understood computer humour.

Garold showed Riff into a smaller lab that was unoccupied except for a few sinks, refrigerators, and a small table. The two took a seat at the table, and Garold pulled out a small box from his green lab coat pocket.

"I'm aware that your older sister was a bit reluctant when she was presented with a device to aid in her vision. I completely understand if you feel the same about this. Anyways, it's for you if you wish to give it a go," said Garold with a warm smile.

He passed Riff the small, cuboid box. It fit in the palm of his hand and had a green ribbon on top. Riff turned the box in his hand, then took off the top.

Inside was a small, black pair of what looked like hair clips with fine antennae that seemed to be moving. Had Garold presented him with bugs?

Riff twisted his face in confusion. "Erm, thanks?"

Garold laughed. "It's a pair of Oidodrums. They'll allow you to hear clearly. They'll come in handy for your upcoming adventure with Project Bakerloo. Flora told me you're going on a mission. Well, go on, try them on. Clip each one to your ear's helix."

Riff clumsily affixed each Oidodrum to one of his ears. Once both were attached, he waited for sound. But nothing happened.

"They have to be paired to your microchip first. Give one of the antennae a little flick," said Garold.

Riff did as he was told and flicked his outer ear. His left wrist started to glow light blue where his microchip was located. Suddenly his ears started to sting, as if he had been bitten where the Oidodrums were.

"Ouch!" Riff exclaimed, grabbing at his ears.

"They're paired," said Garold, clapping his hands together. "Don't worry, that was the Oidodrums stitching themselves into your skin so you don't lose them. Now, let's get them calibrated."

Garold pulled out a tablet and started typing away. "Hear anything yet?"

Riff squeezed his eyes shut in concentration. Nothing. He shook his head.

"No worries, let me just update a few settings." Garold typed away. "Now?"

Once again, Riff concentrated, but no sound came through. He was starting to doubt he'd hear anything at all. Maybe no amount of technology would be able to help him.

Riff shook his head and sat back in his chair with a huff.

"Please, don't get discouraged. Solving problems like this is what I do best. Just give me a moment," Garold said.

As Garold typed away, Riff thought about his hearing days—listening to The Death Brigade every morning, playing in his band at school, bickering with his sisters, his alarm going off in the morning . . . even now he could almost hear the annoying *bleep-bleep-bleep* that used to wake him from his deep slumbers. But the bleeps weren't stopping. He jerked his head in Garold's direction, who was smiling in anticipation. Riff *was* hearing the bleeps that Garold was playing for him.

"Is this real? I can hear it! Ah, my voice! My voice! Whoa, mate! I can hear!" Riff jumped from his chair. The chair's metal feet made a loud screeching noise against the floor, and he covered his ears. He smiled as he heard his breathing, his excited footsteps, and Garold's joyous claps. Riff ran over to Garold and kissed him on the bald part of his head.

The engineer gleefully laughed and hugged him back. "This is great news for both the engineering and deaf communities! But let's sit and go over a few last-minute details."

Riff skipped back to his seat. Garold typed a few things on his tablet. "Okay, so . . ."

Riff noticed how loud the buzzing of the overhead light was. And the welding, hammering, and typing from the other room swelled in his ears. It was a chorus of sounds, and Riff wanted to take it all in.

"Riff?" Garold snapped his fingers in front of his eyes.

"Huh?" said Riff, shaking out of his trance.

Garold chuckled slightly. "I understand that this may all be slightly overwhelming to you. Would you like to take a break?"

"No, sorry. I'll pay attention," said Riff. "It's all just a bit . . . overstimulating."

"You can turn them off at any time. Just shake your head like this," said Garold, demonstrating.

Riff shook his head a few times back and forth, and sure enough, the silence washed through his ears. It felt comforting and familiar.

"Now shake your head again," mouthed Garold.

Riff shook his head, and the buzzing light and all the clamour from the other room rushed into his ear canals again.

Garold continued. "The Oidodrums are now fully calibrated. I have full access to your hearing diagnostics and will be analysing the data that the devices record back to me. I will have several software updates to send through to your microchip over the short term, just to make sure that everything stays perfect. Every time I send one through, you'll hear a high-pitched noise. You don't need to do anything when this happens. The noise will stop once the software update is complete. It lasts for only a few seconds each time."

Riff nodded.

"Any problems, just tap one of the antennae three times, and it will connect the two of us. All understood?" said Garold.

Riff smiled and nodded. He was giddy with excitement and desperately wanted to go show off his device to Matt, Joe, and Ann Lou.

"Great. So, you leave in two days. Are you ready?" asked Garold, lacing his fingers together and resting his chin on them.

Riff's heart sank. Of course he wasn't ready. The excitement of the Oidodrums had momentarily distracted him from thoughts of his impending doom. At least he'd be able to hear for his last two days of life.

"Honestly, no. I don't want to go," said Riff sulkily.

"Well, you won't be alone. You'll obviously have your grandmother accompanying you. And Flora as well," said Garold. Riff sensed a slight nervousness in Garold's voice.

"Flora? Why?"

"She's on the universal communications team, so this is her bread and butter. She'll be making sure that you get to the supernova's location and then to planet Casper safely," said Garold.

"Casper?" said Riff, louder than he meant to. "We're not just coming straight back to Earth afterwards?"

"No, you'll need to give the stardust to the Project Bakerloo team on planet Casper. After which you will probably be a part of the team that sets off to Thera," said Garold.

Riff's mouth hung open. "I—I thought I'd be coming back here."

"I'm sure you will at some point. But these projects here at the ERA are never small tasks," Garold said darkly.

"But . . . but what about Alphabeta? She'll miss her mother," said Riff.

"That she will," said Garold, a tear welling up in his left eye. "Anyways, I've taken up too much of your time today. I'll see you on launch day, and we'll keep in touch through the Oidodrums."

Garold ushered Riff back through the noisy prototyping lab to the hallway, then shook his hand and closed the door.

* * *

Two days later, Riff woke up after a sleepless night. It was launch day. He first worked on waking Knitsy, who grumbled as she woke up, "Save me a seat at the pub, Meg."

Neither of them spoke while getting ready. They walked arm in arm out of the room and toward the Jalopy storeroom on the ground floor. Riff felt Knitsy gripping him extra tightly this morning.

"Do you think we'll be okay?" Knitsy asked hoarsely after a few minutes.

Riff's eyebrows rose in astonishment. It wasn't like his grandmother to express fear. He gripped her tighter. "I'll keep you safe, Nan."

She coughed in response.

"Nan, where is your patch?" Riff asked her sternly, stopping them both in their tracks.

"I don't need it," Knitsy said.

"Yes, you do. Where is it?" Riff repeated.

"How should I know?" said Knitsy, not looking Riff in his eyes.

Riff spent the next twenty minutes back in their dormitory trying to locate her breathing apparatus. He found it in the bin and brushed off the rubbish, then stuck the patch to her arm and affixed the mask around her face.

"If you take this off during the mission, I'll toss you in the bin!" Riff scolded.

Knitsy grumbled but gripped Riff's arm the remainder of the way to the Jalopy storeroom.

Once they arrived at a large sliding door, the pair found a crowd inside, surrounding an old, dusty streetcar. In the crowd, Riff noticed, were Ann Lou, Apollo, Clorin, Matt, Joe, the three Zeeps, President Murphy, Jung-hoon, Delevio, Ricardo with his space transportation team (who looked particularly starved of sleep), and a bunch of other people he didn't recognise.

"They're here!" exclaimed Jung-hoon. He ran over and hugged Riff and Knitsy. "I'm going to miss you both around the lab."

Riff chuckled. "Yeah, I'm sure you will, mate. Things might actually get done for once."

Jung-hoon smirked and squeezed Riff's shoulder.

"Let's hurry this up," snapped Delevio. "Ricardo, give them the debrief."

Ricardo, who seemed to have only one baggy eye open at this point, started reading from his tablet. "Flora Zeep, Griffin McHubbard, and Knitsy McHubbard: You will be taking part in Project Bakerloo's recently added mission, Mission Stardust. Before you is the Jalopy that has been prepared by the space transportation team for this mission. The Jalopy will pilot itself as usual. The crew's primary roles will be to communicate with the ERA base here at the White House, as well as with the Project Bakerloo team based at Schingmaning City on planet Casper; to regulate the temperature on the Jalopy's external surface; to collect the stardust samples whilst in the supernova location; and to direct the Jalopy to the planet Casper base. The team will be awaiting your arrival and has made accommodations for you to continue your work on the project there.

"Flora, your role will be commander. You are in charge of the communications tasks. Griffin, your role will be technician. You are in charge of ensuring the sample of stardust is successfully collected. And Knitsy, your role will be button presser. You are in charge of pressing the buttons that Flora and Griffin tell you to press. And you must not press any other buttons."

Knitsy muttered an expletive under her breath.

Ricardo continued. "Atop the Jalopy is a filter that will collect the sample of pure stardust. The Jalopy will need to fly through the supernova, and a detector on the internal system will alert you when the appropriate sample amount has been collected. The Jalopy is also equipped with heat- and cold-resistant shields that will need to be activated at various times during the flight. Each window has various light spectra blockers built into the glass to prevent corneal and retinal damage.

"The Jalopy hasn't had a proper service due to the lack of time to repair, so there are a few emergency packs, which can be found—"

"We're wasting time again. Let's get the passengers in the Jalopy *now*!" shouted Delevio, so loudly that Ricardo nearly dropped his tablet.

Riff slapped both Matt and Joe on the back in an embrace. "Love you, lads. Keep up the noise around here. It'll drive Delevio mad."

"We got you, mate," Matt said with a warm smile.

President Murphy walked up to Riff and clapped him on the back. "Please bring her home. Do whatever you can," he said with a shaky voice. "I need my Elbina back."

"You and me both," said Riff. He bade President Murphy goodbye with a salute.

Garold shook Riff's hand and reminded him to alert him of any troubles with the Oidodrums. Once Riff made his way to Ann Lou, Apollo, and baby Clorin, his throat tightened.

"Leaving you never gets easier," said Riff to Ann Lou.

"I'll see you soon. This one will need his uncle back," she said, smiling at Clorin. "Can you say goodbye to Uncle Riff?"

Tears welled in Clorin's eyes as he waved a tiny claw and reached for an embrace. Riff took him and hugged him back. "I'll see you soon, big guy. You keep an eye on your mum for me, okay?"

Clorin squealed as he was passed back to Ann Lou. Apollo and Riff did a fist–claw bump.

As Knitsy bid her farewell to Ann Lou, Riff caught a glimpse of Flora saying goodbye to Garold and Alphabeta. Both Flora and Garold had tears in their eyes as they embraced and exchanged their I-love-yous. Riff was saddened at the thought of their family being split up for a while. He empathised with that feeling all too well.

Delevio rather rudely pushed the three passengers into the Jalopy. As the doors of the streetcar closed with a hiss, Riff felt the commotion of the crowd being replaced with the silence of the pressurised cabin.

Flora took her seat at the centre of the control panel at the front of the Jalopy. Riff took the seat to her left, Knitsy the one to her right.

"We're really doing this," Flora said breathlessly.

Riff tightened his mouth and nodded.

The inside of the Jalopy illuminated in green.

"Hello, Knitsy McHubbard, Flora Zeep, and Griffin McHubbard. The Jalopy is ready to depart. Please state your destination," said the calming, soft voice of the Jalopy.

"Spica, a star in the Virgo constellation located within the NGC5468 galaxy," said Flora with a confident tone.

"Enjoy your trip," said the voice of the Jalopy.

And with that, the Jalopy inched forward on the streetcar's wheels away from the crowd. A giant wall came down from the ceiling of the storeroom, creating a barrier between the Jalopy and the crowd. Riff managed to fit in one last wave to his family and friends before the wall shut them out. In front of them, another wall rose to expose the streetcar to the deadly outside environment.

Within seconds, the Jalopy flew into the air. They left the White House behind in a flash. Earth's barren surface grew farther and farther away as they blasted through the atmosphere. Once they reached the darkness of space, Riff felt a mysterious calm wash over him. He'd done this before. Maybe with Flora and Knitsy by his side, they could succeed. And they'd be one step closer to finding Elbina.

Riff smiled at this thought as they flew through the beautiful enigma of dazzling space.

# CHAPTER 7

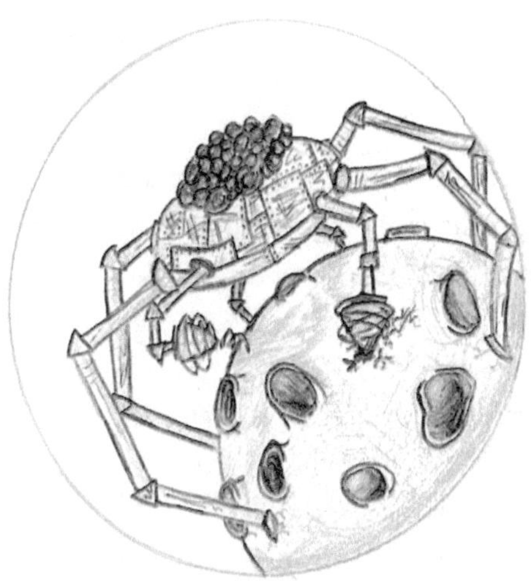

## MISSION STARDUST

As the Jalopy flew at hyperspeed through space, Riff scanned the control panel in front of them. There were loads of buttons, detectors, flashing green lights, and numbers that he didn't know what to do with. Suddenly, Knitsy's role of button pusher seemed slightly more complex than either his or Flora's job. Up ahead of the Jalopy was an extremely bright light that they could see through the front window. It looked like a humongous star, but it was brighter than any star he'd ever seen while flying through space before.

"Flora, what is that?" asked Riff, pointing to the giant star.

"That's where we're going. The Spica supernova," Flora replied.

"It's already visible? From this far away?" asked Riff.

"Supernovas are massive. They can stay bright for weeks, even months," said Flora.

Riff stared at the glowing supernova in awe.

"Zeep to ERA and Casper bases. We are outside of the Milky Way and en route as planned," said Flora into a small microphone in front of her.

"Copy that," replied Ricardo's slightly staticky voice.

"Understood," said another voice that sounded strangely like Tycho's.

Flora focused intently on one of the detectors on the control panel in front of her. It looked like a star map with a green flashing dot.

"What's that?" asked Riff.

"A UPS. Universal Positioning System. It's displaying our route to Spica. The total trip is about two hundred fifty light years," said Flora.

"Oh, so a quick hop over," said Riff.

He could hear light snores from Knitsy's seat.

"Looks like we've lost our button presser," laughed Riff.

"Honestly, the buttons look complicated, but Ricardo's team made sure that the ones we need to press will flash red when it's time to press them. All we have to do is keep an eye on them," said Flora.

"Brilliant," said Riff, peering back at the control panel.

For about half an hour, the three rode in silence except for the occasional loud snore. Even Riff dozed off after a while, but he awoke when the Jalopy shuddered slightly.

"Whoa, what was that?" said Riff, ruffled.

"The Jalopy usually reroutes itself if there's an obstacle incoming. But I didn't see anything on the UPS that looked worthy of rerouting. I'll ask the team." Flora cleared her throat and spoke into the microphone. "Zeep to ERA base. The Jalopy seems to be shaking. Is this a feature we should be aware of?"

Ricardo's voice was a bit more staticky this time around. "No. A repair to the gravitodynamic stabiliser had to be dropped due to time constraints. The risk is low. You'll just notice a bit of turbulence along the way."

Flora and Riff exchanged worried glances. "Seems like something they should have prioritised, in my opinion," Flora said away from the microphone.

The Jalopy continued to shudder as they flew onward. Every so often, they felt a significant jolt. One in particular even caused Knitsy to wake up and slap her cane against Flora's leg.

"Fly straight!" Knitsy barked.

"Nan, the Jalopy is driving itself. It's just a bit turbulent," said Riff.

"Do I need to push any buttons yet?" Knitsy continued.

"No, Nan. We'll tell you when," said Riff.

"What's with that bright light ahead?" said Knitsy, shielding her eyes with a hand. "Can we take a different route?"

The Jalopy decreased in speed as it approached a wall of light. In less than a minute, they would be completely enveloped within the supernova's radius.

"All right, button presser, we need you to be alert!" said Flora, sternly.

Knitsy snorted out of a trance and lifted a knobbly finger.

"Press the red flashing button . . . now!" Flora exclaimed.

Knitsy stabbed a red button just off to her left with great force and a *humph*.

"Great work, Knitsy," smiled Flora. "Zeep to ERA and Casper bases. The Jalopy has entered the Spica supernova region. External temperature remains stable."

"Excellent news," replied Ricardo.

"Glad you haven't exploded yet," said Tycho.

"What was that button for?" asked Riff.

"Jalopies are typically equipped with cold-resistant outer surfaces. We needed the functionality of heat resistance when entering the supernova's region," Flora explained.

"Right," said Riff.

The light surrounding them was surreal, almost heavenly. There was nothing to be seen outside of the windows except bright light.

"Riff, the UPS shows that we're nearing the core of the supernova. Filter collection needs to commence now!" Flora commanded.

"Right," said Riff, hopping up from his chair. He jogged to the centre of the Jalopy, where a large lever hung from the ceiling. He pushed the lever to the left with a grunt.

"Zeep to ERA and Casper bases. Filtration system is operating and collecting stardust!" Flora said gleefully.

"Save me a few grams!" said a quieter voice in the background. It sounded like Jung-hoon's.

"Stay vigilant!" said Tycho.

Riff returned to his seat and watched as the green bar on the detector in front of him rose slowly. He figured it indicated the amount of sample that was being collected.

Flora said into the mic, "Understood. Looks like all is going gr—"

The Jalopy lurched to the left, sending the three passengers tumbling out of their seats. Riff caught Knitsy in his arms as they smashed into the side of the vehicle. The Jalopy started flying in zigzags and shaking violently.

"*Fly straight!*" yelled Knitsy, waving her cane every which way.

"*I'm not flying the Jalopy!*" Flora bellowed back.

The three were pinballing around as the Jalopy continued lurching back and forth. Riff forgot all about the filtration detector until a new indicator lit up red: *Filter obstruction. Please contact your administrator for assistance.*

"Bollocks," he cursed.

Riff used his belt to secure Knitsy to a wall fixture, then began inching back toward his seat, his body at an acute angle to the floor of the Jalopy. He grabbed the back of Flora's seat and held on tightly. Leaning as close to the microphone as he could without poking his eye out, he shouted, rather bouncily, "R-R-Ricardo, we have a sli-i-ight pro-o-oblem!"

Delevio's voice snapped, "Who's speaking? If you don't follow the communications protocols, we have no idea who is contacting us."

"You know who it is, you git! The filter is obstructed, and the Jalopy has gone mad!"

"Pull the—" started Ricardo, and then his voice turned to static noise.

"What? Pull the *what*?" Riff replied.

Nothing but static met his ears. Riff swatted at his ears to see if the Oidodrums just needed to be played with a bit. But nothing changed. The static continued.

"What did he say?" shouted Flora.

The Jalopy was now bouncing so much that they couldn't focus their eyes on the controls.

"He said pull something," shouted Riff. He peered around the Jalopy looking for anything that was obvious to pull, but between the bouncing of the Jalopy and the bright light from the supernova, he could barely see at all.

"W-what about th-that thing up th-there?" Flora said, pointing at a red lever on the ceiling.

Riff tried his best to focus in that direction. Something on the cabin ceiling was blurry and red, and it looked as if it wanted to be pulled.

"There's n-no way I can reach it!" shouted Riff. "The Jalopy is t-too unstable!"

"Use this," said Knitsy, reaching her cane out to him.

Riff reached out his hand and grasped the cane, then stretched his arm out, extending the cane toward the red thing in the ceiling. After a few attempts of swatting and missing, he finally managed to catch the red handle with the cane. He yanked down with as much strength as he could muster. The bouncing continued, but the buzzing behind him stopped. He turned to see that the indicator now read *Obstruction cleared. Sample collection complete.*

Riff swatted the cane once more at the filter lever and pushed it back into its original position.

"How do we get out of here?" yelled Riff, still gripping onto Flora's seat for dear life.

Flora slammed her eyes shut and shouted, "Jalopy, reroute us back to planet Casper!"

The Jalopy stopped suddenly.

The three passengers sat in stunned silence, waiting for something to happen.

"Enjoy your trip," said the calm voice of the Jalopy.

The Jalopy took off suddenly upward, then did a loop-de-loop away from the core of the supernova. The ride, although still bumpy, wasn't nearly as zig-zaggy as before.

Riff helped Knitsy back to her seat. He made sure to keep one hand on a surface at all times, just in case the Jalopy had more randomised flight patterns in mind.

"Zeep to ERA and Casper base," said Flora with a shaky voice and unkempt hair.

They heard a bit of feedback, then only static.

"Zeep to ERA and Casper base," repeated Flora, a bit louder.

Still only static.

"I think we lost them." Flora shrugged. "We'll just have to hope the signal comes back or they're waiting for us."

For the next several minutes, the bright light that had completely surrounded them faded gradually. Once the darkness of space returned into view, Flora opened her mouth to say, "Knitsy, the button!" but Knitsy was already ahead of her. The button for the cold-resistant exterior was reactivated, and the Jalopy accelerated back into hyperspeed.

"Great job, Knitsy," said Flora with a wink.

"Don't get used to it," barked Knitsy.

The Jalopy sailed through space for some time. Riff grew drowsy, and the light, rhythmic snores from Knitsy didn't help him stay alert.

"It's okay if you want to take a nap," said Flora. "The mission is pretty much over. The Jalopy just needs to make it to the Casper base, and we're all done."

"You sure?" asked Riff. "You probably deserve the most sleep of any of us."

"As a new mother, I'm used to sleep deprivation. I'll be awake for many more hours," she smiled.

"All right. Well, if anything interesting happens, wake me up. I've always wanted to see space pirates," Riff said, giddily.

"Arrr," Flora winked.

Riff had been snoozing for at most ten minutes when the Jalopy lurched again. This time, it didn't seem to lose control—it just seemed to stop altogether.

"Riff, good news and bad news," said Flora. "The bad news is that the Jalopy has broken down. The good news is that we're in orbit around a planet. So, if the planet has intelligent life . . . and if that life has achieved space travel, like space pirates, and if they are coincidently roaming around this asteroid belt we're stuck in . . . maybe someone will help us."

Riff jolted up from his chair and pressed his face against the window. All there was to see were millions of miles of asteroids: big, bigger, and gigantic. The Jalopy had managed to collide with one of the smaller asteroids (about the length of a lorry) and wedged itself in a crater. All the flashing lights in the Jalopy had gone out, and there was no noise, not even static from the communication system. There was no telling where they were, since the UPS had also shut down. They were somewhere in the universe, and they were alone.

"What does this say?" asked Knitsy, peering in close to a red flashing indicator.

The text was so faint, and only growing fainter with each flash, but Riff was just able to make out that it read, *Astro-generator out of power.*

"'Out of power?' How do we get more power?" asked Riff, sitting back down and spinning his chair to face Flora.

Flora rubbed her temples in silence, thinking desperately.

"I'm hungry," said Knitsy, finally awoken from her slumber. "Are there any snacks?"

Flora's eyes met Riff's. She said softly, "Do you think your grandmother has any clue what's going on?"

Riff shrugged. "She's usually mental. I think being locked up in the Time Belt for so long kind of sucked the life out of her. In her defence, she is also getting a bit old."

Flora glanced at Knitsy, who was now looking under the controls panel and even under her own skirt for snacks. And then she remembered.

"Hold on, Knitsy has a point," said Flora, leaping from her seat and trotting to the back of the Jalopy. "There should be emergency packs in here somewhere."

Riff watched as Flora searched each row of seats in the dusty old streetcar until she jovially trotted back to her seat carrying a box labelled First Aid Kit.

"Let's see what's in here," said Flora, unlatching the lid of the box and sifting through the contents. "Toffee Twiddlums—"

Knitsy held out an open hand. Flora gave her the box of sticky candies.

"Gumdrop Flumpers—"

Again, Knitsy held out her hand. Flora handed her the multicoloured bag of sweets.

"And a plumple," said Flora, looking at Knitsy in preparation for her to interrupt.

Knitsy didn't seem to notice the fruit.

"Nan," said Riff, "gumdrop me." He opened his mouth wide.

Knitsy tossed an orange gumdrop in an arc toward Riff, and he leaned to the right and caught it perfectly in his mouth. Luckily, this Jalopy, as well as all others stationed on Earth, was equipped with the Universal Union's technology of artificial Earth gravity; otherwise, the gumdrop would be floating around their heads.

"Anything else in there that might help us besides food?" asked Riff through sticky chews.

"Only this," said Flora, holding up a small device. "It's a translometer. It allows any creature with communication skills to understand humans. We obviously have our microchips that audibly translate languages to us and vice versa, but it's limited to the languages of members of the Universal Union."

"Well, do the asteroids communicate? Looks like they're the only things around," said Riff.

"No, unfortunately asteroids aren't sentient beings. Not the ones the ERA has tested so far, at least," said Flora.

The three sat in silence for a while, nibbling on candy and fruit, until Knitsy perked up and pointed a wobbly finger at the window. "Who's that?"

Flora and Riff looked and immediately saw what she was referring to. About three asteroids away was a creature that Riff had never seen before. It looked like a giant spider except that it had six legs instead of eight. It looked metallic, like a robot. Dozens of transparent spheres covered its abdomen.

The three watched in awe as the metal spider attached itself to an asteroid using cuplike appendages on its frontmost and hindmost legs, then drilled into the asteroid with its middle legs. After a few seconds, it pulled the middle legs out of the asteroid and retracted them into its body.

"I know what that is!" said Flora excitedly. "It's a mining droid. I've always wanted to see one. My teammates are going to be so jealous!"

"What's it doing?" asked Riff.

"Its primary role is to mine asteroids. They were developed by the Universal Union when it was first formed to help with funding. The Union would take whatever they mined and sell it for profit. The Union is well funded by its member worlds now, so the mining droid program was dropped."

"Well, what is this one doing if it's not working for the Universal Union?" asked Riff.

"Individuals hire the droids to mine for them. It's completely against the Union's laws, so it's usually done undercover," replied Flora.

"Like the black market, but for space," said Riff. "Cool."

"What're you standing there for?" barked Knitsy, waving her cane. "Get its attention so we can get out of here!"

"Can we communicate with it?" Riff asked Flora.

"I'll try the translometer," she replied.

She picked up the handheld device. It had multiple buttons (one of them red), a digital screen, and a small antenna at one end. Flora pointed the antenna toward the mining droid, and the screen displayed the words *Mining Droid. Would you like to connect with this species?* Flora clicked the red button.

The three watched intently as the droid ceased its drilling and robotically turned its head toward the Jalopy. One of the clear spheres on the droid flickered and then lit up yellow.

"Hello, friend," Flora said aloud. "We are from planet Earth. Can you help us?"

The tip of the translometer's antenna lit up and flickered a few times. More spheres on the droid's back lit up and flickered in different patterns.

"I do not understand," came the translated reply in a mechanical-sounding voice.

"We need to be brought to the nearest civilisation to power up our Jalopy. Can you send help for us?" asked Flora. The antenna flickered more as she spoke.

The droid cocked its head. Spheres on its back flashed yellow. "Are you a customer?" said the droid.

"No. Can you bring us to your master?" asked Flora.

Yellow lights gleamed all over the droid's back, and it detached itself from the asteroid. "Master," it said through the translometer. "I will bring you to Master."

The droid then flew away in a swimming motion with its six legs.

"Where's it going?" asked Knitsy.

"I don't know," said Flora. "I hope it comes back."

About a half hour later, a small army of about ten mining droids swam into view. They surrounded the Jalopy, attached their plungers to it, and lifted it from the crater where it was stuck.

One of the droid's backs glowed with multicoloured lights. "Take them to Master," said the robotic voice.

"*Masterrr*," replied the other droids in unison.

The Jalopy undulated as the mining droids carried it away from the asteroid belt.

"Where do you think they're taking us?" asked Knitsy, her voice slightly shaky. "Where are these blokes from?"

Flora gulped. "They don't have a home planet. Wherever the creature who hired them lives, I guess that's where we're going."

Riff said, "Well, if they're advanced enough to hire mining droids, they should be able to help us."

"Probably," replied Flora. "But will they want to—that's what I'm more worried about. As I said before, hiring out mining droids is illegal. So whoever we're going to be dealing with probably isn't soft and cuddly."

Riff's hands and feet tingled as fear washed through him—a fear that far surpassed his earlier trepidation about having to travel into a supernova. His heart pounded. "So, our lives are in the hands of a bunch of robot space spiders. Bloody brilliant."

# Chapter 8

# The Dark Astromarket

It was soon apparent that the mining droids were carrying the incapacitated Jalopy to the next nearest planet. Riff and Flora were glad that the journey would be short but very nervous about meeting the master of this crew of illicitly hired droids. Knitsy was oblivious to the situation.

The planet was small in comparison to others that Riff had visited in the past. It was all colours of the rainbow: the atmosphere had a yellowish glow, the poles shone orange, and the surrounding planetary regions were vibrant hues of blue, green, and magenta. The entire planet looked smoky, as if it might be just a gas ball. Points of light were arrayed in graceful arcs among the colourful regions. From afar in space, the entire planet looked like a Christmas bauble.

The view out the window of the Jalopy suggested they were heading toward one of the magenta regions. As they entered the planet's atmosphere, they went into a freefall. Riff, Flora, and Knitsy all held tightly to their chairs and the control panel as the Jalopy was buffeted about. They were descending rapidly toward a busy, futuristic-looking city. They watched, fascinated, as more details came into view. What had looked like ground was in fact a cloud layer. Immense cylindrical structures like poles pierced through the clouds, each pole supporting vast flat discs. These discs were at various heights and had flashing lights on their rims. Some of the smaller discs appeared to be landing pads only, while many others supported the infrastructure of busy, futuristic-looking cities with space set aside on their periphery for landings. Interstellar crafts of various sizes were landing on the pads, while smaller service vehicles flew between pads. As the Jalopy neared one of the larger discs, the droids' legs spun like helicopter blades to cushion their descent. The droids then deposited the Jalopy gently on the surface.

Riff peered out the window. The air was a striking magenta colour. "Do you know which planet we're on?" he asked Flora.

"No idea," she replied.

Knitsy snarled, "Why don't you ask the button presser for some advice every once in a while?"

Riff raised an eyebrow. "Do you know where we are, Nan?"

"How should I know?" Knitsy spat back.

The droids detached themselves from the Jalopy, then settled onto the disc surface, which seemed to have a lot of traffic. Riff saw crowds of creatures shuffling in and out of a gigantic building. They were not just one kind of creature, but hundreds, perhaps thousands. Riff didn't recognise any of the species.

"Should we be worried about breathing?" asked Riff, his own breathing rate increasing.

Flora hesitated and gritted her teeth.

"Right, so we either survive and potentially get ourselves in a sticky situation with the robot space spiders, or we suffocate to death and have a laugh about all of this at the pub wherever our spirits go?"

Flora shrugged. "Guess so."

Riff cautiously opened the door of the Jalopy. He slowly took a breath of the foreign air, and to his surprise, his lungs filled as they normally would on Earth. The air tasted sweet, like bubblegum.

"Well, no pub for us," he said, looking back at Knitsy and Flora.

"Damn," said Knitsy, snapping her fingers.

Riff peeked out at the waiting droids. They were standing there in silence, staring at him. Pairs of the translucent spheres flashed every few seconds, as if they were blinking.

"Erm, where do we need to go?" he asked them.

The droids did not react. "Use this," whispered Flora, handing Riff the translometer.

Riff pushed the red button on the device. "Where do we go?" he repeated, and the device's antenna glimmered with light.

One droid's back flashed with lights. "Follow me to Master," it replied.

Knitsy took Riff's arm, and they followed the head droid. Flora accompanied Riff and Knitsy closely as the remainder of the droids trailed them.

The colourful building in the centre of the disc was at least a hundred stories high and had a grand set of marble stairs leading up to the entrance. Swarms of creatures bustled in and out at a constant rate. Some walked out with jingling bags filled to the brim, while others sat on the stairs weeping to themselves. The building resonated with buzzes, rings, jingles, and shouts of excitement from inside.

Riff, Flora, and Knitsy looked up at the sign above the entrance. It bore only indecipherable squiggles until their microchips translated it, and then the word *Casino* appeared in front of their eyes.

"I can't believe I didn't bring any money with me," sighed Knitsy.

The crowd made way for them as the head droid led them up the marble stairs and into the cavernous main lobby. Riff gaped up in awe at the endless array of floors filled with diverse creatures, games, and noises. In the lobby, there were about ten clear tubes arranged in a circle, and they extended up hundreds of stories through the open plan of the casino. They appeared to be lifts that were taking the gamblers where they wanted to go.

Riff was slightly disappointed when the droids led them not to the lifts, but instead to the very back of the casino. They stopped before a door that was being guarded by a pair of tall, muscular creatures with beady eyes and five limbs. Their skin was terribly wrinkled, and each of their limbs held a weapon of some sort.

The guards frowned at the lead droid upon their arrival.

"Why d'ya have company?" asked one of the guards in a husky voice. "This ain't somethin' ya mined."

"They need to see Master," replied the lead droid, its lights flickering on its back.

"You guys got any IDs?" the other guard said.

Riff, Knitsy, and Flora all shook their heads.

"If they go down there, I need to alert the Grand Q'bah," the first guard said.

Riff scrunched his eyebrows. He wasn't sure if he'd heard the guard correctly. What was a Q'bah?

"Let us in," said the droid.

The guards shrugged. One of them opened the door and said, "Have fun."

The guards stepped aside. A set of rickety steps descended into darkness. The lead droid led them down the steps. Riff held Knitsy tightly as they descended, each step creaking along the way. When the door closed behind them, Riff could no longer see anything. Frightened, he halted his and Knitsy's next steps, and Flora bumped into him.

A rumble sounded in front of them, and a minimal amount of light shone up ahead, accompanied by a series of voices and conversations. As their eyes adjusted, they saw that a market lay in front of them. Riff could see many aisles off to his left and right, all filled with vendors selling various products at stalls. The whole area had a very dim and eerie glow to it.

The lead droid led them along the alleyway in front of them. The vendors all looked a bit shady, but perhaps it was just the lighting.

Riff gasped when he saw the advertisements on some of the stalls. *Olfinderian Springs . . . Sinx Tails . . . Pomberian Fingernails.* He watched customers passing briefcases over to the vendors in exchange for these goods. *More like "bads,"* he thought to himself. He wondered what was in those cases.

A large sign hung down above the centre of the market. As Riff focused on the foreign squiggles, the translation appeared:

## The Dark Astromarket
## —All currencies welcome except as noted below—
## Grumplese Fishskin, due to stock market crash
## Time Belt Chroniya, due to its ceasing to exist

"Whoa," Riff heard Flora breathe from behind.

The lead droid arrived at the final vendor in the row, where a sign read *Cipton Eyes.* The vendor behind the stall had a small but perfectly round head and a comically large moustache. His neck was the width of a toothpick, his body big and burly. He wore a black fedora atop his bald head. Jars of twitching, pickling eyeballs lined the shelves behind him.

"Yes?" the vendor growled.

"I have returned, Master. I have the metals and some travellers," said the lead droid, bowing slightly. The rest of the droids behind Riff bowed as well.

"Where's the palladium?" grumbled Moustache.

The lead droid's middle legs retreated in its body, then re-emerged, bringing out a ball of metal. The droid reached out and placed the metal ball on the table in front of Moustache.

Moustache focused on the ball, and it rose into the air. Riff watched, awestruck at the creature's telekinesis skills.

The ball floated over to a scale, then dropped into the pan. Moustache whipped his head around, the hairs of his bushy moustache sticking out straight. "Only forty grams? You're a useless pile of junk, all of you!" he barked. "Get out of my sight!"

"Would you like to purchase more mining time?" asked the droid.

"Why would I? So you can waste it on bringing me stragglers? At this rate, I'll lose all my money! Away with you all!" Moustache shouted.

The lead droid and its comrades scuttled away, leaving Riff, Knitsy, and Flora alone with the angry vendor. Riff couldn't help but feel sorry for the droids, even though he figured they probably didn't have any feelings anyway.

"And what do you want?" Moustache snarled to Riff.

"Erm . . . ehm . . . well, I . . . um . . ." stammered Riff.

"We need help," said Flora, pushing Riff to the side and stepping forward. "Our Jalopy lost power, and we need to get somewhere."

"Well, you got money? Lots and lots of it?" asked Moustache with an arrogant tone.

Another vendor leaned in from the adjoining stall. "Why don't you take one of them as a slave?" they offered.

Moustache eyed Riff up and down with a look of disgust plastered on his face. "You're Earthlings, correct?"

Flora nodded.

Moustache looked at the neighbouring vendor and said, with no attempt at subtlety: "Earthlings aren't going for much these days. Bad economy."

"We don't have any Earth currency, but state what you'd like from us," Flora said.

Moustache looked at her and Knitsy hungrily. "What are those things on your hands? And hanging from your face?"

Flora felt her earrings. "Jewellery. You can have all of it."

Moustache licked his moustache. "Let me see."

Riff saw Knitsy slip her wedding ring into her skirt pocket. He didn't blame her. It was all she had left to remember her husband by. But she then took off her earrings and necklace. Flora unclamped her earrings and wedding ring. Riff removed a bracelet that matched ones that Matt and Joe wore. It hurt his heart, but he knew they would understand. Moustache took the pile of jewellery and used his telekinesis to move the pile to the scale.

Moustache read the scale and did a few calculations, then said, "It's not enough for me to help you."

Rage brimmed inside Riff, and he growled, "It'll be enough when I tell everyone in this market that you're ripping them off."

The neighbouring vendor peeked over.

Moustache glared at Riff. "And why do you accuse me of such atrocities?"

"Creatures from planet Cipto don't have eyes. Their planet is dark. Wherever you got those, they're fakes."

The neighbouring vendor burst out in laughter.

Moustache leaned in close to Riff's face, so close that the moustache hairs tickled his nose. "You trying to put me out of business, boy? Huh?"

"Take the jewellery and help us, or else I'll expose your secret," said Riff as confidently as his shaky voice could muster.

The ends of Moustache's moustache twitched. "Fine," he said curtly. "What do you need?"

"Something to power up an astro-generator," said Flora.

Moustache thought for a few seconds, then called across the row to another stallholder. "Oi, Wejman! You still got some Kilo-209 stomachs for sale?"

Riff and Flora looked sidelong at each other, wondering how a stomach was going to power a Jalopy. Riff recognised the Kilo-209 species as well. He was certain that he'd seen one of the hairy beasts ingest a table at the last Universal Union meeting he'd attended a couple months prior. Perhaps the coupling of immense volume and strength of the stomach fostered a perfect power source, although the thought of using an innocently hungry creature's body part made Riff want to be sick to his own stomach.

Wejman, an orange, very hairy beast, checked his inventory. "One left," he called.

"Get out of my sight and go talk to him," spat Moustache, waving them away.

A slimy customer slunk up to Moustache's stall. "I'll take three jars o' eyes." The customer opened a briefcase that was filled with gold coins.

Moustache and Riff glanced at one another. Riff bowed his head slightly and just said, "Thanks, mate," to Moustache, then walked in the direction of Wejman's stall.

Riff, Knitsy, and Flora had to wait in line to speak to Wejman. His Chewy Partingoose Hooves seemed to be wildly popular. Once they reached the front of the line, Flora stepped up and said, "One Kilo-209 stomach, please." Riff noticed Flora's face had turned slightly green. She, too, wasn't a fan of using the stomach as their power source, but they all knew there was no other choice.

"What can you give me for it?" Wejman chuckled. They couldn't see his face through his thick, orange hair, but every once in a while, a tooth would poke through where a mouth would generally be.

"We gave most of our valuables to that man over there," said Flora, pointing to Moustache. "Perhaps you two could share?"

Wejman laughed even harder this time. "Those stomachs are mighty powerful, with a protein that absorbs the energy of everything the creature has ever eaten. This makes the older ones nearly invincible and incredibly rare. You need an army to take one of them Kilo's down, and most of that army will have been gobbled up with no crumbs to spare. I only have one left. You'd better make me a strong deal."

Riff thought at lightning speed. What did they have that Wejman would want?

Flora appeared to be struggling just as much as Riff was. She searched her pockets but came out short with only a candy wrapper, a plumple core, and a picture of Alphabeta and Garold.

"Get outta here," said Wejman, waving them off.

"We have stardust," said Knitsy, hobbling forward with her cane. Riff started to object, but Flora stilled him.

A dark hole appeared in the middle of Wejman's hairy face, and drool dripped from it like a running tap. "Did you say . . . stardust?"

Knitsy nodded.

A nearby security guard pricked up his ears.

"Pure or matured?" Wejman asked. "Surely it's matured."

"It's pure," said Knitsy.

"I don't believe you," said Wejman.

The security officer arrived at Riff's side and held up three pairs of handcuffs. "Let's take a walk. You, too, Wejman."

"What for?" said Riff.

"I'm taking you to the Grand Q'bah," said the officer.

"What's a Q'bah?" asked Riff.

"That's *Grand* Q'bah to ya," spat the officer. "How very disrespectful."

The guard cuffed Riff, Flora, and a very resistant Knitsy, who kept batting her cane at the guard. He eventually cuffed her, then led the three of them and Wejman to the back of the Dark Astromarket, to another door that was blocked by a guard.

"State your business," said the new guard.

"The Grand Q'bah will want to interrogate these customers," said the officer.

"Interrogate us?" exclaimed Riff. "We haven't done anything wrong!"

"You'll make it worse for us," whispered Flora. "Just go with it."

"I love a good interrogation," chuckled the new guard. "The screams of torture invigorate me."

He stepped aside and allowed the old guard, Riff, Knitsy, Flora, and Wejman to pass through. Another set of stairs downward lay before them, but there was a bright light at the bottom of these stairs.

Once they reached the bottom, Riff's jaw dropped. Before them was the most elaborately decorated room he'd ever seen. It had a red velvet carpet, a high ceiling, and architecture like that of the Victorian era on Earth. Diamond chandeliers hung from the ceiling. The walls were lined with gold columns and elaborately painted *trompe l'oeil* scenes. Riff thought he recognised some of these scenes but wasn't fully convinced. He hadn't paid *that* much attention in art class. One scene depicted gold coins in a fruit bowl, and another with one humanlike figure reaching for a gold bar from a god-like figure. Down the middle of the room stood two rows of royal guards, each holding a jewel-encrusted trident, sword, shield, or mace. At the end of the rows of guards was a throne of sorts, except it didn't look like a chair. It was a giant bathtub.

In the bathtub throne lay a giant slug-like creature. A bejewelled crown rested on his slimy head. The Grand Q'bah appeared to be sleeping. More guards stood around the bathtub and fanned him slowly with great feathery fans as he slept.

When the group arrived at the Grand Q'bah's rostrum, a guard cleared his throat. The fanners ceased fanning, and the slug grumbled awake. Riff saw something flow over the edge of the bathtub as the slug stirred: golden coins.

"Who dares disturb the Grand Q'bah?" rumbled the slug in a nasally voice as he opened his eyes and searched for the annoyance.

"Grand Q'bah," said the security officer, bowing as he spoke, "These customers were overheard—"

"We haven't done anything!" said Riff. "Let us go!"

"Have you any money?" asked the Grand Q'bah. He lifted his plump arms from the bath and started to rub the coins into his skin as if bathing himself.

Flora started to speak. "No, but—"

"One hundred thousand years as my slaves," interrupted the Grand Q'bah. "You two can collect the profits from the casino every night. The old one can rub my feet." The Grand Q'bah lifted a dirty, slimy foot out of the bath. Gold coins fell from between his toes.

"They claim to have pure stardust, Grand Q'bah," said the security officer, stepping forward and bowing again.

The Grand Q'bah's eyes bulged to thrice their size. Veins in his head pulsated as he spoke. "That's not possible."

"We have some in our Jalopy outside," said Flora.

"Bring it to me. I must see it with my own eyes," said the Grand Q'bah. "Although one of you must stay here and tell me how you came across this pure stardust."

"They were simply negotiating a trade at my stall," interjected Wejman. "There's no need to—"

"Silence, peasant!" said the Grand Q'bah.

A guard led Flora and Knitsy to the Grand Q'bah's personal lift off at the side of the room. It was about ten times the diameter of the ones in the casino lobby. They disappeared off to the casino's ground level, while Riff remained with Wejman and the Grand Q'bah.

"Speak!" snapped the Grand Q'bah.

"Erm, well, I'm from planet Earth, and we have this Jalopy that is capable of flying into supernovas, which is where you find pure stardust. We collected some, and then our Jalopy died and we got stranded in an asteroid belt. You probably know the one. We came across some mining droids, and they brought us here. We just need to get our Jalopy going so we can fly out of here and get back on track to planet Casper. Wejman has a Kilo-209 stomach that will help power the astro-generator." Riff's stomach gurgled at the mention of the power source.

"Why were you in search of pure stardust in the first place?" asked the Grand Q'bah.

"We need it for a special Jalopy that will allow us to travel to . . ." Riff paused. He wasn't sure if he should relay the details of Project Bakerloo to a stranger.

"To where?" the Grand Q'bah probed.

"To the sun. The star nearest to Earth . . . My sister is being held captive . . . on the Sun. We're trying to save her," said Riff.

The Grand Q'bah snorted. "I had a sister once."

"What happened to her?" asked Riff.

"I traded her for that chandelier above your head. Best purchase I've ever made," said the Grand Q'bah gleefully. He splashed his limbs in the bathtub, sending coins flying in every direction.

"Who are you exactly?" asked Riff.

"You don't speak to the Grand Q'bah that way!" Wejman interjected.

The slug held up one plump arm toward Wejman. "It's all right, peasant. This prisoner may become richer than you'll ever be—if he really does have pure stardust." The Grand Q'bah lowered his arm and said to Riff, "I am the owner of this casino, and all casinos on planet Baccarat."

"Is that where we are?" asked Riff.

"Yes," replied the Grand Q'bah. "The Dark Astromarket vendors also make money for me in return for extravagant foods, shelter, and protection. They all come from poverty-stricken planets. The market draws in customers from all over the universe. It's the most profitable undercover market in universal history."

"Wow, impressive," said Riff. "Why are you telling me all this? I can just turn you in if I ever manage to escape."

The Grand Q'bah emitted a gurgling laugh. "You just told me your story. I know where you are from and where you're headed. I have plenty of security and access to dangerous weapons that could blow your planet, as well as your sun, to smithereens."

"Ah, fair point," said Riff, gritting his teeth. "But doesn't it make you feel a bit . . . bad? Innocent creatures are being murdered across the universe and having their body parts sold just so you can make money."

"Who's the one in desperate need of a Kilo-209 stomach?" asked the Grand Q'bah slyly.

Riff bowed his head in shame.

Flora, Knitsy, and the guard returned via the lift, and the guard sped over to the Grand Q'bah with a small jar of glowing dust.

"It's real, Grand Q'bah! They weren't lying!" sputtered the guard.

"Bring it to me so I can sniff it," said the Grand Q'bah.

Flora returned to Riff's side.

"I hope you didn't give them all of it," he whispered. "There's no way I'm going back to Spica for more stardust."

"No, that's only a quarter of it," whispered Flora. "That much stardust will surely give them the profits of their dreams. We still have plenty left."

A guard opened the jar, and the Grand Q'bah dipped one of his tentacles into it. He gagged, and then his sluggy eyes bulged again. "I'll be able to buy every moon in the galaxy." Then he sat up straight in his tub and issued his decree. "One Kilo-209 stomach to the Earthlings. One one-millionth of this pure stardust to the peasant, and the rest to me." He bowed his head to Riff, Flora, and Knitsy. "You may leave. Peasant, complete the trade and help them power up their Jalopy."

A guard unshackled Riff, Knitsy, and Flora, and Wejman led them toward the lift. Before getting in, Riff called out, "Thanks, Grand Q'bah."

The Grand Q'bah settled back in his tub. "Good luck with saving your sister. If you're successful, contact me. I know a great chandelier salesman."

Wejman led them up the lift, through the casino, down the marble stairs, and back to their inert Jalopy. He opened up a hatch to reach the astro-generator, pulled out a stomach the size of a beach ball from somewhere under his hair, and affixed it to the generator with a bit of creativity.

"I can't believe he let you go. He's never done that before. Consider yourselves lucky," said Wejman, his eyes bulging through his body hair. "Oh, and your Jalopy should be good to go."

"Thanks for your help. Sorry for the trouble," said Riff.

"'Sorry?' I'm going to be eating the best foods in the universe for the rest of my life because of you. And sleeping on the fluffiest pillows made from the finest fafflin feathers. Thank you!"

Riff, Knitsy, and Flora boarded the Jalopy and took their seats at the control panel.

"Now to see if this actually works," said Flora, taking in a deep breath and holding it.

The Jalopy lit up green. "Hello, Knitsy McHubbard, Flora Zeep, and Griffin McHubbard. The Jalopy is ready to depart. Please state your destination," said the familiar voice of the Jalopy.

"Woohoo!" said Riff.

Flora exhaled, and Knitsy clapped.

"Schingmaning City on planet Casper," Flora said, sounding greatly relieved.

"Enjoy your trip," replied the Jalopy.

They waved to Wejman as the Jalopy rose up from the flat disc holding the casino. They rose into planet Baccarat's upper atmosphere, arrived in outer space, and resumed their journey through the stars.

"Zeep to ERA and Casper base. We are back on track and headed to Casper," announced Flora into her microphone.

The Jalopy soared all the way to planet Casper's solar system in only a few hours without any further turbulence.

<br>

# CHAPTER 9

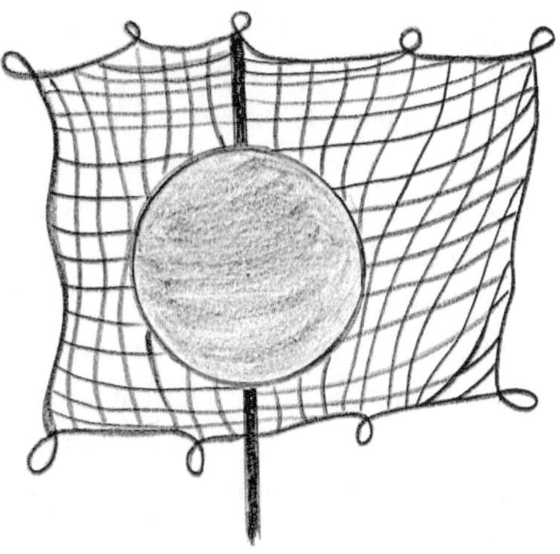

## TROUBLE AT THE BORDER

The streetcar Jalopy headed for planet Casper's binary star system, then homed in on Casper's orbit. Compared to Earth's measly one sun, the two suns of Casper were incredibly beautiful. As they neared the planet, Riff noticed a gargantuan rod sticking out from each of the planet's two poles. Each rod was about thirty times longer than Casper's diameter—comparable to the distance between Earth and its moon.

As the Jalopy drew closer, its crew realised that the rods were holding up a giant net. A Casperian guard was stationed inside each opening in the net. The guards stood on small saucers with T-shaped handlebars, and they wore their badges on frilly hats atop their bulbous heads. Casperians had no need to wear spacesuits because of their anatomy that was highly adaptable to any setting in the known universe.

The openings in the net were plenty large enough for their streetcar Jalopy to fit through, but when the craft tried to fly through, the opening in front of them turned an opaque red and bounced the Jalopy backward. One of the guards who observed their unfortunate rebounding drove his saucer to the front window of the Jalopy and frowned at the inside passengers. His small mouth moved and nasal appendages wiggled.

Flora quickly pushed a button on the control panel in front of her and said, "Sorry, can you repeat that?"

The guard's nasal appendages curled in frustration as his voice echoed through a speaker in front of them. "I said, what brings you here?"

Flora leaned in to her microphone. "We are employees of the Earth Rehabilitation Association. We are working on Project Bakerloo, which is based in Schingmaning City."

The guard turned to another guard who had flown over from the next opening in the net. Their nasal appendages wiggled back and forth in deep conversation.

"We have been alerted to expect you," said the guard in front of them. "Do you have your visa documentation?"

Flora grumbled under her breath. Through gritted teeth, she said, as nicely as possible: "Unfortunately, we did not prepare our documents ahead of time. We apologise profusely. Can you still let us in? The team are expecting us."

"No documents, no entrance. Moronic Earthlings . . . You need to turn around. Don't come back until you have the proper documenta-tion." The guard turned his saucer and started to fly back to his post.

"No, wait!" cried Flora into the microphone. "Please, let us in! We've come such a long way. We need to get in! Please!"

The guard slowly rotated on his saucer and glared at them intensely. "Resisting an officer? We'll need to take you in for further questioning."

"Zeep to Casper base! Is anyone there?" shouted Flora in her microphone. "Zeep to Casper base! We are about to be detained!"

There was no response.

Several Casperian guards swarmed the Jalopy, and within a few seconds, the control panel of the Jalopy went dark again, just as it had when they encountered the mining droids. The guards attached the Jalopy magnetically to their saucers and began guiding it toward the planet's surface.

The original guard tipped his hat with his nasal appendages in a mocking way as they passed by his post.

"What are we going to do?" asked Knitsy, half-awake with fluttering eyes.

"Well, at least we've arrived on the planet. We just need to find the Project Bakerloo team, and we should be fine," said Flora.

Riff wasn't convinced.

They were flown toward one of the colossal rods, which seemed to be stuck through the planet like a kebab skewer. Casper was a well-lit planet, and as they closed in on the landscape, they spotted tall, ornate buildings amid patches of greenery. They descended toward what looked like a town square, but Riff couldn't see any vehicles or pedestrians.

The saucer-mounted guards deposited the Jalopy in front of a grey concrete building. Riff peered out the window at it. It was very plain compared to the beautiful architecture surrounding it. This building also looked neglected, with broken windows and chipped concrete steps that led up to the main entrance. A greasy-looking, long-snouted bird-fish creature was sitting on the bottom step and rocking slowly back and forth.

Riff, Knitsy, and Flora exited the Jalopy with their hands up in surrender, only to be chained together and tugged up the stairs by one of the guards. The other guards flew away with their Jalopy in tow.

"Where are you taking our Jalopy, melonhead?" Knitsy snapped, halting in her tracks.

"Erm, Nan, it's probably best if you don't insult the officers," Riff whispered.

The guard frowned at Knitsy, looking her up and down. "I have a special place for people like you who disobey," he barked.

"You didn't answer my question," Knitsy said firmly, standing as tall as she could with her slightly hunched back. "We have the right to know where our vehicle is going. Don't make me call your mother!"

Riff sighed to himself, trying to imagine the darkest, dingiest, most disgusting room they had available in that awful-looking building, because surely that was where they were about to be taken.

The guard's eyes bugged slightly. His appendages twitched. "My—my mother?"

Knitsy held her chin up high. "You heard me correctly."

The guard's mouth wobbled, and then he fell to his knees. His nasal appendages formed what looked like praying hands. "P-please! Don't call my mother. I haven't finished my weekly quota. If she finds out, she'll send me back to that horrible camp!"

Flora shot a bewildered look at Riff. Riff shrugged and smiled as if to say, "I don't know how she does it."

Knitsy chuckled under her breath before replying, "Then tell us where our Jalopy is going, and where you're taking us."

The guard stood, wiping a tear away with an appendage. "Fine. Your Jalopy is going to the incinerator."

"What?" exclaimed Flora, her startled flinch jostling the chains around them.

"We can't take the risk. All possessions brought to the planet by aliens without the proper paperwork must be destroyed. It's Casperian law," the guard said.

"We need that Jalopy!" begged Flora, walking closer to the guard, pulling Riff and Knitsy along with her. "Surely you can have a Universal Union representative or anyone from this planet look at our Jalopy and see that it's not dangerous. We have special cargo on board that is needed for a very important multi-universe-scale project."

"I'm sorry, there's nothing I can—"

"Moootheeer," Knitsy sang softly.

The guard began to sweat profusely. "Er—actually, there is a form you can fill out. I'll take you to reception."

"Where are we exactly?" asked Riff.

"The immigration holding centre. This is where it's decided whether you are a threat to our planet or just an inferior intelligence who has mistakenly wandered across our border without doing proper research prior to travel."

"I assure you, sir, it's the latter," pleaded Flora, right at the instance that Riff tripped over his own shoelaces. She continued, "We are deeply sorry to have bothered you. We are not a threat to your peaceful community."

"That's what a threat would say," snapped the guard. "Anyway, follow me."

They trudged up the stairs, passing by the strange rocking creature along the way. A half-scaly, half-feathered fin shielded its beady eyes as it grumbled nonsensical phrases under its breath.

"Lumens . . . words per millisecond . . . zygo . . . blip . . ."

After its brief but puzzling monologue, the creature began to sob uncontrollably. Water streamed from its eyes in surprising amounts. A puddle of tears quickly formed, and its fishy tail began swishing back and forth.

The guard and the three chained prisoners entered the immigration holding centre's main lobby, which was even grubbier and more dishevelled than its exterior. Shreds of paper were strewn about, dusty footprints were splattered every which way, and filthy furniture lined the room. Walls of bookshelves stood in the waiting area, where at least fifty creatures sat waiting. Some were absorbed in a book, while others snoozed or talked nervously to a neighbour. A digital sign above a door in the back of the waiting room read:

### *Current wait time:*
### *12 hours 37 minutes*

An old, wrinkly Casperian with her white hair in an updo sat behind a reception desk adjacent to the waiting room.

The guard walked his prisoners to the desk, and he cleared his throat. "Ahem, excuse me, miss?"

The receptionist peered up from her book. "What?" she said in a displeased tone.

"These Earthlings need assigned cells in cell block one-two-G, where they will then wait to sit for THESIS," the guard replied.

The receptionist sat in silence for about two minutes while she finished her book, then proceeded to type something on a tablet in front of her.

"They would also like to fill out Form eight-two-six-F-S-J."

The receptionist *humphed* as she arose from her seat, then dug around under her desk. She emerged with a stack of papers and handed them to Flora without a word.

"May I borrow a pen?" asked Flora.

The receptionist raised her eyebrows.

"Erm . . . a writing utensil. To fill this out," Flora said, raising the stack of paper with difficulty amid her chains.

"Obtuse Earthlings and their lack of functional noses," breathed the receptionist. She shuffled around in a desk drawer, then handed Flora a small stick that must have been the Casperian version of a pen.

Then a buzzer sounded.

"Cells are assigned," snarled the receptionist, picking up her next book to read.

The door in the waiting room unlocked and opened to allow them to enter. As they passed through, Riff heard some of the waiting creatures snarling in discontent. He wondered if they had cut the line. The digital sign now read:

### *Current wait time:*
### *12 hours 40 minutes*

The guard led them down a well-lit but dingy hallway with three rows of cells on each side. A variety of creatures from across the universe inhabited these cell spaces, one or two creatures per cell. Riff was surprised that the cells had no bars or other visible barriers; he wondered why the creatures didn't just make a break for it. But he quickly concluded that there had to be invisible electromagnetic barriers. His guess was confirmed when he saw one brave little creature charge up its limbs by swinging them in circles, then plunge toward the opening of its cell only to be shocked midair and then catapulted to the back of the cell, where it hit the wall hard, and then flopped onto the ground. Riff hoped the creature was okay but after a few seconds, it ruffled its feathers and tried this process again.

Farther down the hall, they saw a cell occupied by two creatures of disparate size. One was so large and squishy that he took up almost the entirety of the cell, while his cellmate was pressed up between him and the invisible barrier. The unfortunately placed cellmate was in a constant state of electrically induced discomfort while the big squishy beast behind it snoozed peacefully.

Near the end of the hallway, the guard stopped. "You," he said, pointing his nose at Knitsy. "In there." He poked a few buttons on a keypad next to her cell, which emitted a sound like a puff of air. Then he uncuffed Knitsy from the chains and pushed her from behind so that she fell face first into the cell. He poked a few more buttons and locked her in with a quick *ZAP*.

"Hey!" Riff shouted, his blood boiling. "You be careful with her!"

"Quiet, you," said the guard, pressing buttons at the cell next door. "Get in there." The guard unshackled Riff, then shoved him into his cell and locked him in.

The guard led Flora to the end of the hallway and roughly hustled her inside her cell. Next, Riff heard rustling and scratching noises. He assumed Flora was filling out the form for the Jalopy. The guard grunted at her in acknowledgement, and Riff heard his footsteps coming back toward his own cell.

Suddenly the ambient light from the hallway dimmed. It was the guard's large head blocking the light. The guard furrowed his brow and said, "It's your turn." He then unlocked the cell.

Riff shrugged and walked forward, glad that his time in jail had lasted only about forty-five seconds. Then the guard's nose smacked him in the face.

"Not you, you dull Earthling. *You!*"

The guard pointed his nose to the back of Riff's cell.

Riff hadn't noticed the small creature trembling in a dark corner by the ceiling. It jiggled in fear, attempting to recede as far into the corner as it could, but the guard's nose extended and tweezed it from its hiding spot.

"No, no, no!" shrieked the small, ocean-blue creature as it held onto the wall with its suction-cup fingers. "Please, let me retake the test!"

"Our testing capabilities are much too robust to require a sample size of more than one test result per candidate. Your result is final." The guard pulled the creature with all his might.

"Noooo!" the creature wailed, losing its grip. When its suction cups gave way, the creature flew above Riff's head, then bounced off the guard's face. The guard caught the poor creature and applied a set of tiny handcuffs to it, then locked the cell again.

As the guard carried the small creature away, its piteous wails receded down the long hallway. An unseen door opened and then closed again, and the wails were silenced.

"Nan, you okay?" Riff called, leaning as close as he could to the barrier without getting zapped. He waited until he heard an uncomfortable groan before sitting back. He hoped Knitsy had a nice cellmate to look after her and was able to sit in a comfortable position. He didn't hear any distress from next door, so he concluded she had fallen asleep.

Riff slumped next to the cell opening and listened to the mumblings of his neighbours on the other side. They were quietly discussing plans to escape something called "blip." There was a constant low rumble in the cell block. No one was causing havoc, but some were clearly in a panic, breathing heavily, while others were just snoring noisily. Before long, Riff was snoring also.

"Psst!"

Riff snoozed lightly, drool dripping from his bottom lip.

"Pssssst!"

Riff scrambled to his knees and looked across the hall at the cells opposite.

No one appeared to be seeking his attention.

*Maybe it was Nan,* he thought. He arched his head and eyeline as close as possible to the opening of the cell, avoiding an electric shock as best he could, and craned his head in the direction of Knitsy's cell. "Nan, I'm here! Are you okay?"

But only the sounds of light snoring were coming from Knitsy's cell.

"Huh?" Riff said, scratching his head.

"PSSSSSSSSST!"

Finally, Riff looked behind him. In the middle of his cell was the creature, or part of one, that was attempting to get his attention. It looked like a small lizard, but its entire left half, from its nose to the tip of its tail, was missing. Riff jumped and bumped his head on the wall.

"Please, I need you to help me!"

As soon as Riff slowed down and realised he wasn't under attack, he stopped to catch his breath. He kept his eyes glued to the shockingly halved creature.

"Where did you come from? And wha-what happened to you?" he asked.

"My other half just got removed from this cell and taken down to BLIP." The creature was ocean-blue, and it dawned on Riff that he or she was exactly half the size of the creature who had been taken away a short while before.

"You're still alive?" Riff asked.

"My kind are able to detach parts of our body when we sense danger. It helps not having a skeletal system."

"What's your name? And where are you from?" asked Riff.

"I'm Panalon, and I'm from planet Salamind." Panalon squished into a curtsy.

"Riff, Earth. Nice to meet you. So, you need help?"

"Yes," said Panalon. "I need to get out of here. I've already lost half my brain, and I plan to use as much of the remainder of it enjoying my holiday to planet Olfinder next month. The wife and I have tickets to see the chorale there. I hear it's mesmerising. I've got to get out of here."

"Well, if I knew how to get out of here, I'd probably already be gone, mate. Sorry to break it to you," said Riff.

Panalon formed into a ball and started to roll to the back corner of the cell.

"Well, it would be nice to have some company," Riff said in an annoyed tone, "in case this is the last conversation either of us ever has."

Panalon stopped rolling. "Fine," he said. "What shall we talk about?"

"Should I be worried about this blip thing?" asked Riff.

"You? No," said Panalon, chuckling to himself. "Trust me, you have nothing to worry about."

Although Riff wasn't sure why Panalon held this opinion, he tried not to let the blip cause him anxiety. Riff tried making a bit more small talk with Panalon, but the small blue creature simply was not interested in talking about anything except how to break out of Casperian jail. Riff spent some alone time listening to The Death Brigade on ChipMusic, the music library stored on his microchip that played the music in his ears like headphones. It had been nearly a decade since he could fully listen to music, and now, thanks to his Oidodrums, he could happily hear all the chords and guttural screams of his favourite band.

He listened to one song called, "Splattering Scarecrows on a Sunday Afternoon," which had a killer drum solo. Riff was air-drumming along to it when he heard a high-pitched ringing sound. Confusion filled his brain because he didn't remember this particular part of the song, so he paused it. After a few seconds, the ringing stopped. Then, it clicked.

"What was that?" asked Panalon, rolling back into view.

"Panalon," said Riff, a smile brewing on his freckled face. "I think I know a way out of here."

Riff turned his pose into a rockstar jump, bumping his head again on the wall. He tapped his ear three times.

# CHAPTER 10

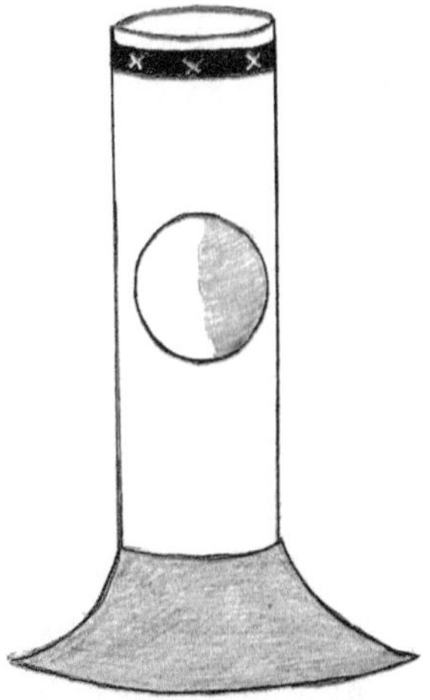

## THESIS

"Garold, can you hear me?" Riff said loudly. "Please, can you help us?"

Riff and Panalon sat in silence for a few moments, neither daring to move.

*Please answer,* thought Riff. *We need help. Please . . .*

Muffled speech came in through Riff's Oidodrums. "Riff, are you there? Did you mean to contact me? I was just sending a software update. There's no need to panic—"

"We need help!" said Riff in a hushed whisper. "My nan, Flora, and I are stuck in the immigration holding centre on planet Casper.

They took our Jalopy. We have to take some kind of test, and then we might get sent to something called a blip. I really don't want to find out what that is."

"My Flora?" Garold sounded as if he were about to cry. "They've got my Flora at the holding centre? B-but this is impossible! Delevio had all of your visa paperwork prepared! Surely he gave it to you before you left."

"No," said Riff with a sigh. "He didn't. I'm honestly not surprised."

"That little . . ."

Garold's sentence faded out as if he were moving out of range of the microphone on his end.

"Can you help us?" Riff repeated.

"Were you able to contact Tycho or any of the other team members at the Casper base?" asked Garold, now back in range.

"No. It seems like our communications were cut off," said Riff.

"Okay. I will alert Tycho to retrieve you. I can transmit your documents to him so you can be released."

"Thanks, mate," Riff said with a sigh of relief.

"And Riff, could you please keep a bit of a better eye on Flora for me?" asked Garold meekly.

Riff was surprised at this slight from Garold. But he could understand where he was coming from. If someone were travelling with his sisters or his grandmother, he would want them to make sure they didn't get a scratch on them. It was only natural for Garold to be worried about his wife.

"Of course. She's been really great, honestly. She's the one keeping me and Nan in line. But I will do everything I can to protect her."

"Thank you," Garold said with a sigh of relief. "I want Alphabeta to have her mother. If I had been allowed to go instead of Flora . . ." Garold's voice cracked.

"I get it," said Riff. "She'll be home in no time."

"Thank you," said Garold.

After they disconnected, Riff and Panalon chatted for a little while longer. Panalon was much more interested in Riff now that there was an escape plan, but eventually the two grew tired and decided to take a snooze. The sounds filling the open hallway weren't necessarily loud, but they were distracting Riff from a peaceful doze. He desperately wished he could turn off the sound, but he was stuck with endless noise from his Oidodrums. Plugging his ears didn't help, but a memory from his initial discussion with Garold when he had presented him with the Oidodrums reminded him that he could silence the world around him. All he had to do was shake his head.

He shook his head and the silence enveloped him like a warm blanket. His anxiety dimmed, and he was asleep within seconds.

* * *

Riff was rattled awake by someone shaking his shoulder vigorously. He wasn't sure how long he'd been asleep, but his guess was at least a few hours, judging from how hungry and thirsty he was and, more notably, how desperately he needed to use the toilet.

He looked up and saw a Casperian standing above him with a large frown on her face. This Casperian, unlike others Riff had seen, had several appendage-like noses on top of her head. She had braided them like hair and secured them with beige bows.

The Casperian started to move her mouth and wiggle her nose, but no sound flowed into Riff's ears. He fixed this by shaking his head to allow the sound to wash in.

"Erm," he croaked. He cleared his throat. "What do you want?"

The Casperian rolled her eyes. "I said, it's time for your test. Come with us." The Casperian's screechy, high-pitched voice was one of the most unpleasant noises Riff had ever heard.

She pointed her nose to the hallway. Riff turned and saw Knitsy and

Flora shackled together with expressions of defeat on their faces. Knitsy looked particularly drained: her hair was unkempt, she had dark circles under her eyes, and her knees were wobblier than usual. She coughed deeply and frequently. It was the first time in a while that Riff had noticed how old she really looked. For as long as Riff had known her, she had been unsteady on her feet, and recently she'd become slightly delusional, yet she always kept things light and humorous and rarely showed any weakness of will. But this time was different. She stared at the floor and didn't say a word. Flora seemed cowed as well, but not nearly in the bad shape that Knitsy was in.

Riff ran to Knitsy and wrapped a strong arm around her waist. He could feel her weight slump into his side with each cough. Her head rested on his shoulder. He thought he might cry. He so desperately wanted to hear her voice. Just something witty—a quip about this Casperian's hair of noses, perhaps, or a smart remark about the wayward curl sticking up from Flora's head or the clump of blue goop on one of Riff's trainers.

The Casperian began wrapping chains around Riff to shackle him.

"Oi, oi!" Riff snapped. "I won't resist you. Just let me hold up my nan."

The Casperian sniffed sharply. "Fine. Follow me, then."

"You know," said Riff, "we're meant to be picked up from here soon."

Flora's expression brightened with hope. Knitsy didn't move an inch. She still slumped in Riff's embrace.

The Casperian's nose popped up. "Oh?" she said, with a flare of distaste. "I have not received word that you will be collected at any time. Besides, the legality in this matter is more pressing. You arrived in our space zone without proper documentation, so you must be tested to assess your threat level. Only then might you be released—assuming you do not pose a threat."

Riff peered nervously at Flora, hoping she'd know how to negotiate with their captor. Flora returned his nervous look and didn't say a word.

He knew very well that he could simply bolt away and leave the women behind. He didn't want to do that, but it was something he would have done in the past. Riff recalled the time when he lived on Antympanica and the GeoLapse invaded. He'd sought refuge at the Cabbaged Egg Inn and Bar, leaving his friends Matt and Joe behind and in serious danger. They were the real heroes who took his sisters and grandmother to safety. Riff had felt horrible about it afterward.

Riff thought of what Garold had asked of him: that he keep Flora safe. He had to make a decision, and fast. *Tycho could arrive any second,* he reasoned. He decided to stall.

"Can you explain the type of technology behind the cell barriers here?" asked Riff brightly.

"Well . . ." The Casperian seemed momentarily surprised. "Certainly. Back in the thirty-ninth century, electricity was manipulated such that it was able to be paired as a mechanical barricade . . ." Cell barrier technology seemed to be a topic of great interest to the Casperian, because she went on about it for at least ten minutes straight.

During the insipid monologue, Riff glanced down and saw Panalon sitting on the toe of his right trainer and squirming in anticipation. When the Casperian turned to point at something, Riff subtly waved his hand to Panalon. The small creature curtsied, then curled up and rolled off his shoe. Riff mouthed, "Have fun on Olfinder." Panalon stuck out a thumbs-up as he rolled down the hallway and out of sight.

Riff felt very proud of himself for outsmarting the Casperian security guard. It was true that Panalon still needed to somehow make it to the exit of the holding centre . . . but that was his problem now.

"Any more questions before we continue?" said the Casperian in a slightly giddier tone than before.

Now Riff was back at square one with the original conundrum. He had to make sure that Flora and Knitsy would be safe. *What is taking Tycho so long?* Riff thought. *He should be here by now.* He could feel Flora's eyes on him. He was so worried about letting her and Garold down.

Riff gulped. He said to the braided Casperian, "No, thank you. That was a very thorough and, erm, fascinating explanation."

Braid nodded, then pulled the chains forward, lurching both Knitsy and Flora into step.

Flora shot Riff a look of surprise.

*She must be angry with my decision,* thought Riff. *Garold will have my head if anything happens to her.* But he had to trust his gut. One thing he did know was that Casperians, although snobbish and slightly discriminatory against other beings, were not a violent community. They weren't very strong physically, only mentally. Still, he'd have to be on his top brain game if he wanted to get them all out of this mess alive. He silently wished Tycho would pop up and whisk them away to safety, even though Tycho regularly shamed them for their inferior intelligence.

Knitsy sputtered and coughed as they walked. Riff held her tighter. As they marched, he tried to catch a glimpse of her upper arm, where her breathing patch was usually affixed. But he couldn't see if it was there or not. She also wasn't wearing the mask around her face.

Braid led them into a small white room, then began detaching their chains. Knitsy wheezed and hacked as her chains were removed, causing Braid to make a face and wipe the cough droplets off her arm with a handkerchief.

When they were all unchained, the guard sat them down around a circular table. The only thing in the room besides the table and chairs was a blank screen on one of the walls.

Braid said, "I'll be right back with the test materials," then stepped out of the room.

Flora turned to Riff, her face scrunched in concern. "Is Tycho coming or not?"

"Yes," said Riff. "Garold told me."

Flora blinked in astonishment. "Y-you've spoken to him? How?"

Riff pointed to his ears.

"Let me talk to him!" Flora said, lunging for Riff's ear. He gently pushed her back into her seat.

"Please, calm down. We can't be throwing ourselves around and making them think we're a threat or violent. You need to trust me."

"Why should I trust you?" Flora croaked as tears filled her eyes. "How do you know we're going to be okay?"

Riff gulped. "I don't."

Flora sat back in her chair in surrender and buried her face in her hands.

Riff turned toward his grandmother. "Nan, are you okay? What's wrong?" He gently shook her shoulders, but she didn't move or say anything.

"You didn't hear?" Flora asked, peering up at him. "The whole cell block heard."

"Heard what?" he said. His heart began to race. "I turned off my Oidodrums for a nap. I don't know for how long exactly. Nan, what's going on?"

Knitsy's body started convulsing every few seconds. Her mouth was tightly closed. Riff realised she was holding back coughs. Eventually she stopped shaking and took a few very shallow breaths. Her eyes met Riff's, and she said weakly, "They took my patch."

Riff's face blanched. Her breathing patch was the only thing that helped her breathe normally. Without it, she had these coughing fits anytime she tried to do anything physical. Riff suddenly realised that the breathing patch was doing much more than helping her breathe . . . it was keeping her alive.

"Why did they take your patch?" he asked. He started digging his fingers into her forearm, as if his subconscious were telling him that the tighter he held her, the less she would cough. Subsequent coughs forced him back into reality, and he released his grip.

"I was 'being reckless,' apparently. All I wanted was a glass of water, or whatever top-shelf gin they had. I was gently tapping my cane against the wall to get their attention—"

A slight curl at one corner of Flora's mouth told Riff that Knitsy's gentle taps had been more like violent raps.

"And someone came, and I told them what I wanted, and after an eternity they came back with some disgusting, wormy sludge that I was expected to drink in order to quiet down. So, I threw it at the guard."

"Nan!" Riff gasped. "You can't throw things at people! Or . . . creatures. It's not very nice."

Knitsy attempted a deep breath. "So then, the watermelon head called in more watermelon heads, and . . . they took my patch."

"I don't get it," Riff seethed. "Why would they do that?" He looked at Flora for guidance.

"I couldn't see what was happening," Flora whispered so Knitsy couldn't hear. "But it sounded like they noticed the patch, or maybe they noticed her trying to hide it. It sounded like they thought it was an intelligence-gathering device. They took it away to investigate it."

"They can't do that to an old lady!" snapped Riff. "Surely if they're as smart as they say they are, they knew straight away what it's for!"

The door handle moved, and Flora and Riff ceased talking.

Braid re-entered the room carrying a handled case. She put it on the table, opened it, and began distributing its contents. "Please affix these to your foreheads," she said, handing out three different-coloured buttons. Next she took out three glass cylinders with flat bases. Each one had a yellow ball resting at the bottom and a red ring traced around the cylinder near the top. Braid placed one cylinder in front of each of them.

When Flora affixed a purple button to her forehead, the yellow ball in her cylinder began to glow.

Knitsy's fingers wobbled as she tried to pick up the button she had been given. Riff laid one hand gently on her arm.

"Just a moment, Nan," said Riff. Then he turned and faced Braid. "Give her back her breathing patch. *Now.*"

Braid narrowed her tennis-ball eyes. "I don't know what you are referring to."

Riff pointed to Knitsy's upper arm and the square region of pale skin where her patch had been. "The patch that she was wearing—and her breathing mask. They were taken away from her. She needs them to breathe!"

"Ah," said Braid, twirling her fingers through her hair. "I believe they have been confiscated for further analysis. They will be returned to her if they are deemed not to be a threat."

"Did you not hear me? She needs them to *live*," Riff pressed. "They aren't a threat to you. But it's a threat to her if she can't wear them."

"We know what Earthlings customarily wear. Those items are not in our Knowledge Vault, so they needed to be removed," Braid continued.

Riff was glad his scruffy hair covered up the Oidodrums. If they tried to remove those, his ears would come off with them. He spoke up, "They're medical devices. That mask was specially made for her. Loads of people on Earth have assistive devices. My sister had—has one that helps her get nutrients into her body because she can't eat." Talking about Elbina caused Riff's chest to tighten. She was the reason they were in this situation. And he'd have done it all over again if it meant that there was a chance of finding her.

"If the devices are not a threat, they will be returned," repeated Braid, her voice rising with anger. "If there are any more interruptions to this test, I will dock your final score."

Riff took a deep breath. "Fine," he said. He pressed his orange button to his forehead. It attached with suction. Then he pressed the green button to Knitsy's forehead. The yellow balls in their cylinders started to glow.

"Excellent," said Braid, poking at a tablet in front of her. "All the sensors are paired."

The screen on the wall now showed three 3-D brain images, each with a colourful dot in the upper left corner that matched colours of the buttons on their foreheads. Flora and Riff's brains looked squishy and full, whereas Knitsy's brain looked a bit shrivelled all over.

"Welcome to THESIS, which stands for Threat of Homeland Examination to Suspend Inferior Species. This test has four sections. Your final THESIS score will determine your disposition. If you do not pose a threat to our society, you must leave immediately on the Jalopy you arrived in and never return. If you do pose a threat, you will be taken to BLIP. Any questions?"

Braid's last question sounded much too cheerful. Riff raised his hand. "Erm, what's the blip?"

"It's not 'the Blip,' it's BLIP—Brain Liquefaction In Progress. Your brain will be transformed to a liquid and stored in our Knowledge Vault for the next generation of Casperians to study," Braid replied.

Riff was starting to rethink his hypothesis that the Casperians weren't a violent community.

"Now I will begin the testing," said Braid. "The first portion of the test is on a subject that was once a favourite on planet Earth: trivia! Griffin McHubbard, the first question is for you."

Riff's eyes bulged. He was terrible at trivia. *My brain doesn't belong in anyone's Knowledge Vault,* he thought. *If they knew what poor marks I got in school, I bet they wouldn't even bother sending me to BLIP.* He wondered how quickly he could get a transcript.

"Draw the tree of planet Casper, then verbally describe the type of fruit that it produces," said Braid, passing him the tablet.

Riff gritted his teeth. He had only ever seen Antympanican greenery before. The majority of the trees there were shaped like giant cones at the base with very dense tops. He decided to just draw one of those and see where it got him. The tablet had different utensils and colours to choose from. Riff chose a sepia brown and drew several cones. Then he switched to a dark green and added a crown of dense greenery to each cone. He slid the tablet back to Braid, who raised an eyebrow.

"Okaaay," she said. "This looks more like the Attalmophus tree species from Antympanica, but please continue with the remainder of the question."

"Right," Riff started. "Well, the tree of Casper is . . . not an Attalmophus tree. It's the . . . Casperophus tree, which grows . . . books?"

Flora couldn't help snickering.

Braid looked unamused. "The tree of Casper is a Zygobroak, which grows fafflin feathers every other spring."

Riff shrugged. "You learn something new every day."

"Knitsy McHubbard, it is your turn," said Braid.

Riff gently shook Knitsy awake, and she coughed and tried to sit up straight.

"How many lumens is the ambient light on Casper?"

Knitsy thought a moment, then said, "Chocolate."

Braid sighed. "Five hundred eighty-five. Casper's orbit around its two suns guarantees a consistent amount of ambient light day and night for reading. Too many or too few lumens would strain our eyes. Five hundred eighty-five is the optimal number of lumens for uninterrupted learning."

Braid turned to Flora. "Which brings me to your question, Flora Zeep. What is the greatest, most ingenious engineering feat of the 312th century?"

Flora's right eye twitched and she held her tongue in her cheek. "Casperian scientists perfected the e-book within a contact lens."

Braid scrunched her eyes at Flora's 3D brain image. "You're lying. Tell the truth."

Flora gulped. "It was the construction of the Casperian polar axis."

"Correct," said Braid. "Why did we need the axis to be built?"

"The mega-density of the axis created a far stronger gravitational pull than Casper's two suns. This made the Casperian solar system geocentric and moved its two stars into figure-eight orbits so they illuminate all parts of Casper consistently and equally at all times."

"Precisely," said Braid. "Very good, Flora."

They all watched as Flora's glowing ball rose about a third of the way from the bottom of the cylinder, drawing closer to the red circle at the top.

"We have reached section two. Griffin, we'll start with you again. Please take this book." Braid handed him a thick book of approximately six hundred pages.

"You have five seconds to read it and give me a brief synopsis. And . . . go!" said Braid.

Riff skipped the cover and found page one, which began: "Umbrierre Unogh: Protozoic Inflammations in the—"

"Your time is up," said Braid, snatching the book from Riff's hands. "Please give me your synopsis."

Riff sat, mouth agape. "Erm, protozoic inflammations."

"Incorrect. It is one of the greatest tragic plays about Casperian physiology, dating from the seventeenth century."

Knitsy fared no better with her book, a history of Casper's successful acquisition of the constellation Trepla.

Both Riff's and Knitsy's yellow balls still rested at the bottoms of their respective cylinders.

Flora's attempt with her book—an analysis for papermakers about the best pulp sources for efficient page turning—raised her ball only about a centimetre.

"Section three," said Braid, clearly unimpressed by the intelligence on display before her. "I will now turn off a portion of each of your brains and ask you to perform a task."

Riff woke up about five minutes later to Braid saying, "Section four." None of their yellow balls had moved.

Braid said: "I will now search your brain for the most traumatising event and let you relive it. Your response to this event will allow me to grade you."

Riff clutched the table. What did she mean by *relive it*? Surely that didn't mean actually reliving it.

A white flash blinded him and everything around him fell silent. He wasn't in the THESIS testing location anymore, but this new place looked so familiar, almost like home to him. He immediately knew it was Antympanica. But what was he doing here?

Small footprints on the muddy path ahead reminded him exactly which event had been chosen for the test. He was reliving a portion of his

Planetary Diagnostic Test—the test he and everyone else on Earth had been administered to determine which planet they'd be sent to. He remembered that these particular footprints belonged to Elbina. Just ahead of him was a giant conical tree, similar to the one he had drawn in section one of THESIS. Numerous branches protruded from about halfway up the tree, and Elbina was crawling along one of them. Riff watched as she tied one of the sleeves of her jumper around a branch and the other around her own neck. Riff knew what he was reliving had been only a simulation, but it still petrified him to witness one of his sisters that close to death. Riff climbed up the tree, knowing very well how this would end, but still instinctively feeling the need to attempt to save her. He tried screaming Elbina's name with every bit of his strength, but no sound came through his vocal cords on the silent planet. After several failed attempts to jump up to the branch where Elbina was situated, he finally got a grip on it. Elbina noticed him, and relief spread across her face. She began crawling toward him, and he thrust out his arm, extending his fingers as far as they could reach, still screaming silent bellows, hoping that this time he might be able to save her. She was a metre away now. Riff lunged toward her, but she fell. Riff screamed, weeping silently for his sister.

Riff hoped the Casperian test would last just a little longer so that he could see Elbina in the McHubbard kitchen again, just as he had following the Planetary Diagnostic Test. Instead, he was brought straight back to the white room in the holding centre. He was sweating profusely and shaking so violently that he had to hold onto the seat of his chair for stability. An overwhelming sadness flooded him. He peered at Knitsy and Flora, who had also just finished reliving their worst memories. They wore similar expressions of pure agony and distress on their faces.

"You have completed THESIS," said Braid. "Thank you for your participation. Griffin and Knitsy McHubbard, you must leave the premises immediately and never return to Casper. Flora Zeep, you will be escorted back to your cell to await your transfer to BLIP for brain liquefaction."

"No!" bellowed Riff, surprised for a moment that his screams now had sound. He noticed the glowing yellow balls in his and Knitsy's cylinders were hovering just short of halfway to the red target circle. Flora's ball, however, had reached the level of the target, indicating she was a threat to Casperian society.

Cuffs on Flora's armrests closed tightly over her wrists, pinning her in her chair. Guards appeared, seemingly out of nowhere, and began hustling Riff and Knitsy out of the room. Flora cried out to Riff, her eyes filled with terror. He had to put up a fight. He had promised Garold.

Something knocked Riff in the back of the head, and he hit the ground hard. The last thing he saw before his eyes fluttered closed was someone he recognised rushing toward them.

"Stop!" the familiar creature called. "I have their documents. They have been cleared. They can leave with me."

It was Tycho.

Relief briefly poured into Riff's chest before he fell unconscious. He dreamt of becoming the Grand Q'bah's slave, having to wash his sluggy body and answer all his weird trivia questions. He got all of them wrong, and with each incorrect answer, another Casperian appendage sprouted from where his nose should have been.

# CHAPTER 11

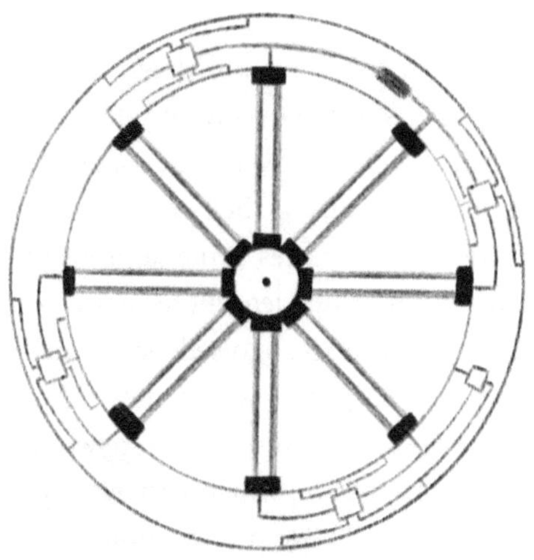

## PROJECT BAKERLOO'S INNOVATION

Riff awoke in an oversized, stiff, but beautiful crimson armchair, surrounded by a library of books from floor to ceiling. His head throbbed where he had been struck, but a bandage had been wrapped around his head to protect the wound. Several Casperians were in this library with him, all reading in similar-looking armchairs or climbing ladders to reach books on high shelves. None of the Casperians was speaking; the only sounds in the room were page turns, the scrunching of armchairs as readers sought more comfortable positions, and the occasional *Ooh* when a Casperian came across something particularly interesting in a text.

Riff was a bit confused. Was he out of the holding centre? Was Flora's brain liquefied? Did Knitsy ever get her breathing patch back?

He popped up from his chair and made a beeline for the nearest exit. The noise of his footsteps elicited looks of annoyance from the Casperians.

Riff charged through the door and down a marble hallway lined with tall columns. The first marble hallway led to another, which led to a courtyard with trees filled with tweeting Casperian birds at their tops and quietly reading Casperians at their bases. From there he roamed through at least three more libraries of the same beauty and tranquillity as the first. He had absolutely no idea where he was going; he just hoped he would run into someone he recognised, or that he'd look lost enough that some kind-hearted Casperian would show him the way to wherever Tycho and the Project Bakerloo team were working.

The current library he was in, which very well could have been the same one he started in for all he knew, was now filled with Casperians. Perhaps what had been teatime back home in the UK was reading time on Casper. Riff started to crave a nice cup of tea—one made by his mother, something he hadn't had in almost eight years.

This thought saddened him as he continued to walk aimlessly through the strange Casperian campus. He remembered how his family used to sit at the kitchen table in the same spots every day. To his right sat Knitsy; then his mum, then Ann Lou, then Luna, and finally Elbina on his left. He could imagine them all doing their usual activities: Knitsy cursing at the news; his mum passing dishes around the table, filling the kitchen with the delicious aromas of heavenly cuisines; Ann Lou twiddling her hockey stick under the table; Elbina adjusting her feeding machine (the Gasser, he used to call it); and Luna silently reading one of her big Braille books. His mental picture of Luna was particularly vivid. She was reading some textbook in preparation for Oxford, where she had been accepted for university. Riff had always admired her thirst for knowledge, which was so much greater than his own. Luna would flip a page . . . sip her tea . . .

"LUNA!" Riff cried, bounding up to his sister. She was sitting in a green velvet armchair, reading.

Several Casperians flicked their noses at Riff.

Luna dropped her book in her lap and tightened her grip on her tea.

"Luna, it's me! Riff," he said, kneeling in front of her. He held out his hands for her to touch as her mouth hung open in astonishment.

"Riff," she breathed with relief. She signed to him. "I heard you'd arrived today. They told me you needed to wake up on your own first. How are you?"

"Never thought I'd say this, but . . . I'm so glad to see you, Sis," he said, smiling broadly.

Luna chuckled, something she didn't often do.

"Also, I can hear now," he said. "The medical engineers at the ERA developed a set of devices for me."

"Wow!" she said. "So, I heard you got stuck at the border. Was everything okay in the end? Flora filled me in a little bit, but she needed to rest."

Riff exhaled with great relief. Flora was safe. Garold wasn't going to kill him.

"The border was just one small event," he began. "So, when we left Earth for the stardust mission . . ." He told her everything about their journey so far: the supernova, getting stranded in an asteroid belt, finding the mining droid, being dragged to the casino, being interrogated by the Grand Q'bah, and their struggles in the holding centre.

After a lengthy technical follow-up statement from Luna regarding the unethical use of mining droids, Riff was desperate to change the subject.

"Anyways, where's Nan?" he asked.

"She's resting. I heard her patch and mask were confiscated. They still haven't returned them," said Luna, balling her fists.

"What?" exclaimed Riff.

More nose flicks from Casperians followed his rising tone.

"They didn't give them back?" he said, slightly quieter. "Why not? They know she isn't a threat!"

"Apparently, whoever investigated was shocked that we 'doltish Earthlings'—I believe that was the verbiage used—are capable of developing such efficacious technology. They transferred it to their Knowledge Vault so they can re-evaluate Earthling intelligence."

"So . . . it's gone?" said Riff, his voice breaking.

Luna nodded, swallowing hard.

"Can't they just make her a patch and a mask? Surely they could whip up new ones in no time," said Riff.

"I'm afraid their priorities don't align with those of an old grandmother from planet Earth," said Luna. "We're lucky they're helping us find Elbina. But they're only viewing this project as the next great engineering feat—to create a multi-universal Jalopy."

"So," Riff's bottom lip quivered. "Nan's going to . . ."

"Don't say it," said Luna, holding up her hand. "I've already alerted the ERA to fabricate a new patch for her and to have it sent here. We just need to spend some time with her. You never know, maybe she'll perk right back up in the meantime. Perhaps the Casperian air will provide her lungs with miraculous health benefits."

Riff raked his fingers through his hair and glared at the Casperians around them. Immediately he felt ashamed of his rudeness, but he was angry with the Casperians. He wanted to grab them by their smug noses, whip them around his head like a lasso, and launch them into the nearest Zygobroak tree. How dare they take away an old woman's assistive devices? And she was helping them! Knitsy was just as much of a team member as the other creatures on Project Bakerloo. They were all working to build a multi-universal Jalopy that could navigate a black hole. He felt outraged and began to pace back and forth in front of Luna.

"I want to go see Nan now. But, what's the progress with the Jalopy build?"

"I'll take you to her," said Luna, "and fill you in on the way."

Riff offered to carry her extremely heavy book. He held the ultra-dense book in one arm and let his other arm hang down by his side. Luna told him which way to go, then touched the back of his free arm lightly as they walked.

"The Jalopy is nearly complete. All it needs is the stardust. Turn right at the end of this hallway. It needs to be tested, though. It hasn't been tested in a real black hole yet. Unfortunately, that test won't be done until the day of the live mission."

"So, this whole thing is a giant risk? We don't even know if it's going to work?" asked Riff.

"Right," said Luna. "Across this courtyard and then to the left."

"How will it be tested?" Riff asked.

"Someone needs to fly through a simulated black hole to a simulated universe. There will be two travellers—but only two, because more weight requires more stardust. If one passenger dies, the other can report back to the team."

"That's cheerful," said Riff.

"It was originally planned to be you and Knitsy, but I don't think she's well enough to fly," said Luna.

"So, will you fly with me?" asked Riff.

Luna smiled. "I'd be happy to."

The eldest McHubbard siblings made their way up a flight of stairs, then down another hallway to Knitsy's room.

Knitsy lay on her side in a small single bed with her hands curled up by her chest. She was asleep, and Riff and Luna sat silently on the bed. Riff noticed a bucket on the floor next to the bed. He nearly gagged when he saw what was in the bottom of it: blood.

"Mack," murmured Knitsy.

"She talks to Grandad in her sleep a lot," Riff whispered to Luna.

Knitsy's eyes fluttered as she repeated "Mack" a few more times. Riff gently caressed her hair while she slept and dreamed of their grandad. He was glad she wasn't coughing, but he worried about what kind of future she was facing. Riff wished he could give all his breaths to Knitsy. She deserved them. But maybe she didn't want them. Riff thought about all the people Knitsy surely missed: Mack; her best friends, Meg and Bowie; and her daughter, Henrietta. Riff hoped she was dreaming of them all in some happy place. Riff and Luna sat quietly with her for another half hour or so before they were due to attend a Project Bakerloo update meeting.

Luna directed Riff to an engineering workshop on the vast campus within Schingmaning City. A team of mostly Casperians and Flora awaited them. Riff smiled to Flora as they walked in.

Tycho approached Riff and Luna. "Welcome to Casper. I trust you found your way without trouble?"

Riff raised an eyebrow. "Mate, you rescued us. I wouldn't say 'without trouble'; alive is more like it, thanks."

"I meant your way to the workshop," said Tycho, already clearly annoyed.

"Oh, yes. Fine, mate," said Riff, embarrassed.

"I'll give you the tour," said Tycho, and he led them farther into the workshop.

The shop reminded Riff of the medical engineering workshop at the ERA. Some engineers with tools he didn't recognise were whacking and hacking away at giant pipes and others were testing the paths of beams of light through large glass lenses with complex shapes. A sea of others coded complex programs on holographic screens. The room was abuzz with activity—until a pleasant ding rang overhead, and then all the Casperians except for Tycho rushed out.

"Reading time," Luna whispered into Riff's ear. He'd guessed right!

Riff was happy that the room was now mostly quiet so he could concentrate on the Jalopy. Tycho led him to a large area of the shop that was entirely empty except for a glass torus resting on the floor. The torus was about the size of a dinner plate. Eight beams of light emerged from the torus at equidistant angles from one another like wheel spokes, meeting at a singular point at the centre.

"Behold!" bellowed Tycho proudly, waving his nose at the torus.

"Nice steering wheel," said Riff. "Where's the rest of it?" He looked around for a giant spaceship with wings, a powerful engine, and maybe even a fiery logo across the body.

"How dare you insult our work?" spat Tycho. "This is the Jalopy we've been developing!"

Riff belly-laughed. "Good one, lad," he said, nudging Tycho playfully on the arm. Tycho was actually a pretty funny guy. It had taken them a while to see eye to eye, but they'd developed quite the banter.

Then Riff caught a glimpse of Luna, who shook her head and gritted her teeth.

He furrowed his brows and peered back at Tycho. "This is the Jalopy? For real? How am I supposed to get in?"

Tycho looked at Flora. "Remind me why he was chosen to co-captain this mission?"

Flora smiled. "Because he's got the heart for it."

"The heart has nothing to do with satisfactory captaincy," muttered Tycho. "If your minuscule Earthling brain has room for concepts beyond your planet's insignificant scientific discoveries, I can show you how this Jalopy works."

Riff heard Luna sniff behind him. Back in the Time Belt, Tycho had regularly insulted Luna's intellect, and she took more offence at that than most. Riff hadn't cared so much.

"Show me," he said.

"Follow me." Tycho leaned down over the wheel Jalopy and dangled his nose over the centre point where the light beams met. Within a second, his entire body shrank down to nothing. Riff gasped and raced up to the Jalopy. Did he go to a different dimension? Was he invisible? He looked around the room to see if anyone else had noticed, but with all the Casperians away for reading time, only Luna and Flora were left to confer with.

"Where did he go?" he asked them.

Luna said, "He's in the Jalopy. You might be able to see him if you look closely."

A confused Riff got down on the floor and peered at the torus. At first he focused on what looked like circuitry inside the glass tube, but then a slight movement drew his eyes to the centre point where the beams met. Something small was waving at him. A long nose attached to a rather round head . . .

"Tycho?" exclaimed Riff, his eyes bulging. A tiny Tycho was standing in a clear glass enclosure atop the point where the eight beams met.

"Get in!" urged Luna.

Riff stared at the torus, then hesitantly held his finger just above the central point where the light beams met. He dangled it there for a few seconds and then touched the point. In a flash he was staring up at giant versions of his sister and Flora. And Tycho looked normal-sized next to him inside the Jalopy.

"When I say, *Follow me*, I expect that you will follow me at that moment, not take your time. We have many universes to explore!" snapped Tycho.

"Well, one in particular," said Riff.

"This is not all about you. We have scientific discoveries to uncover. Let me show you around."

The central point of the wheel Jalopy—the cabin space in which they were standing—was a glass cylinder just large enough for two shrunken human-sized beings to comfortably stand. Two sets of bungee cords were fastened opposite each other to the cabin wall.

"And that's it!" said Tycho proudly.

"Can I see the spokey bits and the outer ring part?" asked Riff.

"Those areas are inaccessible to passengers. We don't want any Earthlings—I mean, any non-Casperian creatures having the opportunity to alter the circuitry that ensures a successful trip."

"How does it work, then?" asked Riff.

"The 'spokey bits' are propellers," said Tycho, pointing at them through the glass. They were clearly visible but distorted by refraction where the cabin's glass wall met the surrounding air. "Currently commissioned Jalopies in the Universal Union use a different type of technology to navigate. They are guided by the Universal Positioning System, which does not anticipate obstacles but instead handles them as they arise, on an 'in the moment' basis. This state-of-the-art Jalopy maps out the entire universe and the trajectories of all objects greater than the Jalopy's size and weight, then uses this map to *anticipate* obstacles. This allows the route to any given location to be plotted with a high degree of precision and accuracy. When the destination requires a route through a black hole, it is imperative that this Jalopy be flown to a specific position of the black hole, or else the journey could be fatal."

Riff gulped. "Right."

"This new Jalopy design also utilises stellar wind—charged particles from stars—to fly faster and more efficiently," Tycho continued.

"And how do you get out of this thing?" asked Riff.

"You simply need to jump in the centre of the cabin," replied Tycho.

Riff's impression of the Jalopy was slowly growing favourable. He was especially proud that his sister was working on this project. He wondered how the project would be going if he were on the team. Probably he'd have mucked something up and his team members would have thrown him in BLIP out of sheer annoyance.

"Is there anything else you want to know?" asked Tycho.

"Why is the cabin so small? There's no room to move around," said Riff.

"When the Jalopy reaches the event horizon of a black hole, the design intent is that the propellers and the peripheral structure break off, leaving just the pilots at the precise destination. We had to make the cabin as small as possible because a black hole pulls all matter to its centre, called a singularity. The cabin wall is made of Graphalattice, the strongest material ever developed. Nothing, not even a black hole, has a chance of rupturing it," Tycho said, patting the wall.

"So, the chances of survival are high, then?" Riff asked in a hopeful tone.

"Oh, not at all!" laughed Tycho. "Only a fool would think that. But with you as pilot for the black hole simulation, we are willing to take the risk."

"Bloody brilliant," snarled Riff. "How do you even make a black hole simulation in the first place?"

"We have a particle accelerator that is able to collide ultra-high-energy particles together. These particles have been gathered from all across the universe. Some of the pure stardust you brought back was included. These particle collisions make black holes. Really, only a little bit of mass and volume are needed to create one. This simulated black hole won't be anywhere near as dense as the black hole portal to Reprisa, but the concept is the same. We'll be ready for the pilot test in twelve hours. Are you ready?" asked Tycho.

"Erm . . ." Riff started.

The odds didn't look good, even with the most intelligent beings in the universe running the project. But Riff's hope was palpable. If there was a chance of developing a Jalopy that could travel to Thera to save his sister, he had to help. He had to prove that the men in his family weren't all evil, like his father and his great-uncle. He would be just as brave as his Grandad Mack . . . as brave as Luna and Elbina and Ann Lou, and their mother and grandmother.

Riff took a deep breath and puffed out his chest. "I'm ready."

# CHAPTER 12

## THE PILOT TEST

That night—which felt like one long, continuous day because of Casper's never-ending light—Riff and Luna slept on chairs in Knitsy's room. They wanted to keep her company, even though she had not regained full alertness at any time since they left the holding centre.

During the night, the siblings took turns watching her while the other dozed. Knitsy coughed lightly as she slept, and they had to make sure she stayed on her side so she could spit out the blood she was coughing up. Riff barely slept a wink, constantly getting back up to fluff her pillows, tuck her blanket in tighter, clean out the bucket beside her bed, and whisper to her that everything would be okay. Luna did the same during the rare moments Riff managed to doze off.

Knitsy talked in her sleep every so often—things like "Hi, Mummy" and "What time is dinner, Mack?" and "Henrietta, the soup is too salty." Riff and Luna felt glad that she was imagining sweet (and salty) scenarios. Neither of them wanted to admit that she was dying. They couldn't believe it because, for one, she had already "died" once previously. The first time they flew in the hourglass Jalopy through the Time Belt on their way to Harvinth, Father Time had taken Knitsy away from them, and they had believed her to be dead. They grieved her loss so intensely then that it seemed impossible to grieve again. Besides, she had not in fact been dead. Surely she would power through this crisis also, and she'd return to her old jovial self, dancing around the room, tapping her cane on walls and people, and enjoying a nice sweet at the end of the day with a cup of tea, all while swearing at anything and anyone who slightly inconvenienced her.

"Have you heard from Garold?" croaked Luna.

Riff knew his sister was as exhausted as he was. He could hear it in her voice.

"Yes, about an hour ago. He said the patch was almost completed. They'll bring it as soon as they can."

"That's good news. I hope he knows to hurry, though." Luna sounded worried.

"I told him to expedite it. He said he would," Riff replied.

The siblings tried to wake Knitsy gently, hoping she might have the energy to take a quick walk or have a cup of tea. Nothing stirred her until Riff opened a pack of biscuits. She fluttered open her eyes, then slowly turned and stared at him.

"Nan!" he yelped. "You're awake!" He rushed to her bedside and held up the bucket, and she coughed up a mouthful of blood. He lightly patted her hair as she spat it into the bucket.

"Nan," Riff said, "the ERA is manufacturing a new patch for you. You'll be feeling better in no time."

"I don't want it," she said weakly.

"Why not?" said Riff. "It's the only way to get you better!"

"I'm tired. I want to rest. I just want to go home," Knitsy said calmly.

Luna bit her lip. "We can send you back to Earth once you get your patch. You're not well enough to travel right now."

"Not that home, love," Knitsy said, a twinkle in her eye.

A gentle ding rang throughout the campus. Reading time.

"Nan, we need to go to the workshop for the Jalopy pilot test now. We'll make sure someone is here to help you. You won't be alone. We shouldn't be gone more than a few hours," said Luna.

"I don't want some melonhead with a string nose and a bad attitude force-feeding me Casperian mush," Knitsy snapped.

She sounded like her old self. Riff breathed a sigh of relief.

"Fine. I'll stay with you," said Luna.

Riff glanced at her. "But the pilot test. How will I know what to do?"

"Tycho will go with you instead," said Luna.

"Nooo, not Tycho," Riff whined.

"He knows how to operate that Jalopy better than anyone else. He'll prepare you well for the actual mission."

Luna was right. They couldn't leave Knitsy alone, as much as she seemed to be improving.

"Okay, fine. I'd better be going, then. Nan, I'll see you when I get back," said Riff. He broke off a small piece of biscuit for her, and she gummed it while Luna poured her some water.

"Good luck," said Luna, hugging Riff. "You'll do great."

Riff kissed Knitsy on the head and she gazed up at him with twinkling eyes. "I love you, darling. Thank you for protecting me." She smiled and reached out a veiny hand. They held hands for a few moments before Riff tipped his cap at the both of them and headed out the door to the engineering workshop.

* * *

In the workshop, he found the Project Bakerloo team circled around a large incubator in the centre of the room. The top of the incubator was a clear dome, and a metallic-looking funnel structure lined its bottom. The wheel Jalopy rested on the top of the dome, and a ladder from the floor to the Jalopy was already in place.

Tycho waltzed up to Riff, flaunting his nose and limbs every which way. He was clearly excited for the groundbreaking event that was about to ensue. "Today's the day! Are you and your wrinkly co-pilot almost ready?"

"Erm . . . My nan is under the weather," said Riff.

Tycho rolled his eyes. "Simpleminded Earthlings and their weak immune systems. Then Luna will accompany you. Where is she?"

"She had other commitments to attend to," said Riff. "But she mentioned that you would be a suitable co-pilot."

Tycho's nose curled into a fist. "What do you mean by 'other commitments?' She was specially chosen to support this team at the drop of a book."

"Please," Riff begged, "trust me. She just can't perform the test today."

"I wasn't planning on surrendering my life today," said Tycho under his breath.

"Well, then, you'll have to take extra care," said Riff.

Tycho turned to the team. "Increase the sensitivity in the strain gauges! Secure the grounding outlets in the propellers!"

The engineers quickly bounced into action.

Once Tycho was confident that each circuit had been quadruple-checked, he demanded a quintuple check. After a brief panic attack, Tycho regained his composure and started up the ladder. Riff followed close behind him.

When they got to the top, Riff could see that the wheel Jalopy was hovering over an open hole in the top of the dome. Riff looked down into the hole and saw only darkness at the centre of the funnel below them. This was probably where the simulated black hole would be initiated.

"Ready?" asked Tycho, his nose almost touching the Jalopy's centre point, where the light beams met.

"Ready, captain," replied Riff. He saluted the team in the room. A few Casperian noses waved back at him.

Together, Riff and Tycho touched the centre point and were shrunk down. Tycho began securing himself to the wall with the bungee cords, and Riff followed suit.

A voice filled Riff's ears, but it was not the usual soothing voice of the kind of Jalopy he was used to. One of the Project Bakerloo engineers had provided the voice for this Jalopy. "The simulation will begin in ten seconds," it said. "Ensure your safety cords are tightly fastened, or else you risk immediate death."

Riff nervously tightened his bungee cords, thinking how humiliating it would be to die during a mere simulation. Tycho appeared a bit nervous as well, but neither of them said a word.

The Jalopy engineer's voice said, "Commencing simulation in three . . . two . . . one."

The ground rumbled beneath them. Through the glass floor of the Jalopy's cabin, Riff could see only darkness. A whipping noise like the blades of a helicopter filled his ears, and the light of the engineering lab greyed slightly. Riff felt the Jalopy descend into the dome and, eventually, into the funnel beneath.

They had officially entered the black hole.

Riff's heart raced, and he gripped his already too tight bungee cords for dear life. He tried to think of happy memories, like bantering with Knitsy and his sisters and playing drums in the GeoLads alongside Matt and Joe. He imagined the thrum of the propellers to be drumbeats that were gradually increasing in tempo, preparing for the drop in an epic rock song.

Everything around him was completely dark in every direction. The Jalopy started to spin, slowly at first, and then gradually increasing in acceleration. Riff shut his eyes as the rumbling grew louder and he thought he might be sick all over Tycho from the spinning. Then he heard an ultra-loud *CRACK*, followed by complete silence. He wondered if the Oidodrums had broken, or if they accidentally interpreted the spinning as a shake of his head. Regardless of the cause, he was thrilled that the sound stopped. It seemed the Jalopy was no longer spinning, either. He took a deep breath and tried to shake off his nausea.

Then he felt his body stretching. All his joints popped, and he couldn't control his limbs. The pressure on every square inch of his body was so intense that he was sure he would be squeezed to death. He tried to scream out for Tycho, but no sound came out. He couldn't breathe anymore. *Perhaps this is the end,* he thought. He just needed to wait for it all to end. He'd be stretched and squashed into a spaghetti string and spun into a knot that would eventually get engulfed by a black hole.

Sound suddenly entered his ears, and a deep breath replenished his lungs. His body snapped back to its original Riff form—perhaps a few millimetres taller now—and he opened his eyes.

There was Tycho in front of him, also gasping for air. Apart from his nose looking slightly longer than before, he was his perfect ordinary self. But more importantly, he was alive.

"It worked!" Tycho exclaimed. "I can't believe it! Casperians have dominated the space travel market! What can't we do?"

Tycho cheered so flamboyantly that Riff couldn't help laughing along with him with equal enthusiasm. He applauded and said, "Well done!"

Riff turned his head as far as he could to the left and right. He could see nothing outside the cabin except grey. "Where are we? This doesn't look like the engineering workshop."

Tycho smiled. "This is a simulated universe. There isn't much here. It's empty space—for now. Another of our latest inventions," he said proudly.

"Neat," said Riff. "How do we get back?"

"The same way we came," replied Tycho. "The team just needs to reboot the black hole."

"But the propellers and the circuitry are gone, right? How will we fly?" asked Riff.

"We won't need to fly. Another simulated black hole will form just above us and pull us in. The final design will be able to regenerate its outer parts. This way, the Jalopy will be able to withstand multiple black hole journeys with its complete form."

"Brilliant."

A few moments later, the engineer's voice filled the Jalopy once again. "If you are indeed alive, we will be rebooting the simulated black hole in ten seconds."

Riff gripped his bungee cords once again and took several deep breaths, knowing those would be difficult to come by in the middle of the black hole.

"Commencing simulation in three . . . two . . . one."

The space above the Jalopy grew dark, and the cabin was pulled upward to meet the simulated black hole's periphery. The rumbling grew louder and louder, and the darkness enveloped them. The sound exited Riff's ears, and his body stretched and squashed. The breathlessness scared him, and his thoughts roamed to Knitsy and how she'd always struggled with breathing because of her coughing fits. A surge of sadness filled him as the Jalopy entered the simulated event horizon. He wished he could be with her back in her room, possibly reading her Casperian epics that would make both of them fall asleep within seconds. But he would return shortly and he could tell her all about his black hole travels.

His bones extended and twisted. He sang Death Brigade songs over and over to himself for comfort, and he pictured each one of his family members at the kitchen table and imagined the feel of drumsticks in his severely outstretched hands . . .

The sound of clapping. A rush of breath and sounds. Riff opened his eyes to a refracted image of the engineering team cheering their arrival.

Whoops and hollers filled his ears, and he grinned at Tycho, who was whipping his nose around in circles.

Tycho undid his bungee cords and said, "I'm going to celebrate with some twenty-eighth-century literature in the poetry library!" He leapt up and exited the Jalopy, leaving Riff to struggle out of his straitjacket of bungee cords.

Once Riff had been freed, he leapt up as Tycho had done and rose back into his normal-sized body. The cheering and joviality of the room continued as he descended the ladder and into the crowd. Riff felt like a hero as he high-fived Casperian noses and fist-bumped a few other creatures' strange body parts. He couldn't wait to tell Luna the news of the project's success, so he ducked out of the room.

Riff rushed down the hall to Knitsy's room and ran in, exclaiming, "We did it! You did it, Luna! I travelled through a black hole!"

He saw Luna leaning over Knitsy's bed. Tears streamed down her eyes and her mouth trembled.

Riff's heart sank. He tapped his Oidodrums three times.

"Riff! Just the lad I wanted to speak with!" exclaimed Garold's jovial voice. "Your grandmother's patch is nearly validated. Is there anything else you need from me?"

Riff couldn't hold his tears back. "Tell Ann Lou to come to Casper immediately."

# Chapter 13

## Celebration of Life

The Casperians working on Project Bakerloo granted Ann Lou an expedited visa. Riff did not interpret it as a kind gesture on the Casperians' part. They were so ecstatic about the success of the pilot test, he could have asked them to incinerate the astronomy library and they would have done it. Nevertheless, Riff and Luna were grateful that they were able to make Ann Lou's arrival proceed smoothly and without any time in the holding centre.

The visa only took one day to process, and once Ann Lou arrived on Casper, Riff recognised her quick footsteps sprinting down the hall to Knitsy's room. Her blonde hair swished into the door. When she saw their grandmother, the colour drained from her skin and her beautiful blue eyes turned aqua with tears.

"What happened?" Ann Lou said as they gathered at Knitsy's bedside.

"She declined quickly after we arrived on Casper," replied Riff. "Her breathing patch was confiscated."

Ann Lou grasped Riff and pulled him toward her with a super-strong grip. He thought she was going to throw him to the ground and pummel him, but instead she embraced him and wept. She then turned to Luna and pulled her in for a hug.

"Is she gone?" Ann Lou said, wiping a tear on her sleeve and kneeling at Knitsy's side.

"No," said Luna. "But she hasn't moved or woken up since yesterday. Her hands are chilly."

Ann Lou placed her right hand on Knitsy's forehead. "She's ice cold."

Riff tucked Knitsy's blankets in a bit tighter around her still body. Knitsy's mouth hung slightly open and her eyelids remained closed. Her hair had been combed earlier by Riff, and it looked just as perfect as it had every day when they were growing up. He grasped one of her hands and Ann Lou grasped the other.

"Do you have the patch?" asked Luna.

Ann Lou shook her head and sighed. "Garold told me this morning that he was unaware of a recent update to the medical device international standard. Apparently, there's a load of documentation that needs to be submitted if a medical device manufactured on Earth leaves Earth. It would be illegal if he would have given it to me. He said it would take at least another month to get the paperwork sorted. He was profusely apologetic."

Riff swallowed hard and he lightly brushed his ears. He was lucky to have been given the Oidodrums in secret. But he wished Knitsy would have been given the chance to receive her medical device over him. The little hope that remained in his heart about Knitsy springing back to life quickly dissipated.

"Should we say a few words?" Ann Lou asked her siblings.

Riff and Luna nodded.

"Nan," said Ann Lou. "I don't want you to worry. It's Ann Lou, Riff, and Luna all here. Elbina and Clorin are here with us in spirit, and so is Mum and Grandad Mack. We all love you so much. I—I—" Ann Lou started to sob.

Luna spoke next. "None of us knows what we would have done without you in our lives. We have loved every moment with you. You were the life of our home in Portsmouth. You always made sure we had enough sweets in our stomachs. You supported us through all of our hobbies. You knew when we were feeling sad. And you cheered us up every time." Luna cried softly, unable to continue.

Riff's stomach felt like there was a brick stuck in it. He gently rubbed Knitsy's hand, as he took a few seconds to think of the words to say to his grandmother.

"Nan, you weren't just our grandmother. You were each of our best friends. You joined in on this great adventure with all of us. You lived on Olfinder, got sucked into the Time Belt, had your soul split into pieces, travelled into a supernova with me . . ." Riff chuckled tearily. "Nan, you lived the most epic life of anyone I've ever met. We are so proud to be your grandchildren."

Ann Lou and Luna nodded and smiled.

"I love you until the end of time, Nan. You can go whenever you're ready. Don't be afraid," Riff added.

Almost as if on cue, Knitsy breathed one last breath. She didn't cough, and she was finally at peace.

* * *

Over the next week, the McHubbard siblings planned a celebration of life for Knitsy while the Project Bakerloo team added the last refinements to the wheel Jalopy. The siblings kept themselves busy making visa arrangements for Earth guests, researching Casperian plants to include in the celebration, and planning a ceremony that would be truly and uniquely Knitsy.

On the day of the celebration, the siblings and Flora waited outside the campus entrance for the Jalopy that was bringing Knitsy's mourners from Earth. In the distance, Riff saw a flying object. He watched its descent and landing. It turned out to be a military transport. Its door opened, and a swarm of people rushed out to greet the McHubbard siblings and Flora: Jung-hoon, Matt, Joe, President Murphy, Garold and Alphabeta Zeep, Apollo, and Clorin. Clorin crawled at an extremely speedy rate toward Riff. Riff picked up his tiny nephew, who hugged him around the neck with his little claws and promptly fell asleep.

"Thank you all for coming such a long way for our nan," announced Ann Lou. "Please follow us to the courtyard."

Ann Lou unlatched the sleeping Clorin from Riff, then led the group through the entrance, down a marble hallway, and into the first courtyard. The courtyard offered a pleasant space: quiet and dotted with Zygobroaks that were abloom with fafflin feathers. Ten chairs surrounded a beautiful coffin made of Zygobroak wood and decorated with origami animals. Flora had used book pages stolen from the whaling library to make the origami. She thought it would be a nice touch since she had so much practice making them for Alphabeta, who loved the look and taste of the decorative paper. Flora did not, however, tell Tycho about the page theft and mutilation.

A lectern closed the circle around the coffin. Everyone took their seats quietly while Riff stood at the lectern and waited until all eyes were focused on him. He felt a bit awkward being the centre of attention, but he reminded himself it was Knitsy who was actually capturing everyone's focus. He was merely guiding everyone through the process.

He cleared his throat and began. "Thanks, everyone, for being here for our nan Knitsy, who passed away peacefully last week. She was just shy of eighty-three and lived a tremendous life. I think everyone here knew her to some degree, and even if you didn't know her well, you knew how crazy she was."

The crowd laughed, easing a bit of the sadness that filled the air.

"Knitsy Hampshire was a beautiful soul who loved many people in her lifetime. She had two best friends growing up, each of whom met a tragic end that she had to endure firsthand. She also was forced to witness the loss of her husband, Mack Gorgan, whilst in the middle of having a child. She loved both her husband and her child with every fibre of her being. Some of you knew my mum, Henrietta, and how similar her determination and will were to Knitsy's."

Jung-hoon bowed his head. He had certainly known Henrietta better than anyone present except for the McHubbard siblings.

"Knitsy raised Henrietta on next to nothing, but with an abundance of love and probably too many sweets. But Knitsy brought her daughter up to become a very loving and powerful woman, and Knitsy continued that level of nurturing as all of her grandchildren were born.

"When Luna was born, Knitsy read to her every morning, noon, and night. When I was born, she sang songs with me and didn't get mad when I banged pots and pans together. When Elbina was born, she taught her to make the perfect cup of tea and cakes to feed the biggest army. And when Ann Lou was born, she played with her and chased her all over the house. Each of us lives on with Knitsy in our hearts.

"My siblings and I each endured our own physical struggles growing up. Knitsy never treated us as disabled or inferior in any way. She treated us as if they were our super powers, and that is the mindset we have carried with us throughout our lives.

"Even though Knitsy was incredibly stubborn, demanded a sweet with nearly every meal, and put many creatures in their place whether they deserved it or not, each of her actions brimmed with love. The last words she said to me were, 'Thank you for protecting me.' Nan, you were the one who protected us. There is so much more to your story than most people know. Without you, we wouldn't have been on, or survived, countless adventures. Can we all raise a glass to honour her spirit?"

Ann Lou was already passing out mugs of a Casperian beverage. It smelled like tea, but Riff kept his expectations in check in case it turned out to be another case of the Cabbaged Eggs. Everyone raised their mystery mugs, including Clorin and Alphabeta, who raised their baby bottles.

"Nan," Riff said as all eyes rested on the coffin, "we love you. Rest in eternal peace with all those who love you dearly. We can't wait to see you again someday if we are so lucky."

"Cheers," the crowd said in unison. Everyone took a sip of their Casperian tea and did their best not to gag.

In keeping with Casperian tradition, Knitsy's coffin rose up off the ground, then accelerated skyward. The mourners watched it recede until it was only a dot flying through space. A gentle wind swept briefly through the courtyard, and fafflin feathers fluttered through the crowd. One feather landed gently on the lectern in front of Riff. He sniffled and picked it up gingerly. The feather followed the general shape of a leaf. Its barbs were fluffy and wispy, and waved gently in the wind.

"Bye, Nan," Riff choked, speaking directly to the feather as a tear streamed down his cheek.

The crowd clapped and rose to embrace one another. Jung-hoon pulled out a bottle of strong-smelling something that he had found stashed in Knitsy's dormitory back at the White House. The crowd cheered and took generous sips (all except Clorin and Alphabeta, of course), and they listened to Earth music from Knitsy's groovy era, the 2160s, and danced the night away in honour of the great Knitsy Hampshire.

# Chapter 14

## The Entrance to Reprisa

"**A**rgh!" yelped Riff, clutching the arms of the chair he had nodded off in. An Oidodrum software update was ringing in his ears.

A swarm of angry Casperian eyes met his gaze, along with Luna's disappointed eyes.

"Sorry," said Riff, blushing and sitting up straight.

"Lucky for us, this is the last meeting you need to fall asleep in before Project Bakerloo is officially complete," snuffled Tycho.

In the weeks since Knitsy's celebration of life, Riff had sat through dozens of unbearably humdrum meetings. He couldn't understand any of the technical jargon, and meetings always went long because of the Casperians' endless fascination with esoteric subjects. Riff couldn't grasp how Luna managed to keep up with everything, but here she was, awake, engaged, and in tune to each meeting.

"What've I missed?" asked Riff, wiping away the sleep from his eyes.

One of the engineers—whose name was Einsty, Riff had recently learned—piped up to summarise. "We were explaining how the Jalopy's mapping software will create a point cloud of coordinates of the universe's topology. This set of coordinates will have a resolution of one micron and will update every five nanoseconds. Because the Reprisa universe is parallel to our own, we'd expect its point cloud to be nearly identical. Copious amounts of time have been spent on this subsystem in order to ensure a maximally efficient and obstacle-free route to the black hole that connects the Coloratura universe to the Reprisa universe, which contains planet Thera."

"So, which black hole is it?" asked Riff, as if he were well acquainted with the universe's black holes.

"Sagittarius A," replied Einsty. "It just so happens to be the black hole at the centre of the Milky Way galaxy—your home galaxy."

"Cool!" exclaimed Riff. "How did you guys figure that out?"

"It was simple, really," said Einsty, excited to explain the complicated scientific details. "All we had to do was build a small-scale map of the universe in our modelling software. The modelling software allows the user to simulate the space-time continuum changes to hypothesise the distances between each respective universe . . ."

Riff slowly drifted into another enjoyable nap and was only awoken at the end of that meeting by Luna.

"Are you ready to head out tomorrow? All the updates to the Jalopy have been completed and are validated to run," she said.

"I guess so," said Riff. "I feel like I have so many questions, though."

"Maybe if you paid some attention during the meetings, you wouldn't have so many questions," snapped Luna.

"No, I mean outside of all this engineery stuff. What do we do when we get to Thera? Where are we supposed to go? How do we find Elbina?" asked Riff.

"The Jalopy has a built-in sensor that detects noises and movements indicative of life. The sensor will activate once we are close to Thera, and the flight path program will use that data to take us to the most inhabited location on the planet. It'll be the best place to start," said Luna.

"But what happens when we get there? Are there any threats or obstacles to be aware of?" said Riff.

Luna shrugged. "I don't know. The Casperians only care about getting us through the black hole. After that, we're on our own."

"First, they incarcerate us and take Nan's breathing patch. Now they can't wait to drop us off in the middle of some random planet in a random universe. Brilliant creatures, those Casperians," muttered Riff.

"Yes, but we're leagues closer to finding Elbina. We owe them big time if we find her," said Luna.

* * *

Riff, Luna, Ann Lou, and Flora ate breakfast together the next morning. The Casperians had served them a dish packed with all the superior nutrients to prevent eye strain for optimum reading time. It was a stew of mashed Gillypump eyes, Swackleback rump, and fafflin feather stems. They miraculously managed to keep it down.

"How're Garold and Alphabeta?" asked Ann Lou, a bit of stew dripping from her chin.

"Good, good. Thanks for asking," replied Flora. "They stopped by planet Coniston for a bit of sightseeing after the funeral. Alphabeta wasn't a huge fan of the Jalopy ride, apparently. She cried the whole time. Drove everyone nuts." Flora laughed.

"How are things at the ERA?" asked Luna.

"Everything seems fine with Garold's team. I probably shouldn't say anything . . . but I've been involved in another project in parallel to this one." She peeked around the room to ensure no one was listening in. "Jung-hoon has been keeping me up to date on some things. Scary things. They're trying to keep the news contained, but I'm afraid it's starting to get out. Delevio doesn't know how to keep his mouth shut. And you three have a right to know for . . . certain reasons."

Riff gulped. "Why didn't Jung-hoon tell me when he was here?"

"He didn't want to burden you. There was a lot going on with the loss of your grandmother and all the anticipation around multi-universe travel. He didn't want to worry you even more," said Flora.

"What's going on?" asked Ann Lou.

Flora leaned in and lowered her voice. "Project Piccadilly has re-opened."

"I've heard of that!" said Riff in a hushed whisper. "Well, I've read about it. I may have been snooping through emails with Matt and Joe a little while ago. I know it has to do with the GeoLapse. Apparently, there's a whole bunch of them still out there."

Luna and Ann Lou grew worried looks on their faces.

Flora nodded. "It's getting worse. They tried to break into the White House. Luckily the ERA has enough security to keep them at bay for a little while. But for the GeoLapse to be that forceful and to cause that much of a stir . . . there's more of them than we thought."

"Do you think there'll be another war on Earth?" asked Riff.

"I wouldn't be surprised. I also wouldn't be surprised if there is more to their plan. You all saw what happened last time, when they took over Cipto, Antympanica, and Olfinder. They have power—power the ERA might not be strong enough to resist."

"What can we do?" asked Ann Lou.

Flora laughed and placed a gentle hand on Ann Lou's shoulder. "You McHubbards are so brave. Still willing to take down the GeoLapse after you've done it once already. You're an incredible family." She smiled at each of them. "You've got quite the journey ahead of you. Leave it to us for now. That's why my time on Casper has come to an end. Project Bakerloo, check. Project Piccadilly . . . uncheck. There's lots of work to do. My ride home will be here soon, so I'd better get my things ready."

She stood up from the table and shook hands with both Ann Lou and Luna.

"Riff," Flora said, extending her arms. "That was quite the adventure we had. Thank you, from the bottom of my heart, for taking such good care of me and your grandmother. You were so brave."

"The pleasure was all mine, Captain Zeep," replied Riff. "Please be careful."

The two shared an embrace, and then Flora exited the room.

"I'm going with you two to Thera, by the way," said Ann Lou.

"What? There's only two seats," snapped Luna.

"I don't care. Elbina needs all of us. What if she's in terrible danger? Do you two really expect you can walk into some dangerous building with giant guards with weapons and get out alive?"

Riff and Luna glanced at one another and replied simultaneously, "No."

"Correct. Which is why I'm going with you."

Riff shrugged. "Makes sense to me."

Luna rolled her eyes and finished her stew.

"How're Apollo and Clorin? Will they be okay with you away for a little while?" asked Riff.

Ann Lou grimaced. "It's going to be difficult for them. Apollo has been such a great father to Clorin, so I know they'll manage. Apollo is keen to sign Clorin up for the children's Pyroll league, but I told him it's too soon. He needs to learn how to catch the ball first. Plus, I think he should learn how to say 'Pyroll' first, let alone any word besides 'no.'"

"His old Uncle Riff taught him how to catch a Pyroll in the Time Belt," Riff said, puffing his chest out proudly.

"Yes, that's true, but he's much younger here than he was there. The

Pyroll is too big for his claws still, so Apollo agreed to start with eggs. There's yolk everywhere," Ann Lou chuckled. "But I trust Apollo with Clorin, and he trusts that I'll come home safely."

Riff felt proud of his youngest sister. She was only twenty but was handling marriage and motherhood better than he could have imagined. He was twenty-three years old and had never even had a girlfriend, although he hoped he would someday.

When they all finished their cups of repulsive Casperian tea, Luna announced, "Time to go." She slung a rucksack over her back and led them to the Jalopy launch site.

The siblings marched to the courtyard nearest the engineering workshop, ready to start their mission to find Elbina. The area was quite the hubbub: paparazzi and journalists from neighbouring planets were jostling for prime locations, the engineers were anxiously chewing on their noses, and Casperians from around the planet were filing in, eager to witness the spectacle about to take place.

Tycho and Einsty greeted Riff and Luna, then ushered them through the parted crowd to the next-generation wheel Jalopy, which was resting upon a very familiar-looking structure—an hourglass.

"Oi," Riff whispered to Luna. "What's with the hourglass?"

Luna sighed in annoyance. "This was discussed at the penultimate meeting. This is the structure that loads the stardust into the engine. This Jalopy is travelling much farther, so more stardust is needed. Plus, it needs to be loaded in a secure way. It's highly explosive in this environment."

"But why an hourglass? I feel like this thing is following us everywhere! Last I saw it, it was in the Time Belt!" said Riff, bewildered. "It seems to have shrunk, though."

"Don't be so thick. It's not the same one. It's not even a Jalopy," said Luna, rolling her eyes.

Riff inspected the hourglass more closely. Luna was correct—this hourglass definitely wasn't the same as the one they had ridden in countless times. It was smaller—the height of it reached Riff's waist. The wheel Jalopy rested atop it like a lid. Inside the hourglass, stardust particles glowed like fireflies as they trailed around entropically, bouncing off the glass walls until they made their way from the bottom section through the cinched area, and into the top. As each particle finally reached the outer periphery of the wheel, it was then absorbed somewhere within the circuitry.

Riff walked around the hourglass watching the sparkling stardust with awe. He was thrilled and proud to see that his efforts within the supernova had been fruitful after all.

Ann Lou followed Riff and Luna up to the Jalopy.

"Excuse me, smaller Earthling," said Tycho, a hint of disdain in his voice. "Move to the spectator area. This area is for Jalopy passengers and engineers only."

"I'm going with them," Ann Lou said confidently.

"There's only space for two," said Tycho, annoyed.

"I'll strap in with her," said Ann Lou, pointing to Luna.

Tycho stepped close to Ann Lou's face and tried to push her back, but his stringy nose was no match for the universal Pyroll champion. "Fine," he growled. "If you corrupt this mission with your grubby little Earthling hand and your . . . anomalous metallic hand, Earth will never receive scientific help from Casper again. Do you understand?"

Ann Lou chuckled. "If I corrupt this mission, I'll be dead, so I won't care."

"How much stardust has been loaded for the journey?" Luna asked.

"Enough to get you to Thera and back. Plus a bit extra, which apparently will be used up by the weight of your extra passenger," Tycho said, snarling in Ann Lou's direction.

"I'm not that heavy!" Ann Lou snapped.

Tycho scowled. "Take your positions. I never thought I would be relying on daft Earthlings for the success of this generation's greatest technological endeavour." He stomped away with his nose furled.

Einsty discussed some final details with the three siblings. He told them what to say when the Jalopy prompted them, and he asked how they wanted their names spelled in textbooks. Riff tried unsuccessfully to get his name recorded as B-I-N-G-O McHubbard. He stuck his tongue out and held up a peace sign for a nearby paparazzo.

Once all the stardust finished collecting in the wheel, the golden hue within the hourglass dimmed. This marked the signal to commence the mission.

The siblings waved to the Project Bakerloo team and received nose waves in return. Even Tycho waved and nodded to them.

The McHubbards each touched the centre of the wheel and shrunk down to the point.

The layout of the cabin still looked the same. The bungee cords, however, had been replaced with a sturdier set of straps. Riff helped Luna strap in and secured Ann Lou in with her so that her back was against Luna's front. Riff strapped himself in on the opposite side. The crowd fell silent in anticipation as the mission was about to begin.

The Jalopy glowed green, that familiar green that they had experienced in every other Jalopy ride. Next, it spoke to them in the soft voice they were accustomed to, which put them slightly more at ease.

"Hello, Luna McHubbard, Griffin McHubbard, and Ann Lou McHubbard. The Jalopy is ready to depart. Please state your destination."

"Planet Thera via Sagittarius A," said Luna confidently.

"Enjoy your trip," said the smooth Jalopy voice.

The wheel Jalopy rumbled and lifted from the top of the hourglass-shaped stardust loader. Through the glass, they could see refracted versions of the Casperian crowd and flashes of the cameras. Riff waved even though there was no chance anyone could see him. The Jalopy rose higher and higher until Riff could just pick out the crowns of the Zygobroaks, which were filled with fafflin feathers at this time of year. The planet's surface fell quickly away, and they broke through the immigration control net just outside the planet's space. As they zoomed onward, Riff could see the mega-dense rod that poked out from the planet's poles. *I may still be a small-brained Earthling,* he thought, *but I know a lot more about Casper now than I used to, whether I like it or not.*

The Jalopy effortlessly and placidly soared through the alluring vastness of space, away from the little yet big-brained planet. Riff admired the nebulas, stars, comets, and all the other celestial objects as they flew nearer and nearer to their home galaxy, the Milky Way, and the black hole at its centre.

Their journey ended up being even quicker than anticipated, thanks to stellar wind gusts: only about an hour.

"Hey, look!" said Riff, excitedly pointing to a familiar object on his right. Through the glass, the McHubbards could pick out planet Earth. The Jalopy slowed from hyperspeed and encircled Earth. Riff wondered if the engineers had purposely plotted a route that would take them within sight of their home planet, but he couldn't imagine Casperians making such a sentimental gesture. Maybe the Jalopy just needed to scan Earth in order to find Thera, Earth's analogue in the Reprisa universe.

Earth had its usual sandy, barren appearance. Patchy brown and black regions reflected the planet's loss of plant life and surface water. But the McHubbards had only ever known Earth as a desert wasteland, so they smiled upon seeing their home. They imagined they could see Portsmouth, UK, where they'd grown up, and Washington, DC, where they'd been living ever since the most recent universal war against the GeoLapse.

Once the Jalopy finished one revolution around Earth, it accelerated back into hyperspeed toward the centre of the Milky Way. After a few more minutes, Riff piped up. "I think we're getting close."

He couldn't see the black hole, but he could hear the propellers whirring much more powerfully than before. Riff gripped his straps tightly. "You won't be able to hear sound in the middle of the black hole. You'll feel yourself stretching, and there'll be a lot of pressure. You won't be able to breathe for a few seconds. Focus on happy memories. Just try not to worry too much, and trust me—I've done this twice already."

His sisters nodded. They looked afraid, but they said nothing. Neither of them wanted to induce panic in the other.

The propellers continued their forceful rotations. Then their cabin began to revolve slowly. This went on for a few minutes—much longer than in the previous simulations Riff had endured. He was already starting to feel sick. Then the cabin started spinning overhead and diagonally, as if they were inside a ball that was rolling every which way. The Jalopy lurched back and forth, and the sparkling starscape around them was quickly transforming into grey, then dark grey, and finally black.

"Is everyone okay?" Ann Lou's shaky voice called.

"I'm okay," Riff called back. He had already slammed his eyes shut, and he was holding a hand in front of his mouth. He thought surely he was going to be sick or pass out. But he didn't want to disappoint his sisters. "You're both doing great. Just keep focusing on happy memories. Don't panic!"

They all screamed with one particular lurch that sent them spinning like a top. The Jalopy had now entered the event horizon of Sagittarius A, and the McHubbards couldn't see anything. Even with their eyes open, they saw no black; it was as if all colour had ceased to exist. An ultra-loud *CRACK* told Riff that the propellers and the outer ring of the Jalopy had broken off. The siblings' shouts to one another had dimmed to a sound quieter than silence.

Riff felt his body being pulled again like before. His bones were popping; his limbs were stretching. These sensations, like the spinning, were a notch above what Riff had experienced previously. In the simulation, the stretching had felt like an uncomfortable yoga pose that lasted for a bit too long. But this was different. Riff felt as if his bones were about to be pulled out of their sockets. His neck twisted so far that he was worried it might snap. The pressure pushed nearly all the air from his lungs, and he was unable to even attempt to take a breath. *Happy memories,* he thought. *Happy—*

Suddenly Riff's upper body twisted so forcefully that he noticed the exact moment when a stabbing pain started in his right shoulder. It was blindingly painful, which momentarily struck him as funny since he was already blind. He was in such horrible, intense pain, and he desperately needed to take a breath. He couldn't summon forth any happy memories; all he could think of was that death was imminent. *I'm a goner. I hope Luna and Ann Lou survive. If anyone can save Elbina, it's them.*

The sound of heaving breaths filled the Jalopy. Riff opened his eyes to see colours and shapes materialising back into view. The scene before him was still a bit blurry. He could feel his lungs decompressing, and he inhaled as deeply as he could. Each new breath seemed to pump his lungs up closer to their normal shape. He started to reach for his straps, but he yelped in pain upon trying to raise his right arm. The ride through the black hole must have dislocated his shoulder.

Once his eyes were readjusted to reality, Riff saw his sisters taking heaving breaths of their own. Luna was rubbing her left knee, and Ann Lou's prosthetic arm had fallen off during the trip, but other than that his sisters emerged from the ordeal with only mild to moderate injuries.

"Is it over?" Ann Lou asked.

"Yes," said Luna, wincing as she shifted her position. "That should be it. How was that compared to the simulation, Riff?"

He wanted to sound strong, but there was no hiding the truth. "Bloody awful."

Something outside their floating cabin started to buzz.

"That'll be the propeller and structural ring regeneration," announced Luna.

Sure enough, through the glass, Riff could just make out the light beam propellers elongating into position. Once all the parts were back in place, the Jalopy started to fly. They had made it. They were in the Reprisa universe, exploring territory that no other resident of Coloratura had ever seen.

"What does it look like out there?" asked Luna.

Riff gingerly unstrapped himself with his left arm from the wall. "Same old, same old," he said, unimpressed with the bespeckled space view. "Nothing out of the ordinary. You sure we got the right black hole? Do you think it spit us out backwards and we're still in Coloratura?"

"No," said Luna. "We'd expect a parallel universe to look similar if not nearly identical to our own. I'm glad it doesn't appear different. That means the correct black hole was chosen."

Ann Lou unstrapped herself and Luna, then worked on reattaching her prosthetic. When the two had finished, Ann Lou peered out through the glass.

"I can't believe we're in a completely different universe," said Ann Lou, her breath wispy with wonder. "Imagine how far we are from home!" Her expression turned solemn. "I'm so far from my little boy." She slumped to the floor and rested her chin in her palms.

Riff patted her on the shoulder. "Clorin would be proud of his mum, auntie, and uncle for going on this adventure. He'll be so impressed when we get home."

"What if we never get home?" Ann Lou asked. "I didn't get a proper goodbye with him. And Apollo . . ." A tear fell from her eye.

"You can't think like that," said Luna curtly. "You sound like you're giving up on Elbs. She doesn't deserve that. We have to give it our all and be optimistic. We've gone through plenty of hardships in our lives."

Ann Lou peered up at Riff for more reassurance. He smiled. "Little sister, you're supposed to be the strong one!"

Ann Lou smirked.

"We should be getting close to Thera," said Luna. "Can you guys see anything that resembles Earth?"

Ann Lou and Riff peered out the glass once more and gasped in unison. There it was. It looked so much like Earth that Riff still wasn't sure they had actually made it to Thera. But he was sure that he and his sisters had just survived a black hole. If it was Earth, he could have a nice rest before trying again. If it was Thera, they were a gargantuan step closer to finding Elbina. His heart leapt at the thought.

"We're almost there, Luna," said Riff. "We've already started the descent."

Riff saw the smile broaden on Luna's face. Not only had she contributed to one of the greatest engineering feats of the age, but she was en route to seeing her best friend again. Riff imagined what Knitsy would be thinking if she saw them all together going on this adventure to save Elbina. Surely she'd be proud, and if she were still alive, she'd be squished in that Jalopy with them. But even though she wasn't there physically, Knitsy was there in spirit. She was present in their hearts, their minds, and their souls. And she would never leave.

# CHAPTER 15

## THERA

Thera's surface, like that of Earth, was a barren wasteland. Riff and Ann Lou described it to Luna as the Jalopy descended: same colours as Earth, no surface water or vegetation, no visible infrastructure.

Growing up on Earth, the McHubbards had never seen the outside. Pollution and the loss of the ozone layer had made the outside environment incompatible with life. Even exposure to sunlight was deadly. Every excursion—to go shopping, for example, or to attend school—was accomplished via tunnels that extended from the doors of buildings to the doors of buses. So the McHubbards didn't know what their street or the outside of their home looked like.

The Jalopy landed in the middle of a residential street on Thera. From inside their glass Jalopy cabin, they looked around with amazement at this sister planet of Earth. Of course they had seen Earth's ruined environment from space, through the windows of Jalopies, but it was quite another thing to see such an environment up close. A gust of wind blew clouds of dust around them, and a big ball that was way too bright to look directly at shone bright through the amber sky.

The street appeared similar in configuration to where they had lived back in the UK. The houses were attached to each other, like town houses. However, the whole street appeared to be abandoned. Windows were broken; doors were boarded up. There was no sign of life.

Riff noticed something else different about this place compared to their childhood home on Earth. "Weird. There are no tunnels. The doors on these houses open straight to the outside."

"Then it should be safe for us to go out there," Luna said.

But Ann Lou was suspicious. "How can we be sure? Thera is a parallel planet to Earth. Doesn't that mean it suffered the same climate crisis?"

"Not necessarily," said Luna. "They definitely have suffered, but the timing of their climate crisis could have been different. Maybe their society is a few decades behind that of Earth. They're generally similar worlds, but that doesn't mean all the details will be perfectly aligned."

"Where is everyone, though? I thought the Jalopy was taking us to the most populous area," said Ann Lou.

"Maybe only one person lives on Thera, and they live in one of these houses," said Riff.

"Well, if one person lived here, it would be Elbina, so that would make things quite simple. We should go explore," said Luna. There was a yearning in her voice.

"Should we wait until we see something move? Just to be cautious?" asked Riff.

"We don't know what to expect. We could end up waiting for a long time. But, if it makes you feel better, we can wait for a little while," replied Luna, sighing.

They waited and watched for about ten minutes, but nothing they could see outside the cabin seemed to be moving. Plus, Riff was growing hungry. "Do you think we should just go? Maybe they have good Earth-like food here somewhere."

Ann Lou and Luna agreed, and the three jumped up in the centre of the cabin and enlarged back into their normal-sized bodies. They each took a deep breath of the Therian air, relieved that it was safe to breathe unlike the air on their own home planet. Luna picked up the wheel Jalopy and nestled it carefully in her rucksack. Then the three started walking down the street.

"It's hot here," said Luna, wiping the sweat from her brow. "But it's good to know it's not too hot to complete our mission."

"Speaking of the mission—how will the Project Bakerloo team know we arrived?" asked Riff.

"They have exact coordinates of the Jalopy. They'll know we made it when they confirm that our location matches the input coordinates. They won't know if we're alive, but they will be celebrating the Jalopy's successful landing. Project Bakerloo is officially a success in their eyes," replied Luna.

The trio continued to stroll down the barren road. Each house they passed looked nearly identical, with just small differences: a more ornate doorknob here, a chunkier window frame there. Once they reached what they thought was the end of the street, they found the road made a tight curve. Around the bend was another row of the nearly identical houses.

"Is it just one long road?" asked Riff.

"What are some of the numbers on the houses?" asked Luna.

"The one we just walked by was 1530. The one just ahead is 1528," Ann Lou replied.

"If it is just one long road, let's follow it to where it starts. Maybe there'll be a town centre," suggested Luna.

"Or the next street," snorted Riff.

Then Ann Lou saw something out of the corner of her eye. Near the end of this new group of houses, just before the street curved again, she saw someone walking.

"Look!" Ann Lou pointed so Riff could see. "There's a person over there. Should we go up to them?"

"What are they doing? What do they look like?" asked Luna, gripping Riff's arm tightly.

Ann Lou squinted and shaded her eyes with her hand. "I think . . . it just looks like a human. Maybe a young woman?"

"Is it Elbina?" Luna said, her voice crescendoing.

"No, she looks a bit older than Elbina would be. And a bit taller," replied Ann Lou.

"She's walking, but her walk doesn't look very human-like," said Riff. "Maybe Therians look like humans but just walk differently."

The distant Therian woman walked ploddingly and robotically, as if her knees and elbows didn't bend. She seemed to be staring straight ahead. A few robotic paces later, she stopped, and her head made a steady, slow scan from right to left, as if she were searching for something. Then, a few seconds later, she resumed her robotic lumbering.

"I'd proceed with caution," said Luna. "As I said earlier, we don't know what to expect."

"Agreed," said Ann Lou. "Let's keep a safe distance. Maybe see where she goes."

The McHubbards ducked into a gap between two sets of town homes and peered out to watch what route the robo-woman took. She covered about half the block, did an about-face, and reached her starting position when they first spotted her.

"She just keeps repeating the same route," whispered Ann Lou. "Do you think she needs help?"

"No," whispered Luna. "Let's keep moving. Stay out of her way."

Riff and Ann Lou obliged, sneaking behind the rest of the houses until they reached the next curve, then peeking out to see the next row of houses. As they went, they saw more of the strangely plodding Therians on patrol. To avoid them, they continued darting into the occasional gap between the rows of houses. The road seemed endless. At one point, Riff threatened to speak to one of them to ask for the nearest loo, but Luna scolded him and told him to just go behind a house.

"What if I get bitten or stung by something?" Riff asked, sounding childish.

"It's more likely that *I* will bite you," Luna snapped. "Make it quick!"

The girls waited semi-impatiently for Riff, and then the three of them continued their current objective. They were successful at avoiding the Therians, and when they rounded the last curve, they found a town centre, as Luna had predicted. The siblings hid behind house number one and observed their surroundings. There were some high street shops, like express grocery stores, clothing shops, restaurants, and bookshops, but these looked as abandoned as the homes had.

"This planet gives me the creeps," whispered Riff.

"Anyone else would probably say the same about visiting Earth for the first time as well. Try to be less judgemental," said Luna.

At the end of the row of shops, an enormously long building came into view. A sign on the building read "IHQ." The exterior of the building was flat and unremarkable, but the structure was colossal compared to the nearby shops and homes. It looked like a warehouse. It was about five stories high, and it was very long and very wide. Outside the building, they could see more robot-people marching around in a disorderly pattern.

"Where do you reckon we should go next?" asked Ann Lou.

Neither Luna nor Riff knew how to respond. They both just shook their heads and hung their mouths open, hoping words would magically flow out with the correct answer.

"Woof!"

"Argh!" yelped Riff, pirouetting into a jump that would put an amateur dancer to shame. "What is that thing?"

A small four-legged creature was sitting at their feet, and a juicy raw steak lay on the ground next to it. The creature resembled an Earth dog in stature and build, but its skin was so perfectly translucent that they could see its internal organs.

"It's a dog!" squealed Ann Lou.

The creature wagged its tail and sat up on its hind legs.

Although the animal looked as if it should have had bones, no bones were visible. All its internal organs squished and bounced around as it moved. The organ dog stuck out its tongue and barked again, causing its brain and eyeballs to bob in a way that was both revolting and cute.

"Look at hiiiiim!" Ann Lou cooed, kneeling down to pet it. "Oh, he has a tag! 'My name is Bisquit. If lost, return to the Cantileery family.'"

Riff gagged. "Ewww, Ann Lou! Don't let that thing lick you!"

Ann Lou said in a deep, playful voice. "Oh, is mighty strong Griffin McHubbard scared of dogs?"

"That's not a dog! It's . . . it's disgusting!" said Riff.

"How dare you speak of Bisquit like that!" snapped Ann Lou. "He's the most normal thing about this planet so far. You should be grateful that he found us."

Bisquit barked in agreement with Ann Lou. She gave him some more pats, and then Luna petted him as well. Riff rolled his eyes as he watched the three of them bond. Bisquit panted with glee, barked joyfully, and picked up his steak. He stared at them, then barked around the steak and started to bound away.

"He wants us to follow him!" Ann Lou called, moving in Bisquit's direction. Luna followed them.

"Follow him where?" shrieked Riff. "What if the robots sent him to lure us in?"

"Then their tactic is working. Come on, we have no other leads. Stay low!" Ann Lou commanded.

"Ughhh!" Having no other options, Riff followed his sisters.

Bisquit guided them through some alleyways, leaping stealthily to avoid being seen by the robot people. The McHubbards weren't as practised as Bisquit in the art of sneakiness, but they managed to get through the first alleyway without trouble. Bisquit tiptoed on his paws as he turned onto the high street. He looked back at the McHubbards to signify that the coast was clear. They followed as discreetly as possible. Riff noticed several robots in the vicinity, but none of them was facing their direction. Bisquit led them to the door of a shop whose sign read Building Blocks. Bisquit slipped in the doorway and waited until all three humans were safely inside.

Riff looked around at the store. It appeared to be a toy store, and he was pleased to see that there weren't any robots shopping there, although he wasn't sure how anyone could shop there considering no one was manning the till. Surprisingly, the toys and other items in the shop didn't seem dusty. It was almost as if someone actually regularly shopped here.

Bisquit slammed into Riff's feet, causing him to stumble back toward the wall.

"Oi, watch it!" Riff snapped at the dog.

"Shhh!" Ann Lou hushed, pointing at the shop window.

Through the window, Riff saw one of the robot people was passing by. It paused in front of the shop, and Riff slunk behind one of the shelves, blending in as much as he could. Ann Lou and Luna flattened themselves against the wall on the opposite side of the store. Bisquit hid behind Riff.

They could see the robot turn its head to the right, looking in their direction as it started to scan. Riff ceased breathing and closed his eyes. He hoped that he hadn't just blown their cover.

Thankfully, the robot didn't detect them. It continued its scan to the other side of the street; still, none of the McHubbards nor Bisquit dared to move or even breathe until it had plodded away.

Bisquit, still carrying his steak, emerged from behind Riff and woofed silently at them to continue following him. The dog really was trying to protect them from something. Riff was impressed by the little dog's courage and street smarts. The dog led them to the back of the shop, where there were a bunch of empty boxes and trunks. He charged up to a trunk in the back corner, flicked the trunk's lid open with his tail, and then jumped inside.

"Huh?" said Riff. He walked up to the trunk and peeked inside. There was a hole about a metre deep with dim lighting, and Bisquit sat at the bottom of the hole, wagging his tail and looking quite pleased with himself. When he had all their attention, he sprinted out of sight. Apparently, the trunk was concealing the entrance to an underground tunnel.

"Let's follow him," said Ann Lou, already heaving herself into the trunk. Once her feet were planted on the ground below, she helped Luna in.

"Are you mad?" sputtered Riff. "Why would we go in a mysterious tunnel? There could be more robots down there!"

"Well, Bisquit helped us successfully avoid the robots thus far, so why not continue to trust him? We're going!" said Ann Lou.

"Oh, I cannot believe they are making me do this, with a bad arm and everything," Riff muttered under his breath as he hobbled into the trunk. "Ow, watch the shoulder!" he grumbled at his sisters when they tried to manoeuvre him inside.

Once Riff was securely in the hole, he closed the lid of the trunk softly so as to avoid alerting any robots who might have been outside. The siblings followed Bisquit down the narrow, torch-lit tunnel, minding their heads as they squatted to get through low parts. The tunnel gradually grew taller as they descended down the path, and eventually they were able to walk standing up. Riff nursed his right shoulder as they walked, and he saw Luna limping slightly. He hoped there would be somewhere to rest soon for both their sakes.

The McHubbards followed the tunnel for a few more minutes in silence and eventually came to a wooden door with a dog flap at the bottom. Bisquit leapt through the dog flap and started woofing to someone.

"Whaddya want, little woofer?"

Bisquit performed a lengthy monologue of yips, yaps, arfs, and bow-wows.

"Yowza! You brought someone back witcha?"

Riff was surprised and relieved to hear that whoever was behind the door was speaking in English.

The wooden door swung open, and two identical, burly, mostly human-looking men with glowing eyes stared back at them. Each held a weapon that was pointed at the McHubbards' faces.

"Who are you and whaddya doin' here? You don' belong here! Shoo!" one shouted.

Bisquit bit the man's trouser leg.

"I don' think they're who we think they are," said the other. Just look at their expressions."

"Please, we come in peace!" said Ann Lou, holding her hands up. Luna followed suit. Riff could only comfortably lift one arm.

"What's two plus one?" the first man said, holding his weapon tighter.

"I really hope it's three in this universe as well," said Luna.

"Yeah, that's righ," said the first man, lowering his weapon. "Yowza, where'd you lot come from?"

"We're travellers from planet Earth in the Coloratura universe. We think our sister was taken hostage here. We've come to save her," said Ann Lou.

The men's jaws dropped. "Yer from a different planet? And universe? Yowza, nice tuh meet you!"

The men took turns shaking the McHubbards' hands, just as normal humans do.

"I'm Thevenin, an' this is my twin brother, Norton."

Upon closer inspection, Riff realised the men's glowing eyes were actually neon-coloured frames of their round spectacles. Thevenin's frames were orange, and Norton's were blue. Otherwise, the twins looked identical, with the same buzzed brown hair, jumbo muscles, and tight-fitting powder-blue T-shirts and jeans. They were reasonably tall, only a few centimetres taller than Riff. Riff couldn't identify any differences at all between these Therian humans and Earth humans.

Ann Lou spoke first. "I'm Ann Lou, this is my sister Luna, and that's my brother Riff. Can you tell us where we are? We followed Bisquit because we had no idea where to start looking for our other sister. We need to talk to someone in town who can give us information."

"Oh, you won' be wantin' any help from the Insomnyus up there, no siree. You've come tuh the right place, my new friends," said Thevenin warmly.

Norton and Bisquit walked farther into the dimly lit, dingy room, and Thevenin motioned for Riff, Luna, and Ann Lou to follow. The room had a sofa in front of a tiny television, which was muted and displaying some cartoon of a giant mouse chasing a tiny cat. Off to the left, a bright light shone from an adjoining room. They peered in and saw a larger room with a bunch of engineering equipment on tables. Just ahead of them in the TV room, Norton and Bisquit stood in front of a stone door with an ornate crest on it. The crest depicted a pair of spectacles, a shovel, and a sphere, with the inscription VISIONARY LABOUR SHAPES OUR FUTURE underneath. Norton pushed the door open, and Bisquit happily yipped as he bounded down the staircase before them, the steak flapping in his mouth.

Riff could hear a clamour as the door opened, and he skipped over to peek through. His jaw dropped as the scene before him unfolded. He was situated at the top floor of an enormous cylindrical space with twenty stories of shops around the perimeter and open space in the middle. It was an entire underground community, buzzing with activity. Riff could see that one floor of shops was dedicated to clothing, another to restaurants, another to grocery stores. Alleyways separated the shops, surely hiding more gems of life. Families laughed together, friends ate sensational-smelling fried foods, children walked out of shops carrying new toys, and everyone seemed . . . happy. These people were all humans just like Riff and his sisters, except they all wore glowing neon spectacles in various colours, just like Thevenin and Norton.

Norton clapped Riff on the back. "Welcome to the bunker."

# Chapter 16

## Meet the Bunker

"Let's walk an' talk. I'll give you the lowdown," said Norton, ushering the McHubbards down the stairs. "Thev'nin, you hold down the fort."

Thevenin nodded. "I'll be watchin' my cartoons," he said, and he closed the stone door behind them.

"No need tuh be afraid," said Norton to the three McHubbard siblings. "Yer all safe here."

Norton led them to a ledge at the bottom of the stairs and gestured out at the magnificent space. "We are what's left of this country. We don' know if there're other bunkers 'round the world, but this is ours. This bunker was built 'bout a hundred years ago, when the Insomnyus took over. Thera was already in a state of emergency with the climate an' all, but humans had bin survivin' just fine above ground. When the Insomnyus took over, humans needed a safe place to hide because they started huntin' 'em in their own homes. The Insomnyus ain't too smart, though. Don' seem tuh really think for themselves. But they don' hold back. They're tougher than they look. So, that's why this is here. Innit a beauty?"

"It's incredible infrastructure," said Luna. "This sounds very in line with what's happened on our planet, Earth; however, our climate crisis is much more advanced, as are our rehabilitation efforts."

"The idea is for us tuh get back tuh the ground level an' start those rehabilitation efforts ourselves," said Norton. "Trouble is, we can' do that with the Insomnyus up there. Thev'nin an' I are the electrical engineers in the bunker. We make all these zany gadgets, hopin' for the day we get tuh use 'em on the Insomnyus. I may look all tough an' scary, but truth is, I'm terrified of those crazies!"

"What sorts of things are you working on?" asked Riff.

"You remember those things we was pointin' at you? Those are what me an' Thev'nin like tuh call our zappers. We designed 'em tuh emit a bolt of electricity and stun the target. Works like a charm," Norton said with a toothy smile. "He an' I are also workin' on a much bigger project at the moment—a type of electric bomb that hits everything in a ten-metre radius with bolts of electricity. Trouble is, the Insomnyus are all spread around town, and we can' deploy the bombs unless we're certain we can get 'em all. But for now, we're callin' it our 'splodey device."

"That's really cool, mate," said Riff. "Where did the Insomnyus come from? Are they all humans, or are they from a different planet?"

Norton shuddered. "Better off askin' someone else in the bunker. As I said, those crazies give me the creeps. I don' even like talkin' 'bout 'em. Every time I do, I have nightmares for a week."

"Do you know everyone who lives here?" asked Luna.

"Mostly. I know everyone's face at the least," replied Norton.

"Our sister was kidnapped, and we have reason to believe that she's hidden here. Do you know an Elbina McHubbard? She's very skinny and wears a little buzzing contraption around her hip. Long, brown hair. Very pale. Soft-spoken," said Luna.

Norton thought for a moment, scratching his chin. "I don' know no Elbina McHubbard, I'm sorry."

"Is there any room for us to stay here while we try to track her down?" asked Ann Lou.

"Of course! Yer all welcome tuh stay here as long as you want. Thev'nin an' I would be happy to help in any way we can. An' I'm sure anyone you meet here will say the same. But first, let's get you set up with some spectacles."

Norton walked them around the curved landing to a lift, which consisted of a small, slightly elevated platform with a thin handrail. They stepped up onto it and huddled together. Built into the handrail were two rows of rusty buttons: four labelled N for north, S for south, E for east, and W for west, and then a series numbered from zero to twenty. Norton pressed W and 18, and the lift carried them horizontally over to the west side of the bunker, then began its eighteen-floor descent. Riff could see at least fifty other lifts in operation, carrying people to all different sections of the bunker.

"Why do we need the glowy spectacles?" asked Ann Lou.

"We wear the spectacles for two reasons. One, so that people of the bunker are easily distinguishable from the Insomnyus. We all take turns goin' out tuh Austere Avenue to collect more resources to keep us goin', and the spectacles make it easier to tell friend from foe. The second reason has more tuh do with optics in general. I'd suggest you ask Spex when he fits you with yer spectacles. He's the pro," said Norton.

An electromagnet halted the lift with a crunch and a clunk. They stepped onto the landing for the western quadrant of floor 18, and Norton pointed to the shop in front of them. It was exploding with glowing colours, and a sign read SPEX'S SPECS. Hordes of people were in the shop picking out new glowing frames and getting their eyes tested. There was a jar of candy-coated chocolate eyeballs for staff to hand out to children who successfully completed their eye exams.

"Spex, my friend!" said Norton, walking up to a tall, skinny young man. He had blonde hair and a thin moustache, and he wore rainbow spectacles that flashed different colours every few seconds.

"Norton, what brings you down to this neck of the woods?" Spex replied, his voice chipper. The two men pulled each other in for a bro hug.

"I've got some customers who need tuh be fitted for spectacles. They're from a different universe!" Norton said, stepping aside and proudly introducing them. "This here is Ann Lou, Riff, and Luna. They'll be staying here for a bit while they search for their sister."

"It's a pleasure to meet you all. Where are you from?" asked Spex.

"Earth, in the Coloratura universe," replied Ann Lou.

"Fascinating! I wasn't aware of any other universes but our own, let alone life on another planet. To that point, I haven't come across the anatomical structure of the Earth eye in my research, but I hope to learn all about it. In the meantime, let's get you fitted!" he said excitedly, jumping into action. "Please, follow me."

Spex manoeuvred his way through the crowd to a back area of the shop that had a small table covered with instruments and a chair in front of it.

"Ann Lou, you first. Come sit," he gestured, patting the arm of the chair.

Ann Lou bounced into the chair.

"I'm going to look at your eyes with this set of binoculars, and you two will be able to see her eyes close up on this screen," he said, pointing to a screen in front of Riff and Luna. "Ann Lou, hold still."

Ann Lou obeyed, and Spex peered through the binoculars. Riff saw Ann Lou's dazzlingly blue eyes pop up on the screen in front of them.

"Lovely, lovely. You're doing great, Ann Lou. I know it's bright, but try your best not to blink. Now, I'll explain to you what I'm doing. This instrument is called a pocket optomniscope. My team and I developed it as an all-in-one optical diagnostic tool. It combines the *power* . . . sorry, optician humour. It combines the capabilities of an autorefractor, a keratometer, and a retinoscope in order to detect the refractive power of your eyes and look for any signs of disease throughout your globes. Then, I can select a set of lenses that will suit your needs. I'm sure Norton already explained why the frames around the clear lenses glow, but from an optician's standpoint, these spectacles are also important medical devices for those living down here in the bunker. You see, our eyes want natural light, which we don't have any of down here. The glowing frames provide the extra light we need to achieve the illusion of natural light. Our eyes also naturally want to look into the distance; that's what keeps the eyes a healthy length. Since the bunker is limited in size, nothing down here is at what you would call an 'infinity' distance, like a horizon, for example. So, without intervention, our eyes would grow longer, which induces what optical specialists call *myopia*—a fancy term for nearsightedness. To avoid this, we have designed special spectacles that not only correct your vision but prevent it from worsening. These designs are really complex optical techniques that the team and I have been working on for a long time."

"See, I told you he'd be the best one tuh ask," said Norton.

"That's amazing," said Luna.

"Ann Lou, you've got very healthy eyes," said Spex. "You must be an outdoorsy girl. Play any sports?"

"I used to play ice hockey, but more recently I was crowned Pyroll champion of the Coloratura universe and Luge Crash champion of the former Time Belt," she said proudly.

"That'll do it," said Spex. "I'm prescribing you a lens design that will maintain your current prescription and give you a few UV blockers in case you spend time out in the sun on Austere Avenue. Riff, would you like to go next?"

Ann Lou and Riff swapped seats, and Riff looked into the optomniscope.

Spex turned some knobs. "You could benefit from spending some more time outside with your sister," he said.

Riff heard Luna and Ann Lou snort from behind him.

"Looks like you have some untreated astigmatism as well as a bit of myopia. I've got just the lenses for you. And, last but not least, Luna!"

Riff guided Luna to the seat. Spex focused the optomniscope, and Riff saw Luna's hazy brown eyes pop up on the screen.

"Wow, Luna, your eyes are . . . stunning," said Spex breathlessly.

"What?" said Luna. "I'm blind."

"That doesn't make your eyes any less beautiful. How long have you had these cataracts?" he asked, leaning back in his chair.

"From a very young age. Over time they just got worse to the point where my vision is now completely gone," said Luna.

"That's incredible. I can tell that you are very comfortable without your vision as well. You get around by using your other senses. Human adaptability is just fascinating, isn't it?" said Spex, a look of wonder spreading across his face.

"Yeah, it is," said Luna, her cheeks reddening.

"I'll tell you what," said Spex. He reached over and gently placed his hand on Luna's. "I have a formula for eye drops that can dissolve the cataracts. I can put you on a lens that will train your eyes, little by little, until they are accustomed to your surroundings. But knowing how well you cope without your vision, I respect your decision if you want to just continue as you have been. I can give you a pair of plano, no-power lenses, so that you can just get a cool pair of frames. What do you think?"

Riff and Ann Lou glanced at one another with excitement. This was the type of treatment Luna had needed years ago but was denied access to. Now she had the opportunity to regain her vision. Riff was sure she wouldn't shut this down, as she had the comparatively crude solution the ERA had offered her before she left for Casper.

"Erm, can I think about it?" asked Luna. Her hand was still covered by Spex's, and she hadn't yet tried to move it.

"Of course. I'll give you the plano lenses, and you can come back anytime if you change your mind," Spex smiled. "All right, you three, go pick out your frames, and then I'll pop your lenses in them!"

After much deliberation, Ann Lou chose light blue frames to match her eyes, Luna chose red, and Riff chose green. Once Spex popped in their lenses, he gave them a few moments to get used to the optical changes.

"My eyes are a bit squiffy," said Riff.

"Give it a few minutes and your brain and eyes will align to figure it out. Let me know if there are any problems. Oh, and Luna, you know where to find me if you ever want more information. Or to just come by and say hello."

Luna blushed almost as brightly as her glowing red spectacles and waved shyly back at him.

Norton led them back to the lift and hit the buttons N and 20. The lift creaked out of its current position and moved along a plane to the northern wing of the bunker, where it then descended two more floors to the bottommost floor.

"Let's see if there's any accommodations available in this section," said Norton, heading in the direction of a sign that read BLOCK A.

The blocks around the cylindrical foundation ranged from A to K, and each was split into even meridians. They strolled to the Block A meridian, which led them down a long hallway lined with doors. Each door had a board on it that identified who lived there. They passed by signs with simple messages such as WELCOME TO THE GOLDMAKER RESIDENCE, and others with messages that made Riff chuckle, such as PETRIS FAMILY: BEWARE OF THE FISH. Riff laughed out loud at one that said QUALSH FAMILY #3. PLEASE MAKE SURE YOU HAVE THE CORRECT QUALSH RESIDENCE BEFORE KNOCKING!

"Aha," said Norton, jogging as he neared the end of the hall. "This one looks empty."

There was no sign on the door to apartment number 30, and the door was unlocked, so Norton ushered them inside. The apartment was in fact completely devoid of humans. It was furnished simply. It reminded Riff of the McHubbard home back in Portsmouth. There was a rickety table and chairs, a compact but functional kitchen, a bathroom, and a sleeping area. Set into the back wall of the apartment were two open sleeping spaces, one beside the other. Riff smiled as he walked around, admiring the comfort. It had been a long while since he had slept somewhere that felt this much like a home.

Norton smiled as he watched the three McHubbards entranced by their new home. "I know it's not much, but you can spruce the place up. There's some grocery stores on the floor above, and some places tuh get decorations on level six. Keys are on the table. An' make sure you write your family name on the sign outside."

"It's perfect," said Ann Lou. "Thank you so much for showing us around."

"My pleasure," nodded Norton. "Need anything else?"

"How do we pay for everything here?" asked Luna.

Riff gulped. He remembered how they had paid for things in the Time Belt: with years off their own lives. He hoped the Therians were less barbaric with their currency.

"Everything's free, Luna lady. Yer generally expected to help out with jobs here an' there as you get more integrated, but don' worry about any o' that now. Just get yerselves comfortable. An' come by anytime to check out the zappers and the 'splodey device."

Norton cackled to himself and waved as he left. Then he poked his head back in the door. "Oh, I almost forgot! Hospital is on level three. You might wanna get that shoulder looked at, Riff." Norton nodded, then walked out of sight.

"Bye, Norton!" the McHubbards called in unison.

The siblings looked at one another in silence for a few moments, taking in all the information they had just learned and the journey they had taken.

It was Riff who broke the silence. "I never want to leave."

"Same," said Ann Lou.

"We need a plan," said Luna. "I know this place seems great, but let's not forget the task at hand."

"Okay, we'll find Elbina, and then stay here forever," said Riff.

"I'm sure I could convince Apollo to bring Clorin here," Ann Lou agreed.

"Plan, now! Focus on the current task!" ordered Luna in frustration. She sat at the table, then pulled out her tablet and started making notes.

"Luna, we have no leads whatsoever," said Ann Lou, tossing her hands around as she spoke. "We need to talk to people. We need to learn more about the Insomnyus. We can't just magically conjure up a plan on command. You have to be patient."

Riff could tell Luna was angry, but not with them—she was angry at the situation. Luna was so good at solving problems on the spot, and the fact that this mystery was taking longer than usual to solve was eating at her. Plus, the fact that it had to do with their missing sister added salt to the burn.

Riff placed a gentle hand on Luna's shoulder. "I'm going to the hospital floor to get my shoulder fixed up. Why don't you come with me? I can tell your knee is hurting. We'll be no use to Elbina if we're injured."

Luna nodded. "Let's head to the hospital, then."

"I'll get some things at the grocery store while you're both out," said Ann Lou.

Before they could move, there was a knock at the door. The siblings stared at one another, confused.

"I'll get it," said Ann Lou.

She opened the door to find a squat, older woman. She had a puff of perfectly coiffed grey hair with a tiny red bow in it, and the turquoise frames of her spectacles were bespeckled with rhinestones. Her cheeks were rosier than apples, and she smiled from ear to ear as she held out a giant platter of cookies.

"Hel-lo!" she chirped, sing-songily. "My name is Mrs. Flumbo. I am your neighbour at apartment twenty-four. I wanted to drop off some of my famous Flumbo Creams to welcome you to Block A!"

"How sweet!" said Ann Lou, taking the platter from her. "Thank you. We're the McHubbard family. We just moved here from a different universe."

Mrs. Flumbo chuckled a high-pitched laugh. "Oh, how I love young people. They are so hip and imaginative! Won't you try a cookie? They are packed with all the love, sugar, and secret ingredients you can imagine!"

Riff jogged over to the door and picked up a cookie for himself. He and Ann Lou each took a bite at the same time. Their faces fell as they tasted the rancid cookies and resisted the urge to spit them out.

"Mmm," said Ann Lou. "That is . . . quite the cookie."

Riff gagged slightly but played it off by rubbing his stomach. "Luna, you must taste this," he said, jogging back to his oldest sister.

Luna sniffed the cookie and took a delicate bite. "Ew!" she spat.

Mrs. Flumbo gasped and clapped her hands to her red cheeks.

Ann Lou improvised. "Don't worry, 'ew' is slang for 'amazing' in our generation!"

Mrs. Flumbo breathed a sigh of relief. "Thank goodness. I'm glad you like them. I'll whip up another batch for you. If you need anything, just stop by my apartment anytime!"

The McHubbards bid the sweet old lady goodbye, and she waddled back to her apartment down the hall.

"I'd take Casperian stew any day over those Flumbo Creams," said Ann Lou, spitting her cookie out in the bin.

The siblings parted ways for a short while. Riff and Luna went to the hospital floor, where they were seen by a Therian doctor almost immediately. Riff received a good old-fashioned chiropractic treatment, and a scream and a few painkillers later, he was good to go. Luna was prescribed a topical ointment for her knee injury. They went straight back to the apartment, where scalding hot cups of tea were waiting for them. Riff decided they had each earned a "giant nap" and leapt into the sleeping space on the left. His shoulder was no longer hurting him; he was in a cosy state of bliss from the hot tea or the painkillers or perhaps a bit of both. Luna passed out on the other bed shortly after. Before starting her own nap, Ann Lou wrote their family name on the sign on their door, which read GREETINGS FROM YOUR OUT-OF-THIS-UNIVERSE NEIGHBOURS, THE MCHUBBARDS!

# CHAPTER 17

## THE CANTILEERY FAMILY

A series of raps and woofs at the front door made Riff snort and awaken.

He sat up and stumbled out of his bed. He felt like he had been asleep for at least a week, and he could have kept going. Riff lumbered over to Luna and Ann Lou, who were sharing a bed and sound asleep, snoring like they belonged on planet Zeezz.

Riff scratched his head as he stumbled to the door, where the knocking and barking continued. He caught a quick glimpse of his hair in the mirror, which was a red, moppy mess and sticking out every which way. He opened the door to see three young women: one a little older than him, one younger, and one who looked about his age. The older one was holding a plate with half of a cooked steak on it. On the floor next to them was Bisquit, who seemed pleased to see Riff as he waltzed up to sniff his socks.

"Bisquit?" said Riff, surprised the dog managed to find his way back to him. "And, erm . . . hi."

Riff didn't often find himself speaking to girls his age other than his sisters. But, in his defence, his sisters weren't scary. All other girls were, though.

"Hello!" said the tallest one. "We heard you just moved in across the hall. We wanted to share some food with you as a welcome." She held the plate out to Riff, who awkwardly took it.

"Thanks. Er, I'm Griffin. Riff for short."

"I'm Meerie-Meerie. These are my younger sisters, Stenolly and Mysco. We live with our grandma, Gwympy, in apartment twenty-nine. We're the Cantileery family."

Stenolly and Mysco waved timidly.

"Oh, we saw your surname on Bisquit's collar. He was the one who led us to the bunker. Saved me and my sisters," said Riff.

"Oh! Well done, Bisquit," Meerie-Meerie said, patting him on the head and causing his brain to bob around.

The Cantileery sisters each had their own unique appearance. Meerie-Meerie was the tallest and the oldest of the sisters. She was trim but muscular. Her dark reddish-brown hair was tied in a long braid, and she wore yellow spectacles. Her spectacle lenses looked a bit different from any Riff had seen so far: the lenses jutted out like bubbles from the frames. Stenolly was notably shorter than Meerie-Meerie and a bit plumper. Her red hair was the exact shade of Riff's, like wildfire, but her hair was bigger. Her curls had curls. She had freckles and wore green spectacles just like Riff. Mysco was the youngest, probably in her early teens. She was athletic, and she seemed to be a bit hyperactive since she was bouncing on her toes as if eager to make her exit. Her straight blonde hair was pulled up in a tight ponytail. She wore white spectacles.

The girls giggled as they watched Bisquit perform a series of tricks, including sit, roll over, and a backflip. Riff couldn't help but notice how pretty Stenolly was. His eyes kept magnetically drawing back to her face. There was something very alluring about her presence.

When Riff finally regained the ability to speak, he opted to look at Bisquit instead of the girls. "You guys should meet my sisters. They're asleep at the moment, but they would be chuffed to meet you, I'm sure."

"That would be splendid!" said Meerie-Meerie. "Bring them over later for dinner. You can all meet Gwympy."

"Er, cool. See you later, then," said Riff.

As the sisters went back inside their apartment across the hall, Riff said, "Thanks for the meat!" He could feel the embarrassment turning his cheeks a deep crimson, so he booked it back inside the apartment.

He took a deep breath with his back against the door. *Why can't I just act normal?* he thought. *Matt and Joe could've taught me a thing or two back in school, but nooo.*

He sighed, then set the plate of steak on the dining table and cut the meat into three pieces. Ann Lou walked up to him, yawning. Riff was displeased to see that her hair didn't look like it had just been rolled around in a tumble dryer, the way his did.

"What's that?" she said, looking confused. "You don't cook."

"Bisquit's family brought us food to welcome us. They live across the hall," said Riff. "There's three sisters that came to say hello. They invited us over to their apartment for dinner."

"What's this about interacting with people?" Luna said as she made her way to the table.

"You had to talk to three girls?" Ann Lou laughed as Riff handed her a slice of steak. "Why wasn't I awake to witness this?"

"I wish you had been there, because I made a fool of myself," moped Riff.

"I'm sure you were fine," said Ann Lou. "Well, isn't this fun! Riff meets three cute girls, and Luna flirted with the optician."

"I did not!" said Luna, shielding her face from Ann Lou.

"Mm-hmm," said Ann Lou with a sneaky grin.

* * *

Two hours before the McHubbards were scheduled to visit the Cantileerys, Riff found himself double- and triple-checking his appearance in the mirror. His hair would absolutely not cooperate and flatten down, and he resigned himself to his fate of perpetual bedhead. Ann Lou came to his rescue and dabbed some water in his hair, which reduced the disarray by at least fifty percent. Luna sat on her bed and read a book as she waited for them to finish.

"Wait, we need to bring something!" exclaimed Ann Lou as she gripped a tuft of Riff's hair.

"Watch it, you're pulling!" whined Riff.

"We can't go over there empty-handed. They already gave us food, and now we're going to waltz over there without bringing them anything? Mum and Nan would be furious with us! We need to make something." Ann Lou raced into the kitchen and started poking through the cupboards. "Of course it's the cook in the family who got kidnapped. The rest of us are useless!"

"What ingredients did you buy?" asked Luna, still tracing her finger along her book.

"Bread, milk, and teabags," replied Ann Lou, yet she kept fishing through the drawers and cupboards, as if a soufflé would magically materialise.

"Remind me to do the shopping next time," said Riff.

"We can't go over there with toast and tea, and certainly not Flumbo Creams," said Luna. "We need to get more food. Plus, Riff won't survive the night on just that."

"Thank you," said Riff. "I will run to the shop. I'll hurry."

Riff ran out the door and down the hallway of Block A apartments, then took the lift up one floor. There were different grocery stores to choose from. He picked the one called "Wegwomans" because it made him laugh.

The general grocery-shopping experience was mostly similar to that on Earth. There were aisles of food, people with carts, and tills near the exit. The carts, however, were not pushed; rather, they were pulled behind the shoppers like wagons by means of straps around the shopper's waist. Riff saw one guy grab a box of pasta and toss it behind him in an arc over his head, assuming it would land in his cart, but the box sailed a bit too far and bonked a child in the head. The child was fine and took the pasta for himself.

Riff buzzed around the store looking for something they could make. Along the way, he noticed a few more differences between this store and the ones on Earth. Instead of kidney beans, there were liver beans. Instead of goat's cheese, there was bear cheese. Instead of natural spring water, there was unnatural spring water. Luckily, these differences were slight, and Riff was not too confused. As Riff pulled his cart through the aisles, an idea gradually formed for what to prepare for the Cantileerys: a classic British roast. He excitedly searched the aisles for ingredients to make Yorkshire puddings, roast potatoes, baked beans, and carrots and peas. He couldn't find the kind of meat that was typical for a British roast, so he opted for a few racks of buffkin. Riff's cart was now quite heavy, and he hauled it toward the tills at a decelerated pace.

He joined one of the lines, then had a thought: *Why is there a till? Norton said everything is free in the bunker. Was he lying to us?* He watched carefully as the customer in front of him completed his transaction. Riff recognised the cashier; it was Mrs. Flumbo. She finished bagging the customer's groceries, then waved and said, "Excellent! Keep up the good nutrition!" The customer took his bags and walked away without paying. Relieved, Riff stepped forward.

Mrs. Flumbo beamed at Riff. "Hello, sweetheart! How did you get on with the rest of the Flumbo Creams? Ready for your next batch?"

A gurgling sound escaped Riff's throat. He caught himself and covered up his *faux pas* by saying, "Always."

"Excellent! Let's see what you have here," said Mrs. Flumbo. She began scanning Riff's selections and placing them in the bagging area, starting with a can of baked beans. "Beans, eh? Let's hope you don't regret that choice." Next were the potatoes. "That's a lot of starch, don't you think?" She continued to editorialise about each item as she scanned and bagged. "Ooh, this won't be good for the appendix. . . . Are you *trying* to kill yourself? . . . Might as well just get the heart attack over and done with." When she finished scanning and bagging all of Riff's items, she glared at him sternly and handed him an itemised list of the medical consequences of each food. "Proper nutrition is crucial for longevity and quality of life. You'd best get a strict regime down pat while you're young. I'm pleased to see that you have carrots, though, dear. Well, save room for more Flumbo Creams! I'll bring them by a bit later!"

* * *

"What are we making?" said Ann Lou as she helped Riff unpack the groceries.

"A roast. Luna, you're on Yorkshire pudding and potato duty. Ann Lou will handle the meat, and I will do the beans and veggies."

"Why do you get the easy stuff?" groused Ann Lou.

"Because I went shopping," said Riff smartly.

The McHubbards bustled and clattered around the kitchen and made the roast as quickly as Earth-humanly possible. In the end, the Yorkshire puddings were a bit flat, the buffkin wasn't very buff, and the peas were a bit too crunchy, but all in all, they had successfully made a roast fit for a tiny army.

They each carried a tray across the hall to the Cantileerys' apartment, number 29. Riff took a deep breath and then knocked on the door. They heard Bisquit barking and quick footsteps approaching. Mysco answered the door with a meek "Hello" and gestured for them to come in.

"Hi, Riff!" said Meerie-Meerie, walking toward him with open arms. She hugged him, and he turned red and awkwardly hugged her back. Ann Lou snickered behind him.

"These must be your sisters!" Meerie-Meerie exclaimed. "So nice to meet you. Welcome to our home!"

Ann Lou and Luna introduced themselves to Mysco, Meerie-Meerie, and Stenolly. Riff noticed that the Cantileery sisters had changed into more formal outfits that matched their spectacles. Mysco wore a white pantsuit, Meerie-Meerie wore a dark yellow blouse and a lighter yellow pair of bell-bottoms, and Stenolly had on a light green shirtdress.

"Make yourselves comfortable," said Meerie-Meerie. And you didn't need to bring anything! That was so kind of you. You can set it all down in the kitchen."

The Cantileerys' apartment had the same kind of kitchen and living room as the McHubbards', but instead of two sleeping spaces, they had four, stacked two by two. Their apartment was also decorated differently, with more colours and scents. Candles were sprinkled around the room, and they had different-coloured curtains closing off their sleeping spaces. A record player played jazzy music.

The Cantileerys had already prepared an amazing spread of food. There were loads of vegetables, a big pot of soup, buttered breads, cakes, pies, and more. The baked goods all looked homemade. Riff wondered if that was because Mrs. Flumbo was short with the Cantileerys when they purchased cakes and pies from Wegwomans.

"Who's this?" Ann Lou said, pointing to a picture of a young boy with moppy brown hair and orange spectacles. Riff noticed many more pictures of this boy spread around the apartment.

"Oh, that's our brother, Fleg. He passed away when he was about ten years old," said Meerie-Meerie, her tone saddening.

"I'm so sorry," said Ann Lou.

Meerie-Meerie smiled sweetly. "It's okay," she said. "He was sick for a long time. There wasn't really anything anyone could do to save him in the end."

"Are these your parents?" asked Ann Lou, pointing to another picture of the Cantileery sisters, Fleg, and a couple who looked like older versions of Fleg and Stenolly.

"Yes, that's them," replied Meerie-Meerie. "They unfortunately passed away as well a few years ago."

"Stop asking about people in pictures," Riff whispered to Ann Lou. She nodded in agreement.

"Shall we sit around and talk? I'd love to know more about you all," said Meerie-Meerie, walking over to their sitting area. It was furnished with two loveseats and two armchairs arranged in a rectangle. Ann Lou and Luna took the armchairs. Meerie-Meerie and Mysco sat on one of the loveseats, and Riff and Stenolly took the other. Stenolly smiled at Riff as they sat down. Her hair was so wild that Riff could feel strands of it tickling his neck. He smirked at Stenolly, then immediately felt embarrassed.

"Sorry for bringing up people you've lost," said Ann Lou. "I didn't mean to stir up any bad emotions."

"No, please don't worry," said Meerie-Meerie. "We want to remember them. That's why we have the pictures. Everyone has endured loss."

"We just lost our grandmother recently. We were very close to her," said Ann Lou.

"My sympathies," said Meerie-Meerie. "We are so privileged to have our Grandma Gwympy still around. You'll meet her later for dinner. She's still working."

"Can I go do something else?" Mysco said, nudging Meerie-Meerie.

"Not yet, we have guests," hushed Meerie-Meerie.

Mysco slumped into the couch.

"What sorts of things do you like to do, Mysco?" asked Riff, feeling bad that she wasn't enjoying herself.

"Um, I like to play sports. I'm in the soccer league in the bunker," Mysco replied.

"Does she mean football?" Riff whispered to Stenolly. Stenolly nodded and smiled.

"Mysco is super talented," said Meerie-Meerie proudly. "It's a soccer league for adults, but they allowed her to join. She's by far the best one on the team."

"Sounds like Ann Lou," said Riff. "You guys would get along. She plays a whole bunch of sports."

"Yeah, maybe we can play soccer together. I've never played and would love to learn," said Ann Lou.

"Sure!" said Mysco, bouncing in her seat. "Let me go grab my ball—"

"After dinner," Meerie-Meerie said hastily, gripping Mysco's arm before she could get away.

"What about you, Stenolly?" said Luna. "What do you like to do?"

Stenolly sat quietly and bowed her head in embarrassment.

"Stenolly is mute," said Meerie-Meerie. "She wasn't always, but ever since Fleg and our parents passed, she doesn't speak anymore. But, to answer your question, Stenolly is very creative. She loves listening to music, and she's quite the dancer."

"Oh, that's really cool," said Riff, mustering up the courage to look Stenolly in the eye for a few fleeting seconds. "What music do you like?"

Stenolly spread her arms wide and smiled.

"Everything? Yeah, me too," replied Riff, matching her smile.

"And you?" said Ann Lou to Meerie-Meerie.

"I love to write poetry and short stories. That's pretty much what I spend all my time doing. But I need these special spectacles in order to do it. I am a very strong hyperope, which means that I am farsighted. Apparently Spex had never seen such a high level of hyperopia before, so he designed these lenses to help me with reading," she said, pointing to her bubble lenses.

"Who are your author inspirations?" asked Luna.

"Oh, a never-ending list, I'm afraid. I can show you my bookshelves later," said Meerie-Meerie. "So, where are you guys from?"

"It's a bit of a long story," chuckled Riff.

"We want to hear everything," said Meerie-Meerie. Mysco and Stenolly perked up in anticipation for his story.

Riff went on to explain that they were from planet Earth, a parallel planet from a parallel universe. He detailed the state of the Earth's environment, the war with the GeoLapse, how they had lost their mother and were sent to live on different planets, and how they ended up in the Time Belt. He covered E. Bowser III, a former resident of Thera, and how she had kidnapped Elbina and sent her here. Then he told them about their Jalopy trip to the supernova for stardust and about the much newer Jalopy that had brought them to Thera.

"Wow!" said Mysco, her hands pressed to her face in awe. "So you guys are aliens from a different universe?"

"Mysco, that's rude!" snapped Meerie-Meerie.

"No, she's correct," said Riff.

"That's an amazing story," said Meerie-Meerie. "I've never heard of E. Bowser the Third. Maybe she was around a long time ago."

"Bowser used her grandmother's time machine to build the Time Belt. Thera must be quite technologically advanced," said Luna.

Meerie-Meerie shrugged. "Possibly. We don't really know what the rest of Thera is like. The bunker is quite detached from the rest of the world. Most of us have lived here our entire lives."

The group sat in silence for a few seconds before Meerie-Meerie filled the void.

"But wow, you're an amazing family to do all of this for your sister. We'd love to help you find her."

Stenolly and Mysco nodded in agreement.

Luna said, "I don't mean to change the subject or anything, but what can you tell us about the Insomnyus? Norton didn't really tell us too much."

"Ooh, I'll answer this one," said Mysco. "The Insomnyus are a group of humans who prey on other humans and steal their dreams. If you get attacked by an Insomnyus, you start to have these really horrible nightmares that make your body so shocked that you are too afraid to sleep. When you eventually go insane, you get these hallucinations that lure you up to Austere Avenue. You're basically a goner at that point—you adopt that robotic lifestyle and prey upon other humans."

"How did that even start?" asked Luna. "Surely someone's behind it for whatever reason."

"No one knows, I'm afraid," sighed Meerie-Meerie. "It's been over a century since Insomnyus started popping up."

"How often do these attacks happen?" asked Ann Lou. "It looks safe down here. Why hasn't anyone been able to put a stop to all this?"

"Some parts of the planet could be relatively free of them; we don't know. We hypothesise that they are mostly concentrated around this area," said Meerie-Meerie. "You probably saw the gigantic building with the IHQ sign on Austere Avenue. That's the 'Insomnyus Headquarters.' In this area, anyway, their numbers have only increased. There's still quite a few people living undercover in those houses behind Austere Avenue, and they get caught quite often. A few people from the bunker have also been caught when they went up for resources," said Mysco.

"So, can a human who is an Insomnyus break free of whatever curse or hold is on their mind?" asked Luna.

Mysco shrugged. "We've never seen anyone who has become an Insomnyus come back to the bunker."

"I don't mean to pry, but by any chance did one of your family members get caught?" asked Luna.

The sisters nodded. "Both of our parents."

"Well, maybe we can help figure out if it's possible to reverse the effects of these attacks and bring people back," said Riff.

"That is a lovely dream. But we've already grieved them," said Meerie-Meerie darkly.

Another few seconds of silence filled the room.

"Should we eat some dinner?" asked Ann Lou.

"That's a great idea. Mysco, tell Gwympy dinner is ready," said Meerie-Meerie.

Mysco hopped up from the couch and ran over to the bedroom area. She climbed a ladder to the top right sleeping space and disappeared behind a tie-dyed curtain. Luna, Ann Lou, and Meerie-Meerie helped set the table, leaving Riff and Stenolly on the couch alone.

Stenolly pointed to the record player. A vinyl record was spinning, and music tooted out of a cone mounted above the player.

Riff inspected it. "I've never seen anything like this before. I'm sure people on Earth had something like it at one point. Check this out," he said, holding up his left wrist. "This is how I listen to music." He tapped his wrist, where his microchip was implanted, then navigated to ChipMusic. He scrolled through his music library and played a song by a random pop artist.

"The music is playing in my ears right now. And if I click this"—he tapped his wrist again—"now you can hear it. It's really cool."

Stenolly laughed and made a funny face, as if to say, "Are you sure about that?"

"Okay, okay, your music player is much cooler than mine. It's very old-fashioned, but I appreciate that it's something you can touch and play with," said Riff.

Stenolly knelt down and pulled a stack of vinyls from a shelf, then held them out to Riff.

"You want me to pick one? Okay, let me have a look," said Riff, kneeling down next to her.

He sorted through Stenolly's collection and took several seconds skimming the text on each jacket and taking in the unique and intricate cover designs. He was impressed at her taste in music, which ranged from pop to heavy metal to R&B (which, on Thera, stood for "radical and bumpy").

Riff chose an album with an illustration of a dove with its wings chained to a dungeon wall. The band's name was The Execution Platoon.

"This one?" he said.

Stenolly held a hand on her heart, then took it from him. She swapped the vinyls, and when the music started to play, Riff felt a wave of peace wash over him. He could hear Meerie-Meerie and Luna groan in the background.

Stenolly discreetly pointed at Meerie-Meerie and then rolled her eyes and stuck her tongue out.

Riff laughed. "Luna hates this kind of music, too."

"This music is disturbing the peace!" blathered an elderly woman's voice.

Stenolly quickly flung the vinyl off of the record player.

An old woman had appeared in the kitchen. She had wavy grey hair with a headband around it. Her spectacles were tie-dye-coloured, and she was wearing colourful jewellery (a lot of it) and a floor-length, sleeveless tie-dye dress.

"McHubbards, this is our Grandma Gwympy. Gwympy, this is Luna, Ann Lou, and Riff," said Meerie-Meerie. "Dinner is ready, so everyone come and sit. Mysco, dim the lights for Gwympy, please."

"Pleased to meet you," said Gwympy in a weak voice. She took a seat at the head of the table. Riff sat on Gwympy's left, and Stenolly sat on Riff's left.

Dishes were passed around the table. Riff prepared three plates for himself: one a full roast, another with bread and a bowl of soup, and the last for cakes and pies. He was so hungry that he didn't care if he looked like a pig in front of the Cantileerys.

"So, Gwympy, what is it that you do for work?" asked Ann Lou.

Gwympy rubbed her temples while she spoke. "I am the bunker's fortune teller."

"Oh, cool," said Riff, his mouth full of bread. "Can you tell me my fortune?"

"Well, to be honest, my fortune-telling abilities are very dependent on how accurate you would like your fortune to be," Gwympy replied.

"I'd prefer fairly accurate, please," said Riff.

"Then it's going to cost you," said Gwympy. "I charge a very hefty price for accuracy."

"We don't have any money," said Riff, deflated.

"Oh, I don't want any money. I prefer medicine," said Gwympy. She now held her head in both hands as if she were in immense pain.

"Medicine? What kind of medicine? Stuff you can get from the hospital?" asked Ann Lou.

"No, that stuff isn't strong enough. Hospital-grade medicine will get you a fortune of about forty percent accuracy."

"I don't need my fortune told that badly," said Riff. He slurped the rest of his soup, leaving the bowl clean.

"Wait. Would you be able to tell us where our sister is?" asked Luna. Ann Lou and Riff dropped their utensils and stared at Gwympy, whose eyes fluttered.

"Of course. But I need the medicine first. That's the only guarantee that what I tell you will be accurate," said Gwympy.

"We'll do anything. What's the medicine and where can we get it?" asked Luna.

"A vial of Tarottriptan at Fadre's Farmacy on Austere Avenue should do the trick," she replied.

"Gwympy, that's really dangerous. I wouldn't encourage them to go up there," said Meerie-Meerie solemnly.

"You're trying to drive away my clientele again! It's as if you want me to be in pain all the damned time. Stay out of my zone!" shouted Gwympy.

"If we were able to get the vials she wants, would she actually be able to tell us the truth?" Luna asked the Cantileery sisters.

The three sisters looked at one another disconcertedly and then nodded. "Yes," said Mysco. "When she's right, she's very right."

"Then it's settled. We'll get you the vial," said Luna. Riff and Ann Lou nodded. Gwympy groaned in relief.

"If I can't stop you, then I will just ask that you listen to me," said Meerie-Meerie. "Go during the daytime. Insomnyus can see just as well at night as they can during the day, so it would be best for you to have optimal lighting. And the smaller your group, the better. Choose one of you to go, and one of us and Bisquit will go with you. We know the streets like the backs of our hands."

"I'll go," Riff volunteered.

"I'll go with you," said Mysco. "I'm the best at sneaking around."

"You're much too young to do something like this," snapped Meerie-Meerie. "I will go with Riff."

"I am not too young! I'm almost thirteen! You never let me go! Please, I promise I'll make sure we're safe," begged Mysco.

Meerie-Meerie sighed and thought for a moment. "Fine. But there can be no dilly-dallying around. Get the vial and get straight back here."

"Yes!" said Mysco.

After dinner, the McHubbards helped the Cantileerys wash up, and then the group separated into smaller groups for various activities. Gwympy took in a client to read their not-so-accurate fortune, Meerie-Meerie showed Luna her bookshelf, Ann Lou and Mysco went to the sports area of the bunker to play soccer, and Stenolly and Riff sat together on her bed and looked at photo albums. She showed him old pictures of herself dancing with her modern dance class, some trophies she had won, and a few of her dance outfits. Riff smiled at each picture.

"Thank you for showing me these," Riff said. He chuckled at a picture where Stenolly had her hair up in a bun. Her hair looked like a beehive that was bulging out of many overstressed hair bands. "Your hair is so . . . unique."

She gave him that funny look again.

"I meant that it's very pretty," Riff said.

She mimed flicking a strand of hair behind her shoulder, which made him laugh.

"Thank you for all being so helpful with finding our sister. I know it's a huge ask for Mysco to go with me. I feel horrible putting her and Bisquit in danger," said Riff.

Stenolly flipped through a photo album to a picture that showed her siblings, including Fleg. She pointed to it and then made a heart with her hands.

"I bet any of you would risk your lives for one another," he said.

She nodded.

"Do you sign?" Riff asked, signing at the same time.

She shook her head.

"I can teach you if you'd like," he said.

She nodded and sat up straighter on the bed.

Riff taught her how to sign the alphabet, as well as a few simple words. She picked them up quickly, and she and Riff had a competition to see who could finger-spell words faster. Although Riff was faster, he regularly misspelled words that Stenolly nailed perfectly.

At the end of the evening, the McHubbards said their goodbyes to the Cantileerys.

"Bye, Ann Lou! See you tomorrow, Riff!" said Mysco, waving excitedly.

"Thank you for coming and for cooking the lovely roast!" said Meerie-Meerie.

"Give our best to Gwympy," said Luna.

Riff waved to the Cantileery sisters. He caught Stenolly's attention before heading out the door.

"Thank you," she signed.

"Good night," he signed back.

As the McHubbards stepped across the hall, another batch of Flumbo Creams waited for them on their doormat.

"We might as well make use of them around the apartment," said

Riff. He went straight to the kitchen and put one of the Flumbo Creams under a table leg to stop the table from wobbling.

The siblings talked as they prepared for bed.

"I *love* them!" exclaimed Ann Lou. "Mysco is like my little twin!"

"I know! And Meerie-Meerie recommended some Therian authors to me," said Luna. "I'm going to the library tomorrow to see if they have any Braille editions of their books."

"Riff, you and Stenolly seemed to hit it off with the music interest," said Ann Lou. "She seems really sweet."

"Yeah, she's nice," said Riff.

"Well, look at that, we've all made a friend today!" said Ann Lou, bouncing on her bed. "Night!"

Riff fell asleep easily that night. All he had to do was imagine Stenolly and him sitting next to a record player, and his mind floated off to a joyous dreamland.

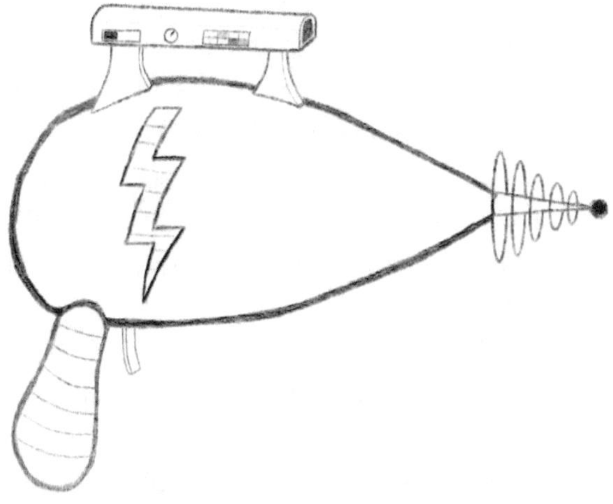

# CHAPTER 18

## FADRE'S FARMACY

The next morning, Stenolly, Mysco, and Bisquit were waiting for Riff in the hallway. When he emerged from his apartment, Riff felt his stomach churn with butterflies upon seeing Stenolly. She was wearing a green jacket, a white T-shirt, and jeans. *Green suits her well,* he thought.

"Good morning," he signed to Stenolly and said to Mysco.

Riff patted Bisquit on the head, and his kidneys and liver jiggled.

"Ready?" asked Mysco.

He nodded, and she and Bisquit led the way down the hall. Riff hung back for a second to see what Stenolly was doing.

She signed "Good luck" to him and waved.

"Thank you. See you later," Riff signed. He smiled and waved to her, then started off after Mysco and Bisquit.

The trio rode the lift up to the zeroth floor of the bunker, then made their way to the stone door where Thevenin and Norton manned the entrance to the bunker. The twins greeted them.

"Little Bisquit! Whaddya doin' up here?" said Thevenin.

For a second, Riff thought he was Norton, but then he remembered that Thevenin was the twin who wore orange spectacles.

"Oh, Miss Mysco, good to see you, darlin'. And Sir Riff!"

"Hi, lads. We're on our way through to Austere Avenue for some supplies," replied Riff.

"Oh, you two'd better be careful!" warned Norton. "Them Insomnyus're gettin' stronger and stronger by the minute. Here—we're givin' everyone one o' these whenever they need tuh go out." Norton passed them each a zapper. They were light blue in colour, and they each had a bulbous chamber with a lightning bolt emblazoned on it. "Bisquit don' need one; he's quick as a flash!"

"Cool!" exclaimed Mysco, her eyes wide as she took the zapper.

"Just aim and press the button, and lightning will strike the target. There's nothing to reload, but it takes a minute or so to recharge," said Thevenin.

"Thank you. We'll be back in a little while," said Riff, saluting them.

"Be careful!" Thevenin and Norton called out in unison.

Riff, Mysco, and Bisquit made their way up the tunnel. As the ceiling of the tunnel became lower, Riff knew they were approaching the end. At the end of the tunnel, Mysco reached up and raised the lid of the trunk just a crack. The coast was clear. She effortlessly pulled herself up and climbed out of the trunk and onto the floor of the Building Blocks toy shop. She took Riff's hand and helped him over the edge, and then Bisquit leapt out of the trunk.

"Thanks," Riff said, getting to his feet. He looked around them and was relieved to see there was still no sign of any Insomnyus in the store.

They carefully tiptoed to the front of the store.

"Which way?" he asked.

Mysco brought a finger to her lips and pointed across the street and to the left.

He gave her a thumbs up.

They held the shop door open a bit, and Bisquit squeezed through. He peered left and right, then wagged his tail twice.

Mysco held up two fingers to Riff.

"There's two Insomnyus out there?" Riff whispered.

Mysco hushed him again and nodded.

Bisquit then took off running across the street. Mysco yanked Riff's arm, and the two ran out of the toy shop and across Austere Avenue. Riff could see one Insomnyus to their left who was facing away from them, and another to their right who was turning down an alleyway. They had timed their getaway perfectly.

Once across the street, the trio needed to make their way down the avenue. Bisquit led them on a zigzagging series of back alleys, stops, and starts to avoid being seen by the Insomnyus. Several times he stopped for a wee. Riff quickly learned that he could predict when this would happen by watching the size of Bisquit's bladder.

They reached the back of a building, and Mysco started jabbing her finger toward it rapid-fire.

"Fadre's?" Riff mouthed.

Mysco nodded.

The three slunk down an alleyway next to Fadre's Farmacy with their backs to the wall. Once Bisquit reached the main avenue and gave them the go-ahead, the two bolted from the alleyway, and they ran inside Fadre's. Riff and Mysco leaned against the nearest wall to take a breather. Bisquit met them there a few seconds later.

Mysco pointed to the far back of the store and mouthed, "Vial."

Riff peered up over a tall shelf of medicine, then gasped and pulled Mysco down to the ground. "Insomnyus," he mouthed.

Her face blanched.

The pharmacy was colossal in comparison to the toy store. It was one large maze of aisles, and Insomnyus were scattered all throughout the store layout. Riff's heart was pounding so hard he feared it might give away their hiding location.

Riff and Mysco followed Bisquit along the aisles, retreating when necessary to avoid being seen. They had made it about halfway to the pharmacy counter in the back when Riff and Mysco found themselves in a slightly sticky situation. Two Insomnyus were closing in on them, one from the front and one from behind. Bisquit ducked easily into a space on a bottom shelf, but Riff and Mysco had nowhere to run. Riff panicked and simply ducked down where they stood and covered his head, which didn't do them any good. Mysco had the brilliant idea to toss pill bottles behind each of the Insomnyus to draw their attention and lure them in the opposite direction. She tossed the first bottle forward in a high arc. It landed behind the first Insomnyus, who made a quick turnaround to investigate the source. This caused the Insomnyus behind them to charge forward in curiosity, but when Mysco threw another bottle behind it, it turned around and hobbled in the opposite direction. Their pathway was now clear. Mysco urged Riff up from his duck-and-cover position, and they hurried around the next corner.

After a few more close calls, the trio successfully reached the back of the store, where the Tarottriptan was stored. Unfortunately, it was behind a glass door that required a key to open.

"Get your zapper ready," Riff whispered to Mysco.

She nodded and held up the zapper, defending Riff's back. Bisquit took up a position next to her. Riff walked up to the glass that stood between him and the Tarottriptan and took a deep breath. He knew chaos was about to erupt, but it had to be done for Elbina. He aimed the hilt of his zapper at the glass and struck it hard, sending shards of glass everywhere. A series of alarms began blaring. He snatched three vials of Tarottriptan and stuffed them into a trouser pocket.

Riff and Mysco turned around and saw that every Insomnyus in Fadre's Farmacy was staggering full speed in their direction. The centres of their eyes were blinking red, exactly as if an LED had been installed behind each pupil. Their mouths were opening and closing rhythmically, and Riff realised with horror that the alarm sounds were coming from inside their heads.

"Zap them now!" he shouted, holding up his zapper and pushing the button.

Both his and Mysco's zappers shot out powerful bolts of electricity, which paired with the chests of the nearest two Insomnyus and sent them flying backwards. They crashed into shelves and seemed temporarily incapacitated, twitching slightly. The other Insomnyus were not dissuaded; they kept plodding straight toward Riff, Mysco, and Bisquit.

With their immediate path cleared, they split up and raced down the outermost aisles toward the exit of Fadre's Farmacy, pushing shelves over as they ran. The obstacles slowed the Insomnyus down slightly but did nothing to disrupt their focus. They merely changed direction and plodded through or over the debris toward their prey.

Bisquit reached the front door first and waited there patiently, unwilling to leave his comrades behind. Mysco and Riff zapped another pair of Insomnyus, then ran to the door. Mysco grabbed Riff's hand, and they followed Bisquit out of the store.

Riff and Mysco looked around them. The avenue was now full of Insomnyus. Hundreds of them were flooding into the street and heading straight for Fadre's Farmacy. Riff wondered if their alarms had triggered all existing Insomnyus, or just the ones in the area. Whichever case it was, there were way more of them than Riff had initially anticipated.

Mysco sent another lightning bolt toward the nearest Insomnyus. It knocked him down and seemed to stun the ones behind him, allowing Bisquit, Mysco, and Riff to duck into the alleyway next to Fadre's. Mysco, still holding Riff's hand, hurtled down the alley and turned left at the end. Riff was tripping over himself and trying his best not to slow her down.

As they raced along the backs of the shops, Mysco spotted a pile of wooden crates. She let go of Riff and started stacking the crates to make a fort for them to hide in. Bisquit hid inside one of the crates, and the humans completed the barricade just in time to keep themselves hidden. Insomnyus began seeping out of the alleyways and searching behind shops.

Riff and Mysco held their breaths as they watched through the cracks of the crates. Luckily, the crates were sufficient cover. The Insomnyus were not searching thoroughly, they were merely looking for targets in plain sight. As long as Riff, Mysco, and Bisquit stayed hidden and quiet, they would be safe.

Riff thought about Mysco's parents, who were somewhere in the mix of brainwashed humans on Thera. It was entirely possible that they were nearby right now, trying to find and attack their own daughter. Riff wondered if Mysco had even fully processed the situation. It couldn't be easy for her.

The trio waited for a long while until the Insomnyus dispersed. Bisquit was the one who checked that the coast was clear, then quietly whimpered to alert them to emerge.

"I can't believe we made it out alive," Mysco said quietly, trembling as she began moving the crates.

"It was all because of you," said Riff as he lifted a particularly heavy crate, clearing a path for Mysco to get out. "Thank you for your quick thinking."

"Let's head back. Meerie-Meerie will be worried sick that we've been gone so long," Mysco said.

The three were quite careful on their way back to Building Blocks. They saw only a few Insomnyus doing routine patrols. Once they reached the shop just across the street from Building Blocks, Bisquit gave the go-ahead to run across the street. Mysco followed Bisquit across, and within about ten seconds, both were in the entryway to Building Blocks. Mysco turned to speak to Riff and was surprised to see that he wasn't with them. He was still on the other side of the street.

Mysco beckoned with her hand for him to hurry up, but Riff was not watching her. He was fixated on a single Insomnyus to his left, about twenty metres away from him. The Insomnyus was doing a slow right-to-left scan of her route.

Riff started to lift his zapper, but when he got a clear look at the Insomnyus's face, his heart sank and his arms dropped to his side. She had wispy brown hair and pale skin. She started plodding toward him again. Despite her robotic movements, Riff recognised her thin, frail build. Alas, the Insomnyus on duty just a short distance away from Riff was the entire reason he, Luna, and Ann Lou had come to this planet.

"Elbina," Riff said a bit louder than he should have. "Elbina, I'm right here. It's your brother, Riff." He took one step toward her and waved his hands.

Mysco darted out from the safety of Building Blocks, raced across the street, and slammed into Riff. She gripped his collar and pulled on it with every fibre of her being. "Riff, no! She doesn't know you! You've got to get away!"

"She's my sister," said Riff. "She'll know me." He began pushing Mysco gently away.

"She won't!" said Mysco, struggling. "Listen to me!"

"Elbina," Riff repeated. "Elbina, can you hear me?"

Elbina stopped for another scan. She was now only ten metres away. She started the scan on her right, and slowly revolved her head until it reached the centre, when she discontinued the scan.

"It's me!" said Riff, the desperation rising in his voice. "You know me. Elbina, you know me!"

Elbina's mouth opened, and she stared at Riff for about a second. Then her eyes flashed red and an alarm sounded from her mouth.

Bisquit ran to Riff and began tugging his trouser leg to pull him toward Building Blocks.

"We can't go there, Bisquit! They can't know our hiding place," shouted Mysco. "We need to run!" She began pulling Riff along the sidewalk.

Riff allowed himself to be pulled along, yet he was still entranced by the sight of his sister, hoping against hope that his sister would come to and realise that she had just been under a spell of some sort.

Then Elbina began loping toward them with a viciousness that Riff had never seen in her. She was the sweetest little sister in the world. In the universe. In all the universes! She was incapable of malice. How could this be happening?

"Snap out of it, Riff! She'll turn you into an Insomnyus in the blink of an eye," shouted Mysco.

Riff ran with Mysco down an alleyway only to find that the end was blocked off by a high stack of crates. They turned back, but Elbina had already started down the alleyway. They were trapped.

"Riff, please!" pleaded Mysco, crouching into the foetal position and holding Bisquit close to her chest.

Riff teared up as Elbina approached. This wasn't his sister anymore. She barely looked like herself. The Elbina he'd known would never hurt anyone. Clearly there was only one thing to do. Riff wondered if his head was screwed on correctly, but he went with his gut and raised the zapper. Elbina was only a few metres away now, and hordes of Insomnyus were already piling into the alleyway.

"Mysco, climb!" shouted Riff. "Elbs . . . I'm so sorry." He closed his eyes and zapped her, sending her ploughing into the line of Insomnyus behind them. Now was their chance to escape. He ran to Mysco.

Bisquit was already halfway up the mountain of crates.

"You first," said Mysco. "I have a plan."

Riff obeyed and followed Bisquit onto the crates. They were a bit wobbly but proved easy to climb. They made it safely to the top, then waited for their comrade.

As Mysco climbed the crates, she periodically turned and held up her zapper, waiting for the right time to use it. When the Insomnyus reached the stack of crates and crowded below her, she zapped them. Then she resumed climbing, tossing adjacent crates off the pile as she went.

Riff and Bisquit descended the pile of crates and could hear Mysco climbing on the opposite side. Then her blonde hair peeked up over the top. Just as Riff reached out a hand toward her, she screamed in terror and was immediately pulled back down.

"Mysco!" yelled Riff.

Bisquit then hopped back up to the top of the crate mountain, growled, and let out a supersonic bark that was so loud that Riff fell to the ground and had to cover his ears. When Bisquit reappeared, he was dragging Mysco by her sweatshirt and pulling her over and down the mountain of crates to safety.

Riff helped Mysco in her descent to the bottom of the crates. Once she regained her footing she was clearly spooked. She was trembling and struggling to stay up. Her lower legs had bloody scratches on them. Bisquit looked exhausted.

"Mysco," said Riff, "are you all right?"

"I think so," she said in a shaky voice. "Good boy, Bisquit . . . good boy."

"I'll hide you." Riff lifted Mysco into a crate, then put Bisquit in with her and closed the lid. Then he hid himself in another crate and watched through the cracks for any trailing Insomnyus.

He waited there for a long while. Guilt flooded him. He had zapped his own little sister. It didn't matter that she wasn't of a sound mind; he still felt terrible. And what would Ann Lou and Luna think of him? He wondered if he hurt Elbina when he zapped her, but something twigged in his brain, reminding him of what Norton had said: that the zappers merely stunned their targets. That made him feel slightly better. He hoped Luna and Ann Lou would understand.

And Meerie-Meerie and Stenolly—what would they do to him when they found out Mysco had been injured? She had escaped, thanks to Bisquit . . . but Riff still felt bad that they'd gotten Mysco involved. Just like on Casper, when he had wanted so badly to protect Flora and Knitsy in the holding centre, he wished he had been able to save Mysco from harm. He wished he had been injured instead of her.

Bisquit's whimpers from the crate adjacent brought Riff back from his thoughts. Riff took one last look through a crack to check for Insomnyus and saw none. He quietly opened the lid of his crate and got out. Then he opened the lid of the other crate. Bisquit and Mysco were trembling in fear.

"The coast is clear. Let's get out of here," said Riff. He lifted Bisquit out first, then Mysco.

"Okay," said Mysco. She still looked spooked, but she was able to walk.

Mysco held onto Riff's arm as they followed Bisquit back through a series of alleyways toward Building Blocks. As they walked speedily along, Riff kept his eyes off Austere Avenue in case Elbina was back on duty. He didn't want to be tempted to try to speak to her again. He didn't want to put his companions in any more danger.

The trio made it safely inside the toy store and rushed to the trunk that concealed the entrance to the bunker. Riff helped Mysco and Bisquit inside, then climbed in and securely closed the lid behind them. They staggered down the tunnel, slowly regaining a sense of safety. Riff breathed a sigh of relief once the wooden door to Thevenin and Norton's post came into view.

Bisquit sat down wearily at the wooden door. His usually bouncy internal organs sank to the bottom of his body.

"Is Bisquit going to be okay?" said Riff.

"Yes," said Mysco. "His ultrabark uses up most of his energy. He just needs to sleep and recharge. Lots of treats will help, too."

Bisquit's ears perked up upon hearing the T-word.

Mysco said, "I've only ever seen him use his ultrabark once before. His breed is very protective. They use their ultrabark when someone in their family is in grave danger."

"How is it that he knows where to go? He seems to understand English," said Riff.

"He's very smart," said Mysco. "My dad found him as a stray one time when he went up to Austere Avenue for resources years ago. Bisquit is unlike any other pet in the bunker. We think he's the only one of his kind. He is very independent and prefers going up to Austere Avenue by himself to get resources for our family. That's why you found him up there when you first arrived."

"He's a good boy," said Riff.

Bisquit wagged his tail weakly.

The trio knocked on Thevenin and Norton's door, and the twins let them in.

"I hope you didn't need tuh use the zappers," said Thevenin, taking the weapons from Riff and Mysco.

"Unfortunately, we did," said Mysco. "But they saved our lives. And we got what we went up there for."

Norton opened the stone door for them. "Man, I hate those Insomnyus creeps. Glad you guys are okay. Go get some rest."

Riff and Mysco thanked the twins, then proceeded into the bunker. On the lift ride down, Riff noticed that Mysco seemed a bit unsteady on her feet.

"Are you sure you're okay?" asked Riff.

"I'll be fine," said Mysco. "I just need some rest."

"Thank you for going with me," said Riff. He pulled the vials of Tarottriptan from his trouser pocket. "I guess we don't need these anymore."

"Why not?" said Mysco. "Now you can go see Gwympy and get her prediction."

"But we don't need it anymore," said Riff. "We know where Elbina is now."

"I know, and I'm really sorry about your sister," said Mysco, now leaning on the lift railing for support. "But Gwympy might be able to help you figure out if there's a way to save her."

The trio hopped off the lift at Block A. Their sisters were all sitting together at the end of the hallway.

"There they are!" shouted Ann Lou, running up to them.

"Thank goodness! I thought you were dead!" Meerie-Meerie cried, wiping away tears.

Hugs were exchanged all around. Riff felt a tingle up his spine when Stenolly hugged him. He held her an extra second longer than he did the others.

"What happened?" asked Luna. "Did you get the vial?"

Riff held up the three vials he had stored in his pocket.

"Excellent!" said Luna. "Let's ask Gwympy where Elbina is!"

"That's the other thing," said Riff. "We might have . . . solved that mystery." Tears flooded his eyes.

"What are you talking about?" asked Ann Lou.

Riff completely broke down. He fell to his knees and sobbed. He could hear Mysco putting the pieces together for their sisters. Between sobs, he heard Mysco say "Elbina" and "Insomnyus." He heard the other girls gasp.

Ann Lou and Luna sat on either side of Riff and embraced him while he cried and Mysco told the remainder of the story. When she got to the part about Riff zapping Elbina, both of them whispered reassurances to him.

"You did the right thing," said a teary Luna.

"Elbina would understand," said Ann Lou.

Mysco then explained how Bisquit used his ultrabark to take down a horde of Insomnyus. Riff could see Stenolly holding the little dog tightly in her arms. Mysco proceeded to show the others the scratches on her legs. "Bisquit saved my life."

Meerie-Meerie cried and embraced her youngest sister. "You are never going up there again!" she scolded her. "I can't believe they did this to you. We need to get you to the hospital!"

"I'm fine," said Mysco. "It's only a few little scratches."

"I don't care if they gave you high-fives and kisses! You're going!" said Meerie-Meerie, still holding a firm grip on her sister.

"I swear, I'm fine. I just want to get some rest."

"Well . . . all right. But I'm keeping my eyes on you," said Meerie-Meerie sternly.

"We can see Gwympy tomorrow," said Ann Lou.

"Come over in the morning," said Meerie-Meerie.

Mysco went to Riff and held her hand out. He took it and rose to his feet. Mysco pulled him in for an embrace. "Gwympy will help you. I promise," she whispered.

"Thank you. I hope you're okay," was all Riff could utter to the brave girl.

The McHubbard sisters helped Riff inside and talked him into sipping some tea and taking a few bites of toast before heading to bed. Once he consumed his small but homey meal, Ann Lou and Luna tucked him in, then went to the kitchen to talk. Riff eventually fell asleep listening to the soothing sounds of his sisters' voices.

*　*　*

A high-pitched scream woke the McHubbards up that night.

"What was that?" said Luna frantically, hopping from her bed.

"I dunno," said Riff, listening intently.

The screaming continued. It was full of fear, and it was coming from across the hall.

"Do you think it's one of the Cantileerys?" asked Ann Lou.

Dread filled Riff's body. An awful possibility had been lurking in the back of his mind, and he didn't want to face it.

He gulped. "I think Mysco is having a nightmare."

# CHAPTER 19

## GWYMPY'S PREDICTIONS

Riff banged on the Cantileerys' door as soon as he figured out that the source of the screaming was Mysco. His sisters stood with him, wanting to help in any way they could. A worried-looking Stenolly answered the door, and Riff had to swallow his feelings and jump straight to the point.

"Is Mysco okay?" he blurted.

Stenolly ushered them in and brought them to the couch in the living area, where Mysco lay screaming and sweating. Meerie-Meerie and Gwympy were standing over her. Meerie-Meerie dabbed her forehead with a flannel and murmured loving words.

"Can we help?" asked Ann Lou.

Meerie-Meerie whipped her head around. "No! Riff, you've done enough already." She glared at him as if he'd hurt her or her family, which he felt like he had. Why hadn't he taken better care of Mysco? Why had he stood there on Austere Avenue like an idiot and put Mysco's and Bisquit's lives on the line?

Stenolly gripped Riff's hand. *At least she doesn't hate me,* he thought.

Gwympy started pacing back and forth, holding her head in her hands and muttering to herself. "I can feel it; it's on the tip of my brain."

"There has to be some way to help her," said Luna. "I can go to the library. I can do some research on the Insomnyus."

"There's *nothing* you can do," croaked Meerie-Meerie, now glaring at Luna. "You don't understand. She's changing. She's becoming one of them. That's another one of my family gone!" Meerie-Meerie charged at Riff and slapped him across the face.

Riff knew better than to retaliate. Ann Lou and Stenolly stepped in and were able to pull Meerie-Meerie away from him.

"I know my brother had no intention of any of this happening to Mysco," Ann Lou said sternly. "You can't blame him for this. Our sister is an Insomnyus. He just thought maybe he could break through to her. I would have done the same thing. I bet anything that you would have as well."

Meerie-Meerie trembled with anger. "I surely wouldn't be that stupid. You don't know the Insomnyus like we do."

"How much time before Mysco fully transforms?" said Luna.

"I—I don't know. Could be a few days," said Meerie-Meerie.

"Can Gwympy help us?" asked Luna. "Maybe she can tell us something about the Insomnyus."

Gwympy sat in a chair and held her head in her hands, clearly in agony. "Do you have the vial?" she asked.

"Yes," said Riff.

"Let's go tell a fortune then, shall we?" Gwympy smiled through the pain with a mysterious twinkle in her eye.

"I'll stay with Mysco," snapped Meerie-Meerie. "You all get out of my sight." She resumed attending to Mysco, who was whimpering and clawing at her head.

Gwympy stood wobblishly and led the remainder of them up the ladder and behind a tie-dyed curtain to her sleeping area. The tiny room smelled of a mixture of perfumes, candles, and incense, which Stenolly was now lighting for her grandmother. Instead of a bed, Gwympy had a small wooden desk. On the desk were several decks of oracle cards, assorted crystals, a pink rabbit's foot, seven shamrocks, and a crystal ball in an elaborate stand. Gwympy sat behind the desk and summoned everyone to gather in front of it. She then shuffled her oracle cards, rubbed the rabbit's foot under her nose, and ate one of the shamrocks.

"The vial," she said, closing her eyes and reaching a hand out to Riff.

Riff handed her one of the vials. She snatched it from his grip, popped open the top, and downed every last drop.

"Aughhh!" Gwympy groaned. "The spirits! They're coming. Spirits, may you take me to your internal mirror and reveal the truth to . . . what's your name again?"

"Erm, Riff McHubbard. But they can call me Griffin if they'd prefer."

"Reveal the truth to Grafflin McFlubbin's deepest and most desperate desires of the unknown."

Gwympy held one hand to her head while the other one waved over the crystal ball. "Ahhh, the clearing! The torment that blocks my imaginative spirit has been dissolved. The truths are seeping into my soul. Spirits, will you provide me with the tools and resources to convey Gronffin MaClubbird's truth?" Gwympy then waved both her hands above the crystal ball in a way that resembled a child trying to swim for the first time.

Riff and Ann Lou eyed one another. Stenolly tapped Riff's arm, then gave him a reassuring glance and a thumbs up.

"Gruffin!" Gwympy exclaimed, her eyes now bugged out. Her voice sounded strong, unlike that of normal, non-spirit-wielding Gwympy. She reached for Riff and clasped his wrist. A bit of white smoke formed in the crystal ball. The white smoke expanded until it filled the ball, and then colours bubbled up from the centre until the crystal ball resembled an eye with an orange iris and a tiny pupil. Riff flinched when the eye blinked.

Gwympy exclaimed, "The Insomnyus are alive, but not enough to survive. The Athenaeum holds each victim's brain, but into whom do they all drain? A monster so sinister, a creature, a visitor. He calls himself Fantasly, a being of brutality. He can be beat, but it can't be a small feat. A simple zap to the lobe will cause Fantasly to explode. Once he's gone, there will be a new dawn. The bunker can be made obsolete, and we can go to the street."

Gwympy tossed her head back and breathed deeply. She let go of Riff and pulled her hands back to her head. The eye in the crystal ball dissolved, and the sphere was completely clear again.

"You don't happen to be a descendant of the Bowser family, by any chance?" asked Luna with an air of worry.

Riff's thoughts mirrored hers. Gwympy's rhyming chant sounded exactly like that of E. Bowser III, the evil ruler of the Time Belt . . . the same ruler who had kidnapped Elbina and sent her here to become an Insomnyus.

"Bosnan?" asked Gwympy.

"No, Bowser," Luna clarified.

Gwympy didn't reply. She only held her head in her hands, wincing in agony.

Luna spoke up again. "It just sounded like—"

"Drop it, Luna. Does any of that information she relayed mean anything?" asked Riff.

Ann Lou shook her head as Luna thought. Riff felt a tap on his shoulder. Stenolly finger-spelled "IHQ" to them, then mimed reading a book.

"Erm, something to do with IHQ and books," said Riff.

"The Athenaeum must be in IHQ!" exclaimed Luna.

"What's an Athenaeum?" asked Ann Lou.

"It's like a library. It sounds like Fantasly could be the culprit behind the Insomnyus. Gwympy provided us with some possible clues to defeat him, which I'll have to take some time to mull over," said Luna.

"This Fantasly sounds like a piece of work," said Riff. "Why do you reckon he's turning everyone into robots?"

"Probably the same reason the GeoLapse do what they do. For power," replied Luna.

"Right," said Riff, glumly.

Gwympy moaned and grumbled in her chair. "Do you have any more Tarottriptan?" she asked in her usual weak voice.

"Sure," said Riff, placing another vial on her desk.

"I think a reading is coming through for you three," she said, pointing a knobbly finger at the McHubbards. "This will do the trick."

The McHubbards held their breaths as Gwympy downed the second vial of Tarottriptan. This time, she appeared much more focused. She concentrated all of her energy on the crystal ball as it filled with white smoke, then became an eye once more.

"This doesn't happen often. Spirits are trying to relay a message. They are trying to warn you," she continued.

Gwympy closed her eyes and took several deep breaths, followed by a groan of relief. "I can see it all now, and I have enough energy to show you. Please, focus your attention on the crystal ball."

At first Riff was unsure as to what he should be looking at. Then the eye's pupil expanded until the entire ball was filled with black, and a clear image formed. Then the contents of the image began to move, as if they were seeing through the eyes of some unknown person who was walking around in a carpeted room. Riff had no idea whose sight they were following or anything of that sort. But as the person walked through a doorway and into a long hall, a crawling sensation climbed Riff's spine. He knew exactly where the person was: the White House in Washington, DC.

* * *

An unknown man traipsed around the White House like he owned the place, screaming and yelling at employees in green lab coats to put their hands up and obey his every command.

"Come on, fellas!" the man called to a group of people behind him. The group wore all black and bore the letters GL in gold on their chests.

Several of the man's black-suited cronies charged forward, their weapons drawn, and ordered the staff in lab coats to get on their knees.

"Who's gonna talk?" said the man in a loud, authoritative voice. "Where are the McHubbards?"

No one said a word.

The man circled around the bruised ERA staff. He bent down to a few of them and laughed in their faces. Then he stood over a man whose badge read DR. JUNG-HOON KANG. "You know anything, *Mister* Kang?" said the man, tracing his baton along Jung-hoon's jawline.

"Nothing," Jung-hoon replied.

"What about you?" said one of the black-suited men. He was standing over a pair of humans with their heads bowed. "Zeep. What a funny name. What do you know?"

"Nothing," replied Garold and Flora in unison.

"Someone must know something," said the man in charge. "I'll tell you what. If someone tells me where the McHubbards are, I won't tell my guys to destroy your labs and all of your precious little science kits. Instead, I will be very generous and give you something in return: a life outside of your crummy little homes and your dead-end jobs. Suits to roam around as you please. Endless food and drink. The promise of prosperity, power, and anything else you could possibly imagine. Now, I will ask one more time before my men tear this place down, causing each of you a very painful death and the sure destruction of any scientific breakthroughs you have made. Where are the McHubbards?"

The man walked past Matt and Joe, who also said nothing. He then stopped in front of Delevio, knelt down, and placed a firm hand on Delevio's shoulder. Delevio was trembling.

"Dr. Delevio, surely you know something. Has my speech struck a chord with you? I can give you a suit at any time, and you can join us. Just tell me where they are." The man's grip tightened on Delevio's shoulder.

Delevio's mouth twitched and he winced in pain as the man's grip inched toward his neck. "Th-they're on planet Thera."

"And where is that?" asked the man calmly.

"In the Reprisa universe. They took a Casperian-engineered Jalopy through the black hole at the centre of the Milky Way galaxy," Delevio muttered.

"The Casperians have figured out how to travel between universes?" the man said incredulously.

"Yes," replied Delevio, now trembling violently. "They have made several new Jalopies that can do it."

"Fellas," said the man, standing up, yanking Delevio by the neck as he rose. "We have a new frontier to explore. We've been focusing our efforts at the wrong scale. The GeoLapse are about to go multi-universal!"

Cheers erupted behind him.

"C-can I come with you?" Delevio asked meekly.

"I don't need a coward on my team. Kill him," the man commanded.

As the man turned away from the ERA staff, Delevio's pleading voice was followed by gagging, then silence, and then the thump of a body hitting the floor.

The man in charge passed by a mirror briefly. He had thick, moppy white hair. A circle was tattooed around his right eye. A scar ran down his left cheek, and one of his front teeth was missing—but whatever threats or hardships had marred his face, clearly they were in the past. Everybody listened to him now. This was a man with no fear.

* * *

Gwympy flung her head back and immediately snoozed herself into a deep sleep. The eye within the crystal ball returned to its clear, smokeless form. The last of the incense had burned out.

Riff, Ann Lou, and Luna all looked at one another, fear plastered on each of their faces.

"Our dad the murderer is coming to visit? Can't wait," said Ann Lou, quivering.

"He might not get here," said Luna. "I don't believe the Casperians would just give them a Jalopy."

"The GeoLapse aren't exactly going to ask nicely," said Riff, matter-of-factly. "In fact, they don't usually ask for anything."

"Well, it's going to take them some time to get to us. We need to focus on what's happening right now. Mysco and Elbina need help. We have to take down Fantasly first," said Luna.

The rest of the group nodded in agreement.

Riff, Ann Lou, Luna, and Stenolly quietly exited Gwympy's room and went back to the living room. Meerie-Meerie was reading a book to Mysco. Mysco still couldn't sleep, and she looked pale and clammy. Ann Lou updated Meerie-Meerie and Mysco on both of Gwympy's predictions. Riff winced when she mentioned the part about their father and the rest of the GeoLapse potentially storming planet Thera, and he was worried that Meerie-Meerie might react poorly to the added bad news, but she took it better than expected, given the circumstances.

"I was quite curious about your father. You had only mentioned your mother previously. I'm sorry to hear that. But let's tackle one objective at a time. Where do you go from here?" Meerie-Meerie said as calmly as she could.

"We should start with the Athenaeum in IHQ. It's our strongest lead from Gwympy's prediction," said Luna.

"I agree with you. Definitely start with the Athenaeum. But Mysco cannot help you this time, and I need to stay here with her. I'd advise not to take Bisquit either. Mysco would be devastated if anything happened to him. And Stenolly shouldn't put herself at risk, either—"

Stenolly slammed her foot down and glared at her eldest sister.

Meerie-Meerie groaned. "Fine. Stenolly, if you really want to, you can make your own decisions. But please—have a plan. You need to be properly armed. The bunker needs to be alerted about the possibility of a GeoLapse attack. If you charge off to the Athenaeum with no plan, you're just asking to get killed. Take ample time to prepare."

The McHubbards agreed and bid goodnight to the Cantileerys. Ann Lou cheered Mysco up slightly with the promise of their playing soccer together the following day.

Stenolly stopped Riff before he left and signed, "Teach more tomorrow?"

Riff smiled. "Yes, we can practise as much as you'd like." He hugged her goodnight. The butterflies in his stomach flew him back to his apartment.

When he was cosied up in bed a few minutes later, Riff once again fell asleep to sweet thoughts of Stenolly. Every thought started and ended with her. He dreamed of her dancing while he drummed a beat for her. It was just the two of them in Riff's old room in England. Even though it was only a dream, Riff hoped that he and Stenolly would be able to share such a moment someday. It would never be at the home he'd grown up in, but that didn't matter. All he knew was that whenever she was next to him, he felt at peace. He felt an understanding. He felt someone who loved all the same things he did and saw the world in the same way. He felt love.

# CHAPTER 20

## STENOLLY'S OVERTURE

Over the next week, word spread quickly around the bunker about the impending arrival of GeoLapse from the parallel planet Earth. In general, the bunkerians were more than willing to involve themselves and provide defence if needed: Thevenin and Norton hermited themselves in their workshop to work on the 'splodey device. The adult soccer league began offering classes on special kicks and defences that might come in handy in a brawl. Mrs. Flumbo organised volunteers to cook nutritious meals for the security staff, who were working extra hours. The bunker's library set up a special display of books about the Athenaeum and IHQ, which there were only three in total (they were a children's fantasy trilogy), and Luna and Meerie-Meerie scoured nearly every page of them as well as the rest of the library books in their spare time when they weren't at the hospital visiting with Mysco.

While most were preparing for the worst, Riff and Stenolly spent most of their free time together practising sign language. Stenolly was a quick learner, and it made her and Riff's communication stronger and deeper. They found themselves signing into the late hours of the night as they talked about music, learned about one another's planets, and reminisced about their childhoods—which were surprisingly similar, given that they had both lived indoors for most of their lives. Riff's feelings for Stenolly were growing every day, but he didn't dare tell her. He'd never been in a relationship before, and he didn't know if Stenolly even felt the same way. There were times when he'd catch her looking at him in what seemed like a more-than-friends way—and she seemed genuinely interested in learning as much as she could about him. But he couldn't risk telling her how he felt. They had become such close friends, and he didn't want to lose her. If it meant hiding his feelings and still being able to have her in his life as his friend, he'd surely keep it that way, no questions asked.

On this particular mid-June evening, the pair were conversing about Stenolly's favourite dances when she asked, "Can I dance for you?"

Riff smiled excitedly. "I would love that."

Stenolly flipped through the stack of records, picked out a colourful vinyl, and placed it gently on the record player.

The vinyl spun, and music started to play. It was piano music, ethereal and filled with gentle harmonies, like music meant to help someone fall asleep. Chords and resonant frequencies filled Riff's ears as Stenolly gracefully glided around the living room, extending her arms above her head and pointing her toes. Her eyes were closed, and she breathed in and out with each movement.

Riff watched, mesmerised by Stenolly's dance. Her movements were slow and controlled, and her balance was unbelievable when she stood on the tips of her toes. Her leaps made her seem to float, and her landings were as light as if she were the weight of a fafflin feather. Her hair bounced in sync with her movements, adding to the spectacle of the performance. Riff was entranced.

The music ended, and Stenolly dipped into a bow and curtsied to Riff.

He couldn't help but smile and clap for her. "Beautiful," he signed.

She waltzed over to the record player and put on something a bit more upbeat and jazzier. She beckoned for him to join her.

"No," Riff said, sinking deeper into the couch and crossing his legs. "I don't dance."

"Then I'll teach you," she signed in reply. She held her hand out for him to take.

Riff bit his lip. No one had ever seen him dance. Perhaps Ann Lou had a time or two when they were kids and she would charge into his room in the morning to turn his music down, but other than that, Riff McHubbard did not dance in front of anyone. He even had a hard time watching himself in the mirror!

"I dunno," he said.

"No one is here," said Stenolly.

It was true. Luna and Meerie-Meerie were at the hospital visiting Mysco, Ann Lou was out kicking a ball somewhere and being extroverted, and Gwympy was sleeping, as he deduced from the hog-like snores honking from behind the tie-dyed curtain over her bedroom.

"Please," Stenolly urged.

Riff sighed in surrender and stood up from the sofa. He took her hand, which felt warm and welcoming. She led him into a jive style of ballroom dance. When she lifted his hand up high, he bent down (being substantially taller than her) and twirled underneath. He couldn't keep up with her quick steps, but he improvised as best he could, which sent her into a fit of giggles. Riff was delighted when she laughed out loud; he felt privileged to hear her voice firsthand. It was a rarity and a pleasure few others got to experience.

They danced for a little while longer. Riff stepped on Stenolly's toes a few times and almost tripped over the sofa once, but after about half an hour his stumbling decreased and the two were dancing in sync. Finally, Riff collapsed onto the sofa, taking in deep breaths.

"That was a workout," he laughed. "I'm good for a few weeks now."

"You're a good dancer," she signed.

"That's the biggest lie you've ever told," he replied.

"Well, perhaps," she smiled.

The vinyl stopped spinning, and the two sat in silence for a little while. Riff started to casually put his arm around Stenolly's shoulders; however, he managed to tangle one of the buttons on his jacket in her curls, after which he decided he wasn't smooth enough to make a move after all.

"I'm going to go," he said, hopping up.

"We'll sort out a plan soon for the Athenaeum," said Stenolly.

"Yes. See you later," said Riff.

Stenolly walked up to Riff and stood close to him. He was so afraid of making a fool of himself that he didn't dare to breathe or move. Then she gently put her arms around his waist, and he hugged her back. They stayed like that briefly. He could feel both their hearts beating rather fast.

*She must be winded from the dancing is all*, he thought, trying to push away the urge to hold her for any longer.

Blushing, Riff let go of her and walked out the door, releasing his held breath as soon as she shut the door behind him. He stepped across the hall to his own door and opened it, sighing heavily, rethinking his and Stenolly's parting. His thoughts were interrupted when he saw Luna and Spex sitting at their kitchen table.

"Riff!" exclaimed Spex, his zany spectacle frames flashing. "What a surprise!"

"To see me in my own apartment?" said Riff. "What're you doing here?"

"I brought over some additional information about the treatment system that may be helpful for Luna's condition. I've only just arrived, so I can give you both the rundown if you'd like," he replied.

"Sure," said Riff, pulling up a chair next to Luna. "You okay with this?" he asked Luna.

"Yes. I requested the information," said Luna, twiddling her fingers. "It's been in the back of my mind ever since we received the spectacles. I figure that if it's low risk, it might be of interest, especially if it means I can be of more help with saving Elbina."

Riff could tell she was nervous. He sat closer to her and patted her shoulder.

"I can definitely reassure you," said Spex. In front of him was a small bottle of clear liquid and two round lenses. He held up the bottle. "This is the solution that dissolves the cataracts. You put a drop in each eye three times per day for a week, and the cataracts disappear. The only side effect you may experience is light sensitivity, but that will lessen as your eyes adjust."

"And the lenses?" asked Luna.

"In healthy eyes, certain eye muscles enable the crystalline lens within the eye to focus on near and far objects in a process called accommodation. Once your cataracts are dissolved, your eyes won't be able to accommodate right away; you'll need to gradually strengthen the muscles involved because they've weakened over time. These lenses have state-of-the-art adaptive optics that retrain your eyes to utilise the eye muscles for accommodation. The lenses will change shape depending on what you are focusing on, near or far, to allow for clear vision. Initially the lenses will provide more correction so as not to strain your eye muscles. Over time, the amount of correction slowly decreases, allowing your eye muscles to strengthen gradually."

"That sounds amazing!" said Riff. "This is exactly what you've needed from the beginning, Luna!"

Luna didn't appear as convinced as her brother. She continued to fidget with her fingers.

"May I ask about the reasons for your hesitation?" asked Spex. "Perhaps I can answer questions about the technology to put your mind at ease."

Luna shook her head. "I trust you—I mean, your design. It's fascinating, truly. I know that these opportunities are few and far between . . . but I've always been quite proud of myself for how well I've adapted to my vision loss and how little impact it has had on the way I live. I don't want to lose the thing that has made me different. The thing that has made me special."

"Luna," said Riff, placing his hand over her still-fidgeting hands, "you will always be special. It doesn't go away just because there's an opportunity presented to you that might make your life a bit easier. You're taking a very brave step in order to help find Elbina."

Spex nodded and smiled.

Luna beamed. "Thank you both."

"Shall I swap out your lenses and you can administer your first dose of drops?" asked Spex.

"Go for it," said Luna, confidently.

Spex popped out the plano lenses in Luna's red frames, then pressed her new lenses into place. He handed her the bottle of drops, and she easily applied her first dose of treatment to dissolve her cataracts and restore her vision.

"Anything yet?" asked Riff, only seconds after the first dose.

"Hmm, nothing," said Luna.

"You won't notice anything until tomorrow. Expect to see general shapes over the next few days, followed by a few days of light sensitivity. You will get used to it, I promise," said Spex warmly.

"Will I have my vision back in a few days? That's when we're going to the Athenaeum," said Luna.

"Technically, you can expedite the treatment. Take five doses per day, but no more than that. And you must limit eye movement. I have a pair of spectacles you can wear during the first few days of treatment to negate nystagmus—rapid and involuntary eye movements. Perhaps those will help. I will retrieve them. Would you by any chance like to come with me, Luna? We can grab a bite to eat and talk more. I'd love to recommend some reading material. I have plenty of scientific papers that I think you might enjoy," said Spex, smoothly.

Luna's expression brightened, and her cheeks turned rosy. "I'd love to." She grabbed her book, and she and Spex left the apartment.

"Ahh, alone time," said Riff, heading toward his bed.

His eyes had been closed for barely ten seconds when Ann Lou walked in. He peered out the gap in his recently acquired music note-themed curtain and saw that her normally pin-straight hair was slightly dishevelled and she had a bruise on her right knee. Worried, Riff sat up quickly and whipped open his curtain, only to find Ann Lou smiling.

"What happened to you?" asked Riff.

"Soccer," she beamed. "Well, football."

"You having fun beating everyone to a pulp?" asked Riff.

"Yup," she replied. "Although I really wish I had more of an opportunity to play with Mysco. I'm going to visit her in the hospital after I fix my hair. Want to come with me?"

Riff groaned. All he wanted to do was have a lie-down, but he still felt very guilty and responsible for what had happened to Mysco on Austere Avenue.

"Sure," he replied.

"Where's Luna? I'm sure she'd want to join, too," said Ann Lou.

"Luna is on a date with the jolly glasses lad," said Riff.

"A *date*?" said Ann Lou, gasping. "We have to spy!"

"Nooo way! I don't want to see any romantic happenings with any of you. You are all still my little sisters, and no one must ever touch you. Apollo is still on my hit list," said Riff, crossing his arms and huffing.

"Well, you certainly sound like Apollo," snorted Ann Lou. "And Luna is your big little sister?"

"I don't care how much older she is, she is too young to be involved with anyone in front of me," declared Riff.

"Oh, grow up," said Ann Lou, combing her hair. "We're forced to watch you and Stenolly gush over each other all the time."

"What're you talking about?" snapped Riff, his cheeks reddening.

"Oh, please! You two are obsessed with each other. Have you kissed her yet?" asked Ann Lou.

"I would do nothing of the sort!" said Riff, taken aback. "She's not interested in me."

Ann Lou raised an eyebrow at him. "Really? Are you right in the head? I bet she could kiss you and profess her love for you, and you *still* wouldn't believe that she likes you."

"For all we know, it could be Therian tradition to kiss and profess love to a friend," said Riff.

"Ahh, yes. You are mental," snickered Ann Lou.

Riff rushed to the mirror where she was braiding her hair. "You think she likes me?"

"No," said Ann Lou sarcastically. "I think she spends every waking moment with you because she has nothing better to do with her life. She must *despise* you."

"Should I tell her? How do I tell her?" asked Riff, gripping Ann Lou's prosthetic arm.

"Just tell her! That's what Apollo did to me," said Ann Lou.

"Oh, no. Firstly, Apollo is a hunky Epitonian who is in shape, athletic, and suave. All things that I am not. Secondly, I'm not good with words. I'm actually quite deplorable with them," said Riff.

"'Deplorable' is a good word," said Ann Lou.

"I only know that one because Luna said I smelled deplorable this morning, and she wasn't saying it in a nice tone," said Riff.

"Then tell her how you feel without words. Perhaps with a gesture that would be meaningful to her. Make her dinner or something like that. Girls love food!" said Ann Lou.

"A gesture . . . okay, I can do that," he said.

"Let's go see Mysco. I need to tell her about the kick we learned today," said Ann Lou.

She sprinted a few steps toward the door and jumped, kicking one leg into the air and then swinging the other one even higher up. Riff kept a healthy distance from her as they left the apartment.

Riff and Ann Lou made their way to the lift and up to the third level. Ann Lou guided Riff through the hospital corridors, around patients' beds, and directly through the middle of a group of healthcare professionals who were mesmerised by a patient whose nose had grown to the size and rotundness of a skeebamelon.

Ann Lou burst through a set of doors labelled Lost Causes Unit, and Riff followed her. The hallways changed from a sterile white colour to a dull grey.

"You'd think they would at least spruce this unit up with some colour for the poor sods who are stuck here," said Ann Lou, sounding disgusted.

They rounded a corner, and then Ann Lou gently knocked on the frosted glass of the first door on the left.

A blurry image of Meerie-Meerie approached. She opened the door and gestured for them to enter. "Welcome to the LCU," she said dismally.

Riff's heart sank as he walked in. The room was as dismal as the hall, and Mysco lay trembling in the bed. Meerie-Meerie whispered to them, "She gets a little spooked whenever people come in." Then she rushed back to Mysco's side and tended to her, stroking her hair gently to calm her down.

"How's she doing?" asked Ann Lou.

"She hasn't slept in days. Reality seems to be slipping away from her. She keeps having panic attacks and hyperventilating, so the nurses hooked her up to this apparatus to maintain regular breathing patterns."

Riff walked to Mysco's bedside. A breathing mask hid most of her face, but she stared at Riff with a clear look of terror in her eyes. He watched as her breaths escalated. Riff started to touch Mysco's hand to reassure her, but Meerie-Meerie slapped it away.

"Don't touch her!" she snapped. "She doesn't trust anyone right now. She can't tell the difference between one of her friends and a stranger."

"Is there anything the doctors can do?" asked Ann Lou.

"No," said Meerie-Meerie, looking back at Mysco. "She's nearly gone. It's just a matter of time before she leaves."

"Why can't you hold her back?" asked Riff.

"Because the Insomnyus are expecting her. If she doesn't arrive at the moment she officially changes over, they will come looking for her. They broke the skin when they attacked her, so they know her scent. They'd easily find her and discover the bunker."

"Then we need to go with her," said Ann Lou. "She might lead us to Fantasly."

"She'll be too dangerous. We'd need to keep a safe distance. Sweet little Mysco," said Meerie-Meerie, a tear falling down her cheek.

Riff said, "That's probably the safest way for us to do this, then. We follow Mysco to Austere Avenue. Obviously the Insomnyus won't attack her, since she'll be one of them—"

"Don't say that!" Meerie-Meerie snapped. She jumped to her feet and pointed a stern finger in Riff's face. "Don't say things like that in her presence! In fact, don't say them in front of any of us. You have no idea what Stenolly and I are going through!"

Riff breathed calmly. "I do know what you're going through. Our sister is an Insomnyus, too. But we're going to save her and Mysco. If we don't, I'll die trying."

Meerie-Meerie stepped back from Riff and slumped into a chair. She nodded and squeezed her temples with her fingers and stayed still for a while.

* * *

Back at the McHubbard apartment the next evening, Ann Lou helped Riff tie a bowtie around his neck. He attempted to pat down his hair, but the moppiness was too strong for any amount of mousse to tame.

"I look like a mess," he pouted.

"You look adorable. Now hold still," Ann Lou replied, pulling the tie into its knot.

Riff gagged. "Ack, are you trying to kill me before the date even starts? Loosen it!"

"You are such a drama king," Ann Lou said, rolling her eyes. "Luna, how was your date yesterday? Any words of wisdom for our brother as he embarks on a new journey?"

"It wasn't a date," Luna called from her bed as she trailed her finger across the page of a book, a library book that Spex had recommended.

"How is it that the both of you are so completely clueless when it comes to dating? For goodness' sake, even Elbina does better than you!" Ann Lou laughed.

"Spex just thinks I'm interesting because of my vision, that's all," said Luna. "He's able to use me as inspiration for new designs."

"I think that he has a bit more substance than that," said Ann Lou. "I'll work on you next. But you, Riff: you are officially ready for your date. Now go get your girl!" Ann Lou cheered.

Riff exhaled, took one last look in the mirror, picked up the droopy flowers he'd chosen from the bunker garden, and saluted his sisters. "I shall channel the energy of the great Ann Lou McHubbard. Wish me luck."

As he walked to the door, he heard Luna call out, "Don't channel too much of her energy, or else Clorin might have a cousin soon."

"Hey!" he shot back. Ann Lou's hooting was the last thing he heard before he hastily shut the door.

Riff knocked on the Cantileerys' door and waited nervously, gripping the flowers with sweaty palms. He was pleased to see Stenolly open the door to greet him, but she looked distressed. Her eyes were puffy, as if she had been crying.

"Erm, hello," he said. The monologue he had prepared suddenly dissipated into his garbled mind. "You all right?"

"Not really. I just got home from visiting Mysco. It's difficult to see her like this," she signed.

"I visited her as well. I'm so sorry you're going through this," signed Riff.

"Thanks for coming by. Why are you dressed so nicely?" she asked.

"I wanted to ask if you have time to come on a date with me?" he signed back.

She stared back at him in confusion and replied, "On a what? I don't know that word."

"Oh," he said aloud. "Erm, date. This is the sign for date," he said, demonstrating. He then handed her the flowers.

Stenolly's face brightened up, and she took the flowers graciously. "I would love to go on a date with you. Let me change quickly," she signed, and then she sprinted to her room, her wildfire hair bouncing behind her.

Riff stepped in the doorway and paced back and forth as he waited. Out of the corner of his eye, he saw Gwympy sitting at the kitchen table, holding her head and wincing in pain.

"Evening, Gwympy," Riff said, nodding in her direction.

"Who are you again?" she asked, squinting at him.

"Griffin McHubbard, from across the hall," he replied.

"Ah, yes, you retrieved the Tarottriptan for me," said Gwympy.

There was an awkward pause that lasted for a few moments, and then Riff broke the silence.

"Gwympy, I've been wondering . . . do you know if there's a timeline for when the GeoLapse will arrive on Thera? Or whether they will be successful?"

"What's that?" asked Gwympy, still holding her head.

"The prediction you made. We saw the GeoLapse coming after me and my sisters," said Riff.

"Grufftin, the more accurate the reading, the less I remember about it. I could give you a half-arsed one if you'd like," she said with one eye open.

"I guess something is better than nothing," he replied, pulling up a chair next to her.

Gwympy raised one hand to the spirits and closed her eyes. "Spirits!" she exclaimed in a tired tone. "Answer the boy's question." She swirled her arm around his head, then swatted the air.

Riff held his breath and waited patiently for an answer.

Gwympy finally opened her eyes and said very seriously, "Sometime between tomorrow and twenty years from now."

Riff exhaled in annoyance and pushed his chair away from the table. He almost said, "That was half-arsed, all right," but that would have been rude. He didn't want the thought of his father and the GeoLapse to ruin his special evening anyways.

Riff decided to pass the time by flipping through Stenolly's record collection. Once he was halfway through the piano ballads section, she appeared from behind her bedroom curtain. Riff stood to greet her, and his jaw dropped. She wore a beautiful forest green jumpsuit and ballerina shoes. Her green handbag matched her outfit and the frames of her spectacles. Her hair was tied into a bun that looked like a puffy round bush on top of her head. Riff thought she looked just as beautiful as ever, and he smiled as she walked up to him.

Stenolly waved to Gwympy as they strode toward the door. Riff nodded at the old woman, and she shouted after them, "Have her home by breakfast!"

As Riff led Stenolly down the hall toward the lift, he couldn't find any words. How did he get so lucky to be holding the arm of this beautiful woman? He hoped he could manage not to ruin the evening. She was already enduring enough stress; she didn't need him adding to it.

"Where are we going for our date?" Stenolly signed, gazing into his eyes sweetly.

"You'll see," replied Riff. "By the way, you look beautiful. You always do."

"Thank you," replied Stenolly, blushing.

Block A was quiet in the evenings, and this evening was no different. They took the lift up to level fifteen, where all the school classrooms were situated. Riff and Stenolly moseyed to a room labelled Miss Treble's Music Room. Riff opened the door of the darkened classroom, then flipped the light switch, revealing colourfully decorated walls and musical instruments galore. There was a piano at the head of the room—most likely played by Miss Treble as she led the school children in endless verses of Therian nursery rhymes.

Set up in the middle of the room were a drum set and an acoustic guitar. To anyone not entirely familiar with the instruments, they looked pretty much identical to their Earth counterparts—but to a practised musician, they were worlds different. On the drum set, the cymbals were where the toms would be, the bass drum was where the snare would be, and the snare was where the cymbals would be. The guitar's differences weren't as obvious as the drum set, but the strings were made of an indestructible Therian metal, which came in handy with the razor-sharp metal pick. Riff had also connected a looper pedal and a small speaker to this guitar.

Riff ushered Stenolly to have a seat in a beanbag chair that he had previously set up in front of the instruments. He felt so nervous that the blood in his body was draining from his fingers, and he had to keep rubbing his hands together to keep them warm and ready for his performance. Intrusive thoughts continuously penetrated his mind, deflating his plan to show Stenolly just how much he cared for her and how similar they were. He did his best to push the thoughts away and focused on the music he had prepared.

Riff took the acoustic guitar and signed to Stenolly, "I really enjoyed when you shared your passion for dancing with me. I want to return the favour and show you a bit of me as well."

Stenolly's face lit up, and she sat upright in the beanbag chair and focused solely on Riff. Normally Riff wasn't afraid to play music, especially when Matt and Joe were around. The three of them could play around anyone and he'd be calm, whether it be their entire school, a celebrity, or even an axe murderer. He didn't care what any of those people thought of him. But he cared very much about the opinion of the person before him now.

Thankfully for Riff, Matt had taught him a few tidbits on guitar. Riff took a deep breath and held the Therian guitar in position.

Riff played a simple tune in four measures. It was slow, rhythmic, and tranquil. Then he tapped the looper pedal with his foot and stopped playing. The first tune continued to play through the amplifier, and he started his second tune, harmonising with the first tune. After another four measures, he hit the looper pedal again. The two harmonising tunes continued playing from the amplifier. Next he played a faster sequence of notes, a melody to his overture. It was simple but colourful. The guitar sang with all the tenderness that Stenolly made him feel. He closed his eyes as he played. He imagined him and her sitting together listening to the record player, and his music resonating from it. Visions of tender moments and playful adventures lit up their eyes as the music narrated their story. The low bassline notes resembled their hearts beating as one, and the high melodies were the two of them imagining their lives together, travelling and playing music.

Riff tapped the looper pedal again and the three guitar tunes continued to play. He opened his eyes and saw that Stenolly's focus had not budged. He breathed a sigh of relief that she hadn't dashed out of the classroom when he wasn't looking.

Now, he was going to show her an even deeper side of him. As the guitar lines continued looping, he moved a metre to the right and sat at the Therian drum set. He felt surprisingly comfortable at it despite its unfamiliar configuration. Instead of banging on the drums with his head in the Therian fashion, Riff opted for some wooden sporks that he'd found in a trunk of percussion instruments by the wall. When he felt the sporks in his hands, a combination of warmth and sadness washed over him. He so dearly missed his friends from back home and yearned to play with them again. Riff always admired his friends for their musicality and creative originality. Each jam session was different but equally as fun and impressive. Sometimes the beat would be heavy metal, just like their favourite band, and other times it ventured to a lighter, more pop-like route. But he needed to push that thought out of his head, because the music he was playing now was meant to be passionate and romantic. He played a simple beat on the bass drum, then built upon that with a more complex pattern. When he had that down, he filled in the spaces in the melody with riffs. He felt the music enveloping his body, and his mind was transported to the clouds. Stenolly was present with him in the clouds. This time, she was dancing along to his music. When Riff opened his eyes this time, Stenolly was dancing in front of him. She twirled and fluttered around the room, her hair bounding beautifully to the beat. She was clearly in a musical trance as well. Riff smiled as he kept playing.

After an impressive finish, Riff set down his spork sticks. As the three guitar lines continued their conversation through the looper, Riff walked up to Stenolly and reached out a hand. She completed a twirl, then saw his extended hand and took it in hers. She led him into a slower dance along to the guitar, and he followed as best he could. She dipped him a few times, making him laugh out loud. In addition to being creative and confident as a dancer, she was also surprisingly strong. They laughed when Riff tripped over the beanbag chair, pulling them both down into it. The guitar continued to loop as they gazed into one another's eyes.

Riff had to say something, even though he felt like he was about to be sick. He signed to her. "I find it really difficult to express myself outside of music. But I want you to know that I really like you. Not just as a friend, but as much more. I've never felt this connected to another person before, and I think everything about you is perfect and amazing." He watched her face as she absorbed this information. Her expression was so soft and loving, but he wasn't sure how to interpret it. Maybe she just felt bad for him.

He continued signing. "It's okay if you don't feel the same way. I just couldn't hold it in anymore. I think you're bloody brilliant."

Stenolly smiled brightly and signed back. "I am so thankful for you. I've had a very difficult time conversing with people since my brother died and my parents were taken. My sisters can usually tell what I'm trying to convey, but not on a deep, personal level. You seem to understand me better than anyone. It feels like our souls talk through music. Thank you for offering me the opportunity to have a connection again."

Riff smiled as butterflies rose in his stomach.

"I also really like you," Stenolly added.

The butterflies in his stomach soared up and out of his body. He was overjoyed and in a state of euphoria he'd never experienced before. He pulled Stenolly's face gently toward his, and they shared their first kiss. It felt symphonic, invigorating, and warm. He had no idea if he was kissing her even remotely correctly, but she wasn't pulling away, so he didn't either. Riff felt so connected to Stenolly in that moment. He hoped this connection would never dim—but honestly, how could it?

Finally the kiss ended, and they leaned back from each other.

An idea popped into Riff's head. He dug in his trouser pocket. "For you, my lady, to always remember this moment," he said, holding out his guitar pick. "Be careful, though. It's extremely sharp. I cut myself twice while practicing earlier."

Stenolly beamed as she graciously accepted the pick in her palm. "I don't think I could ever forget this moment," she signed.

Riff's elation was interrupted by the grumbling of his stomach. He asked: "Hungry?"

Stenolly nodded. "I know just the place."

They stood up, and she took his hand and they skipped blissfully out of the classroom and took the lift to level eight, where all the restaurants were located. There was one all-night restaurant: Jonee'z Diner. A few late-night customers were feasting on burgers, chips, and shakes.

Riff and Stenolly devoured their meals. Riff couldn't help but grin proudly as he sipped his skeebamelon shake. He'd secretly dreamed of an evening like this, and he couldn't think of anyone better to share it with. They spent the rest of their evening at the diner, laughing and sampling Therian delicacies. Riff tried fairquat rings, a shrew shake, and a bigwudgy cake. He let Stenolly finish the cake—mainly because it was her favourite, but also because it tasted like mushrooms and lemon, two flavours that he couldn't get on board with mixing.

They strolled happily back to Block A. When they stopped in the hallway between their apartment doors, Riff kissed Stenolly's hand and twirled her on the spot.

"Thank you for a wonderful night," Stenolly signed. "I feel on top of the world. Same thing tomorrow night?"

Riff chuckled. "Anything you want."

"Thanks again for the memory," she signed, holding up the guitar pick. "I'll keep it close."

They hugged goodbye, shared a small kiss, and parted ways.

Riff opened the door to his apartment and felt a vast array of emotions: love, merriment, eagerness for the future, and longing. He missed her already, and he was determined that each day they spent together would be more special for her than the last.

Ann Lou popped out of bed. It was obvious that she had been anxiously awaiting his arrival home. As she tiptoed over to him, he could hear Luna's light snores from her bed.

"So, how did it go?" Ann Lou whispered excitedly.

"It was perfect," Riff beamed.

Ann Lou bounced around the kitchen, whisper-chanting, "Riff's got a girlfriend, Riff's got a girlfriend!"

Riff relayed most of the details of their evening to Ann Lou over steaming cups of tea before they both said goodnight. He omitted only the dance they had shared in the music room. He wanted to keep something just between him and Stenolly—their own little secret musical synchrony.

# CHAPTER 21

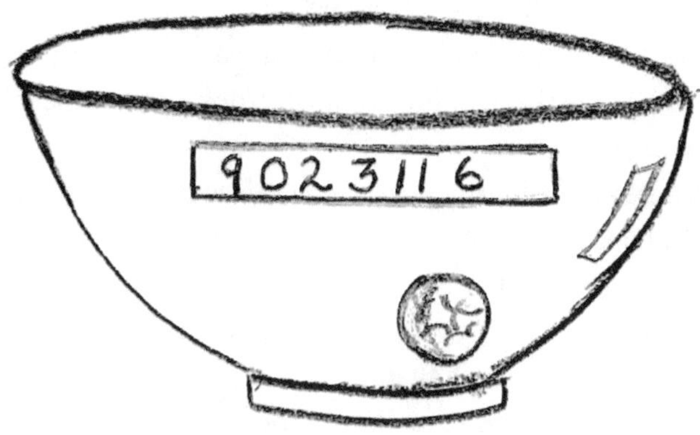

# THE ATHENAEUM

The McHubbards awoke the next morning to the sound of knocking and barking at their door. Ann Lou hurried to the door and opened it to see Stenolly and Bisquit looking terribly distressed. Riff tumbled out of his own bed upon seeing Stenolly and barrelled toward them.

"What's wrong?" asked Ann Lou.

Bisquit barked twice. Stenolly finger-spelled, "Mysco."

"Is she going up to Austere Avenue?" asked Riff with a shaky voice.

Stenolly gulped and signed, "Soon."

"We need to go, then! We'll meet you at the hospital!" shouted Riff, already running back into his bedroom area and tossing on a pair of trousers and a jumper.

To Riff's surprise, he caught sight of Luna checking her hair in the mirror.

"Y-you can see?" Riff asked, astonished.

"A little," Luna said, smiling as she patted down one unruly wavy tress. "I can see the shape of my head! And look—is that the table? And the refrigerator?"

Riff grinned as he hastily put on a pair of socks. He wished so badly that he and Luna could spend more time talking about this momentous milestone. But they both knew they needed to attend to Mysco.

The McHubbard siblings stuffed toast in their mouths and chugged piping hot cups of tea. Less than three minutes after Stenolly's knock, they were all dressed and ready to go. The siblings barrelled down the Block A hallway and leapt onto the nearest lift, even though nearly an entire school class was already huddled on it.

As the lift started moving, an alarm blared throughout the bunker, and everyone they could see on the levels above them stopped walking and dashed into the nearest commercial entrance. The children on the lift seemed terrified.

"What's that alarm for?" Ann Lou asked a small girl she was squished next to.

"Someone is becoming an Insomnyus. We have to give them space to leave," said the girl gravely.

The lift slowly and creakily carried the children to their classrooms on level fifteen. There, they all jumped off quickly and dashed to the nearest classroom, where, hopefully, they would be safe. The lift continued its ascent to level three, and once it arrived, the McHubbards leapt off and swiftly headed toward the hospital entrance. Ann Lou once again guided Riff and Luna through the maze of hospital corridors. If Ann Lou hadn't been there, they could have found Mysco's room just by following the sound of her screams. Healthcare professionals bowed their heads in sorrow as they cleared hallways, pushing other patients that were lying in gurneys into various rooms to make the path clear.

"You can't go in there!" a doctor shouted after the siblings as they bounded through the LCU doors, but the doctor didn't chase after them.

Inside the LCU, the screams were piercing. Riff's heart sank as he listened to Mysco's pain. As they approached Mysco's room, Riff saw Stenolly in a doorway diagonally opposite, beckoning to them. The McHubbards crept into the room with her.

"We need to stay clear of Mysco's room," signed Stenolly. "She's going to leave any minute."

"Where's Meerie-Meerie?" Luna asked, looking around.

"She's still in there. She won't give up trying to get Mysco to stay. The doctors warned her, but she just won't listen," Stenolly replied.

Riff saw Bisquit shaking in fear, his internal organs vibrating along. He held the dog close and petted him, which calmed him down slightly.

They could hear someone speaking amid the screams from the room across the hall. "Mysco, please listen to me! It's your big sister, Meerie-Meerie. And just across the hall is your other big sister, Stenolly. Your favourite little buddy Bisquit is there, too. We all love you!"

Mysco's screams continued unabated. Riff felt horrible that he wasn't able to help. He continued to hold little Bisquit close to his chest.

"I promise to always stay by your side! I will never leave you. Do you understand? You're still one of us, Mysco. Here, in your heart! Don't let them take you! You are stronger than all of them!" Meerie-Meerie continued.

Suddenly, Mysco's screams stopped.

Riff poked his head out of the door in confusion. The hallway was still devoid of any people or medical equipment. "What's going on?" he whispered to Stenolly.

He looked at Stenolly, who was sobbing silently. Riff could only guess that this meant it was over. Mysco had transitioned over from being a human to an Insomnyus. He took Stenolly's hand and squeezed it.

"Mysco, can you hear me?" said a slightly calmer Meerie-Meerie. "If you can hear me, move your eyes, squeeze my hand, do anything you can!"

More silence.

"Mysco, please just—*Mysco, no!*" cried Meerie-Meerie.

Riff could hear the sounds of a struggle. He instinctively popped up from his crouching position, but he was yanked back down by both Stenolly and Bisquit.

"She needs help!" Riff yapped, hoarsely.

"Mysco is dangerous!" Stenolly signed sternly. "She's much stronger than any of us now. You need to stay out of her way!"

"But Meerie-Meerie!" cried Riff.

"She's smart. She's been through this before, with our parents. Trust me," said Stenolly.

Riff kept his eyes on the open door across the hall and listened intently. He heard Meerie-Meerie struggling, then quick footsteps started toward them, and Meerie-Meerie dashed out of the doorway with tears streaming down her cheeks. She ran to Stenolly, and they embraced in a fit of tears.

The McHubbards peeked out of the door and heard slow footsteps in Mysco's room. The door to her room opened, and there stood Mysco with a vacant expression on her face. Riff noted that she wasn't moving quite as robotically as the Insomnyus he had encountered on Austere Avenue, but she definitely wasn't acting like her old self.

Mysco turned right outside of the door and trod at a fervent pace toward the exit of the LCU. She didn't care to check her surroundings; she was solely focused on leaving.

"Please tell me you have a plan devised," said a petrified Meerie-Meerie.

"We have to follow her," whispered Riff. "I'm afraid once we get to Austere Avenue, there really isn't much we can prepare for."

"We need to keep a healthy distance from her, or she'll be suspicious," warned Meerie-Meerie.

"Agreed, but we can't lose her. Let's move!" commanded Ann Lou, leading the group through the doorway and into the hall.

The McHubbards and the Cantileerys followed Mysco as quietly and stealthily as they could, staying at least twenty metres behind her. They spotted healthcare professionals peeking out of rooms to see if the coast was clear. Luna gave them confirmation with a thumbs up.

Once they were outside the hospital, Riff watched as Mysco rode a lift all the way up to the zeroth floor to the entrance to the bunker. It was strange to see the bunker so empty at this time of the morning. Usually, the walkways would have been filled with children going to school, people starting work, and the aromas of coffee and breakfast foods wafting around the entirety of the bunker—but there was none of that this morning, just the deafening alarm warning people to remain sheltered.

Ann Lou led the group to a nearby lift, and they started up after Mysco. She was gazing up at her exit, focused on her imminent departure. When she dismounted the lift, she started up the stairs toward Thevenin and Norton's workshop. Riff hoped that the brothers had made their way to safety as well.

Once Mysco had cleared the bunker entrance and begun her walk through the tunnel, Ann Lou led the group up to the entrance. To their surprise, Thevenin and Norton were trembling as they hid under a workspace table in the back room.

"She gone?" Thevenin uttered.

"She's on her way out. You're safe," said Ann Lou.

"Yowza—Mysco? Poor little gal. She didn't deserve that type o' endin'," sniffled Norton.

"Where're y'all goin'?" asked Thevenin as the twins crawled out from under the table.

"We're going after her. We need to find out the secrets of the Insomnyus. It's the only way to help our sisters," said Riff, gesturing to the Cantileerys.

Norton screeched in terror. "You can' go out there all by yerselves!"

"We have to!" said Ann Lou sternly. "I'd bet either of you would do the same for each other!"

Thevenin and Norton looked at one another and said in unison, "No, we wouldn.'"

"But we do have some things you might find useful while yer up there," added Thevenin.

Norton went to a cabinet, shuffled some items around, and returned with a zapper for each of them.

"An' here," said Thevenin, "is generation one of this bad boy." He handed Riff a tiny, black box.

"What's this?" Riff asked, opening the lid.

"Careful with that!" said Thevenin, slapping the lid closed. "That's the 'splodey device. We only got one, so you need to use it at just the right moment, and *only* if you need to."

Riff gently placed the box in his back pocket.

"How does it work?" asked Ann Lou.

"It 'splodes!" said Norton theatrically, spreading his arms. "It releases powerful currents of electricity to everything around it. But yer also at risk when you detonate it. Y'all'd better take these."

Norton handed them each a pair of long rubber gloves. He even had two pairs of mini socks prepared for Bisquit to wear on his paws.

"Fantastic, thank you!" said Ann Lou. "We'd best be going, or else we'll lose track of Mysco."

"We won' hold y'all up anymore. But please, be careful. Use the zappers at any opportunity. If you run into trouble, come straight back," said Thevenin.

"Will do. Thank you, lads," said Riff as they went through the wooden door.

Riff led the others down the tunnel in a quick sprint. They could just see Mysco's legs dangling up ahead, indicating that she was pulling herself up into the trunk at Building Blocks. The light that shone through the trunk dimmed, then disappeared as she closed the trunk.

"Hurry!" Riff urged.

They arrived at the end of the tunnel, and Bisquit offered to be the first to enter the store above. Riff held the trunk lid open just enough for a peek, and he saw Mysco exiting the store.

"Up you go." Riff hoisted the dog up into the trunk, and Bisquit leapt from his arms and landed safely on the floor.

Riff climbed up and out next, then turned to help the girls up. Bisquit growled from behind him.

"What's wrong, boy?" whispered Ann Lou, kneeling down and patting the dog's head.

Bisquit stared out the store window and continued his light growls. Outside, on Austere Avenue, an army of Insomnyus were marching past. After they were gone, Riff carefully opened the door of the store, made sure the coast was clear, and then looked in the direction the horde had gone. In the distance he could see Mysco's blonde hair. She was at the head of the group.

"It looks like they're all following her to IHQ," said Riff. "Maybe we can sneak in behind them and they'll be too focused on Mysco to notice."

"That makes this venture slightly easier," said Ann Lou.

Out of the corner of his eye, Riff saw something glinting in the sunlight. It was so subtle he almost ignored it. But he flicked his eyes over to it, then retreated into Building Blocks and closed the door.

"Everybody down!" he commanded.

Everyone obeyed and lay on their stomachs, including little Bisquit.

"What's wrong?" whispered Luna.

"GeoLapse," Riff whispered back. "They made it. They're patrolling the streets."

Almost on cue, a pair of GeoLapse ran past Building Blocks. They appeared slightly perplexed, looking every which way and holding their batons and other weaponry at the ready. The GeoLapse had never been known for their cleverness, more for brute force and strong presence.

"How do we get past them?" asked Ann Lou, peeking through the window.

"It looks like they're following the Insomnyus. If we hold back a bit, we may still be able to sneak in behind them," said Meerie-Meerie.

"Right. Let's move, then. I don't see any other GeoLapse down the road. Maybe it's just those two," said Riff, slowly standing up.

"Bisquit and I will lead," said Ann Lou. "Riff and Stenolly, you stay behind Luna and Meerie-Meerie and keep an eye out for any stray Insomnyus or GeoLapse."

Bisquit yipped and joined Ann Lou at the front of their group. The rest of them obeyed and assumed their positions as they exited the store and dashed down one of the alleys off Austere Avenue. Bisquit led them on a back-alley route to minimise their chances of being seen.

As they approached the end of Austere Avenue, the colossal fortress of IHQ towered above them. They poked their heads around the final shop at the corner of the avenue and watched as a long line of Insomnyus marched through the front entranceway. They were followed closely by several dozen GeoLapse. The McHubbards and the Cantileerys stayed quiet and covert until the last of the GeoLapse had entered IHQ. Riff heard sniffles in front of him. Meerie-Meerie was trembling, and Stenolly embraced her.

"There's still hope," said Luna warmly.

Riff said, "We can do this."

"Let's move," Ann Lou ordered in a soft voice. They walked swiftly but quietly to IHQ and lined up against the front wall where they couldn't be seen through the entrance.

Riff peeked around one last time down the avenue and the alley they had come up from. No one was following them. "Good from the back," he said.

The group dashed through the door into a rather drab-looking lobby. Two staircases were situated at the far end of the lobby. A sign on the wall between the staircases read:

## *Athenaeum ↗*
## *↙ Fantasly's Lair*

"There it is!" exclaimed Riff. "Up the stairs!"

"We can't just barge up the stairs," snapped Luna. "We need to be more discreet."

"Where else can we go besides Fantasly's Lair?" asked Meerie-Meerie.

"There's a directory over there," signed Stenolly. "Just by the lift." She pointed toward a placard on a side wall next to a set of rusty grey doors.

Riff and Stenolly jogged over to the lift, and the others followed. Riff read the directory aloud:

| | |
|---|---|
| *Basement:* | *Offices (staff only)* |
| *Ground Level:* | *Main Lobby* |
| *Level 1:* | *Athenaeum* |
| *Levels 2–4:* | *Library Stacks* |
| *Level 5:* | *Rafters (staff only)* |

"We should go to the rafters. We may be able to spy from there," said Luna.

"What if the Insomnyus are waiting for us when the lift door opens? Or what if some are on patrol in the rafters?" asked Ann Lou.

Luna pondered for a moment. "Everyone stand against the wall with your zappers at the ready. Riff, take off your spectacles. If the Insomnyus are in the lift, you won't immediately look like an intruder to them. Then we can zap them before they get too close to you."

Riff stood aghast. "Me? Why me?"

Luna threw Riff a disappointed look.

Riff sighed. "Fine. You're right. I'll do it. But please act quickly. If they can smell fear, I'm a dead man."

The rest of the group agreed and assumed their positions against the wall with zappers held at the ready. Riff removed his spectacles and held them behind his back. He pushed the ↑ button with a trembling finger to call the lift. After a dull *ding*, the doors creaked open. Riff stood as still as his trembling body could stand for a few seconds, but no one was on the lift.

Riff sucked in a breath of air and ushered the rest of the group in. Once they were all piled in, Riff jabbed the 5 button. The lift creaked into motion. The ascent was slightly rough, as if the lift hadn't been maintained in years. They watched the floor counter nervously.

"Everyone against the wall, and keep your zappers ready," said Luna. "Riff, less shaking this time."

"I have to do this again?" whined Riff.

Stenolly brushed his arm affectionately. Riff looked into her eyes and nodded. He wanted his sisters and the Cantileerys to trust him. He could do it.

Everyone assumed their positions once again. Riff wore a theatrically deadened look on his face, but once the lift door opened on the fifth and topmost floor, no one was present in the shadowy space of the rafters.

Riff relaxed his face and breathed a sigh of relief. "All clear," he whispered.

A high-pitched buzz was accompanied by the more distant rumble of a crowd. They stepped from the lift onto a narrow walkway, and the doors closed behind them. Stenolly held Riff's hand. Bisquit stayed close by Meerie-Meerie. Ann Lou and Luna took the first courageous steps out of the lift.

The walkway ran around the perimeter of the space. In the centre was a truss of steel beams linking the exterior walls to the roof. Electric lights hung from the underside of the truss, brightly illuminating the space below but leaving the rafter space in relative darkness.

"It's so dark up here, I can't see much," whispered Luna.

"Neither can I," said Riff.

Ann Lou tiptoed to the edge of the walkway. Holding onto a steel beam, she peered over the edge of the walkway and down through the roof truss into the Athenaeum. Then she crouched and looked back at the others.

"Mysco is down there," she mouthed.

The others crept out to where Ann Lou was. The Athenaeum reminded Riff of the layout of the bunker, except this space was boxy instead of cylindrical. The second, third, and fourth levels were filled with rows of pink, glowing objects. The floor of the first level was packed almost wall to wall with Insomnyus. GeoLapse were guarding the perimeter and the entrance to the stairwell.

It took Riff only a few seconds to identify the small figure of Mysco. Her prominent blonde hair stuck out as she stood on a dais in front of the dense crowd of Insomnyus. He looked for Elbina in the crowd. He couldn't find her, but he was appalled to see numerous black-suited GeoLapse standing amidst the Insomnyus. It was not just a few GeoLapse who had come to Thera on a scouting mission; it was a small army of them.

"Why are the GeoLapse just standing there?" Riff asked.

Before the McHubbards and Cantileerys could confer, the lights dimmed suddenly. The effect was startling for the group, as they were very close to the lighting just below them. On the spotlit dais, they saw Mysco being joined by a round pink creature who towered over her.

"Is that a giant . . . brain?" whispered Ann Lou.

Riff squinted to focus on the creature. "It sure looks like it," he whispered back.

Then the brain began to speak. Its booming voice reverberated through the Athenaeum.

"Now that we've all arrived and settled down, I wanted to welcome you all back to my Athenaeum. Most of you present today have been here before, and some of you, many times. We do have a few guests in our midst, and one guest of honour in particular. But before that, I wanted to thank the Insomnyus here before me.

"The Insomnyus are what continue to make planet Thera a more knowledgeable place. Without your help, I wouldn't be the astute, universally omnipotent being that I am today. What a waste for each individual human to have their own brain confined within their skull! The rarity of great scientific discoveries is proof that one brain working on its own is simply not enough.

"But Thera is not settling for mediocrity. I, Fantasly of the Amygdala galaxy, am collecting all of your knowledge into one archive. Thera's knowledge will be mirrored into my mind and merged with that of an ever-growing number of worlds to create one knowledge base containing all the knowledge in the universe!

"With the help of external technology, I rededicated this Athenaeum to host my knowledge base. The collection has only continued to expand, thanks to all of your involuntary participation. We now accept our guest of honour, Insomnyus number 9023116, to our cohort! I look forward to all the knowledge you will provide, although you do seem a bit young and naive to contribute anything novel."

Fantasly laughed heartily, and the Insomnyus joined in with robotic laughs of their own.

To his left, Riff could see Meerie-Meerie shaking her head.

"No matter," Fantasly continued. "I must save you by taking your brain's contents into my own. Let us begin the brain drain process! You two up front, I think you both will want to take part in the draining of this new recruit."

Two Insomnyus stepped forward: a middle-aged man with moppy brown hair and a middle-aged woman with curly, fiery red hair. Meerie-Meerie and Stenolly choked back sobs. Riff squeezed Stenolly's hand. When she looked him in the eyes, tears were streaming down her cheeks. She held up a shaky hand and signed, "Our parents."

Riff's heart sank. He had some idea what they were going through, having seen his own mother as an empty husk on Mortalok in the Time Belt. But he thought what Stenolly and Meerie-Meerie were going through had to be even worse. Their parents weren't dead; they were hostages in their own still-living bodies. He couldn't imagine what seeing his mother in this state would do to him. His father, on the other hand, was probably in the Athenaeum somewhere, and that thought hadn't twigged until Stenolly mentioned her parents. He'd been told he looked just like his father, and the thought that he might catch a glimpse of him now made Riff sick to his stomach. He averted his eyes temporarily from the crowd below.

On the dais, the stone-faced Cantileery parents each held onto one of Mysco's arms. Then the entire dais began mechanically rising slowly. The McHubbards and non-Insomnyus Cantileerys backed away slightly from the edge of the walkway to avoid being seen. The dais rose, tracked by the spotlight, all the way to the fourth floor. A walkway materialised one tile at a time out of the side of the dais and connected to the fourth floor, and the Cantileery parents robotically led their daughter across it and onto the floor, closely followed by the slithering Fantasly.

Riff could see Fantasly more clearly now. Nestled under his frontal lobe were a pair of eyeballs. Riff winced at the sight of the eyeballs, which were attached to Fantasly's brainy body by their optic nerves. He had a long, thick, medulla that trailed behind him like a snake as he slithered forward.

The crowd below watched as Fantasly and the Insomnyus Cantileerys walked past a few rows of stacks. Each aisle was lined with chairs, each of which had a glass bowl above it containing what looked like a single glowing pink light bulb. Mysco was led to a chair under some loose tubes that hung from an empty glass bowl.

The parents sat Mysco down on the chair. Now that Mysco was on the fourth floor, it was much easier for Riff to see her face. He detected a slight fear in her expression that the other Insomnyus didn't have. They never really emoted at all, actually. She didn't look fully human, but it seemed to Riff that a little part of her was still very much alive. Riff squeezed Stenolly's hand again, but she and her sister had both turned away from the scene unfolding one level below them.

"Begin!" boomed Fantasly.

The parents hooked the loose tubes to Mysco's head, then stood back next to Fantasly. Riff watched as the expression on Mysco's face changed from slight fear to confusion as pink sludge flowed from her head through the tubes and up into the glass bowl above her head. The pink sludge started amassing in the centre of the bowl. The confused look on Mysco's face was now replaced with the typical Insomnyus expression, devoid of emotion, knowingness, and any sense of control. Mysco's brain matter buzzed and sizzled in the bowl as it assumed a spherical shape, and then it began to glow.

"Let's all officially congratulate Insomnyus 9023116 on her induction! The process is complete—her brain is mine!"

Claps from the Insomnyus below followed Fantasly's celebratory remarks. Their claps were slow and simultaneous, an eerie, soulless response to Mysco's brain drain. Riff's stomach churned at the sound.

"You are now under my control," boomed Fantasly, "and are responsible for completing such tasks as your post requires. You will be patrolling the odd-numbered side of Orchard Lane from house numbers 3001 to 3049, inclusive. Good luck on your human-hunting adventures. Now, BACK TO WORK!"

Upon the final command, Fantasly's demeanour changed and he flicked his medulla like a whip, catching Mysco square across the face. She did not flinch but obediently stood up and walked back toward the dais to descend, leave the Athenaeum, and assume her duties. The rest of the Insomnyus on the first floor turned around and began flooding down the stairs to resume their various posts around the town.

The group in the rafters waited until every last soul had exited the Athenaeum before they reviewed what had just unfolded. The McHubbards helped the Cantileerys to their feet and pulled them in for a long embrace.

"What are we going to do?" sobbed Meerie-Meerie. "They sucked her brain out. How can she ever get it back?" Meerie-Meerie started to hyperventilate, and Stenolly held her tightly to calm her down.

"I could be wrong, but from what I can see, it doesn't look like it was her whole brain," said Luna in a comforting tone. "The glowing spheres don't look large enough to be a human brain. I'd bet anything that she still has a part of her brain left within her skull. I think there's a chance that we can get her and your parents back to being human."

"Do you really think so? Will they be the same?" asked Meerie-Meerie, desperation written all over her face.

"I don't think we'll know until we try," said Luna.

"We just have to hope for the best," said Ann Lou. "Elbina and Mysco would do anything to save any of us, and we will do everything we can to save them."

"Where do we start?" asked Riff.

Luna's eyes bulged. "Gwympy's first prediction! It all makes sense now," she said excitedly.

Luna's sudden burst of excitement spread to Bisquit, who stood up from scratching his ear, and then trotted around Luna as he happily panted.

"Remind us," said Riff, puzzled.

Luna's eyes shone with excitement at her breakthrough. "Gwympy said, 'A simple zap to the lobe will cause Fantasly to explode. Once he's gone, there will be a new dawn.' So, how do we take down Fantasly? With this," she said grinning, holding up her own zapper. "We have to go to his lair."

"I was hoping you wouldn't say that," Riff said, his shoulders slumping. "And what about the GeoLapse?"

"I think we need to split up. The bunker needs to be warned in case we need more defence. One group goes to the bunker and the other group goes to the lair," said Luna.

Riff turned to Stenolly. "You need to get back to the bunker. I can't have you in any more danger out here."

Stenolly shook her head and took Riff's hand. With the other, she signed, "I'm staying."

"Me too," said Ann Lou. "Luna, your skills are better suited to planning at the bunker, I'm sorry to say. Same with you, Meerie-Meerie."

The two girls nodded in agreement.

"Bisquit, can you lead us home safely?" said Meerie-Meerie.

The little dog skipped forward with a small bark and hopped back in the direction of the lift.

Together, they swiftly made their way back to the lift. Once they were inside, Luna pushed the G button.

At the lobby level, Meerie-Meerie, Luna, and Bisquit got out, then waved and woofed their goodbyes as the lift doors started to close between them and Ann Lou, Riff, and Stenolly.

"Be safe!" Luna called to them, a worried look in her eyes.

"You too," said Riff, nodding to them.

As the doors closed, Stenolly pushed the 4 button. "I need to make a quick stop," she signed.

Ann Lou turned to Stenolly. "Are you sure you want to do this?"

Stenolly nodded and signed, "I have to."

They exited the lift at level 4, and Stenolly led them around the periphery of the walkway. Riff's skin crawled as they passed by endless rows of glowing brain fragments. The only light in the Athenaeum now was the glow of thousands of brains.

They found Mysco's chair. A plaque on it read NUMBER 9023116. A number was all that was left to remember Mysco by.

Stenolly laid her hand against the glass bowl and held it there, as if trying to have a last few fleeting moments of connection with her sister. To Riff's surprise, Mysco's brain flickered. He looked closely at the centre of the round brain and saw images of Mysco-like movies. She was laughing with her sisters, then blowing out candles on a cake, then running with a soccer ball and scoring a goal. All these beautiful memories that Mysco had once held were right in front of them, trapped away from the safety of her own body.

Riff placed a gentle hand on Stenolly's back. She stepped away from Mysco's brain and pulled him into a tight embrace, crying into his shoulder.

"We're going to save her, don't worry, darling," he whispered into her ear.

"Riff," said Ann Lou in a croaky voice.

Riff turned and saw that Ann Lou was about halfway down the row of brains, staring intently at one of them.

Riff and Stenolly went to her side. The brain of number 9022095 was flickering with images of a young woman laughing in the arms of a man she clearly loved. The images then switched to a younger version of the girl sitting at a kitchen table that Riff and Ann Lou recognised all too well. Then they saw themselves at the table with her.

Seeing himself in the images ripped Riff's heart into shreds. Part of Elbina was right in front of him. She was so close to him—the closest she had been since they were in the Time Belt. He needed to save his sister. She deserved a second chance to experience these joyful and peaceful memories, and he was more determined than ever to make sure that happened. He laid a hand on Ann Lou's shoulder.

"Let's go get our Elbs back."

Riff, Ann Lou, and Stenolly looked once more toward what remained of their sisters, then walked back to the lift. Riff pressed the call button. When the rusty doors opened, they saw a tall, lean figure clad in black in the lift, staring at them. Riff, Stenolly, and Ann Lou were frozen with fear. Then the figure's mouth curled into a crooked smile, baring a front tooth whose neighbour was missing. It was a man with white hair, a circle tattoo around his right eye, and a scar on his left cheek. Riff gulped. For the first time in twenty years, he was face to face with his father.

# Fantasly's Lair

Valents tutted. "You don't look like our robotic friends. Fantasly won't like hearing that intruders are running roughshod around his Athenaeum. Get 'em, lads!"

Two GeoLapse jumped out from behind Valents and grabbed Riff, Ann Lou, and Stenolly. Riff and Stenolly were easily detained and zip-tied by one of Valents's cronies, but Ann Lou put up a fairly respectable fight with the second one. She shoved him away, then grabbed her zapper and pushed the button, sending her attacker flying into one of the chairs in the nearest aisle of brains. His head struck the glass bowl, shattering it. Brain goop from the bowl landed on the GeoLapse's head, making him look like a cracked egg. He shook it off, sending brain goop in every direction, then got right up and charged back at Ann Lou as if nothing had happened.

She pushed the zapper's button again, but the zapper hadn't yet fully recharged. With the extra few seconds of pause that he had won, the GeoLapse body-slammed Ann Lou, and in a flash her wrists were shackled behind her back.

Valents snatched up their zappers and equipped them to his own belt. He then got right up in Riff's face. "Who are you, and why are you parading about the Athenaeum unescorted?" he spat.

Riff winced as drops of spit hit his face. "We . . . got lost," he said.

Valents eyed him, hungry for more information. "Lost from where? Are there more of you?"

"No, we're . . . travellers from planet . . . Zoiskatchewan," said Riff, starting to sweat uncomfortably.

"That's odd. You look very similar to humans. Are you sure you aren't from here? Or perhaps from a faraway planet called Earth?" said Valents.

"Nope, definitely not a human. Zoiskatchewanese creatures take the form of whoever is around them," said Riff. He knew what Ann Lou was probably thinking: something along the lines of *You bloody idiot!*

"Hmm," said Valents pensively. "I don't think I believe you. But I know someone who can confirm my suspicions. Let's go and have a quick little chat with Fantasly, eh?"

Valents and his cronies pushed the prisoners into the lift. As they rode down to the basement floor, Ann Lou's GeoLapse captor wrapped her hair around his hand and pulled hard, while Riff and Stenolly's bloke pinned them by their necks against the wall of the lift.

"I'd like our hostages to stay alive until we get to the lair," snapped Valents.

The GeoLapse immediately loosened their grips, and Riff and Stenolly gasped and sucked in large gulps of air.

At the basement level, the lift doors opened onto a riot of colour. Pulsating streams of pink and blue neon lights lined a long cylindrical tunnel. Valents ordered everyone off the lift, and his GeoLapse thugs began pushing their captives forward. The neon lights throbbed as if propelling them down the tunnel. Worse, the tunnel's diameter was pinched in every few metres, creating ridges that they had to step over as they walked. Riff noticed the tunnel went uphill, then downhill again, followed by a long, more gradual upward curve. His captor found pleasure in pushing Riff over each ridge, causing him to stumble throughout the strange passageway.

The end of the passageway sloped upward, and the neon tubes flowed through an opening barely a metre wide and into a sort of vault.

"Fantasly!" called Valents in a singsong voice. "Come out and see what I've brought you!"

A few seconds later, Fantasly's pink, brainy body pressed against the opening to the vault, then pushed through it with a wet pop.

"Who is it?" grumbled Fantasly. "I don't like to be disturbed when I am collecting new information!"

"I understand, but since we are working together now, I need you to confirm something for me," said Valents, a hint of impatience in his voice.

"Fine," snarled Fantasly.

"Have you heard of planet Zoiskatchewan?" Valents asked.

Fantasly snorted. "Of course. It's several galaxies down the road."

"Oh," said Valents, shocked. "That's where this lot hail from."

Fantasly looked Riff, Ann Lou, and Stenolly up and down, then laughed heartily. "I do appreciate a good joke from time to time. No, these aren't Zoiskatchewanese."

"Then who are they?" Valents said, his face purpling.

Fantasly squinted and stared into the eyes of each prisoner for a few seconds. "Data exists for all three. This one here is named Stenolly Cantileery. Three sources tell me she is of Therian descent."

Valents peered at Stenolly menacingly, then said, "She's no use to me. Keep going."

Riff felt a burning sensation in his body. Hearing someone—his own *father*—say something negative about Stenolly made him want to lash out. But he needed to stay calm, or else they were all at risk of being in more trouble than they already were.

Fantasly's bulging eyes now bore into Ann Lou. "This one is Ann Lou McHubbard. Two sources tell me she is from the planet Earth, which is located in the Coloratura universe."

"Ann Lou . . ." mused Valents, turning toward her. "That name is so . . . unusual."

"And the last one is Griffin McHubbard. Two sources tell me that he is also from planet Earth in the same universe," Fantasly said in a strained voice. He slumped slightly, tired from his knowledge searching.

"Griffin. . . . Do you have a nickname, by any chance?" asked Valents, his tone gradually falling softer.

"No, I prefer to be addressed formally," said Riff, a little too quickly.

"Oh, yes—and the boy prefers to be called Riff," said Fantasly, now slumped to the floor.

"Damn you, brain," Riff muttered under his breath.

Valents grinned. "So, your mother went into hiding and changed your surname but not your given names. It's almost as if she were on the GeoLapse's side all along, just waiting for you all to be captured. Well done, my dear Henrietta."

"She's dead because of you!" Riff exploded. "You and your blokes killed her!"

Valents laughed a maniacal, evil laugh. "She had it coming for a long time. She didn't want our family to survive. I was going to provide you kids with endless food, riches, access to the outside world, and survival skills. But no, she decided that I was 'endangering the whole family,' 'an unfit father,' and a load of other bollocks."

"Don't speak about our mother that way!" Ann Lou shouted. "She was the most incredible parent we could have ever asked for. You, on the other hand, are a monster!"

Valents mimed being stabbed in the heart. "My baby, Ann Lou! I never even got to meet you, and you call me such a horrid thing?"

"You are not our father!" Ann Lou cried.

"You all could have used a father; I can guarantee that. I bet your mother forced you to grow up with her own insufferable mother as well. That old, oafish woman never spoke a kind word about me once in my life."

"That's because Knitsy knew what was best for us, and she knew that it wasn't you. Knitsy raised us with dignity, morality, and love," said Ann Lou.

"You know, you aren't the brightest of the bunch. Tell me, where's Luna? I bet she can talk some sense into you all. And dear, sweet Albino," Valents said, holding his hands over where his heart should be, although the McHubbards weren't convinced he had one.

"It's Elbina, and your friend over here has already made an Insomnyus of her," snapped Ann Lou, tossing her head in Fantasly's direction.

"What are you doing here, anyways?" asked Riff.

"I'm so glad you asked, son," said Valents, causing Riff to cringe. "I'm here to find you. I heard there was a clan of McHubbards who were foiling our plans. I just didn't know anything else about them or where to find them. But lucky for me, one of your friends gave up your little hiding spot, and now I get to reunite with my children."

"Delevio isn't our friend. No friend of ours would have sold us out," said Riff.

"It doesn't matter to me who your friends are. All that matters is that you're here, and now I can kill you," Valents smiled.

"You'd kill us?" sputtered Ann Lou. "Have you no heart?"

"You're quite the hypocrite, Ann Lou. You and your siblings concocted the heartless plan that wiped out most of my men. We've had to step up recruitment to replace them."

*Woe is you,* thought Riff. *Tell us all your problems!* Then it struck him that he could buy time by keeping Valents talking. "Why are you working with Fantasly?"

Valents replied eagerly. "Ah, yes. Fantasly is a happy consequence, a bonus of our mission here. When I learned of his knowledge base, I proposed that he share the technology with us so that we can utilise it on Earth. It will greatly streamline our recruitment process. In return, we provide extra security on Thera."

Ann Lou glanced at Riff, then chimed in: "How so?"

As Valents rambled on about recruitment and brain drain technology needs, Riff remembered the 'splodey device in his back pocket. He just needed to figure out how to get to it. Somehow, they had to get their hands free.

Fantasly finally quivered from his spot and slithered back into his cave opening. Valents was now speaking directly to Ann Lou. "On the subject of recruitment, I could spare you from death. You have a choice, you know. You can still join me."

"Never!" said Ann Lou.

Valents chuckled and turned to Stenolly. "Well, how about your friend here? Can I tempt you with a luxurious GeoLapse lifestyle?"

Stenolly's brows furrowed. She shook her head boldly.

Valents walked up close to Stenolly. "Well, if you're so militant about it, then why don't you speak up for yourself?"

Stenolly bared her teeth in a grimace.

"She doesn't speak. She signs with her hands," Riff said sternly. An idea was brewing in his mind.

Valents snorted and turned to Stenolly's captor. "Release her. I want to talk to her."

The GeoLapse obeyed and cut Stenolly's zip-ties. She brought her hands forward and stretched her wrists.

Valents smiled. "See? I can be forgiving. Now, I believe you can do me a favour. Join me."

Stenolly signed something to Valents. Riff had to hold himself back from chortling. Stenolly had remembered every one of the swear words he taught her in one of their last sign sessions.

"She said, erm, she needs more information," lied Riff.

Valents clasped his hands together loudly, making everyone in the room jump. "Let me start with the living conditions: your own personal quarters with soft, comfortable beds, and a five-star service all day and all night . . ." As Valents droned on, Stenolly caught Riff's gaze, as if asking what to do. Riff pointed with his shackled hands up to his back pocket, where the 'splodey device was. He darted his eyes behind him and then back to Stenolly. Her eyes brightened, and she knew what she had to do.

Ann Lou was catching on to their plan as well. She continued the work of stalling Valents and his cronies. "Personally, if I were to join the GeoLapse, I'd need a place to train for combat. Can you show me some moves that you've learned?" she asked with fake enthusiasm.

The two GeoLapse behind the captives grunted in reply and swaggered over to Valents's side. The three of them posed in defensive stances.

"This one is called the 'Swirl'," Valents explained. "Malco, if you'll assist me as offence. Digby, you'll be the opposition."

Valents put Digby in a headlock, while Malco picked up Digby's legs. Valents and Malco started spinning Digby in circles faster and faster, eventually dropping him simultaneously. Digby stood up and hobbled in a disorderly fashion, eventually falling back to the ground.

"Inspiring," said Ann Lou. "Show me another."

While Valents showed Ann Lou step-by-step how to execute the "Gong", Stenolly swung behind Riff and plucked the small box from Riff's back pocket. She opened the lid and pulled out what looked like an ice hockey puck with a red button on the top. Stenolly peered quickly at Riff, who nodded to her. She jabbed the button on the 'splodey device, then lobbed it toward Fantasly's lair.

"What the—" started Valents, who held Malco's arms in an uncomfortable twist behind his back.

The 'splodey device sailed through the air and perfectly arced into Fantasly's enclosure.

"RUN!" shouted Riff.

*BOOM!* Shrapnel from the 'splodey device and pink ooze blew toward them as they stumbled away.

Stenolly ran ahead of Ann Lou and Riff, waving a small object above her head. Riff gasped—it was the guitar pick he gifted her on their date. The three stopped briefly enough for Stenolly to cut through the others' zip-ties. Their hands freed, they ran for the lift at the end of the passageway. The neon lights above flickered and buzzed loudly.

Riff looked behind him while he ran. No one was following. *We lost them,* he thought, huffing and puffing with all his might to make it to the exit unseen.

"Take the stairs!" he called to Ann Lou and Stenolly, and the three of them barrelled up the staircase.

They whizzed through the empty lobby but skidded to a halt when they reached the doors. Just outside, hordes of Insomnyus were milling around and acting very strange. Instead of their usual robotic movements and predefined pathways, they all appeared lost. Some held their heads and spun in circles, others were crawling on the ground as if searching for something, and one lady had gotten her head stuck in a barrel outside of a store called Tuns o' Butts.

"What's wrong with them?" asked Ann Lou.

Abruptly, all the power went out in IHQ, and Riff watched as all the Insomnyus outside on Austere Avenue suddenly fell to the ground in a wave.

"Are they dead?" signed Stenolly.

"Only one way to find out," said Riff, tearing into a run.

He ran to the first Insomnyus in his path, a young man about his age with long, sandy hair in a ponytail.

"Mate?" Riff said, shaking the man. He didn't respond.

Stenolly bent down and felt his wrist for a few seconds. Then she signed, "He's alive."

"Come on, mate! Wake up! Can you hear me?" Riff shook him with more vigour this time, and the man's eyes started to flicker.

"He's awake!" Riff exclaimed with joy. "Come on, open your eyes."

The man fluttered his eyes open and stared at Riff with both awe and confusion. He tried to speak, but his voice cracked. He cleared his throat. "Where am I?"

"You're on Austere Avenue, the street above the bunker. What's your name?" asked Riff.

"Er, I dunno," the man replied. He looked sad, then frustrated.

"Don't worry, you've just woken up after a long time. You're safe now. We'll get you some help," Riff assured him. "We'll be back soon."

Riff stood and beckoned to the girls to follow him. "We have to get back to the bunker. We can alert everyone that the Insomnyus are waking up. Fantasly's done for!"

"Do you think Elbina is here somewhere? And Mysco?" asked Ann Lou, jogging beside him.

"They have to be," Riff said, breathlessly.

Riff thought it felt very strange but liberating to be able to run down Austere Avenue without worry of being attacked by the Insomnyus. With Fantasly gone, the inhabitants of the bunker could move up to the surface again. He couldn't believe that he, Ann Lou, and Stenolly had managed to pull this mission off!

They made their way through Building Blocks, into the trunk, down the tunnel, and into Thevenin and Norton's workshop.

"Yowza, yer back!" Thevenin launched himself up from the sofa, with Norton just behind.

"The 'splodey device did it. The Insomnyus are all waking up, thanks to you lot!" said Riff.

"Whaddya mean, wakin' up?" Norton asked suspiciously.

"They're back to life! No more brain control!" said Ann Lou.

The brothers stared at one another in amazement. "Mamaw's back!" they cried.

"Do you have a way to alert the bunker?" asked Riff.

"Sure, here you go! Tell the world the good news!" exclaimed Thevenin. On a table rested a device similar to an old-fashioned Earth telephone except with no dial. Thevenin picked up the handset from its cradle and handed it to Riff.

"You want to do the honours?" Riff asked Ann Lou.

She smiled giddily and snatched the handset. "Attention bunker. This is a message from Ann Lou McHubbard of Block A, apartment thirty. My brother, Riff, and our friend Stenolly Cantileery just returned safely from IHQ on Austere Avenue. We went there to find the source of the Insomnyus and put a stop to it, and I'm very happy to announce that we did just that. We have just confirmed that those previously captured as Insomnyus are now waking up and free from the reins of the evil entity that was previously controlling their minds.

"We need volunteers to come up to retrieve the awoken, give them immediate medical attention, and start reuniting them with their loved ones."

A few moments of silence quickly transformed into a confused buzz, escalating to the point of cheers and thunderous applause filling the air from the bunker below. The bunker boomed as people started racing up the lifts almost immediately. Healthcare professionals carried stretchers, bottles of water, snacks, and teddy buffkin to help remind the former Insomnyus of home.

"Y'all better get outta the way! There's gonna be a stampede!" shouted Norton.

"We might as well go with them to help! Come with us, maybe you'll find your Mamaw," Ann Lou urged the two burly men.

Thevenin and Norton led the stampede of bunkerians through the tunnel and up and out of the trunk in Building Blocks. They spread out on Austere Avenue, and everyone began flinging the awoken onto stretchers and splashing water on their faces. Some of the awoken took their teddies with many thanks, hugging them as they were carried back to the safety of the bunker. Others were a bit hesitant to go with the strangers, but snacks were offered, and they obliged after tasting a few Crunchie Cats.

Riff, Ann Lou, and Stenolly stayed close together as they moved through the crowd, trying their best to find anyone they recognised.

"Elbina? Mysco?" called Ann Lou.

It was hopeless trying to hear anything with everyone shouting at the top of their lungs for their loved ones. Riff regretted not having provided a more organised plan, but at least there were many willing volunteers. It was heartwarming but not surprising to see the support, as most people in the bunker had lost a loved one to the Insomnyus, much as Earth's inhabitants knew the GeoLapse all too well.

"The last time we saw Elbina, she was patrolling just over there," Stenolly alerted Riff.

"Right, let's check there," he said, heading straight in the direction that Stenolly suggested.

"Elbina!" Riff couldn't help but call out her name in hopes that she was listening for it.

He peered down alleyways and was forced to dodge a few incoming stretchers carrying the awoken, but Elbina was still nowhere to be found.

"Riff, I think there's someone over there," said Ann Lou, pointing to an alleyway to their left. At the end of it, someone had piled up bundles of sacks like a barricade.

Ann Lou was correct—someone was behind the sacks, sitting against the wall, holding her head, and dizzily looking around.

"It's Elbs!" shrieked Riff. He sprinted down the alleyway and knelt down in front of her.

"Elbina, it's Riff. Are you okay?" Riff blubbered. He couldn't help but grasp onto her shoulders. He didn't want to overwhelm her, but he wanted so desperately to hug her again.

"Elbina! We found you!" Ann Lou cried, propping herself next to Riff. She gripped Elbina's leg.

Elbina stared at them. She tried forming words but seemed to have trouble saying anything. She continued to hold her head.

"It's okay, take your time. Start by saying your name," said Riff.

Elbina looked around, frightened. She curled up her legs and held them to her chest.

"Elbina, it's okay. You're alive and free from Fantasly and E. Bowser the Third and every other evil force. You're safe," said Riff.

Elbina batted his hands away from her shoulders. "G-get away!" she stammered.

"I think she just needs a moment," Ann Lou whispered to Riff.

"Can you say our names?" Riff pried, desperate for some reassurance that she was with them.

"I d-don't know you," Elbina said softly. She continued to retreat from her siblings.

"But . . . I'm your brother. And this is your sister," said Riff, his heart sinking.

Elbina shook her head. She tried to stand, but she quickly fell back down on the ground.

"Let us help you back to the bunker," Ann Lou said, reaching out for Elbina's bony arms.

"Leave me alone!" Elbina shouted.

"Oi, you need help?" a nurse from the bunker shouted from the top end of the alley.

The nurse and a partner raced down to them, wrestled Elbina onto a stretcher, and started to carry her away.

"Don't give her any snacks or water—she can't digest anything!" Ann Lou shouted after them.

Riff stood still, his heart shattered. Stenolly hugged him, and Ann Lou joined soon after.

"She doesn't know who we are anymore. Fantasly stole her memories," said Riff, tears streaming down his face. "She's gone."

# CHAPTER 23

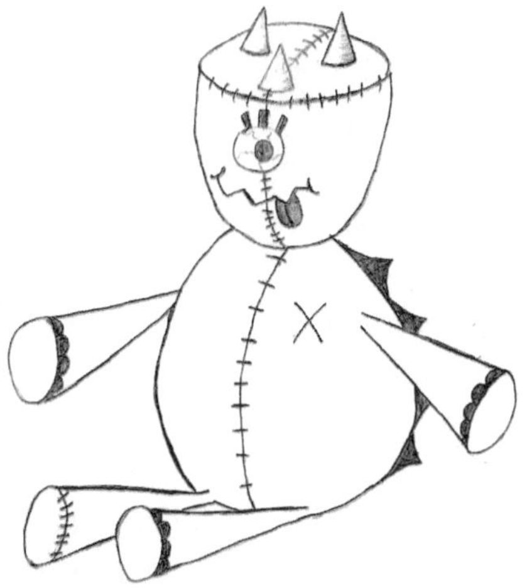

## INSOMNYUS REUNITED

The next morning in apartment A-30, Riff sat at the kitchen table with his sisters and a cup of tea that Luna made for each of them. The three sat in silence for the first half of their tea, but it was Ann Lou who eventually broke the silence.

"Did you visit her yet?" she asked Luna.

Luna nodded. "It was the worst experience that I could have ever imagined."

"Maybe it'll take a little while for her brain to reconfigure itself. She's been through a lot," said Ann Lou.

Luna shook her head. "Each of the Insomnyus had a part of their brain forcibly taken from them. They weren't able to get it back before Fantasly was destroyed. In many cases, I'm afraid we will find that the missing piece was critical to their memory storage."

"Have you heard from Stenolly about Mysco? Did they find her or their parents?" Ann Lou asked Riff.

He shook his head. "I haven't had the energy to talk to anyone since we saw Elbina yesterday." He swigged the last of his tea, wincing at the tea leaves that had sunk to the bottom, and slumped in his chair. "I feel so messed up."

"You need to talk to your girlfriend!" said Ann Lou, sternly. "You can't be one of those lads who just retreats when there's a difficult situation. Besides, she's going through the exact same thing. You might as well be there for each other rather than sulking by yourself."

Riff sighed. "You're right. I should go find her. But what are we going to do? Is there any hope that Elbina will remember us?"

He and Ann Lou instinctively looked to Luna to solve the problem at hand.

Luna said, "I think we just need to wait it out. Hopefully Elbina will get through her anger phase, but it's only because she's scared and confused. The best thing to do is not overwhelm her with too much information, especially startling information such as telling her about family she doesn't remember. Let's stick to small things for now, like her name, age, where she is right now, et cetera."

"Speaking of family who might not remember us, I need to get back to my little Clorin soon. Now that Elbina is back with us, when can we go home?" asked Ann Lou.

Luna pondered for a few moments. "She probably needs to get adjusted to the Therian environment first before she's packed into a Jalopy that travels through a black hole that tries to stretch her into spaghetti. It's probably best for her mental wellbeing. I tested her on reading and writing, which she can still do. It's really just the core memories that she struggles with."

Ann Lou slapped her palms on the table. "We have to wait until she remembers everything that has ever happened in her life? I have a husband and a child to get home to!"

"Yeah, and I have . . . two best friends to get back to," said Riff.

"And I, no one," said Luna.

"Come on, you two," sneered Ann Lou. "Clorin and Apollo miss you both terribly."

Luna and Riff each raised an eyebrow.

"Okay, Apollo is a rock, and he's fine. Clorin misses you terribly," said Ann Lou. "Which is why we need to go home!"

"We shouldn't be much longer," said Luna. "Spex and I spoke to the hospital staff last night about devising a plan for the awoken. It's called PIRT—Previous Insomnyus Re-entry Therapy. It should help them quickly get back on their feet and inserted into a societal structure."

"Oh, you and Spex came up with it together?" Ann Lou teased.

"It's not like that," Luna said, waving her hand. "I'm not interested."

"You certainly are!" Ann Lou blurted. "Your face turns red as a tomato every time his name is brought up!"

"Just drop it, okay? I'm not interested, end of story," said Luna.

"I bet if Elbina were here, you'd tell her all the juicy secrets," said Ann Lou, crossing her arms.

"Okay, I've had enough boy talk for today," said Riff, scooting his chair out. "I'm going to find Stenolly."

"Wait," said Ann Lou. "There's one more thing I want to talk to you both about."

Riff sat back down. "What is it?"

"Erm . . . Dad," she said softly.

Riff shook his head. "He's not our father anymore. He lost that privilege as soon as he left Mum and joined the GeoLapse."

"I know, and I'm sorry to bring it up," said Ann Lou. "But isn't it strange that the GeoLapse just kind of disappeared? Do you think Dad—Valents—died with Fantasly in the explosion?"

"I hope so," said Riff, unperturbed.

"It is a bit strange," said Luna. "Were any other of the GeoLapse in the lair with Valents?"

Riff shook his head. "Only the two goons who helped him capture us."

Luna sat back in her chair and closed her eyes. "They may well be out there, whether or not they have Valents to lead them."

Riff's throat tightened. The thought terrified him. Even after all he and his family had gone through, it seemed almost impossible to shake the GeoLapse's murderous clutches.

"We need to stay alert. I'll warn Thevenin and Norton to stay vigilant in case anything suspicious arises. The bunker needs to be prepared. I'll catch up with you two later," said Luna, standing from her chair and heading out the door.

"Well, that was a pleasant conversation," said Ann Lou. "I can't believe Valents is that mental to turn his own children in—"

"Will you stop connecting us and him together?" Riff shouted, balling his hands into fists. "He's not our dad, and we certainly aren't his children!" He stood and loudly pushed his chair back under the table. He stormed out of the apartment, slamming the door behind him, and he stomped across the hall, pounding on the Cantileery's door.

No answer.

He grumbled to himself as he continued storming down the hallway and up the lift to the hospital level. The lifts to and from the hospital level had been jam-packed ever since the night before. Families were scrambling to reunite with their loved ones, but instead of the happy reunions that Riff had imagined, most of the visitors emerged from the hospital with depressed and gloomy auras. It turned out almost all of them were enduring the same grief as Riff and his sisters were: the grief of losing a loved one even though, physically, the loved one was back in their arms.

Besides families and friends of the awoken, more awoken arrived in stretchers throughout the next day, carried by volunteers from the bunker. The hospital was well over capacity, so many volunteers were recruited to work as stand-in nurses and doctors. As Riff squeezed through the crowds of depressed and disoriented people, he noticed one stand-in doctor, a young girl who couldn't have been more than five years old, sticking a bandage on the forehead of a patient who had been admitted for a broken leg.

"Riff!" called a voice from a room as he passed by.

He turned on his heels and peeked in. There was Meerie-Meerie, beckoning to him. The entire Cantileery clan was there. Mysco and her parents lay asleep in three beds, and Meerie-Meerie, Gwympy, and Stenolly were watching over them. Stenolly's eyes met Riff's with a deep yearning. Riff smiled shyly at her, quite caught off guard by her beauty, but he couldn't get himself too distracted now.

Riff squeezed into the room and went to Stenolly's side. "You all right?" he said, gently brushing her hand with his out of sight of the others.

"You guys did it!" said Meerie-Meerie, her eyes wet. "I never thought I'd see them again. Thank you!"

"You're the happiest person in here," said Riff, surprised. "Can they remember everything?"

"No," said Meerie-Meerie. "But I'm relieved that they're safe. That's all I ever wanted. Have you visited your sister yet?"

Riff scrunched up his face. "Not yet. My sisters have. I was on my way to see her."

"Well, maybe it would be best if you didn't go alone. Stenolly can go with you for support. It might make things a bit more comfortable for you and Elbina. But before you go, we'd like you to meet our mother, Elmeria, and our father, Joland." Meerie-Meerie gently shook each of them awake, and her parents looked around the room in confusion.

"Elmeria and Joland, meet Riff," said Meerie-Meerie, gesturing.

"Pleasure to meet you," said Riff, nodding to them.

"I'm Joland, right?" asked Elmeria.

"You are Elmeria. But you were so close to getting it correct this time!" Meerie-Meerie said cheerfully.

Gwympy rolled her eyes. "I'm too old to do this parenting thing again."

"Gwympy, your negative presence is distressing to everyone in the room. Please go back home if you are going to continue complaining," said Meerie-Meerie in a strict tone.

"Fine, I'll leave. I have a blasted headache anyways," said Gwympy as she walked out the door.

"We should be going as well," said Riff, holding Stenolly's hand as they started walking to the door.

"Why is that man pulling that woman's hand? He's trying to steal her!" yelled a frightened Elmeria.

"No, Elmeria. Riff and Stenolly are in *love*. That is what people in love do. You and Joland are actually in love as well," said Meerie-Meerie, encouragingly.

Elmeria and Joland gawped at one another and exclaimed, "Ew!" perfectly in sync.

Stenolly waved to her family as she and Riff left the room. Before he could find the way to Elbina's room, he pulled her into a nearby equipment closet and gave her a deeply passionate kiss. She stayed there close to him, giving him all the same energy in return. Once they came up for a breath, he signed to her, "I wanted someplace quiet to talk."

"Talk?" she signed back, tossing him a sensual look.

"Well, I wanted to kiss you a lot and then talk," he said, smiling. He kissed her gently on the lips. "I didn't want you to think I was ignoring you last night. I've just been having a difficult time processing everything that's been going on. I know you're in the same position, so I want you to know that I'm here for you if you need to let off some steam or discuss anything."

Stenolly put one hand around Riff's waist. "I appreciate that. It's okay if you need time to grieve. But Elbina is here. You just need to help her get back on her feet. I am also here for you if you need anyone to talk to."

"Thank you," said Riff. "Oh, and what Meerie-Meerie said back in the room—"

"Don't worry. You don't need to feel that way yet," signed Stenolly.

"But I do. I feel it with every ounce of me. I've never felt this way about anyone in my entire life. I had to travel to another universe to find you, and I'm so grateful that you were here waiting for me. Stenolly, I love you," blurted Riff. The feelings exploded out of him. He didn't even know he was capable of speaking to a person in that way, but the words and the feelings spewed out of him so naturally.

Stenolly pulled him in closer and held up her hand in a single hand gesture for a few seconds. "I love you."

Riff chirped with glee and wrapped his arms around Stenolly. He kissed her and scrunched his fingers through her beautiful locks of red hair. He felt her heartbeat matching his, as if they were becoming one unit.

The closet door opened, and a confused volunteer doctor stared at the kissing couple for a few seconds.

"Um, is this the bathroom?" said the teenage boy.

"No, mate. Afraid not," said Riff, staring at the boy while holding Stenolly's face in his hands.

"Right. Sorry!" The teenager closed the door gently on them.

After a few seconds of silence, Riff and Stenolly broke into hysterical laughter. They laughed until they were doubled over and had to hold each other up. After a few minutes of giggling together, they ended up in a swaying embrace.

Riff broke the silence. "I bet Elbina could use a bit of cheering up, too."

Stenolly nodded and opened the closet door. "Let's go."

The pair made their way to Elbina's room, which was at the very end of the same hallway on the opposite side. Riff was pleased to hear a very familiar buzzing just as he reached the outside of her door. He walked in and said, "Hi, you have a visitor."

Elbina sat up in her bed, holding a teddy buffkin close to her chest. Her bony body vibrated as her Gasser contraption transformed solid nutrients into gases and infused them via her respiratory system. It was the only way she could get nutrients without getting sick. Riff was pleased to see she was using it. It looked as if Spex had visited her as well, judging from the neon yellow spectacles she wore.

"I saw you yesterday," Elbina croaked. "What do you want with me?"

Riff tried to maintain a light-hearted face while he spoke to his younger sister. "I apologise that I scared you yesterday. I didn't mean any harm. I just want to . . . be your friend."

Elbina eased slightly. "My friend?"

"Yes. My name is Riff, and this is Stenolly. We both live here," said Riff calmly. He and Stenolly walked to Elbina's bedside.

Elbina began to talk more freely. "A girl came in last night and told me that we're underground. She was tall and wore red spectacles. She brought me some books. She was really nice. I just don't remember her name." Elbina repeatedly began hitting her forehead.

"Don't hurt yourself!" said Riff, gently guiding her hands away from her head. "Her name was Luna. You can ask us any questions and we will answer them for you."

"My brain feels like it's muddy—like there's all this information buried somewhere, but I can't access it. It's very frustrating," she said, slumping back into her bed.

"I bet it's very difficult. But you aren't alone. There are a lot of other people in the same situation as you. Plus, Luna has set up a programme for people like you to help you remember things."

"Can you tell me anything that I may not know?" a doe-eyed Elbina asked.

"Erm," Riff started, thinking of the advice Luna gave him: to stick to basic information for now. "There's a lot. But starting small is the best way to move forward. Do you remember your name?"

Elbina nodded proudly. "Luna told me that my name is Elbina and I am twenty-two years old. My birthday is February eighth."

"Very good!" said Riff. "What about hobbies? Do you remember any of those?"

Elbina pondered for a moment and then sadness washed over her. "I don't remember."

"That's okay, because I can tell you that you used to like to cook, and you were learning French. You were very good at both of those things," said Riff.

"Hmm, I don't think I remember how to do either of those things," said Elbina.

"Once you get discharged, I'll take you to my and Luna's apartment, and we can all cook together. Does that sound fun?" said Riff.

Elbina shrugged. "I guess. But I'll probably have to go home to my family when I get out of here. I'm sorry that we probably won't have too much of a chance to get to know one another."

Riff and Stenolly looked sidelong at one another. "Erm, yeah, that's right. I'm sure your family misses you."

Elbina looked dreamily at the ceiling. "I wish I knew where they were. Maybe they'll come looking for me. I wonder what my mother and father are like. Maybe they're teachers or famous chess players! Maybe I have siblings and we live in a mansion on the moon! The possibilities are endless!"

Riff thought it best not to burst her temporary happy bubble. If he broke the news that her mother was dead, her father was an infamous and murderous terrorist who was trying to take over the omniverse, and that they used to live in a cramped home in Portsmouth, UK, which wasn't nearly as exciting as the moon, she might not be too happy with him. Although maybe she would be happy about having three siblings.

Over the next few days, Riff, Luna, and Ann Lou spent most of their hours with Elbina, and swapped in turns every so often to the Cantileery room to visit with Mysco. Luna and Spex's PIRT programme proved a major success among the awoken: although their memories weren't coming back, they were starting to remember things they had been told since reawakening, and they were picking up useful skills such as sports, music, cooking, and language courses taught by volunteers in the bunker. A lot of the awoken's frustrations were defused as they learned new things and busied themselves with jobs around the bunker. Mysco and Elbina were employed as waitresses at Jonee'z Diner, although Elbina concluded within the first day that she didn't care much for handling food.

To the McHubbards' dismay, Elbina's boss, Jonee himself, called them in one day to discuss Elbina's abominable behaviour at work. He reported that she was careless with orders, she spoke rudely to customers, and she had stolen things.

"I don't think you're talking about Elbina McHubbard," said Luna.

"Small, bony girl who buzzes twenty-four seven?" Jonee clarified.

Luna nodded.

"That's the one. She took my Game Girl straight out of my front jeans pocket just yesterday! At least she's not subtle about it, so she'll never get away with it if she keeps up her current tactics," Jonee chuckled. "Unfortunately, I'm going to have to let her go."

Once Elbina was granted a full discharge from the hospital, the McHubbards invited her to stay at their apartment while she waited for her family to pick her up. The first evening in their apartment, Elbina slept soundly on the sofa after a long day at Wegwomans in her new role. The other three siblings quietly discussed her progress at the kitchen table.

"I think we should tell her that we're her family now. She's improved since she first came to the bunker," whispered Ann Lou.

"I think you're right," said Luna. "Her participation in PIRT has been exceptional. She's socialising and finding out the types of activities that she enjoys . . . to some extent."

"She's definitely not the same person that she was before, though," said Ann Lou, peering at Elbina snoozing away. "She hates cooking and has no interest in any of the language classes."

"She has taken to playing chess," said Luna, optimistically.

"But old Elbina would never in a billion years have played chess," snapped Ann Lou. "Plus, she's turning into a klepto!"

"Did she give back Mrs. Flumbo's refrigerator yet?" asked Riff.

"She couldn't even get it out the door, so everything was resolved in the end," Luna said.

"Luna," said Ann Lou, "you have to stop brushing these things off. It's not normal behaviour. Do you need to add a 'being a nice person' section to PIRT?"

"PIRT is perfectly structured and doesn't need any alterations!" Luna barked.

Ann Lou continued. "Take Mysco as a second example. I tried playing soccer with her yesterday and passed her the ball. Instead of her usual kick-flip receive, she grabbed the ball with her hands and chucked it at the coach!"

Riff burst into laughter. Ann Lou whacked him on the shoulder.

"These are very normal behaviours when people are transitioning back into society after a traumatic event," said Luna calmly. "She needs her community to grant her patience and understanding while her brain reconfigures itself to its new environment and her forthcoming life."

"Speaking of forthcoming life, I say we just tell her a different life story," said Riff. "She's really hoping that her mum and dad are coming to pick her up and bring her back to their mansion on the moon."

"So we lie to her, get her hopes up, and then send her back into a spiral when her parents don't show up?" snapped Luna.

Riff stared blankly. "Um . . . good point. I didn't think the whole thing through."

"Clearly," snorted Luna.

"So, it's settled. We tell her we're family, and then we go home," said Ann Lou.

"I can't just leave Stenolly," said Riff. "Maybe you two should go with Elbina, and I'll stay here."

"Griffin McHubbard, we did not travel to a completely different universe to find one sibling, only to leave another one behind," Ann Lou said sternly.

Suddenly an ear-splitting alarm shrieked around the bunker. Elbina awoke in a frenzy and rushed over to her siblings at the kitchen table, clutching her teddy buffkin for support.

"What's that noise?" she said in a worried tone, covering an ear.

Riff's heart dropped. The last time they had heard that alarm was when Mysco transformed into an Insomnyus.

# CHAPTER 24

## BATTLE IN THE BUNKER

"Is there another Insomnyus?" Ann Lou yelled over the blaring alarm.

"There can't be. Fantasly's dead!" shouted Riff. "You three stay here. I'll go check it out!"

Riff, heart racing and limbs trembling, approached the apartment door and poked his head outside. A majority of the neighbours in Block A had the same idea, and they all peered puzzlingly at one another, their heads turning back and forth.

"What can you see?" Mrs. Flumbo asked Mr. Goldmaker in apartment A-1.

Mr. Goldmaker, a middle-aged balding man with a particularly pointy nose, timidly shuffled out of his apartment and investigated the central bunker area. Then he flung his hands to his face in horror and turned to his neighbours, shaking violently. "It's just as Luna McHubbard warned us. The evil Earth-dwellers with the black suits are storming the bunker!"

A calamitous uproar travelled down the hall like a wave as the news spread all the way to the McHubbards' apartment.

"What is it?" Luna called from the kitchen.

Riff turned to his sisters, his face ashen. "GeoLapse. They're here."

"Time to execute BRAGL," commanded Luna, jumping from her seat and picking up various kitchen utensils.

"BRAGL?" scoffed Ann Lou. "Another programme you and Spex came up with?"

"Precisely. Bunker Resistance Against GeoLapse. The outline was efficiently delivered to all bunkerians while you both were at IHQ," said Luna, passing Ann Lou a spatula, Elbina a pair of tongs, and Riff a set of measuring spoons. She took a masher for herself.

"I'd rather defend myself than bake the GeoLapse a succulent pan of brownies," snorted Riff, exchanging his measuring spoons for a rolling pin.

"Take whatever you want. The bunker doesn't have any weaponry, so everyone needs to improvise," said Luna, switching to her teaching voice. "Everyone is well versed on BRAGL except for the awoken and you two. There is a strict outline to follow. First in the six-step process: Awareness. Look both ways before moving. Hold your weapon at the base with your dominant hand—"

"I think the window for education has closed," said Ann Lou, putting her trainers on. "Riff and I took down the Insomnyus leader; I think we'll be okay."

"Fine. If you need help, ask anyone in the bunker to relay the six steps. Everyone has been tested on the concept," said Luna, slightly deflated that her siblings weren't interested in her defensive strategies.

"All right, listen up," said Ann Lou in a commanding tone. "We need to split up. The GeoLapse are after us, and we can't give them any reason to capture all of us in one fell swoop. Luna, you stay on one of the lower floors—"

"Why do you get to make a plan if I can't tell you what mine is?" Luna said crossly.

"Because by the time you finish telling us your plan, the GeoLapse will have torn the place down!" Ann Lou snapped. She continued on with her orders. "Riff, you take the upper floors. I'll take the entrance-way to the bunker to give Thevenin and Norton some backup."

"What about me? I want to help!" Elbina said, waving her tongs in the air.

"You stay here," ordered Ann Lou. "I don't think you're fit enough to fight anyone at this time."

"You're not the boss of me!" spat Elbina. "How dare you tell me what I can and cannot do? You barely know me!" Elbina angrily laced up her own trainers, then quietly asked Riff to remind her how to do the loop-de-loop portion of the knot-tying sequence.

"Let her help," urged Luna. "She's got every right to fight back."

Ann Lou shot her older sister a menacing glance and exhaled. "Fine. You can go to Wegwomans and keep watch from the back of the store."

Elbina, all laced up, nodded and sprang to the door, only to be caught by Riff at the last second.

"Hey, let go!" Elbina clawed at him with her fingernails, leaving scratch marks on his arm.

"I just wanted to say . . ." Riff paused, swallowing hard. "I want you all to be as safe as you possibly can. We're a really strong team, and although we fight sometimes, we have to remember why we're here in the first place, and the respect we have for one another. I love you, sisters."

Ann Lou and Luna's face softened. Elbina's face scrunched in disgust.

"I love you," Ann Lou said, glancing at each of her siblings.

Luna's mouth pursed, her throat tightening. "I love you, too."

"We don't say that often enough. But I know we all feel it," said Ann Lou, holding Luna's hand.

Elbina stared at each of them with a bewildered expression. "I don't know any of you well enough to say anything like that." She tugged her arm away from Riff's grasp and bolted out the door.

"She'll come around," said Luna.

"Let's go! The bunker needs help," said Ann Lou, already halfway out the door.

Luna and Riff followed and set off for their predefined positions within the bunker. Riff paused as he reached the mouth of the central bunker at the start of Block A. On all twenty floors above, he could see and hear cantankerous scenes of brutality between the GeoLapse and the bunker community. Dark figures zipped across levels, swiping batons and other brutal weaponry at innocent people. Clings and clangs filled his ears as spatulas, vases, and mops were used in defence against the GeoLapse's attacks. Even small children were involved in the brave fight. One little girl subtly tied the laces of a GeoLapse's shoes together. When the GeoLapse lunged forward, he tripped and rolled into the side of a bin.

A fellow bunkerian shouldered Riff as they ran past, quickly disengaging Riff from his trance. Riff held his rolling pin ahead of him and ran to the nearest lift, where a GeoLapse greeted him with a smirk. Riff dodged the GeoLapse's attack, then leapt onto the lift and got it moving before the fallen GeoLapse could get up and strike again.

The lift seemed to be chugging along slower than usual. As it passed level ten, Riff saw a GeoLapse charge to the edge of the railing and throw something that looked like a small rock. It struck the lift and exploded. The lift was still rising, but now in short, violent bursts.

Riff managed to exit the lift on level six unscathed. He wasn't sure which way to turn or how he could possibly help. He eventually decided on following a series of screams that he heard within the depths of the home goods store, Doilies. He searched the aisles of buffkin pillows and corduroy bin bags for the source of the screams until he found a group of schoolchildren quivering in the carpet section of the store. Three GeoLapse taunted and teased the small children and laughed maniacally as their fears amplified.

"Oi, losers!" blurted Riff, holding his rolling pin wobblishly in his right hand.

The GeoLapse ceased their chortling and turned to face their new target.

"How very courageous you all are, picking on children less than half your size. You let them go!" Riff shouted.

"We hoped some poor sod like you would come to their rescue to give us more of a challenge," the middle GeoLapse said huskily. "Kill him, boys. And make sure the kids get a good view of it."

The GeoLapse on either side lunged forward and swung their batons in Riff's direction. Riff swivelled out of the way and threw his rolling pin at one of them, more out of fright than defence. He managed to hit one of them square in the head, knocking him unconscious.

"Don't let him get away!" shouted the leader.

Riff started hurling buffkin pillows off the racks at the charging GeoLapse. Although not super effective at doing any damage, the pillows distracted the attackers enough that the children could crawl away. They formed their own small plan and began to kick the middle GeoLapse to the ground. Some jumped on his stomach to keep him down while others bound his hands and feet with rainbow yarn. Once they had him secured, the youngest child stuffed the remainder of the rainbow yarn ball in his mouth.

The last GeoLapse continued after Riff, who zigzagged through the aisles, accidentally sending baubles, crystal plates, and other sumptuous-looking decorations crashing to the floor. Once Riff reached the greeting cards section, he attempted to hurdle over the aisle to put more distance between him and his attacker. An unfortunate misstep caused him to slip back down to the floor, and his foot was caught by his pursuer. The swing of a GeoLapse baton connected with Riff's shin, causing him to howl in pain. Riff kicked as hard as he could, shook the GeoLapse off, and pushed a rotating display of cards over on him. Rather than looking back, Riff ran as fast as he could and dashed out of the store.

He spent the next half hour aiding bunkerians on level six with their defensive tactics. He quickly learned that the optimal move was to strike the GeoLapse from behind with any random object he could find. His most notable success was with a cello bow, which flexed and ended up trapping the GeoLapse's head between the bow hair and the stick.

As he was looking for his next target, Riff caught sight of bright beams of light sweeping around the bunker. He rushed to the railing to identify the source. Sure enough, twelve floors down, he saw a contraption emitting bright lights just outside of Spex's Specs. The contraption consisted of a giant magnifying glass that refracted bright lights to a single pinhole, and Spex and Luna sat atop it, running the controls. Riff could see Luna pointing out oncoming GeoLapse, after which Spex would steer the contraption in that direction, dazzling the target or causing a burn sufficient to send the GeoLapse running in the other direction. They managed to thwart several GeoLapse attacks in the span of the minute Riff watched them.

"Look out below!" shouted a voice from above.

Riff looked up just in time to see Thevenin, Norton, and Ann Lou battling a group of GeoLapse six levels up. He could just make out the sounds of electric zaps, probably from Thevenin and Norton's zappers, and then the shouts of a GeoLapse as he fell from the top ledge of the bunker.

Hopefulness filled Riff's core as he saw the significant contributions his sisters were making to the welfare of the bunkerians. Maybe they actually had a chance of coming out of this alive and ridding themselves of the GeoLapse . . . forever.

A loud ringing filled the air of the bunker via the public address system, followed by the sound of a man clearing his throat.

"Attention to my men and the opposing forces of this bunker," said a voice.

The bunker fell silent. No one moved an inch except to orient their heads in the direction of the announcement. The ounce of hope Riff had felt only minutes ago vanished. He knew this voice. He had wanted to believe its owner was dead. But he was wrong. It was Valents.

"I'd like my men to transfer their focus to the primary objective of why we travelled here in the first place. Find the McHubbards. Find all four of them, and bring them to me—alive."

Riff didn't dare move. He wasn't sure if the GeoLapse knew what he and his sisters looked like. They weren't the brightest bunch, and he wouldn't have been surprised if the GeoLapse ended up dragging four lost grandmas up to wherever Valents was hiding.

The man's voice continued. "Now, if the McHubbards want to expedite this process, they may turn themselves in to me. That way, no one will be harmed and all of the bunker community can go back to living in peace. Anyone who tries to aid the McHubbards will be killed. Find me at the entrance to the bunker." Valents paused for a few seconds. "Oh, would you look at this! One of them has already been honourable enough to show up without any resistance. I await the rest of the McHubbards with the sincerest anticipation. Men, continue your search, and don't hold back."

A plasticky clunk terminated the announcement. For a few hesitant moments, the bunkerians and the GeoLapse peered at one another in puzzlement. Riff's stomach dropped at the thought that a bunkerian might recognise him and turn him in. After all, the McHubbards were the reason that the GeoLapse were here at all.

Riff caught Mrs. Flumbo's eye. She was clinging to the railing one level above. She shook her head at him subtly. At first Riff thought that she was angry with him, but then she winked. She was trying to tell him to stay hidden. The bunker wanted to fight back.

But which of his sisters had already turned herself in to Valents? Riff couldn't possibly leave one of them alone with him. Who knew what his plans were!

*It must be Ann Lou,* Riff thought. *She's positioned at the top with Thevenin and Norton.*

With a roar, the GeoLapse resumed their fighting. Riff peered down to Luna's level and saw her riding up a lift with Elbina in hand. When the lift reached Riff's level, Luna ordered, "Get in."

Riff obeyed, and Luna pressed buttons to take them to the zeroth level.

"So, it was Ann Lou," said Riff. "Do you think this is a bad idea, going up there and turning ourselves in?"

"Of course it's a bad idea," said Luna. "But it's the right thing to do. We have to face Valents ourselves and avenge Mum, and most of Earth's population. Ann Lou was brave to turn herself in so quickly."

Elbina struggled in an attempt to jump off the lift. She lifted a leg over the railing and leaned forward.

"What are you doing?" Riff scolded her, pulling her back inside the handrail. "You'll get yourself killed if you jump!"

"Why are you holding me hostage? Why do you want to hand me over to some stranger?" Elbina asked them angrily.

"Because . . . Luna, you tell her. She listens to you," said Riff.

Elbina turned to Luna with an irate expression. "Well?" she said impatiently.

Luna took a deep breath. "Because the four of us are siblings. The man who is the horrible leader of the GeoLapse is our father."

Elbina's eyes widened. "My father is here to get me?"

"No, he's here to kill you. We have to take him down as a family so that the GeoLapse will disband and disappear," said Luna.

Elbina pondered the information that Luna had presented to her. She neither spoke nor attempted to jump off the lift for the remainder of the ride up.

Once the three siblings reached the top level, Riff saw Thevenin and

Norton at the base of the stairs that led to their workshop. He rushed over to them and saw Norton kneeling over Thevenin, who was resting his bleeding head against the wall.

"Is he all right?" asked Riff, crouching next to Norton.

"He jus' needs some restin' time. He was out there zap-zap-zappin' away," said Norton, his voice croaking.

"He needs medical attention," said Luna. "His head . . ."

Thevenin groaned in pain and quivered as Norton held him upright. "We'll go down there once this mess is over with," Norton said. "He wouldn't wanna take someone's place in the hospital anyways. Where're y'all goin'?"

"We came to see Valents," said Riff, quietly so that Valents couldn't hear them from up the stairs.

Norton gasped. "Yowza, you can't turn yerselves in! I won't let you!" He held out a zapper and pointed it at them, but his hand shook violently.

"We appreciate your kindness to us, but this is something we have to do. You all have covered for us without a second thought," said Riff.

"But . . . you can' go. Y'all are my friends. Y'all are everyone's friends," sobbed Norton.

"We're going to be okay. Trust us. We have a plan," said Luna.

Norton nodded and lowered his zapper. "If anyone has a good plan, it's you, Luna. Be careful up there."

The siblings waved to Thevenin and Norton, then started up the stairs to the workshop.

"So, what's the plan?" Riff whispered to Luna.

"No idea," she replied.

# CHAPTER 25

## ELBINA'S DECISION

Luna pushed the stone door open and crept into Thevenin and Norton's dimly lit workshop, followed closely by Riff and Elbina. Ann Lou sat silently weeping on the sofa, her hands and feet bound. When she saw them walk in, she sobbed out loud.

"They're here!" called a GeoLapse, whom Riff recognised as Malco. He held a baton in front of him, prepared to fight.

A shadow emerged from the back room of the workshop. Valents stood, grinning maliciously at Riff, Luna, and Elbina.

"I'm so glad you decided to join me," he said in a baleful manner. "Alert the men," he said condescendingly to Digby, who was guarding him.

Digby went to the announcement phone and picked up the handset. "Stand down," he said, then hung up and returned to Valents's side.

The stone door opened, and a horde of GeoLapse started crowding into the bunker.

"Wait in the tunnel. I have a feeling we'll be leaving soon," Valents ordered. "Aren't I a kind father?" he said to his children. "I told you my men would leave your friends alone if you came for a simple visit. You should be thanking me."

"Over my dead body!" shouted Ann Lou, trembling.

Valents formed a theatrical expression of hurt on his face. "My darling baby Ann Lou! Don't say such hurtful things to your father."

"Leave her alone," growled Luna.

"And my two other daughters are here!" Valents said, rushing over to Luna and Elbina. "My, my, Luna. Aren't you tall! You remember all those bedtime stories we used to read together? I've heard you're a clever girl. You owe all that to me."

Luna shivered. "I'm not sure 'Dolls and Balls' type reading material is the real reason I am the way that I am today."

"And Elbina," exclaimed Valents, wrapping his arms around Elbina's shoulders. "You have the same sweet little-girl face that you've always had." He gently patted her cheek. Elbina smiled brightly at him.

"Don't touch them!" Riff shouted. "What do you want from us?"

"Firstly, restrain them!" commanded Valents.

Malco, Digby, and a third GeoLapse pounced on the three McHubbards. Luna and Riff put up as much of a fight as they could in the small amount of reaction time available, but it wasn't enough to save themselves from restraints on their hands and feet. Elbina, on the other hand, held her arms out for the third GeoLapse to tie her up. She stared at Valents with what seemed to Riff like a mix of mystification and adoration. The siblings were squished on the sofa next to Ann Lou and held down by their captors. Valents paced back and forth in front of them. "Tsk, tsk, not very robust fighters. That's okay . . . after a little while, you'll learn the ropes," said Valents.

"What are you talking about?" asked Riff, baring his teeth.

"Oh, sorry—did I forget to mention that you will be joining as new recruits of the GeoLapse?" said Valents.

"And if we refuse?" sneered Ann Lou.

Valents shrugged his shoulders. "I'll kill you."

"Why are you so interested in us now, after twenty years of abandonment?" asked Luna.

Valents leaned down to Luna and shouted in her face. "Because the four of you have single-handedly foiled our most fruitful takeover of the universe! We had plans to restore order on Earth and to work with the ERA to rehabilitate the environment. We wanted to transfer our knowledge to other planets in the Universal Union in order to establish trust and universal companionship. But then you four went and eradicated our bases on Earth. We had to work hard and fast to rebuild our foundation to preserve the core values of the GeoLapse's mission."

Riff snorted. "That's the biggest load of bollocks I've ever heard!"

Valents held a hand to Riff's neck and squeezed. "How dare my own son speak to me like that?"

"I . . . can't . . . breathe," Riff choked. His face turned purple.

"Let go of him!" screamed Ann Lou.

Valents complied. "Ann Lou, sweetheart, you've just reminded me. I think I have a much better way of convincing you that joining us is the best decision—for you and for all of humanity. Come!"

The surrounding GeoLapse grabbed each of the McHubbards by the collars and dragged them to the back room.

Stenolly, Mysco, and Meerie-Meerie were hanging by their arms from the ceiling. A gag was stuffed in each of their mouths and wrapped around their heads. Riff and Stenolly made eye contact, and every feeling in Riff's body fell numb. "No!" he screamed, and then he collapsed to the floor.

"Keep him upright!" Valents bellowed at Riff's captor.

Malco pulled Riff to his feet by his collar, choking him again in the process. Tears streamed down his cheeks.

"Please, let them go. If you ever do one thing for me as a father, do this. Please. PLEASE!" Riff begged through sobs.

"Ah, I knew this might be the best bait to lure you in. I'll tell you what, Riff. I'll let them go, but only if you agree to join the GeoLapse. If you refuse, both you and your friends will die," said Valents.

Riff gulped. Neither situation would allow him and Stenolly to live out any of his dreams. Their time together would be cut short—something he had never imagined would happen.

"What about my girls?" Valents continued, circling the four siblings. "My dear, sweet girls. Will you do the right thing to save your friends?"

"Are you really my father?" asked Elbina.

Valents stood in front of her, smiled, and put his grimy hands on her shoulders. "Yes. I remember the day you were born. February eighth, 2206. You were always tiny; you came out at just two kilos. What a beautiful day that was for me and your mother."

"I want to go home with you," said Elbina. "I can start my life over again."

"Now that's the spirit I'm looking for," said Valents, untying Elbina's restraints. "You are going to live a life of riches, something you've always wanted, I'm sure. Food galore, and as much drink as your tiny brain can possibly imagine."

Riff, Ann Lou, and Luna glanced at one another. Even though they understood what had been done to her brain, it was hard to fathom how their sister could trust such a horrid man.

"Elbina, don't listen to him. He's lying to you," said Riff.

"No, you're the one lying to me," Elbina snapped. "None of you told me we were siblings until just before we got here. Dad has been completely honest from the start. I knew he'd come save me!"

"I told you we were siblings when I found you on Austere Avenue!" Riff boomed. "You didn't believe me!"

"Give me a break! You have no idea what I've been through!" Elbina shouted.

Valents clapped his hands. "This is exactly the vigour we are looking for in the GeoLapse. Well done, Elbina. I'm proud of you for taking this leap to continue the family legacy. You know, your great-grandfather and your grand-uncle were also a part of this fantastic organisation. I know they would be ecstatic for you."

"I'm excited to learn more," said Elbina.

"Would you like to choose one of your friends to join you?" Valents gestured toward the Cantileerys.

"Mysco," said Elbina. "We worked together briefly, and it would be nice to have someone with a similar traumatic experience by my side."

"Excellent choice." Valents walked over to where Mysco hung. "Elbina, would you be so kind as to help me?"

Elbina skipped over to Mysco's other side and untied her hand restraints. Mysco fell to the floor, unable even to hold herself up with her arms. Elbina removed the gag from her friend's mouth and helped her to her feet.

"How do you feel about joining our organisation, Mysco? And about the exhilaration of unlimited power?" asked Valents.

Mysco shrugged. "Sure. This place is a dump anyways. I could use an excuse to get out and see the world."

"See the world?" Valents laughed, and his cronies followed suit. "My dear, you will see the universe, and many more universes after that! Your adventure has only just begun!"

Stenolly and Meerie-Meerie struggled and groaned through their gags.

Valents turned back to the McHubbards. "Won't you release them from their misery? Join me. Join your sister. She needs her family."

There was only one way Riff could logically answer Valents's request: he had to join the GeoLapse. It was the only way to save the Cantileerys.

Riff opened his mouth to speak, but words did not come.

"Yes?" Valents said, his evil smile only centimetres away from Riff's face.

"I'll . . . join you," Riff muttered, defeated.

Ann Lou and Luna gasped. Even Stenolly's eyes widened.

"Excellent! That's my boy," said Valents, clapping him on the back and starting to untie his restraints.

"On one condition," Riff continued.

Valents looked taken aback. Anger filled his body and he curled his hands into fists. "How dare you attempt to bargain with me?" Before Valents could lash out further, he paused. He thought that he should listen to his son. After all, he wanted the boy to join him. The girls, in Valents's mind, wouldn't be as useful, especially in combat. "What is your condition?"

"You let the rest of them go. My sisters and the Cantileerys. I won't join you otherwise." Riff stared aggressively at his father.

Valents pondered for a moment. "Well, I'm not backing down on the current recruits," he said, nodding toward Elbina and Mysco. "But I'll accept your condition. Welcome to the team." Valents reached out his hand.

When Riff was free of restraints, he hesitantly held out his hand. Valents took it and dug his dirty fingernails into Riff's hand as he pulled him close. "You're mine now," he whispered darkly. He smelled Valents's rotten breath. He was trapped. There was no life left to live if he had to become one of the GeoLapse. But he had no other choice.

Behind him, Riff heard tiny footfalls, much too tiny to be a human's. Riff peeked around his shoulder to see Bisquit bounding forward. Bisquit stopped, then growled and started inching toward Valents.

Valents recoiled at the sight of the dog's transparent skin. He let go of Riff's hand and backed away. "What in the world is that?"

"It's just my dog," said Mysco. "Come here, boy."

Bisquit growled at Mysco and Elbina, sending them several steps back.

"Get rid of the beast," said Valents to his cronies.

The GeoLapse standing behind Riff, Ann Lou, and Luna came out from behind the sofa and followed the dog to where he had cornered Elbina and Mysco.

"Come here, little buddy," said Digby in a cutesy voice, bending down to grab him.

Bisquit yipped and bit his would-be captor on the leg. Digby howled in pain and crumpled to the floor.

"Are you kidding me? It's a little dog! Just grab the boneheaded thing," Valents whined. He lunged to grab Bisquit himself but missed.

Riff saw Bisquit's brain convulse visibly under his transparent skin. There was a plan of attack ready; Riff could feel it. He gently pulled Ann Lou and Luna back a few steps to give the dog some space. Bisquit had every threat in the room cornered now: Valents, Elbina, Mysco, and the three GeoLapse. The others were safely behind him.

"Bisquit," said Mysco, timidly stepping forward toward him. "You're my best friend, or so I've been told. You wouldn't turn on me like this, would you?"

Bisquit shut his eyes, then lifted his head and let out a supersonic ultrabark. Riff, Ann Lou, and Luna were knocked to the floor but not seriously hurt. Bisquit's direct targets were thrown against the wall and knocked unconscious—all except for Valents, who appeared concussed. He tried dizzily to stand.

"Good boy, Bisquit!" said Riff, getting up. He started to untie Ann Lou.

Bisquit dragged his tired body under Stenolly and Meerie-Meerie and yipped weakly.

"I'm coming!" Riff said. He finished freeing Ann Lou, and she started untying Luna.

Riff ran to Stenolly, untied her gently, and helped her to her feet. "Are you all right?" he cried, pulling Stenolly in for an embrace.

"No time, Riff! Help Meerie-Meerie!" shouted Luna.

Riff obeyed and worked on untying the oldest Cantileery sister.

"We need to contact security straight away! I'll find them!" said Ann Lou, already halfway out the door and into the bunker. Luna followed her.

Bisquit pawed weakly at Meerie-Meerie's ankle. Meerie-Meerie scooped up the small dog. "I need to get you home!" She rushed after Luna.

Riff grabbed a wrench and started toward Elbina. Stenolly pulled him back. "What are you doing? We have to get out of here!"

"I'm not leaving our sisters. Not after everything we've all been through trying to get them back."

Valents grabbed Riff forcefully by the wrist. "You're not taking her!" he shouted. He winced and grabbed his head with his other hand. "She's my daughter!"

"You're no father to her or any of us!" Riff swiped the wrench at Valents. It hit him on the head, knocking him back to the floor.

"Backup! I need backup!" Valents called, blood dripping from his head and mouth.

Five GeoLapse barrelled into the workshop from the tunnel to aid Valents. They shoved Riff into a corner and beat him until he was nearly unconscious.

As Riff tried to fend off the blows, he saw a flash of red hair fighting against the evil forces. The flash of red hair ended up next to Riff on the ground.

"Stenolly?" Riff moaned. He reached out feebly for her hand.

The last words Riff heard echoing in his brain were from Valents. "Get the men and the girls out of here! Don't forget my son!"

Thumps and thuds sounded around Riff. He couldn't see what was happening. His brain felt fuzzy, and his vision and hearing were blurred. He felt himself being dragged backwards by his collar, and then everything turned to black.

# CHAPTER 26

## A Message from the Beyond

Riff fluttered his eyes open to see Ann Lou, Luna, Stenolly, and one of the doctors from the hospital standing over him. He was lying on the sofa, but he couldn't remember how he got there. He noticed with alarm that half of Stenolly's head was bandaged. She smiled at him, and his worries faded, replaced by a feeling of warmth. She looked slightly comical with half of her fuzzy hair poking out wildly and the other half bundled up under her wrappings.

"Have him take these, and make sure he gets plenty of rest over the next few days," a doctor told Luna, and then disappeared from view.

"Hey there, sleepyhead," said Ann Lou, beaming. She handed him a cup of tea.

"Where am I?" said Riff, taking the cup.

"We're in the apartment," replied Ann Lou. "You've been out for a couple days. You got a nasty blow to the head. I'm sorry I wasn't up there to help." Her expression grew glum.

"But how did Stenolly and I get out of there?" asked Riff. He looked to Stenolly.

She finger-spelled the answer. "Thevenin and Norton."

"Did security catch Valents? Where's Elbina? And Mysco? Did they get away safely?" asked Riff. Energy and adrenaline started flowing back into his system. He sat upright in bed and watched the girls' nervous expressions.

"We don't know where they are. The GeoLapse were all gone by the time we got back up to the workshop. There was no sign of anyone except you and Stenolly. They even checked Austere Avenue. Nothing," said Ann Lou.

"We lost them again," said Riff, slamming a fist on the duvet and spilling a bit of tea. "Are we ever going to get her back?"

"Maybe in time her memories will return. But right now she's yearning for her parents. She may still be healing from the damage to her brain. We'll know more when we see her again . . . if we see her again," said Luna gravely.

"Don't say it like that. We're going to find her," said Riff.

"But what if she stays this way forever? What if her life's purpose was to join the GeoLapse all along?" asked Ann Lou.

Riff shook his head. "This isn't her fault. Part of her brain was forced out of her head!"

"I don't know how long she'll last as a GeoLapse. Valents made it sound like such a comfortable life, but I'm not sure that's truly the case," said Luna.

Every heart in the room had a hole in it, but especially Luna's. Riff could feel her pain through her body language. Her brain was working in overdrive as she processed all the horrible possibilities of Elbina's new life.

"I need to go help Meerie-Meerie set up for the party. Excuse me," and Luna dashed away and out of the apartment.

"What party?" asked Riff.

"It's Mysco's thirteenth birthday today. We wanted to celebrate in her honour," signed Stenolly.

"I'd better get ready, then," said Riff. He turned slightly and winced. "Would someone be able to help me get changed?"

"That's a girlfriend duty, not a sister one," said Ann Lou, leaving the room.

Once Riff was all spruced up, Ann Lou and Stenolly walked him across the hall to the Cantileery apartment. Bisquit, who had now fully recovered from his latest ultrabark, greeted them at the door. His eyes and lungs bobbled as he panted with excitement at seeing his friends. He pawed Ann Lou's leg, and she gave him a few head scratches before he led them all to the dining area.

Drinks and platters of food were laid out on the colourfully decorated table. Guests filled the apartment, including Elmeria and Joland Cantileery; Mysco's classmates and her soccer team; a few of the Block A neighbours, including Mrs. Flumbo and Mr. Goldmaker; Norton; Spex; and a few other bunkerians whom the McHubbards knew only by their faces.

Stenolly and Ann Lou sat Riff in a chair with Norton to his right, then went to help Meerie-Meerie and Luna put the last-minute touches on the decorations. Norton barely noticed Riff sitting next to him. He just sat staring at his plate, which held a small cupcake with white frosting, the same colour as Mysco's spectacle frames.

"Norton, nice to see you," said Riff.

Norton nodded shyly in return.

Riff continued. "I owe you and Thevenin big time, mate. I heard you both got me and Stenolly out of the workshop just in time. I don't think 'thank you' quite covers it."

Norton mustered up a weak smile. "That's what friends are for."

"How's Thevenin holding up?"

Norton turned toward Riff, his face expressionless. "You didn' hear?"

Riff's heart sank. "No, what happened?"

"We was gettin' you two outta the workshop, when one of them bad guys crept up behind Thev'nin and started a brawl. He already wasn' in a good state. There was nothin' I could do to save him." He cleared his throat, and his eyes turned glassy. "He's gone."

"Norton . . . I'm so sorry," said Riff. He couldn't fight the tears. The thought of losing Elbina to the GeoLapse was hard to bear, but at least she would still be alive. Norton's brother—his twin brother—was gone. This new source of misery threatened to overwhelm Riff. He feared if he had to take in much more, he'd never be able to feel joy again.

Norton gently patted Riff's shoulder. "Naw, he gave it his all, Thev'nin did. He's always been the braver of us two. Now I gotta live my life a bit more like him. Gotta be strong for Mamaw now that she's back. But she hasn' really been the same, you know what I mean? She's a bit more . . . devious. But I'm sure that's what happens when you get old, anyways."

"Where's my mashed skeebamelon?" shouted Gwympy as she sat down at the head of the table, a few chairs down from Riff.

Norton stifled a laugh; it was probably the first time since Thevenin's passing that he'd even wanted to smile.

Meerie-Meerie placed a giant, three-tiered white cake at the centre of the table with thirteen lit candles atop it. "All right, everyone! Find your seats at the table. Who would like to start the birthday song?" Meerie-Meerie asked the crowd. She was using her happy voice, but her face wore a look of sadness.

One of Mysco's school friends raised her hand.

"Take it away, Blinkie," said Meerie-Meerie.

Blinkie started to sing her verse along to a Celtic-style tune. "She stubbed my toe and pinched my nose, and washed my dog with tar. She broke my bike and toys alike, have a wicked birthday, Mysco!" Blinkie blew one candle out, then pointed to someone on the soccer team.

Mysco's teammate sang the next verse in a similar fashion. "She stole my crayons and tripped my gran, and ate my mom's dessert. She blew up the shed, no sorry was said, have a wicked birthday, Mysco!" The soccer player blew out another candle and pointed to another teammate to sing the third verse.

"Strange song for a birthday," Riff whispered to Stenolly.

She giggled and signed in reply, "It's a tradition to sing one verse for each year of age. So, there's thirteen verses of Mysco doing all these devious things."

"I didn't think Mysco had it in her to trip someone's gran," Riff signed, chuckling.

Stenolly laughed again. "Therians believe only the wicked live the longest, so singing about wicked things gives them good luck for many more birthdays."

Riff smiled. "That's brilliant. People from Earth usually sing a happy song with many fewer verses."

Stenolly pretended to act horrified. "That's basically asking for death!"

They laughed together and held hands under the table for the remainder of Mysco's wicked birthday song.

Gwympy finished the thirteenth verse with, "She locked my ring inside the thing where Daddy stores his socks. She let the sociopath sit in the bath, have a wicked birthday, Mysco!"

After a few whoops and cheers, the celebratory air quickly dissipated. Guests made their rounds to the McHubbards and the Cantileerys (including Bisquit) to express concern about Elbina and Mysco. They all offered to help with the search, and each family thanked the bunkerians for their kindness.

Guests gradually filtered out until only the McHubbards and the Cantileerys remained at the table munching on the last of the birthday snacks. Elmeria and Joland left next. They still technically lived at the hospital (now in separate rooms because of their growing distaste for one another). Bisquit was tired out from running in circles with Mysco's friends and the soccer team, and he lay paws-up in front of the sofa, snoozing away.

Gwympy sat at the head of the table, clearly wincing in pain.

"Is this one a bad headache?" asked Meerie-Meerie.

"Particularly," Gwympy grimaced. "It usually means that I have a warning message from spirits." She craned her neck. "It's for you three." She pointed a knobbly finger at Riff, Ann Lou, and Luna. "I believe you have one vial of Tarottriptan left. Do you want your message or not?" Gwympy asked.

The McHubbards looked at one another, speechless.

Gwympy stood up from her chair. "I can't stand this pain any longer. I'm going to my room." Then she rushed to her bedroom, climbed up the ladder with great difficulty, and disappeared behind the rainbow curtain.

"Well come on, let's see what she has to say!" blurted Ann Lou. She rushed after Gwympy.

Riff dashed to his room across the hall to grab the last vial of Gwympy's preferred headache remedy. He and Luna joined Gwympy in her room. Stenolly and Meerie-Meerie weren't about to miss an epic reading, so they crammed into Gwympy's room as well.

Riff handed over the vial, and Gwympy downed it. She sat back, feeling the relief wash over her. The crystal ball formed white smoke that eventually turned into the eye with the orange iris.

"Please, focus your attention on the crystal ball." Gwympy waved her hands over it.

Just as during their previous reading, the eye's pupil expanded until the entire crystal ball was filled with black. This time, the ball stayed black and no image formed for them to watch. No one moved a muscle as they waited for something to happen.

"Luna? Riff? Ann Lou? Is that you?" said a woman's voice.

Riff knew the voice. It reminded him of home.

"Mum?" he said weakly.

"Yes, darling, it's me," replied Henrietta.

"H-how are you talking to us?" said Ann Lou, her voice trembling.

"I'm afraid that's a rather complicated subject. I have an urgent message to relay to you." Henrietta's voice sounded distressed. "It's the GeoLapse. They're coming after the ghosts."

"What do you mean?" asked Luna.

"We've been watching them. We know their plans. They want to take over the ghost dimension. If they can get to us, they can manipulate all the living. You are in grave danger, and so are we," Henrietta said solemnly.

"G-ghosts are r-real?" stammered Riff.

"We're as real as you believe we are," replied Henrietta.

"How do we help you?" asked Ann Lou.

"If you can save your sister, you can save everyone."

"What does Elbina have to do with this?" asked Riff.

"Valents has a plan for her. If she executes it, it will devastate us all."

"How do we find her?" asked Ann Lou.

"Get the ERA involved. They will help you. Especially Jung-hoon," Henrietta replied. "This is all I can say for now. The connection is dwindling. Each of you has been so courageous since you left Earth all those years ago. I hope you know I've been with you every step of the way."

"We'll try our best," said Riff, tearfully. "We miss you."

"I miss you, my darlings. Thank you for taking such good care of Knitsy as well. She's here with me."

"Take those GeoLapse nitwits down, my loves!" called a voice from farther away that sounded exactly like Knitsy's.

"We love you so much," Henrietta continued. "We will be with you the whole journey. Be safe."

"Love you," said Ann Lou.

The black of the pupil faded until the crystal ball was clear again.

Meerie-Meerie ushered the rest of them out of the room so that Gwympy could snooze. The Cantileerys guided the stunned McHubbards into the living room to sit down.

"That was quite the reading. I can't imagine how you must be feeling," said Meerie-Meerie, sympathetically.

"Do you think that was really Mum?" asked Ann Lou.

Riff nodded. "Her voice was so genuine. I felt a warmth that has been missing ever since we left her on Earth."

"I don't doubt that the GeoLapse already have another plan in place, this time on a much grander scale and targeting those we love and hold most dear," said Luna.

"Elbina will be playing a large role in this as well, whether willingly or not," added Riff.

Luna shook her head. "It's not willingly. I think our sisters are still deep within their bodies somewhere, and if we get them out, maybe we can finally put a stop to the GeoLapse."

"So, where do we go next?" asked Ann Lou.

"Let's start by going home. Jung-hoon can help us track the GeoLapse's movements," said Luna.

Riff nodded and turned to Stenolly. "I'm so sorry that I can't stay here. I have to go back to Earth to help my mum."

Stenolly lifted an eyebrow. "You think you're going without me?"

A smile broadened on Riff's face. "You want to come?"

Stenolly snorted. "Of course I'm coming! My sister needs help, too. I can't let you do all the saving by yourself."

Riff gripped her hand and held it tightly. He turned to Meerie-Meerie. "Would you want to come as well?"

Meerie-Meerie shook her head. "Someone needs to stay back and keep an eye on our parents and Gwympy. I'll be okay to do it on my own. Besides, I'll be able to keep an eye on you through Gwympy's readings. But you need to promise to visit," she said, with an understanding smile.

"Oh, and I think Bisquit might like to accompany you. He clearly loves you McHubbards. He wouldn't release an ultrabark for just anyone. I think he misses his Mysco and would like to help bring her home."

"Yay, Bisquit!" exclaimed Ann Lou.

Upon hearing his name, Bisquit awoke from his slumber, ran to Ann Lou, and jumped on her lap.

"Are you and Spex on track with BAAT?" Luna asked Meerie-Meerie.

"A *third* programme?" Ann Lou blurted, tossing her hands up in the air. "What on Thera is BAAT? And when did you have time to plan all these?"

"It's Bunker to Austere Avenue Transfer. There's no Insomnyus to threaten the Therians anymore, so they can move back aboveground," said Meerie-Meerie, her eyes twinkling. "Thanks to you all."

* * *

The next morning, Riff, Ann Lou, Luna, Stenolly, and Bisquit were scheduled to depart from planet Thera. The McHubbards cleaned out their apartment and erased the sign on their door. They met the Cantileerys at the entrance to the bunker and found Norton working in his back workshop. It seemed strange to see only one of the brothers present.

Norton saw them and stopped welding. "Where're y'all goin'?"

"We're leaving," said Riff. "We wanted to say goodbye."

"Yowza, yer leavin' already?" Norton said, tossing his goggles and protective equipment on the floor. "Did you make yer rounds tuh everyone?"

"No, we'd prefer to make a discreet exit. We don't want to bother anyone," said Luna.

Norton looked bewildered. "Y'all saved us from the Insomnyus leader! And y'all have become our friends. I won't let y'all leave without a proper goodbye. Thev'nin would want me to do this."

Norton clambered over to the announcement phone and picked up the handset. "Attention, bunker: the McHubbards, Lady Stenolly Cantileery, and big buddy Bisquit are headin' out today on a whirlwind adventure. Let's give 'em a proper goodbye." He replaced the handset in its cradle. "Let's go up."

They followed Norton through the tunnel, out of the trunk, through Building Blocks, and out onto Austere Avenue, which was free of evil forces. Luna pulled out the wheel Jalopy from her rucksack and placed it in the centre of the avenue.

Within fifteen minutes, the entire bunker had emerged from underground and assembled on the avenue. The rounds of goodbyes commenced. Mrs. Flumbo presented them with a batch of Flumbo Creams. The soccer team clapped Ann Lou on the back for showing them all a few Pyroll-inspired special moves to incorporate into their games. Norton offered them each a zapper, but they declined when Luna pointed out that they might interfere with the Jalopy's circuitry. Their neighbours from Block A gave them all hugs.

Spex then delivered an impromptu and heartfelt goodbye speech. "Luna, you've enchanted me from the beginning. Your eyes reeled me into a sea of emotions that I didn't realise that I could feel for someone. Will you promise to come visit me someday, so that we can continue to devise community-wide programmes, solve the myopia pandemic, and possibly venture into the romantic realm?"

Riff clasped his hands over his mouth to hold in his laughter.

Luna chuckled and smiled at her friend. "I appreciate the offer. The first two sound exhilarating, so perhaps one day we could make them happen. However, the last one might need to be prioritised a bit farther down the list. I think I'll be a bit too busy for . . . er . . . many years."

"Understood," said Spex, bowing to her. "Until next time."

"Goodbye," said a tearful Meerie-Meerie to Stenolly and Bisquit, holding them both close. "You two watch out for each other, okay?"

Stenolly nodded and Bisquit yipped. Stenolly gave Gwympy and each of her parents a hug goodbye, and her mother replied with, "It was a pleasure to meet you."

"Time to go," said Luna. "Circle the Jalopy."

Riff, Ann Lou, Stenolly, and Bisquit obeyed and stood in a tight circle around the tiny wheel. They bent low and touched the centre point, shrinking themselves down into the Jalopy's small cabin. Stenolly couldn't believe her eyes; she stared with wonder at the Jalopy's walls and the outside.

"Get ready for a whole load of new adventures," Riff said, kissing her on the cheek.

Luna and Ann Lou strapped in on one side of the Jalopy, and Stenolly, Bisquit, and Riff secured themselves on the other. The Jalopy glowed green and said, "Hello, Luna McHubbard, Griffin McHubbard, Stenolly Cantileery, Ann Lou McHubbard, and Prince Bisquit of Clan Whellivan. The Jalopy is ready to depart. Please state your destination."

"The White House, Washington DC, Earth, via Sagittarius A," replied Luna.

"Enjoy your trip," said the Jalopy's calming voice.

The Jalopy rose from Austere Avenue, and each of the passengers watched through the glass with melancholy. The crowd of bunkerians waved goodbye to them, and the sea of Therians grew smaller and smaller as they ascended into the atmosphere. Within seconds, Thera was no more than a pinpoint in the blackness of space.

"Who knew Bisquit was a prince!" exclaimed Ann Lou. "You're such a cool dog!"

Bisquit yipped with glee.

Riff heard Stenolly silently weeping as they flew away from her home planet. He held her tightly and whispered, "We'll be back. We can visit anytime you'd like, okay?" She nodded and snuggled up closer in his embrace. "Oh, one more thing," Riff added. "Let me give you the lowdown about what it's like going through a black hole."

* * *

Ann Lou's prosthetic popped off during the ride through the black hole. Stenolly's hair emerged ultra-knotted, Riff's and Luna's necks were slightly stiff, and Bisquit's kidneys got tangled up with his lungs. But there were no major injuries.

The Jalopy entered Earth's solar system, then neared the sandy planet the McHubbards called home. They watched as the craft descended into the atmosphere and the barren ground drew closer and closer. Seconds later, the White House came into view. The Jalopy approached the giant air lock from which Riff, Knitsy, and Flora had departed in the streetcar Jalopy when they left Earth for Mission Stardust, and the door opened, allowing the Jalopy to fly in. Then the door closed behind them, creating a seal between the building and the outside. An interior door opened in front of them, and the Jalopy chugged in to the centre of the workshop and touched down on the floor.

"We're back!" Riff shrieked with excitement. "Welcome to our home, Cantileerys," he said patting Bisquit's head.

They unstrapped themselves, and Riff showed Stenolly how to leap to exit the Jalopy. For a few seconds, the workshop was empty, but running footfalls soon transformed into an exasperated Jung-hoon, who jogged forward to greet them.

"I saw you coming on the Jalopy radar!" he exclaimed, embracing the McHubbards. "Where's Elbina?"

"We have loads to tell you, but first, can you please get us some Nectarine Nuttys and a round of tea?" pleaded Riff.

Jung-hoon fulfilled Riff's request, and they moved into his lab to debrief their entire adventure.

"Before you begin your tale, you should know that I am now the director of the ERA. Delevio . . . I'll tell you about that later. The point is, you may speak freely. You need not worry about the previous director lurking around and hearing things that he shouldn't be hearing," said Jung-hoon.

"Congratulations!" said Ann Lou. "Mum would be thrilled."

Jung-hoon bowed. "That is too kind of a compliment. It was an unfortunate circumstance, but I stepped up in honour of her. If I can do the job a quarter as well as she did, I will be pleased. But I digress . . . tell me your story."

Riff and Ann Lou did all the talking. Whenever one of them ran out of breath from speaking so rapidly, the other would continue the story. Once Ann Lou finished the portion of the story about their mother's message from the beyond, Riff could see the sadness wash over Jung-hoon's face.

"That must have been terrible to hear her in such distress. I always wanted to believe that those who pass on are granted instantaneous and eternal peace. Not everyone believes in these sorts of concepts, of course. But to find out that the ghosts are in misery and serious trouble . . . How do we help them?"

"Mum said you would know how to locate the GeoLapse. It has something to do with Elbina," said Luna.

Jung-hoon beamed. "Your mother is kind. The fact that she still has faith in me is beyond an honour." His tone turned pensive. "It sounds like we may need to pretend to be on the GeoLapse's side to gain their trust, just as we did previously when humans were all moved to different planets about eight years ago."

"We need a mole," said Riff. "Someone to gain their trust and report back to us."

Jung-hoon nodded. "Sounds like we have a new project on our hands. Project Jubilee."

* * *

Later that evening, Riff, Luna, Ann Lou, Stenolly, and Bisquit were greeted by friends and family while they ate dinner in Danforth

Commons. Clorin was so excited that he didn't know whose arms to run into first. He zigzagged three ways between Ann Lou, Riff, and Luna, but eventually he made the right decision and jumped into his mother's arms.

"Aww, that's my boy!" said Ann Lou as she cradled him in her arms.

"You're back," said Apollo huskily. He picked Ann Lou up off the floor as he hugged her. He was trembling. "I didn't th-think you'd be gone that long."

Riff was surprised to see the Epitonian sobbing into Ann Lou's shoulder.

"It's okay, my love. I'm home now," Ann Lou replied, hugging him tightly.

"Good to see you, Riff," someone said behind Riff.

He turned to see the Zeep family. Both Garold and Flora had slight bruising on their faces and arms, but they were their usual pleasant selves. He shook their hands and gave Alphabeta a tickle.

"Good to have you back," said Flora, smiling.

President Hayden Murphy gave Riff a nod and a handshake. Hayden's forced smile quickly transformed into a look of distress and concern. "Is she okay?" he said in a hoarse voice. His lip wobbled and his eyes welled with tears.

Riff sighed. "She's alive. We'll get her back. I promise."

Hayden wiped away a tear. "I'll do anything I can to help. I'll use my power of veto, pass a few laws, or even get the Rhothgans to provide backup. You name it."

"Thanks, mate. I know she misses you. The old Elbina is still there. I can feel it," Riff said softly.

Hayden patted Riff's shoulder with a real smile this time, and walked away to speak with Jung-hoon.

Riff led Stenolly by the hand over to meet Matt and Joe. "Lads, this is the divine Stenolly Cantileery of planet Thera. Make fun of me all you want, but I have fallen deeply in love."

Joe nodded and waved. Matt reached out a hand and said, "Pleasure to meet you, Stenolly. You play music?"

She shook her head and smiled.

"We've got ourselves a dancer, though," said Riff.

"Excellent. We've just written a rock ballad. It would go perfectly with a ballet component," said Matt.

As Matt and Joe tried to interest Stenolly in joining the GeoLads, Riff sat back and cast his eyes around the room full of friends and family. He loved them all wholly, but he couldn't help thinking about those he'd lost: his mother and Knitsy. Even though they were with him in ghostly form, a void remained ever-present in his heart. There was still one sister whom he needed back in his life to fill this emptiness.

Through the pain of these thoughts, he managed a smile as he glanced at each of his favourite people. His capacity to love had reached record heights since meeting Stenolly and making so many new friends at the bunker. Love seemed to unleash a power within him that he hadn't known he possessed, and it was the sole reason that he could continue the fight to bring his family back together.

# Acknowledgments

Thank you to the team at DartFrog Books for making the third instalment of *The Jalopy Chronicles* a reality. A big thanks goes out to Suanne for managing all of the Jalopy books so far, Chris and Tracy for their fantastic work on the cover design that stayed true to the series, Amy for her line edit and advice that elegantly pulled the story together, Andrew for the diligent final proofread, and Simona for putting all the puzzle pieces together in a wonderful format.

You might notice the list of illustrators continues to grow. Lucky for me, they are all family members of mine. My cousin Elyzabeth and my mom Brigid are now seasoned chapter illustrators for the books, and in my opinion, the drawings remain the best part of the series. We also have a new artist on board – my talented fiancé, Martin! Welcome to the team! I love the different styles you all bring forth and the incredible creativity and heart you put into your art. Here is a list of each of their drawings:

- Elyzabeth: cover page and chapters 1, 2, 7, 8, 15, and 25
- Brigid: chapters 6, 9, 16, 19-22, 24, and 26
- Martin: chapters 5, 11-13, and 18
- I have also done a few drawings, and if you'd like to have a laugh, check out chapters 3, 4, 10, 14, 17, and 23

Thanks to my friends and family who keep passing the books along to their own friends and family. Every time one of you tells me that you know someone, especially a child, who is reading and enjoying the book, my heart soars.

Thanks as always to my momager for spreading the word and cheerleading the book through every phase, from writing the draft to reading the final product.

Thank you to my dad who specifically asked for a villain named "Grand Q'bah". Ask and you shall receive. I love all the ideas!

Thank you to Martin for talking through some of the plot lines with me and brainstorming the wacky things that the McHubbards encounter. The exposure to Futurama and Star Wars has also provided some great inspiration. We've already got some great ideas for book 4!

To my readers – your time spent on reading my stories means the world! I hope you enjoy the third instalment of *The Jalopy Chronicles* and look forward to the fourth and final book!

# About the Author

Caeli Ennis crafted the story of the McHubbard Family in her small flat in Southampton, England, during the COVID-19 pandemic. She is originally from snowy Buffalo, New York, where she enjoys nothing more than spending the summertime at the cottage on Lake Erie with her family and friends. Caeli sought to build characters with physical disabilities to prove to readers that anyone and everyone can help save the universe, as she most personally identifies with Luna's visual obstacles. She works as a Development Engineer and in her free time she plays cello in the local orchestra and loves to travel, eat, and game with her fiancé, Martin (one of this book's exceptional chapter illustrators).